The unicorn is noble;
    He keeps him safe and high
Upon a narrow path and steep
    Climbing to the sky;
And there no man can take him;
    He scorns the hunter's dart
And only a virgin's magic power
    Shall tame his haughty heart.

From a medieval German folksong

Special Collections From Ace Science Fiction and Fantasy

BASILISK, *edited by Ellen Kushner*

DRAGONS OF LIGHT *and* DRAGONS OF DARKNESS, *edited by Orson Scott Card*

ELSEWHERE I, II, *and* III, *edited by Terri Windling and Mark Alan Arnold*

MAGICATS! *edited by Jack Dann and Gardner Dozois*

MAGIC FOR SALE, *edited by Avram Davidson*

THE MAGIC GOES AWAY *and* THE MAGIC MAY RETURN, *edited by Larry Niven*

UNICORNS! *edited by Jack Dann and Gardner Dozois*

UNICORNS!

EDITED BY
JACK DANN & GARDNER DOZOIS

ACE FANTASY BOOKS
NEW YORK

Dedication: For David Hartwell

The editors would like to thank the following people for their help and support:

Virginia Kidd, David Hartwell, Trina King, Edward Ferman, Susan Casper, Jeanne Carpenter, Tom and Vivian Smith, Mark Owings, Perry Knowlton, Diane Zagerman, Tom Whitehead of the Special Collections Department of the Paley Library at Temple University, J. B. Post of the Map Department of the Free Library of Philadelphia, Ellen Kushner, Fred Fisher, Michael Swanwick, Stuart Schiff, Pat LoBrutto, Al Sarranionio, Bob Walters, Tess Kissinger, Elizabeth A. Lynn, Brian W. Aldiss, Avram Davidson, Ellen Datlow, George Scithers, George Zebrowski, Brian Perry of Fat Cat Books (263 Main Street, Johnson City, New York 13790), and special thanks to our own editor, Susan Allison.

UNICORNS!

An Ace Fantasy Book / published by arrangement with
the editors

PRINTING HISTORY
Ace Original / May 1982
Fifth printing / June 1984

ISBN: 0-441-85443-5

Ace Fantasy Books are published by The Berkley Publishing Group,
200 Madison Avenue, New York, New York 10016.
PRINTED IN THE UNITED STATES OF AMERICA

ACKNOWLEDGMENTS

Acknowledgment is made for permission to print the following material:

"The Spoor of the Unicorn: *An Adventure in Unhistory*" by Avram Davidson. Copyright © 1982 by Avram Davidson.

"The Silken Swift" by Theodore Sturgeon. Copyright © 1953 by Ballantine Books, © 1979 by Theodore Sturgeon. Reprinted by permission of the author and the author's agent, Kirby McCauley.

"Eudoric's Unicorn" by L. Sprague de Camp. Copyright © 1977 by DAW Books, Inc. Reprinted by permission of the author and the author's agent, Eleanor Wood, Spectrum Literary Agency.

"The Flight of the Horse" by Larry Niven. Copyright © 1969 by Mercury Press, Inc. First published in *The Magazine of Fantasy and Science Fiction*, October, 1969. Reprinted by permission of the author.

"On the Downhill Side" by Harlan Ellison, from the author's collection *Deathbird Stories*. Copyright © 1972 by Harlan Ellison. Reprinted with permission of, and by arrangement with, the author and the author's agent, Richard Curtis Associates, Inc., New York. All rights reserved.

"The Night of the Unicorn" by Thomas Burnett Swann. Copyright © 1975 by April R. Derleth and Walden W. Derleth. First published in *Nameless Places* (Arkham House, 1975). Reprinted by permission of Margaret Gaines Swann.

"Mythological Beast" by Stephen R. Donaldson. Copyright © 1978 by Mercury Press, Inc. First published in *The Magazine of Fantasy and Science Fiction*, January, 1979. Reprinted by permission of the author.

"The Final Quarry" by Eric Norden. Copyright © 1970 by Mercury Press, Inc. First published in *The Magazine of Fantasy and Science Fiction*, May, 1970. Reprinted by permission of the author.

"Elfleda" by Vonda N. McIntyre. Copyright © 1981 by Vonda N. McIntyre. First published in *New Dimensions 12* (Timescape/Pocket Books). Reprinted by permission of the author and the author's agent, Francis Collins.

"The White Donkey" by Ursula K. Le Guin. Copyright © 1980. First published in *TriQuarterly 49*. Reprinted by permission of the author and the author's agent, Virginia Kidd.

"Unicorn Variations" by Roger Zelazny. Copyright © 1981 by Davis Publications, Inc. First published in *Isaac Asimov's Science Fiction Magazine*, April 13, 1981. Reprinted by permission of the author.

CONTENTS

AVRAM DAVIDSON
  The Spoor of the Unicorn : 1
THEODORE STURGEON
  The Silken Swift : 29
L. SPRAGUE DE CAMP
  Eudoric's Unicorn : 55
LARRY NIVEN
  The Flight of the Horse : 77
HARLAN ELLISON
  On the Downhill Side : 96
THOMAS BURNETT SWANN
  The Night of the Unicorn : 116
STEPHEN R. DONALDSON
  Mythological Beast : 124
ERIC NORDEN
  The Final Quarry : 149
VONDA N. MCINTYRE
  Elfleda : 176
URSULA K. LE GUIN
  The White Donkey : 193
ROGER ZELAZNY
  Unicorn Variation : 198
GARDNER DOZOIS
  The Sacrifice : 231

FRANK OWEN
    The Unicorn : 236
GENE WOLFE
    The Woman the Unicorn Loved : 247
BEV EVANS
    The Forsaken : 271
T. H. WHITE
    The Unicorn : 286

Introduction to
Avram Davidson's
"The Spoor of the Unicorn":

Avram Davidson has for too long been underrated as a writer, in spite of his well-deserved Hugo (for that mad little classic, "Or All the Seas with Oysters," detailing the sex-cycles of coat hangers and safety pins), his almost endless list of fine short fiction, his erudite and highly-entertaining novels, and the demonstrable fact that he is one of the most eloquent and individual voices in modern letters. Good as Davidson has always been, in the last few years he's gotten even better: his recent series of stories about the bizarre exploits of Doctor Engelbert Eszterhazy (collected in *The Enquiries of Doctor Eszterhazy)* and the strange adventures of Jack Limekiller (as yet uncollected, alas) are Davidson at the very height of his considerable powers, and must be counted as some of the very finest work produced in the seventies, in any genre. In the last few years a few long-unavailable Davidson books have come back into print again—the novels *Rogue Dragon, The Kar Chee Reign,* and *Masters of the Maze,* and the collection *Or All the Seas with Oysters*—and it may be that Davidson is on the brink of finally getting the sort of recognition and critical attention that he deserves. Davidson's other books include *The Phoenix and the Mirror*, *Rork!*, *The Enemy of My Enemy*, *Clash of Star-Kings*, *Joyleg* (with the late Ward Moore), and *Peregrine: Primus*. His most recent books are *Peregrine: Secundus*, a novel, and the collections *The Best of Avram Davidson*, *The Redward Edward Papers*, and *Strange Seas and Shores*.

Here, in an essay especially commissioned for this anthology—one of a series of "Adventures in Unhistory" that Davidson has been writing, examining curious and little-known areas of history and folklore—Davidson brings his customary wit and erudition to bear in a search for that most elusive of all animals—the unicorn.

THE SPOOR OF THE UNICORN

An Adventure in Unhistory

Avram Davidson

In that one of the ADVENTURES IN UNHISTORY called *An Abundance of Dragons,* I declared that although the wombat is real and the dragon is not, nobody knows what a wombat looks like and everyone knows what a dragon looks like. Also, a unicorn. Platonian comment in re the Archetype would be of interest here, as to what Plato said about the unicorn, lo! it is that he said nothing. So far as *I* know. So evidently I am free to paraphrase, to wit, Somewhere there is a heavenly or archetypal unicorn, for if there were not, how would we have been able to formulate the image of one here below? Perhaps it is the function of this Adventure to show how; easy does it, though, Plato was the pupil of Socrates, and we all know what happened to *him*. Don't we.

Whenever I ask myself, in any situation, "Where to begin?" the answer always comes from Charles Fort: "In measuring a circle, one begins anywhere." After that, no matter what digressions, it is merely a matter of getting back to it. And I begin with a quotation from Jorge Luis Borges's *Book of Imaginary Beings* (with Margaret Guerrero, tr. by N. T. di Giovanni, Avon, 1960, N.Y.). "To the Chinese, the heavens are hemispherical and the earth quadrangular, and so, in the Tortoise with its curved upper shell and flat lower shell, they find an image or mould of the world. Moreover, Tortoises share in cosmic longevity; it is therefore fitting that they should be included among the spiritually endowed creatures (together with the unicorn, the dragon, the phoenix, and the tiger) and that soothsayers read the future in the pattern of

3

their shells.'' It might not in the normal, everyday, course of events have occurred to you that the unicorn was related in any way to the tortoise, the dragon, the phoenix and the tiger; let alone that it is (as each of them is) ''a spiritually endowed creature.'' But now you know. We have begun to measure our circle. Onward.

Having already accepted that the subject of this Adventure is not merely a fancy horse with a spirally-wound horn, going tap-it-a-trot across beautifully-broidered tapestries in order to lay its lovely head in the lap of a lovely maiden, you may be prepared to obey the order, *Now hear this:* ''The unicorn was also a symbol frequently used by the alchemists, and it represented Mercury and the Lion. It was intermingled with the Eagle and the Dragon, and, during the Middle Ages, was regarded as the sign of the Holy Spirit. The unicorn represented divine power, both in its negative and destructive aspects as well as in its creative manifestations.'' The *this* which you have now heard is not from Borges, nor does it refer to that much mis-used matter, The Wisdom of the East. It is from *A Pictorial History of Magic and the Supernatural,* by Maurice Bessy (Spring Books, U.K., 1960). I am of a reasonable surety that this was translated from the French, and if anyone knows who the translator was, please let me know. Monsieur Bessy, like a great many writers . . . like far too many writers . . . is likely to state casually as facts things which are likelier to have been purely his own opinions, but there is nothing I can do about that; 22 years after publication, ''Clean up your act, Bessy!''—what would it accomplish? Faint transatlantic echoes of *Merde, alors!, Eh, ta soeur!, Comme ça?, blague!,* and other Gallic impertinences; never mind. Doubtless the same thing might equally be said of many another writer; just keep this in mind as you read his book.

The important thing is to note how the dainty hoof of the

one-horned beasty has already crossed the Euro-Asian land mass from one end to another: long, long ago. Keep *this* in mind, too: ''Near the field Helyon in the Holy Land is a river Mara [Hebrew, *bitter*], whose bitter waters Moses struck with his staff and made sweet, so that the children of Israel could drink thereof. [Not exactly what the Bible says: but close.] Even now, *now* being 1389, ''evil and unclean spirits poison it after the going down of the sun, but in the morning after the powers of darkness have disappeared, the unicorn comes from the sea and dips its horn in the stream, and thereby expels and neutralizes the poison, so that the other animals can drink of it during the day.'' Our authority for this useful information is ''the pilgrim, John of Herse.'' And how do I know *that?* Do I have his parchment journal lying by my side, no I don't, I know it because I have faith in the one who quotes him: Clark E. Firestone, in a wonderful book, *The Coasts of Illusion*, A Study of Travel Tales (Harper, '24). That is the way which items such as this are usually written, though it mayn't be fully known that such is the case. Not every author of something called, let us say, and we might safely say, as I'm making this up, *Gadzooks and Genzel-worms,* is going to tell you point-blank that he found out something in a book from the East Weewaw (Wis.) Public Library, let alone tell you *what* book. I fear that the author of *Gadzooks and Genzel-worms* is simply going to abstract his info and slip it to you as though it had been scraped off the wall of a tomb in Khartoum by the author himself. Well, why not. Old stuff. Of course at one time writers felt that the more titles and authors they could quote, the more impressive-sounding their own works were. Many an antique author is known by name only because a long-later one quoted him. However, gradually, a slyer note crept into the great game. ''Ambergris,'' a later writer may state casually, ''though

usually assumed to be the by-product of the indigestion of
the sperm-whale, was far more often produced in a
pickled-pigs' feet factory in Bratislava.'' (I'm making this
up, for pity's sake! Don't *quote* me.)—thus giving the
impression that he, personally, found this out in the course
of fatiguing researches in, of course, Bratislava . . .
whereas, actually, *no:* he simply extracted it from a slim
little volume entitled *Pickled Pigs-Feet Through the
Ages,* the Farmers Wife Press, East Weewaw, Wisconsin,
1893, where he had found it after being driven by rain into
the public library whilst waiting for his transmission to be
fixed.

I, however, will level with you. Only maybe not.

I am not sure when this began. Even the great Gibbon
indulged in it; all those immensely impressive footnotes,
Slawkenbergius, xxi, 13; Berzelius, xxx, 121; Isidore of
Isphahan *contra* Manichaeus, vl. 3—etc etc etc—you
think Gibbon actually *read* them all? No ho ho. Gibbon
lifted the refs. in toto from others. And when he presented
vol. ii of the great *Decline and Fall* to His Royal Highness
William Duke of Gloucester whose Patronage of Learning, and all the rest of it, HRH exclaiming, ''Another
demned thick square book? Scribble, scribble, scribble,
eh Mr. Gibbon?''—why, people sneered behind their lace
jabots, called HRH ''Silly Billy.'' Only maybe he wasn't
so silly. Being younger brother to George III is not absolute proof of feeble-mindedness. Almost, though. Well,
and how do I know all *this*? I read it. Somewhere. Forget
just where. Couple of places. Nyaa.

Meanwhile. Back to the Spoor of the Unicorn, which
has already led us to classical Chinese uranology,
medieval European alchemy, and ancient Hebrew
history—however, take note, and take careful note: although the Pilgrim John of Herse connects the unicorn
with the Biblical account of Moses, he speaks of the

unicorn as living in his, John's, own present time . . . not in the time of the Bible. This distinction is to be blurred, ere we have finished trekking this fabulous spoor.

Onward.

However. Ere we onward, note also that the unicorn makes its appearance only at the break of day, and it does not bathe in the stream; it suffices, evidently, for it to dip its horn in it. The key words, however, do not include *water*. The key words are *night, poison,* and *horn*. Remember.

With a cold, stern look all around, intent to smother any possible snickers, I ask, "What is it which we most commonly do at night?" The answer I promote is not, Listen to the radio, Eat a Dagwood sandwich, or, Call my Mother in East Weewaw, Wis.—it is, *Sleep*. Of course we sometimes sleep at other times as well. Sleep may well indeed be Nature's sweet restorer. But sometimes it is induced for other purposes than simply catching forty, in order to rise like a giant refreshed and go out and sell more Life and Casualty insurance than any other guy in the District. I will not cite you some sources which, at first sight, may seem to have nothing to do with unicorns . . . but if I were to cite, merely sources which specifically refer to them, why, you might simply go and read them for yourself. Anyone, after all, can go peek in the catalog (or, increasingly, the microfiche—harder on the eyes, easier on the feet) under *U*. The value of this Adventure, if value it has, is to bring before you things gleaned from fields seemingly foreign to the subject. This next field is entitled, *Folklore in the English and Scottish Ballads,* L.C. Wimberly, Dover, NY, '65 (reprinted from the edition of 1928).

In Scandinavian analogues of *Lady Isabel and the Elf-Knight* . . . the demon-lover's sleep is induced

by the power of runes, to match which we find in the
Scottish ballad . . . a soporific ''sma charm'':
  She stroaked him sae fast, the nearer he did creep.
  Wi a sma charm she lulld him fast asleep.
Among the several devices, again, which the woman
employs in order to get the murderer into her power,
the original would seem to be her inducing him to lay
his head in her lap, which gives her the opportunity
(by use of charms or runes) . . . to put him into a
deep sleep.

  According to the Swedish *Sömp-runorna* and the
Danish *Sövnerunerne,* which tells a story somewhat
similar to *The Broomfield Hill* . . . a maiden puts a
man to sleep by the aid of rune charms and so preserves her chastity.
[foot-note: For other examples of rune-slumber and
sleep-thorns in romance, ballad, and tale, see Child
[Ballads] . . .]

Very well, you've been very patient, you've read it,
you've read it all: what does it have to do with unicorns?
Well, the unicorn in John of Herse appears only just after
night has departed, night is connected with sleep, sleep is
magically induced by a lady's getting a fellow's head into
her lap, and that is the downfall of the unicorn: lays he
down that puissant head in that chaste lap, it's off to sleep
he goes. And awakes in chains. So to speak. —What?
Absurd? Preposterous? My dear people, this is *all* preposterous and absurd. No, it *won't* Sell Flour, no, it *has*
nothing to do with our Dwindling Natural Resources; it is
*Po*etry, it is *Ro*mance, and it is also an incredibly complex
account of one of the many complexities of nonsense
which from ancient times have perplexed and led astray
the minds of man- and womankind. Let us say in its favor
that though it is nonsense, it is gorgeous nonsense, and it

does not lead us down slow cold steps to worship a tyrant in his tomb; and that at least there have never been Unicorn Riots, Unicorn Wars, Unicorn Persecutions, Unicorn Plagues, Unicorn Famines. A scholar in his study studying unicorns will encompass no one's death in the sacred names of Science and Technology. Perhaps we are where we are because we have no more unicorns. Onward.

I have quoted Charles Fort to the effect that — But let me go back a bit. *Sleep-thorns*. What do thorns do? They prick, and draw blood. What do *horns* do? They gore. And draw much blood. Unicorns, thorns, horns, chastity, maidens, virgins, blood, sleep.

Back to Charles Fort, and . . . But, say. Who *was* Charles Fort? He was a roly-poly man with a walrus moustache who, having inherited a competence, spent the rest of his life copying odd stuff, damned odd stuff, out of books, magazines, and newspapers; writing them down on slips of paper and file-cards, filling thousands of shoe-boxes in his Bronx apartment with this data, which, eventually, he drew off into 4 of the damnedest, oddest books ever compiled: *Lo!, Wild Talents, New Lands,* and *The Book of the Damned*. For a very long time nobody much read these books, and in the meanwhile Charles Fort died. Read them if you can find them. They are absurd and fascinating. They have, specifically, nothing to do with unicorns. This was the man who said, "One measures a circle, beginning anywhere."

However, the spoor of the unicorn does not lead us altogether in a circle; if even time must have a stop (must it?), then even the spoor of the unicorn must have a beginning.

There was in Constantinople in the 9th century a holy and scholarly man named Photius, who was in fact the Patriarch of that city, "New Rome," capital of the Eastern Roman (or "Byzantine," a word its people did not use)

Empire. Things must have been placid at least for some considerable while in Photius's times. He did not have his beard torn out nor his nose cut off nor his eyes blinded, neither was he burned alive . . . at least I don't *think* he was burned alive; if somebody knows for a fact that the Patriarch Photius was burned alive, let me know, please. With all this peace and quiet at his disposal, Photius was able to devote himself to abstracting the works of Ctesias, a fellow-Greek and fellow-scholar who had lived almost 1300 years before him. Ctesias, in retirement, did not spend his golden years puttering around the house: he wrote a *History of Persia,* in 23 "books," a meaningless unit of measurement, now mostly all of it down the tube of time; and a work which we know as the *Indica.* Aristotle knew of Ctesias, but did not think much of him; what we know of what Ctesias knew, or thought he knew, we owe to His Holiness, Photius, Patriarch Oecumenical; or, more specifically, to his abstracts from the *Indica.* And so, rather than pretend that I have an excellent working knowledge of Greek, a language which I *flunked,* forty years ago, boys and girls! forty years ago—I shall quote what is perhaps the beginning of it all (only maybe not), and quote it from the properest place from which to quote: *The Lore of the Unicorn,* by Odell Shepard, Houghton Mifflin, Boston '30. And here it be.

There are in India certain wild asses which are as large as horses, and larger. Their bodies are white, their heads dark red, and their eyes dark blue. *They have a horn on the forehead which is about a foot and a half in length.* The dust filed from this horn is administered in a potion as a protection against deadly drugs. The base of this horn, for some two hands'-breadth above the brow, is pure white; the upper part is sharp and of a vivid crimson . . . and the remainder, or middle portion, is black. Those who drink out of these horns, made into drinking vessels, are not subject, they say, to convulsions or to the holy disease [epilepsy]. Indeed, they are immune even to poisons if, either before or after swallowing such, they drink wine, water, or anything else, from these beakers.

The date? The year 400+ or − before the Common Era will do. It may be said, then, that at this date the unicorn enters written history. You will note that it is not the single horn, as such, which most occupies the attention of Ctesias: it is the curative powers thereof. It ought to be noted, in this connection, that Ctesias, unlike many Greeks who had gone into Persia, was not a military but a medical man. And even as early as his time, and even as late as, say, the 18th century, in the eyes of many the chief importance of a physician was to save people from poison.

I don't refer here to fear of accidental poisoning, such as properly concerns us all, and against which (in theory) a network of Poison Control Centers have been set up, reachable by one's local police in a matter of seconds: no. I refer to a personal fear of being personally poisoned. It is said that the easy ritual of wine-tasting derives from the slow, ceremonious sampling of the Big Man's food and drink. If power tends to corrupt—and it does—so does the envy and the fear of power. And the desire to achieve it. If one were, say, 500 or 1000 years ago, desirous to remove from office one's chief, be he sacred or secular, one did not go out and ask people to sign a Recall petition; neither was it always feasible to hire an assassin. It was popularly believed that anyone who held high office was liable to be poisoned. What to do about it?

Recall that forensic medicine was all but non-existent, and that medical science itself, with its belief in the Four

Humours, its absolute ignorance of the world beneath the microscope, was—we now realize—all but impotent to provide real help to those really ill. Or, for that matter, when people died, to say from what they really died. Violent death was of course obvious, and so was death by any of the great plagues recognized as such . . . and that was, by and large, about *it*. But it was not recognized that that was about *it*. The stroke, the heart attack, the wasting diseases, and—and most of all—food poisoning (the "ptomaine poisoning" of my childhood) . . . none of these were always and clearly recognized as what they really were.

If the bishop fell into convulsions, if the duke died whilst dining, if the king ate a spoonful of preserves insufficiently preserved: no one said, "Botulism." Everyone was likelier to say, "Poisoning." When, indeed, somebody did not say, "Witchcraft."

Therefore, it was of immense importance to know that there was a way to avoid vicious intromission into one's food supply, and if this way lay via the use of the horn of a mysterious creature which in life galloped over the mysterious soil of far-off lands, why, how wonderful! Hardly anyone asked, "How do you know?" The usual question was, "How much does it cost?" And the answer was, "Plenty." *A wand of unicorn's horn,* Shepard says, *sold for 20 times its weight in gold* . . . If, therefore, a sovereign who used it regularly, lived to die of what was recognizable as old age, this was all to the credit of the unicorn's potent horn. If, however, unlike Mithridates, the king did not "die old," but, after a mere tenth helping of everything on the table during the heat of summer, turned crimson, made funny noises, and fell face forward into the stewed eels: why, what could have *caused* it? The answer was fairly obvious: poison. And . . . but . . . the

king's unicorn wand? His drinking cup of unicorn's horn?
It was a fake. Wasn't that obvious? Sure it was.

Unicorn was merely the chief-most of many substances
used in this ceaseless war against doses from the black
bottle. Petrarch, taking some time off from Laura, or
perhaps Cicero (he made an immense journey to find a rare
copy of a book by the Latin lawyer-orator . . . only to
find, also, that there was hardly any ink to copy it with and
probably the xerox was broken), noted of a certain poten-
tate the precautions he had taken "against secret plots;
between the wines and the viands project the livid horns of
serpents skilfully fastened to little gilded trees, so that it is
a wonder to see how Death himself stands guard, as it were
in the very strong-hold of pleasure, against the death of
this miserable man."

Leaving the horned serpent for a while, let us return a
moment to old Dr. Ctesias, there in his retirement home in
Cnidus, alternately exciting and boring the neighbors with
his tales of foreign parts and the great wonders thereof: he
had been the personal physician of the Great King of
Persia, and from Persia it was but a spit in the right wind to
India. Now, *India,* by obvious definition, one would
think, is the land of the *Indus* River; only maybe not.
maybe the river was so-named because it was in India.
One measures a circle . . . However. It has been said
that, "India, to Ctesias, is the Himalayas and Tibet."
Maybe so. Well, let's see, then, let's try this on for size
and style: "Somewhere in the Himalayas and Tibet is a
certain wild ass as large as a horse, and maybe larger."
Well, with an eye more to zoology than geography, one
might say that this a description of the onager, or wild ass;
perhaps of that other Asian wild ass, the kiang: ¿Quien
sabe? I am not a specialist in wild asses. Of course, when
we read that these beast had horns "on the forehead" we

realize that we have left zoology almost past the possibility of returning, and the length of the alleged horn is irrelevant. That there were one-horned beasts somewhere in them there parts is certain, for there still are, if they have not all been extirpated by the wonderful picturesque natives so busy enjoying their independence from imperialist constraint that they may soon have extirpated all their larger wild life and even a good deal of the smaller, too.

It is of course easier for us to preach conservation to them than it is for them to appreciate it. When a native of Nepal (which is in the Himalayas, or was, last I looked) sees a rhinoceros, he does not immediately think of how magnificent and increasingly rare it is; he immediately thinks (as does his African and Indonesian counterpart) of how much *meat* it is; next he thinks of all the damage it does to his crops (plenty), and he never thinks such thoughts as, "Well, maybe I shouldn't be planting my crops in rhino country;" and then he thinks of the *horn*, which is actually not a horn as the horn of the antelope is a horn, but a mass of compressed hair-tissue . . . or something like that . . . he doesn't care about that, neither does the horn-buyer. What they care about is that there are quite a lot of elderly Chinese gentlemen who, not yet being resigned to inability to achieve an erection, are willing to pay plenty for the medicine which will, they believe, make this possible. *Blamm!* It is a seller's market, and if the horn doesn't nowadays fetch 20 times its weight in gold, still, it fetches plenty. How come? How come that after all these years people are still paying plenty for a substance which doesn't do what is claimed for it?—namely, allowing old Mr. Wong to Get It Up. Kindly remember all those long centuries in which people paid plenty for it under the belief that it would prevent and cure poisoning. If "the origin of illness is in the mind," then so is its prevention and cure. —Yes, but what gives them such an idea? Mr. Wong, Mr.

Ong, Mr. Dong, *et al.*? Well, the idea is already there. How did it originate? I say, simply, that it is simple. Horn = Horny.

Very well, very well. But why did they describe the rhinoceros as an ass? Because, those unfamiliar with either Linnaean or Aristotelian ideas of categories, faced with new creatures, naturally describe in terms of old creatures. The sea-cow is not a cow, the sea-horse is not a horse, the Rocky Mountain goat is not a goat, the bison isn't really a buffalo; and neither, really, is the North American elk an elk. Going farther back into history than the time of Ctesias, we find the horse being described, early on, as "the ass of the east." The wild ass, by which one does not mean those poor stunted feral burro which, despite inroads made by starvation and disease, continue to destroy land-cover in many a western canyon; the wild ass is considerably larger than its domestic donkey cousin or the latter's run-wild descendants; but now enough about the wild ass.

The glamor of the unicorn, that is, of it as a particularly graceful and lovely creature, belongs largely to the Renaissance; the ancient world was impressed, but it was differently impressed. Here is our old friend Solinus, called (often) "Pliny's ape," and in fact almost improving on Pliny: here he is, in an older translation by Arthur Golding: *"Atrocissimum est monoceros"* —oops! that's not Golding, that's Solinus; still, you must admit that *Atrocissimum est monoceros* sounds more impressive than *Omnia Gallia est in tres partes* and the rest of it; *"But the cruelest is the Unicorne, a Monster that belloweth horrible, bodyed like a horse, footed like an elephant, tayled like a swyne, and headed like a stagge. His horne stikketh out of the midds of his forehead, of a wonderful brightness about four feet long* [It has *grown,* you see, since the earlier report of Ctesias; *eh,* Mr. Wong, Mr. Ong, and Mr.

Dong? Hmmm.] *so sharp that whatsoever he pusheth at,
he striketh it through easily. He is never caught alive;
kylled he may be, but taken he cannot bee."* Note that
there is here no mention at all of the matter of his being
taken by a virgin. That came later.

And when, long later, it came to be realized that there
was an animal, the rhinoceros, which, like the unicorn,
had one horn—did this immediately dissipate the legend,
relegating the unicorn to the realm of myth? No it didn't.
The rhinoceros was one animal, the unicorn another. Besides: sometimes the rhinoceros (read *nose-horn*) had
more than one horn. You *see?*

Physiologus (not his real name), that fairly early Christian writer who (most likely) lived in Alexandria and probably invented the Bestiary; Physiologus said that the unicorn was about the size of a goat-kid. Having swelled, it
now shrinks. *Uh*-oh, Mr. Wong, Mr. Ong, Mr. Dong!
This could not be endured. Just as the unicorn could not be
tolerated to be as large as the rhino, so it could not be
endured to be as small as a kid. The human mind, by a
series of trials and errors, finally figured out what the right
size of the unicorn was, and there it still is, on the other
side of the British lion, both of them holding up the Royal
Arms. You don't believe me, go look. I don't recall
having seen any ancient Greek or Roman *picture* of a
unicorn, either graved on pottery or painted on walls; but
in one of the murals of Pompeii is a centaur: how big is it?
oh, about the size of a goat-kid . . . in comparison to the
man-figure before whom it stands. Do I mean to imply a
connection? no I don't. The centaur was "merely" mythical; the unicorn was medicinal as well. Do you know about
St. Hildegarde? Do you know about Bingen on the Rhine?
Course you don't.

It was the custom in our public schools during the last
century and partly into this, to give those children capable
of it a "piece," often but not always a poem, to memorize

during the week, and to recite, usually on Friday afternoon, "in assembly." *The* assembly was not merely a gathering, it was a hall in the school building (is it still? they don't tell me these things); there we would gather to salute the Flag, listen to a Psalm being read, and receive instruction from the Principal. Sometimes this was limited to orders to eschew the syllables *Om* and *Yup;* on one Memorable Scene he directed all girls and women teachers to Leave the Assembly: the doors being reported firmly closed, he smote the table in front of him and cried, "This practice of throwing paper towels in the urinals must *stop!*"

Also, poems and other "pieces" were recited. One favorite began (searching the dimmest corners of memory), *"A soldier of the Legion lay dying in Algiers / There was dearth of woman's nursing, there was dearth of woman's tears. . . ."* And at each verse's end the dying soldier reminds us that he was *"born in Bingen, dear Bingen on the Rhine."* Other favorites included *Darius Green and His Flying Machine; There's Nothing To Laugh At, As I Can See, / If You'd Been Stung By A Bumble-Bee . . .* and, of course, a late-comer but a stayer: Joyce Kilmer's *Trees.* The science of reciting well had a name, it was called Elocution, my late Cousin Tootsie taught Elocution, and when this became unfashionable, she re-emerged as a Speech Therapist. Good one, too. Nowadays kids are not subjected to this harsh discipline, and, instead of reciting long poems, they drink, dope, smash windows, shoot out lights, wreck cars, knock up their eleven year old girlfriends, and set fire to churches. Progress, this is called. Progress.

Very well, Hildegarde was from Bingen, she was a nun, a physician, and a visionary. Shepard tells us that:

Hildegarde believed that not the horn alone of the unicorn but the whole animal was medicinal; under its horn, she says, it has a piece of metal as transparent as glass in which a man may see his face; she tells how to make an unguent of the yolks of eggs and powdered unicorn's liver, which . . . is a sovereign cure for leprosy—''unless the leper happens to be one whom Death is determined to have or else one whom God will not allow to be cured. [. . . .] A belt made from unicorn's skin, she says, will preserve one from fevers, and boots of the same material assure one of sound legs and immunity from plague. All this is good to know, and it comes from one who, as head of a large religious house, had the health of a whole community in her keeping.

As to where Mother Superior *got* her unicorn parts from, I am sure I do not know. Certainly it is easy to laugh and sneer. Once I saw a reproduction from an illuminated Ms which St. Hildegarde had either painted herself or directed a painter to execute; it showed things which I can best, though inadequately, describe as turrets, or castellations; I brought and showed it to an ophthamologist, asked what he thought. He said that he thought he agreed with the caption. ''Probably they are migraine constructs. Why do you ask?'' I said, because from time to time my eyes would become sun-dazzled by flashes of light and that things very much like the ones in St. Hildy's Ms would wiggle within them. Dr What examined my eyes fore and aft. ''It is my diagnosis,'' he said, thoughtfully, ''that you suffer from migraine, fortunately a mild form. Take the pills I'm going to prescribe, as directed.'' I did, they worked, the label says they consist of caffeine and phenobarbital and ergot: if they also, and surreptitiously, contain unicorn, well, *I* wouldn't be surprised.

When ''a whole unicorn's horn [was] worth six or seven thousand ducats'' there was a temptation to get one's money back before the interest mounted too high; anyone who has seen, even today, people casually swapping pills, will acknowledge a fairly widespread belief that what is good for one thing may likely be good for another; an old-time country pharmacist told me of the woman who used to come in once a year to ask for "A quarter's worth of mixed pills for my children." Ought to be no surprise, then, to learn that unicorn's horn, also known as *licorn* or *alicorn,* "had an important place in the *materia medica* . . . prescribed as a cure for all poisons, for fever, for bites of mad dogs and scorpions, for falling sickness, worms, fluxes, loss of memory, the plague, and prolongation of youth. Charlatans were even known to assert that it could raise the dead." Absurd? Take a look at the other items included in the medieval *materia medica*—with the possible exception of worms, nothing was available which was of any use, really, for any of the ailments mentioned. But this doesn't mean that they were useless. (Do I contradict myself? Very well, then, I contradict myself. I am vast, I contain multitudes.) A 19th C. cartoon by the great Daumier shows a sick man with a physician on each side. Says the homeopath, "My patients die of the disease." Says the allopath, "My patients die of the medicine." Says the patient, "*A moi c'est égal,* it's all the same to me." Sometimes, of course, the patients recovered; this was sometimes due to a sound constitution, a weak form of infection, or factors unknown; sometimes it was due to an absence of fear, itself one of the great killers. And if "the medicine," no matter what it contained, provided confidence, confidence would drive away fear. Often.

Well, well, very well, then. Here we have unicorn's horn. But, there being, really, I am afraid, no such actual thing as a unicorn—what *were* all those people taking, who thought they were taking unicorn's horn (alicorn,

licorn?) *What* were they applying to the food and drink on those lavish tables? *Bezoar-stone, snake's-tongue, terra sigilata, eagle-stone, snake-stone, toad-stone, cerastes, vulture's and raven's claw, vulture's claw, rhino horn, walrus tusks, stalactites, stalagmites, powdered stag's horn, tongue-stone, burnt horn, whalebone, limestone, fossils* . . . This list may pose as many questions as it answers. *Bezoar-stone,* for example, is a concretion which may be found in the tummies of turtles and of serpents as well as in those of cattle and goats. In my *"Adventure in Unhistory,* An Abundance of Dragons" (IASFM, July 6, 1981), I have attempted to connect it with the so-called treasure-hoards of precious stones guarded by the Great Worm. *Snake's tongue* may have been, indeed, snake's tongue; *similia similibus curantur,* like cures like, the poisonous tongue of a snake was—obviously—good against poison; the fact that the venom of a venomous snake is not distilled through its tongue was not fully realized. *Tongue-stone* was "really the petrified tooth of a shark;" Shepard doesn't say which shark; Fred, maybe. *Terra sigilata* means "sealed earth." The earth was taken from a place in the island of Lemnos for well over 2,000 years, stamped with whatsoever signs, and used for cups, as well as being eaten. One of the signs was the sign of the unicorn. Perhaps the consumption of the *terra sigilata* may be associated with the phenomena variously called pica, geophagy, or clay eating; Shepard doesn't say; *I* say. Also the earth was certainly one of the "native earths," largely (perhaps) aluminum silicate, used in modern times for stomach ailments such as ileitis. *Eagle-stone* is also a concretion (look up "concretion"); old John D. Rockefeller used to carry one in his pocket to keep off rheumatism, and, possibly, competition and trust-busting; for the last 40-odd years of his life he lived on *milk,* poor-rich guy, his stomach being able to hold nothing stronger—you think it's a cinch, being the richest man in the world?—popular belief says it was mother's milk, sceptics say it was merely that of mother goats. Maybe he should have tried *terra sigilata*, or one of its successors.

Toad-stones, despite Shakespeare's assurance that "the toad, ugly and venomous, Wears yet a precious jewel in its head," were actually "the fossilized teeth of the sting-ray."—And so on. As for fossils, if, as often, these were fossilized bones, the calcium content might well have been useful to the consumer.

However. When we read of the alicorns being some-times seven feet long, and sometimes decorated with silver and with gold, clearly we are not dealing with some nugget extracted from the belly of a goat, nor with a fossilized fish-tooth, a walrus tusk, or a concretion able to fit into a pocket . . . even a millionaire's pocket. Nor was it a cerastes, or viper's horn . . . what? A horned *snake?* Isn't this about as fabulous as a horned (as distinct from a horny) jack-ass? Let us to Webster's Collegiate (I use no other), what does it say, it says

ce-ras' tēs [L. a horned serpent, fr. Gr. kerastēs, horned, fr *keras,* horn] A venomous viper . . . of the Near East, having a horny process over each eye;— hence often called *horned viper*.

Well, I snum. Whether or not Herodotus snummed, I can't say, but he referred to "horned asses," too . . . and, clearly, his creatures were not rhino. What were they? Don't you wish you knew? Stick around. Rome wasn't built in a day. *Andrea Bacci . . . says that in his time a pound of* powdered *alicorn was commonly sold in Flor-ence for 1,536 crowns, the worth of a pound of gold at the time being 148 crowns.* More than they pay *me.* Of course,

I'm not working. I'm just writing. ("Are you working these days, Avram? Or just writing?") And if you knew how many years I have been accumulating these data, you would shake your heads in shame at the mere trifle you have paid to read it. Onward.

The learned Mr. Robert Silverberg, in his monumental *Prester John,* gives us the following report:

> Byzantine writers testify to the continuing power of Axumite Ethiopia in the 5th and 6th centuries. Ethiopian ambassadors were in attendance at the courts of Constantinople, Persia, India, and Ceylon. Ethiopian caravans spanned the desert route to Egypt and went up from Yemen across Arabia to Mesopotamia; Ethiopian vessels were active in the Red Sea. Kosmas Indicopleustes, who visited Ethiopia about 525, set down a vivid account of the great expeditions of traders sent from the Axumite capital every other year to the Ethiopian interior to bargain for gold, offering the primitive natives salt, iron, and cattle in return. Kosmas also told of the king's palace at Axum, with four great towers topped by four *statues of unicorns,* and marvelled at the tame elephants and giraffes in the palace courtyard.

Were these the unicorns of Ctesias, from far-off India? If the ambassadors of Axumite Ethiopia went as far as Ceylon, a commerce with India would not be out of the question;—or, on the other hand, were these unicorns the "horned asses" mentioned by Herodotus as being "in the eastern side of Libya, where the wanderers [i.e. nomads] live"? The name of the modern nation of Libya is a fairly recent borrowing of the ancient Greek term which included most of cisequatorial Africa aside from Egypt. Perhaps we shall find out. Perhaps not. Who knows what we shall find.

''I saw 32 unicorns there. This is an amazingly fierce creature, in every way similar to a fine horse, except that it has a stag's head, feet like an elephant, the tail of a boar, and a black horn on its forehead, six or seven feet long, which generally hangs down like a turkey-cock's comb. When it wishes to fight or use it in any other way, it raises it stiff and straight. I saw one of them in the company of several other wild animals, purifying a fountain with its horn. [. . .] The unicorn purified the water of pools and springs from any dirt or poison in them, so that these various animals could drink in safety after it.''

Who saw? One Reverend Father François Rabelais, M.D., is our source here, in his book *Gargantua and Pantagruel* (Penguin, 1955). As old Rabelais was a funny fellow, it is likely that he is funning here; despite the quotations from Solinus and ''the pilgrim John of Herse.'' *There is always more in a work of art than its creator intended,* says Marianne Thalmann; and it is certain that in the reference to the ''horn . . . which generally hangs down like a turkey-cock's comb . . . [and sometimes is raised] stiff and straight'' there is more intended than the good father's religious superiors intended he should intend; eh, Mr. Wong, Mr. Ong, Mr. Dong?

And surely it is now time to state that in the whole legend of the unicorn and the virgin (recall that it is a small *v,* and that we are dealing merely with a popular legend and not with any article of religious belief) there is scarcely a trace of mysticism, that the allegory or metaphor is purely, I would not wish to say ''impurely,'' a phallic one; that the horn which sometimes hangs down and sometimes rises stiffly erect is the same phallus which every male mammal has—or, for that matter, largely (ho ho) every male vertebrate—that, whether or not Ovid was correct in stating, ''after coitus all animals are sad,'' it is certainly correct that after coitus all phalluses are flaccid.

The whole thing was merely a tolerable joke which got, so to speak, out of hand; scarcely did one know it, before it had entered the realm of metaphor and art. The savage creature persuaded to lay its fierce-horned head in the virgin's (maiden's) lap, after which it fell asleep and was easily captured—what else is this but that which everyone knows as a commonplace? the pricking of the sleep-thorn? Samson shorn in the arms of Delilah as he slept? Sisera, sleeping, slain by Jael? Need we go on? Not really.

In Europe (merely to sum up) the horned unicorn yields to the charms of sex. In Asia the unicorn's horn gives capacity to prolong sex. To this day in southern Italy, *corno*, or "horn," refers to the penis, to the horn-shaped charm so puissant against all magic, and to magic—in its malign form—itself. I've said it once, and once again and no more say it I will: horn = horny.

Rapidly to ascend to a higher sphere, have I not hinted that there may have been Biblical elements in the legend of the unicorn? I have. There are verses. *God hath brought them out of Egypt; he hath as it were the strength of an unicorn*, Num. 23:22 (a marginal note—*wild oxx*). The them/he in question seems to be Jacob/Israel. *Will the unicorn be willing to serve thee, or abide by thy crib? Canst thou bind the unicorn with his band in the furrow? or will he harrow the valleys after thee? Wilst thou trust him because his strength is great? or wilt thou leave thy labour to him? Wilt thou believe him, that he will bring home thy seed, and gather it into thy barn?* Job, 39:9-12. These are among the great many rhetorical questions in the great Book of Job. And, to swing back to both Ctesias and Herodotus, earlier in the 39th Chapter of Job we find this: *Who hath sent out the wild ass free? or who hath loosed the bands of the wild ass? Whose house I have made the wilderness, and the barren land his dwellings*. However . . .

Let us recollect that the Bible was not originally issued in English, and take note that every Biblical use of *unicorn* is in the Old Testament, which came out, the first time around, in Hebrew. The world used was *re'em,* pronounced *rem,* and Bible scholars seem to agree that it really means "wild ox;" so say the Jewish translations, and so says a marginal note in the (Nelson) edition of the King James, or Protestant, version from which I have quoted. Other verses, which I have not quoted, seem to emphasize the *horn*—except sometimes, sigh, it is *horns.* Nowhere does the Bible indicate that this beast has only one horn. The implication must have entered via the Latin and the Greek translations, both of which had been revised after the first one(s); it is not possible for me, writing with the valor of ignorance, to say at which date implication of single-hornedness entered the texts—certainly, though, after the time of Ctesias or Herodotus. I conjecture visions of a translation committee wondering what *re'em* is, considering that it was anyway a horned animal living in the wilderness and not domesticable, and deciding that it might be the unicorn.

And that's as far as I go.

As for the moon, the fancied resemblance of the crescent moon to horns enters the symbolism of mankind earlier than we are able to trace; as for the pollution or poisoning caused by nocturnal demons, we have here, I think, a conflation of nightmares and wet dreams with the same half-awareness of the origin of a major plague which has given us the word malaria: *mal aria,* bad air. Webster's Collegiate again,

> *archaic:* air infected with a noxious substance capable of causing disease.

As I have expressed my simple but certain conviction

that 'horny' = 'horn,' and that 'horn' = 'horny,' it will come not as a shock when I state further that behind the 'poisons of the night' may well lie the so-called 'nocturnal pollution' which consists of, simply, the phenomena well-known to every man and boy under the common term of 'wet dream'—that is, a dream of sexual intercourse which results in an emission of semen. As for water, there was the obvious fact that water sometimes, often, *was* polluted (and what do I mean, "*was*"?), plus the not so obvious fact of stagnant water harboring mosquitoes which sometimes spread disease.

Let me attempt my reconstruction, then. The crescent moon rises and sets over a body of water, that is, *it dips its horn in it*. By day time many of the mosquitoes have gone back to their ponds and marshes, therefore the day is healthier than the night, that is, *the dipping of the horn has purified the water*. All horns are powerful, the rarer they are the more powerful they are, that of the unicorn is the rarest and thus the most powerful, so *if you dip the unicorn's horn in water it will purify the water*. Pollution is poison, and so *the unicorn's horn will both prevent and cure poisoning*.

Q.E.D.

Many items, we have seen, were passed as unicorn (licorn, alicorn), but the one which became recognized as unicorn's horn, the most obvious and excellent, was the long, straight, spirally one. There was nothing else really like it, it was obviously . . . well, whatever it was . . . and, by Jove! It looked like it damned well ought to *be* the horn of the unicorn. —And, after it had been so depicted in art long enough, the matter came to admit of no doubt. *Until*.

Until someone began to do a little book-keeping. The unicorn, it was generally accepted, lived in the south and the south-east. *Hot* countries. Yes? Yes. So . . . how come . . . how come that all the best—and, in fact, all the spirally—horns—came from the *north?* This question was long in being asked and was long in being answered; when the answer finally came, sometime in the 1600s, the effect was devastating: *"The unicorn's horn is the tooth of a fish which lives in the great northern ocean!"* —or, in modern terms, it is the tusk of the narwhal or narwhale. Back to Webster's Collegiate:

> tusk . . . 1. an elongated greatly enlarged tooth that projects when the mouth is closed and serves for digging food or as a weapon . . .

and

> nar-whal *also* nar-wal . . . or nar-whale . . . an arctic cetacean (*Monodon monoceros*) about 20 feet long with the male having a long twisted ivory tusk of commercial value.

Only, any longer, not *that* damned valuable! For, you see, it was not the innate value of the article which gave it its value; it was the belief that the article came from the magical land-animal which gave it its value; if it was not from the unicorn then it had no more value than if it had come from, say, the hippo. Ivory, although valuable, was, after all, merely valuable as ivory. The elephant could cure nothing, neither could the hippo, neither could the walrus, and so, certainly, neither could this damned Norwegian dolphin . . . or whatever it was . . . And after that, it was down-hill all the way.

The narwhale is born with the roots for two tusks, but only one of them grows out? Who cares. There is an antelope called the oryx with a long spiral horn, or horns, and sometimes one breaks off, or if viewed in profile the two look like one single horn? Who cares. It is possible to transplant the horn-buds of a bull-calf to the middle of its forehead so that it will have one centrally-located horn? Who cares. If the puissant horn was not in fact grown upon the brow of a classy-looking horse-like creature in a remote wilderness and taken after its capture by a virgin—if it was merely a damned *fish*-tooth washed upon a barren strand somewhere in Scandinavia . . . why . . . then . . . the hell with it.

Who cares.

Nobody.

After that, all the work of scientific scepticism and empiric investigation was largely beside the point. After that, the merchants of Venice, who had made many a killing in unicorn horn, after that, after asking the familiar question of *What news on the Rialto?*—the Venetian commercial district—did not bother to quote unicorn. Probably they quoted, instead, spaghetti. Which, after all, if not as romantic, is certainly a lot tastier.

Please pass the grated cheese.

Introduction to Theodore Sturgeon's "The Silken Swift":

Theodore Sturgeon is one of the true giants of the field, a seminal figure whose influence on the development of SF itself is hard to overestimate. Whether he was writing for John W. Campbell's *Astounding* during the "Golden Age" of the forties, or for Horace L. Gold's *Galaxy* during the fifties, or for the original anthologies of the sixties and seventies (or for *F&SF*, or *Playboy*, or . . .), Sturgeon has for more than forty years been in the business of producing stylish, innovative, and poetically-intense fiction. Sturgeon was one of the best short story writers ever to work in the genre, and even a partial listing of his short fiction will include major stories that helped to expand the boundaries of the SF story and push it in the direction of artistic maturity: "It," "Microcosmic God," "Killdozer," "Bianca's Hands," "The Other Celia," "Maturity," "The Other Man," and the brilliant "Baby is Three," one of the best novellas of the fifties. "Baby is Three" was eventually expanded into Sturgeon's most famous and influential novel, *More than Human*. Sturgeon's other books include the novels *Some of Your Blood*, *Venus Plus X*, *The Dreaming Jewels*, and the collections *A Touch of Strange, Caviar,* and *The Worlds of Theodore Sturgeon.* His most recent books are the collections *The Stars are the Styx* and *The Golden Helix.*

In ''The Silken Swift,'' one of the most renowned of all unicorn stories, he explores the subtle differences between those who are blind and those who will not see.

THE SILKEN SWIFT

Theodore Sturgeon

THERE'S a village by the Bogs, and in the village is a Great House. In the Great House lived a squire who had land and treasures and, for a daughter, Rita.

In the village lived Del, whose voice was a thunder in the inn when he drank there; whose corded, cabled body was golden-skinned, and whose hair flung challenges back to the sun.

Deep in the Bogs, which were brackish, there was a pool of purest water, shaded by willows and wide-wondering aspen, cupped by banks of a moss most marvellously blue. Here grew mandrake, and there were strange pipings in mid-summer. No one ever heard them but a quiet girl whose beauty was so very contained that none of it showed. Her name was Barbara.

There was a green evening, breathless with growth, when Del took his usual way down the lane beside the manor and saw a white shadow adrift inside the tall iron pickets. He stopped, and the shadow approached, and became Rita. "Slip around to the gate," she said, "and I'll open it for you."

She wore a gown like a cloud and a silver circlet round her head. Night was caught in her hair, moonlight in her face, and in her great eyes, secrets swam.

Del said, "I have no business with the squire."

"He's gone," she said. "I've sent the servants away. Come to the gate."

"I need no gate." He leaped and caught the top bar of the fence, and in a continuous fluid motion went high and across and down beside her. She looked at his arms, one, the other; then up at his hair. She pressed her small hands

31

tight together and made a little laugh, and then she was
gone through the tailored trees, lightly, swiftly, not
looking back. He followed, one step for three of hers,
keeping pace with a new pounding in the sides of his neck.
They crossed a flower bed and a wide marble terrace.
There was an open door, and when he passed through it he
stopped, for she was nowhere in sight. Then the door
clicked shut behind him and he whirled. She was there, her
back to the panel, laughing up at him in the dimness. He
thought she would come to him then, but instead she
twisted by, close, her eyes on his. She smelt of violets and
sandalwood. He followed her into the great hall, quite
dark but full of the subdued lights of polished wood,
cloisonné, tooled leather and gold-threaded tapestry. She
flung open another door, and they were in a small room
with a carpet made of rosy silences, and a candle-lit table.
Two places were set, each with five different crystal
glasses and old silver as prodigally used as the iron
pickets outside. Six teakwood steps rose to a great oval
window. "The moon," she said, "will rise for us there."

She motioned him to a chair and crossed to a sideboard,
where there was a rack of decanters—ruby wine and
white; one with a strange brown bead; pink, and amber.
She took down the first and poured. Then she lifted the
silver domes from the salvers on the table, and a magic of
fragrance filled the air. There were smoking sweets and
savories, rare seafood and slivers of fowl, and morsels of
strange meat wrapped in flower petals, spitted with
foreign fruits and tiny soft seashells. All about were
spices, each like a separate voice in the distant murmur of
a crowd: saffron and sesame, cumin and marjoram and
mace.

And all the while Del watched her in wonder, seeing
how the candles left the moonlight in her face, and how

completely she trusted her hands, which did such deftness without supervision—so composed she was, for all the silent secret laughter that tugged at her lips, for all the bright dark mysteries that swirled and swam within her.

They ate, and the oval window yellowed and darkened while the candlelight grew bright. She poured another wine, and another, and with the courses of the meal they were as May to the crocus and as frost to the apple.

Del knew it was alchemy and he yielded to it without questions. That which was purposely over-sweet would be piquantly cut; this induced thirst would, with exquisite timing, be quenched. He knew she was watching him; he knew she was aware of the heat in his cheeks and the tingle at his fingertips. His wonder grew, but he was not afraid.

In all this time she spoke hardly a word; but at last the feast was over and they rose. She touched a silken rope on the wall, and panelling slid aside. The table rolled silently into some ingenious recess and the panel returned. She waved him to an L-shaped couch in one corner, and as he sat close to her, she turned and took down the lute whcih hung on the wall behind her. He had his moment of confusion; his arms were ready for her, but not for the instrument as well. Her eyes sparkled, but her composure was unshaken.

Now she spoke, while her fingers strolled and danced on the lute, and her words marched and wandered in and about the music. She had a thousand voices, so that he wondered which of them was truly hers. Sometimes she sang; sometimes it was a wordless crooning. She seemed at times remote from him, puzzled at the turn the music was taking, and at other times she seemed to hear the pulsing roar in his eardrums, and she played laughing syncopations to it. She sang words which he almost understood:

> *Bee to blossom, honey dew,*
> *Claw to mouse, and rain to tree,*
> *Moon to midnight, I to you;*
> *Sun to starlight, you to me . . .*

and she sang something wordless:

> *Ake ya rundefle, rundefle fye,*
> *Orel ya rundefle kown,*
> *En yea, en yea, ya bunderbee bye*
> *En sor, en see, en sown.*

which he also almost understood.

In still another voice she told him the story of a great hairy spider and a little pink girl who found it between the leaves of a half-open book; and at first he was all fright and pity for the girl, but then she went on to tell of what the spider suffered, with his home disrupted by this yawping giant, and so vividly did she tell of it that at the end he was laughing at himself and all but crying for the poor spider.

So the hours slipped by, and suddenly, between songs, she was in his arms; and in the instant she had twisted up and away from him, leaving him gasping. She said, in still a new voice, sober and low, "No, Del. We must wait for the moon."

His thighs ached and he realized that he had half-risen, arms out, hands clutching and feeling the extraordinary fabric of her gown though it was gone from them; and he sank back to the couch with an odd, faint sound that was wrong for the room. He flexed his fingers and, reluctantly, the sensation of white gossamer left them. At last he looked across at her and she laughed and leapt high lightly, and it was as if she stopped in midair to stretch for a moment before she alighted beside him, bent and kissed his mouth, and leapt away.

The roaring in his ears was greater, and at this it seemed to acquire a tangible weight. His head bowed; he tucked his knuckles into the upper curve of his eye sockets and rested his elbows on his knees. He could hear the sweet sussurrus of Rita's gown as she moved about the room; he could sense the violets and sandalwood. She was dancing, immersed in the joy of movement and of his nearness. She made her own music, humming, sometimes whispering to the melodies in her mind.

And at length he became aware that she had stopped; he could hear nothing, though he knew she was still near. Heavily he raised his head. She was in the center of the room, balanced like a huge white moth, her eyes quite dark now with their secrets quiet. She was staring at the window, poised, waiting.

He followed her gaze. The big oval was black no longer, but dusted over with silver light. Del rose slowly. The dust was a mist, a loom, and then, at one edge, there was a shard of the moon itself creeping and growing.

Because Del stopped breathing, he could hear her breathe; it was rapid and so deep it faintly strummed her versatile vocal cords.

"Rita . . ."

Without answering she ran to the sideboard and filled two small glasses. She gave him one, then, "Wait," she breathed, "oh, wait!"

Spellbound, he waited while the white stain crept across the window. He understood suddenly that he must be still until the great oval was completely filled with direct moonlight, and this helped him, because it set a foreseeable limit to his waiting; and it hurt him, because nothing in life, he thought, had ever moved so slowly. He had a moment of rebellion, in which he damned himself for falling in with her complex pacing; but with it he realized that now the darker silver was wasting away, now it was a finger's breadth, and now a thread, and now, and *now*—.

She made a brittle feline cry and sprang up the dark steps to the window. So bright was the light that her body was a jet cameo against it. So delicately wrought was her gown that he could see the epaulettes of silver light the moon gave her. She was so beautiful his eyes stung.

"Drink," she whispered. "Drink with me, darling, darling . . ."

For an instant he did not understand her at all, and only gradually did he become aware of the little glass he held. He raised it toward her and drank. And of all the twists and titillations of taste he had had this night, this was the most startling; for it had no taste at all, almost no substance, and a temperature almost exactly that of blood. He looked stupidly down at the glass and back up at the girl. He thought that she had turned about and was watching him, though he could not be sure, since her silhouette was the same.

And then he had his second of unbearable shock, for the light went out.

The moon was gone, the window, the room. Rita was gone.

For a stunned instant he stood tautly, stretching his eyes wide. He made a sound that was not a word. He dropped the glass and pressed his palms to his eyes, feeling them blink, feeling the stiff silk of his lashes against them. Then he snatched the hands away, and it was still dark, and more than dark; this was not a blackness. This was like trying to see with an elbow or with a tongue; it was not black, it was *Nothingness*.

He fell to his knees.

Rita laughed.

An odd, alert part of his mind seized on the laugh and understood it, and horror and fury spread through his whole being; for this was the laugh which had been tugging at her lips all evening, and it was a hard, cruel, self-assured laugh. And at the same time, because of the anger or in spite of it, desire exploded whitely within him. He moved toward the sound, groping, mouthing. There was a quick, faint series of rustling sounds from the steps, and then a light, strong web fell around him. He struck out at it, and recognized it for the unforgettable thing it was—her robe. He caught at it, ripped it, stamped upon it. He heard her bare feet run lightly down and past him, and lunged, and caught nothing. He stood, gasping painfully.

She laughed again.

"I'm blind," he said hoarsely. "Rita, I'm blind!"

"I know," she said coolly, close beside him. And again she laughed.

"What have you done to me?"

"I've watched you be a dirty animal of a man," she said.

He grunted and lunged again. His knees struck something—a chair, a cabinet—and he fell heavily. He thought he touched her foot.

"Here, lover, here!" she taunted.

He fumbled about for the thing which had tripped him, found it, used it to help him upright again. He peered uselessly about.

"Here, lover!"

He leaped, and crashed into the door jamb: cheekbone, collarbone, hip-bone, ankle were one straight blaze of pain. He clung to the polished wood.

After a time he said, in agony, "Why?"

"No man has ever touched me and none ever will," she sang. Her breath was on his cheek. He reached and touched nothing, and then he heard her leap from her perch on a statue's pedestal by the door, where she had stood high and leaned over to speak.

No pain, no blindness, not even the understanding that

it was her witch's brew working in him could quell the wild desire he felt at her nearness. Nothing could tame the fury that shook him as she laughed. He staggered after her, bellowing.

She danced around him, laughing. Once she pushed him into a clattering rack of fire-irons. Once she caught his elbow from behind and spun him. And once, incredibly, she sprang past him and, in midair, kissed him again on the mouth.

He descended into Hell, surrounded by the small, sure patter of bare feet and sweet cool laughter. He rushed and crashed, he crouched and bled and whimpered like a hound. His roaring and blundering took an echo, and that must have been the great hall. Then there were walls that seemed more than unyielding; they struck back. And there were panels to lean against, gasping, which became opening doors as he leaned. And always the black nothingness, the writhing temptation of the pat-pat of firm flesh on smooth stones, and the ravening fury.

It was cooler, and there was no echo. He became aware of the whisper of the wind through trees. The balcony, he thought; and then, right in his ear, so that he felt her warm breath, "Come, lover . . ." and he sprang. He sprang and missed, and instead of sprawling on the terrace, there was nothing, and nothing, and nothing, and then, when he least expected it, a shower of cruel thumps as he rolled down the marble steps.

He must have had a shred of consciousness left, for he was vaguely aware of the approach of her bare feet, and of the small, cautious hand that touched his shoulder and moved to his mouth, and then his chest. Then it was withdrawn, and either she laughed or the sound was still in his mind.

Deep in the Bogs, which were brackish, there was a pool of purest water, shaded by willows and wide-

wondering aspens, cupped by banks of a moss most marvellously blue. Here grew mandrake, and there were
strange pipings in mid-summer. No one ever heard them
but a quiet girl whose beauty was so very contained that
none of it showed. Her name was Barbara.

No one noticed Barbara, no one lived with her, no one
cared. And Barbara's life was very full, for she was born
to receive. Others are born wishing to receive, so they wear
bright masks and make attractive sounds like cicadas and
operettas, so others will be forced, one way or another, to
give to them. But Barbara's receptors were wide open, and
always had been, so that she needed no substitute for
sunlight through a tulip petal, or the sound of morning-
glories climbing, or the tangy sweet smell of formic acid
which is the only death cry possible to an ant, or any other
of the thousand things overlooked by folk who can only
wish to receive. Barbara had a garden and an orchard, and
took things in to market when she cared to, and the rest of
the time she spent in taking what was given. Weeds grew
in her garden, but since they were welcomed, they grew
only where they could keep the watermelons from being
sunburned. The rabbits were welcome, so they kept to the
two rows of carrots, the one of lettuce, and the one of
tomato vines which were planted for them, and they left
the rest alone. Goldenrod shot up beside the bean hills to
lend a hand upward, and the birds ate only the figs and
peaches from the waviest top branches, and in return
patrolled the lower ones for caterpillars and egg-laying
flies. And if a fruit stayed green for two weeks longer until
Barbara had time to go to market, or if a mole could
channel moisture to the roots of the corn, why it was the
least they could do.

For a brace of years Barbara had wandered more and
more, impelled by a thing she could not name—if indeed
she was aware of it at all. She knew only that over-the-rise

was a strange and friendly place, and that it was a fine thing on arriving there to find another rise to go over. It may very well be that she now needed someone to love, for loving is a most receiving thing, as anyone can attest who has been loved without returning it. It is the one who is loved who must give and give. And she found her love, not in her wandering, but at the market. The shape of her love, his colors and sounds, were so much with her that when she saw him first it was without surprise; and thereafter, for a very long while, it was quite enough that he lived. He gave to her by being alive, by setting the air athrum with his mighty voice, by his stride, which was, for a man afoot, the exact analog of what the horseman calls a "perfect seat."

After seeing him, of course, she received twice and twice again as much as ever before. A tree was straight and tall for the magnificent sake of being straight and tall, but wasn't straightness a part of him, and being tall? The oriole gave more now than song, and the hawk more than walking the wind, for had they not hearts like his, warm blood and his same striving to keep it so for tomorrow? And more and more, over-the-rise was the place for her, for only there could there be more and still more things like him.

But when she found the pure pool in the brackish Bogs, there was no more over-the-rise for her. It was a place without hardness or hate, where the aspens trembled only for wonder, and where all contentment was rewarded. Every single rabbit there was *the* champion nose-twinkler, and every waterbird could stand on one leg the longest, and proud of it. Shelf-fungi hung to the willow-trunks, making that certain, single purple of which the sunset is incapable, and a tanager and a cardinal gravely granted one another his definition of "red."

Here Barbara brought a heart light with happiness, large

with love, and set it down on the blue moss. And since the
loving heart can receive more than anything else, so it is
most needed, and Barbara took the best bird songs, and the
richest colors, and the deepest peace, and all the other
things which are most worth giving. The chipmunks
brought her nuts when she was hungry and the prettiest
stones when she was not. A green snake explained to her,
in pantomime, how a river of jewels may flow uphill, and
three mad otters described how a bundle of joy may slip
and slide down and down and be all the more joyful for it.
And there was the magic moment when a midge hovered,
and then a honeybee, and then a bumblebee, and at last a
hummingbird; and there they hung, playing a chord in A
sharp minor.

Then one day the pool fell silent, and Barbara learned
why the water was pure.

The aspens stopped trembling.

The rabbits all came out of the thicket and clustered on
the blue bank, backs straight, ears up, and all their noses as
still as coral.

The waterbirds stepped backwards, like courtiers, and
stopped on the brink with their heads turned sidewise, one
eye closed, the better to see with the other.

The chipmunks respectfully emptied their cheek
pouches, scrubbed their paws together and tucked them
out of sight; then stood still as tent pegs.

The pressure of growth around the pool ceased: the very
grass waited.

The last sound of all to be heard—and by then it was
very quiet—was the soft *whick!* of an owl's eyelids as it
awoke to watch.

He came like a cloud, the earth cupping itself to take
each of his golden hooves. He stopped on the bank and
lowered his head, and for a brief moment his eyes met
Barbara's, and she looked into a second universe of wis-

dom and compassion. Then there was the arch of the magnificent neck, the blinding flash of his golden horn.

And he drank, and he was gone. Everyone knows the water is pure, where the unicorn drinks.

How long had he been there? How long gone? Did time wait too, like the grass?

"And couldn't he stay?" she wept. "Couldn't he stay?"

To have seen the unicorn is a sad thing; one might never see him more. But then—to have seen the unicorn!

She began to make a song.

It was late when Barbara came in from the Bogs, so late the moon was bleached with cold and fleeing to the horizon. She struck the highroad just below the Great House and turned to pass it and go out to her garden house.

Near the locked main gate an animal was barking. A sick animal, a big animal . . .

Barbara could see in the dark better than most, and soon saw the creature clinging to the gate, climbing, uttering that coughing moan as it went. At the top it slipped, fell outward, dangled; then there was a ripping sound, and it fell heavily to the ground and lay still and quiet.

She ran to it, and it began to make the sound again. It was a man, and he was weeping.

It was her love, her love, who was tall and straight and so very alive—her love, battered and bleeding, puffy, broken, his clothes torn, crying.

Now of all times was the time for a lover to receive, to take from the loved one his pain, his trouble, his fear. "Oh, hush, hush," she whispered, her hands touching his bruised face like swift feathers. "It's all over now. It's all over."

She turned him over on his back and knelt to bring him up sitting. She lifted one of his thick arms around her shoulder. He was very heavy, but she was very strong. When he was upright, gasping weakly, she looked up and down the road in the waning moonlight. Nothing, no one. The Great House was dark. Across the road, though, was a meadow with high hedgerows which might break the wind a little.

"Come, my love, my dear love," she whispered. He trembled violently.

All but carrying him, she got him across the road, over the shallow ditch, and through a gap in the hedge. She almost fell with him there. She gritted her teeth and set him down gently. She let him lean against the hedge, and then ran and swept up great armfuls of sweet broom. She made a tight springy bundle of it and set it on the ground beside him, and put a corner of her cloak over it, and gently lowered his head until it was pillowed. She folded the rest of the cloak about him. He was very cold.

There was no water near, and she dared not leave him. With her kerchief she cleaned some of the blood from his face. He was still very cold. He said, "You devil. You rotten little devil."

"Shh." She crept in beside him and cradled his head. "You'll be warm in a minute."

"Stand still," he growled. "Keep running away."

"I won't run away," she whispered. "Oh, my darling, you've been hurt, so hurt. I won't leave you. I promise I won't leave you."

He lay very still. He made the growling sound again.

"I'll tell you a lovely thing," she said softly. "Listen to me, think about the lovely thing," she crooned.

"There's a place in the bog, a pool of pure water, where the trees live beautifully, willow and aspen and birch, where everything is peaceful, my darling, and the flowers grow without tearing their petals. The moss is blue and the water is like diamonds."

"You tell me stories in a thousand voices," he muttered.

"Shh. Listen, my darling. This isn't a story, it's a real

place. Four miles north and a little west, and you can see
the trees from the ridge with the two dwarf oaks. And I
know why the water is pure!'' she cried gladly. ''I know
why!''

He said nothing. He took a deep breath and it hurt him,
for he shuddered painfully.

''The unicorn drinks there,'' she whispered. ''I *saw*
him!''

Still he said nothing. She said, ''I made a song about it.
Listen, this is the song I made:

> *And He—suddenly gleamed! My dazzled eyes*
> *Coming from outer sunshine to this green*
> *And secret gloaming, met without surprise*
> *The vision. Only after, when the sheen*
> *And Splendor of his going fled away,*
> *I knew amazement, wonder and despair,*
> *That he should come—and pass—and would not stay,*
> *The Silken-swift—the gloriously Fair!*
> *That he should come—and pass—and would not stay,*
> *So that, forever after, I must go,*
> *Take the long road that mounts against the day,*
> *Travelling in the hope that I shall know*
> *Again that lifted moment, high and sweet,*
> *Somewhere—on purple moor or windy hill—*
> *Remembering still his wild and delicate feet,*
> *The magic and the dream—remembering still!*

His breathing was more regular. She said, ''I truly *saw*
him!''

''I'm blind,'' he said. ''Blind, I'm blind.''

''Oh, my dear . . .''

He fumbled for her hand, found it. For a long moment
he held it. Then, slowly, he brought up his other hand and

with them both he felt her hand, turned it about, squeezed it. Suddenly he grunted, half sitting. "You're here."

"Of course, darling. Of course I'm here."

"Why?" he shouted. "Why? *Why?* Why all of this? Why blind me?" He sat up, mouthing, and put his great hand on her throat. "Why do all that if . . ." The words ran together into an animal noise. Wine and witchery, anger and agony boiled in his veins.

Once she cried out.

Once she sobbed.

"Now," he said, "You'll catch no unicorns. Get away from me." He cuffed her.

"You're mad. You're sick," she cried.

"Get away," he said ominously.

Terrified, she rose. He took the cloak and hurled it after her. It almost toppled her as she ran away, crying silently.

After a long time, from behind the hedge, the sick, coughing sobs began again.

Three weeks later Rita was in the market when a hard hand took her upper arm and pressed her into the angle of a cottage wall. She did not start. She flashed her eyes upward and recognized him, and then said composedly, "Don't touch me."

"I need you to tell me something," he said. "And tell me you *will!*" His voice was as hard as his hand.

"I'll tell you anything you like," she said. "But don't touch me."

He hesitated, then released her. She turned to him casually. "What is it?" Her gaze darted across his face and its almost-healed scars. The small smile tugged at one corner of her mouth.

His eyes were slits. "I have to know this: why did you make up all that . . . prettiness, that food, that poison . . . just for me? You could have had me for less."

She smiled. "Just for you? It was your turn, that's all."

He was genuinely surprised. "It's happened before?"

She nodded. "Whenever it's the full of the moon—and the squire's away."

"You're lying!"

"You forget yourself!" she said sharply. Then, smiling, "It is the truth, though."

"I'd've heard talk—"

"Would you now? And tell me—how many of your friends know about your humiliating adventure?"

He hung his head.

She nodded. "You see? They go away until they're healed, and they come back and say nothing. And they always will."

"You're a devil . . . why do you do it? Why?"

"I told you," she said openly. "I'm a woman and I act like a woman in my own way. No man will ever touch me, though. I am virgin and shall remain so."

"You're *what?*" he roared.

She held up a restraining, ladylike glove. "Please," she said, pained.

"Listen," he said, quietly now, but with such intensity that for once she stepped back a pace. He closed his eyes, thinking hard. "You told me—the pool, the pool of the unicorn, and a song, wait. 'The Silken-swift, the gloriously Fair . . .' Remember? And then I—I saw to it that *you'd* never catch a unicorn!"

She shook her head, complete candor in her face. "I like that, 'the Silken-swift.' Pretty. But believe me—no! That isn't mine."

He put his face close to hers, and though it was barely a whisper, it came out like bullets. "Liar! Liar! I couldn't forget. I was sick, I was hurt, I was poisoned, but I know what I did!" He turned on his heel and strode away.

She put the thumb of her glove against her upper teeth for a second, then ran after him. ''Del!''

He stopped but, rudely, would not turn. She rounded him, faced him. ''I'll not have you believing that of me—it's the one thing I have left,'' she said tremulously.

He made no attempt to conceal his surprise. She controlled her expression with a visible effort, and said, ''Please. Tell me a little more—just about the pool, the song, whatever it was.''

''You don't remember?''

''I don't *know!*'' she flashed. She was deeply agitated.

He said with mock patience, ''You told me of a unicorn pool out on the Bogs. You said you had seen *him* drink there. You made a song about it. And then I—''

''Where? Where was this?''

''You forget so soon?''

''Where? Where did it happen?''

''In the meadow, across the road from your gate, where you followed me,'' he said. ''Where my sight came back to me, when the sun came up.''

She looked at him blankly, and slowly her face changed. First the imprisoned smile struggling to be free, and then—she was herself again, and she laughed. She laughed a great ringing peal of the laughter that had plagued him so, and she did not stop until he put one hand behind his back, then the other, and she saw his shoulders swell with the effort to keep from striking her dead.

''You animal!'' she said, goodhumoredly. ''Do you know what you've done? Oh, you . . . you *animal!*'' She glanced around to see that there were no ears to hear her. ''I left you at the foot of the terrace steps,'' she told him. Her eyes sparkled. ''Inside the gates, you understand? And you . . .''

''Don't laugh,'' he said quietly.

She did not laugh. ''That was someone else out there.

Who, I can't imagine. But it wasn't I.''

He paled. ''You followed me out.''

''On my soul I did not,'' she said soberly. Then she quelled another laugh.

''That can't be,'' he said. ''I couldn't have . . .''

''But you were blind, blind and crazy, Del-my-lover!''

''Squire's daughter, take care,'' he hissed. Then he pulled his big hand through his hair. ''It can't be. It's three weeks; I'd have been accused . . .''

''There are those who wouldn't,'' she smiled. ''Or—perhaps she will, in time.''

''There has never been a woman so foul,'' he said evenly, looking her straight in the eye. ''You're lying—you know you're lying.''

''What must I do to prove it—aside from that which I'll have no man do?''

His lip curled. ''Catch the unicorn,'' he said.

''If I did, you'd believe I was virgin?''

''I must,'' he admitted. He turned away, then said, over his shoulder, ''But—*you?*''

She watched him thoughtfully until he left the marketplace. Her eyes sparkled; then she walked briskly to the goldsmith's, where she ordered a bridle of woven gold.

If the unicorn pool lay in the Bogs nearby, Rita reasoned, someone who was familiar with that brackish wasteland must know of it. And when she made a list in her mind of those few who travelled the Bogs, she knew whom to ask. With that, the other deduction came readily. Her laughter drew stares as she moved through the marketplace.

By the vegetable stall she stopped. The girl looked up patiently.

Rita stood swinging one expensive glove against the

other wrist, half-smiling. "So you're the one." She studied the plain, inward-turning, peaceful face until Barbara had to turn her eyes away. Rita said, without further preamble, "I want you to show me the unicorn pool in two weeks."

Barbara looked up again, and now it was Rita who dropped her eyes. Rita said, "I can have someone else find it, of course. If you'd rather not." She spoke very clearly, and people turned to listen. They looked from Barbara to Rita and back again, and they waited.

"I don't mind," said Barbara faintly. As soon as Rita had left, smiling, she packed up her things and went silently back to her house.

The goldsmith, of course, made no secret of such an extraordinary commission; and that, plus the gossips who had overheard Rita talking to Barbara, made the expedition into a cavalcade. The whole village turned out to see; the boys kept firmly in check so that Rita might lead the way; the young bloods ranged behind her (some a little less carefree than they might be) and others snickering behind their hands. Behind them the girls, one or two a little pale, others eager as cats to see the squire's daughter fail, and perhaps even . . . but then, only she had the golden bridle.

She carried it casually, but casualness could not hide it, for it was not wrapped, and it swung and blazed in the sun. She wore a flowing white robe, trimmed a little short so that she might negotiate the rough bogland; she had on a golden girdle and little gold sandals, and a gold chain bound her head and hair like a coronet.

Barbara walked quietly a little behind Rita, closed in with her own thoughts. Not once did she look at Del, who strode somberly by himself.

Rita halted a moment and let Barbara catch up, then walked beside her. "Tell me," she said quietly, "why did you come? It needn't have been you."

"I'm his friend," Barbara said. She quickly touched the bridle with her finger. "The unicorn."

"Oh," said Rita. "The unicorn." She looked archly at the other girl. "You wouldn't betray all your friends, would you?"

Barbara looked at her thoughtfully, without anger. "If—when you catch the unicorn," she said carefully, "what will you do with him?"

"What an amazing question! I shall keep him, of course!"

"I thought I might persuade you to let him go."

Rita smiled, and hung the bridle on her other arm. "You could never do that."

"I know," said Barbara. "But I thought I might, so that's why I came." And before Rita could answer, she dropped behind again.

The last ridge, the one which overlooked the unicorn pool, saw a series of gasps as the ranks of villagers topped it, one after the other, and saw what lay below; and it was indeed beautiful.

Surprisingly, it was Del who took it upon himself to call out, in his great voice, "Everyone wait here!" And everyone did; the top of the ridge filled slowly, from one side to the other, with craning, murmuring people. And then Del bounded after Rita and Barbara.

Barabara said, "I'll stop here."

"Wait," said Rita, imperiously. Of Del she demanded, "What are you coming for?"

"To see fair play," he growled. "The little I know of witchcraft makes me like none of it."

"Very well," she said calmly. Then she smiled her

very own smile. "Since you insist, I'd rather enjoy Barbara's company too."

Barbara hesitated. "Come, he won't hurt you, girl," said Rita. "He doesn't know you exist."

"Oh," said Barbara, wonderingly.

Del said gruffly, "I do so. She has the vegetable stall."

Rita smiled at Barbara, the secrets bright in her eyes. Barbara said nothing, but came with them.

"You should go back, you know," Rita said silkily to Del, when she could. "Haven't you been humiliated enough yet?"

He did not answer.

She said, "Stubborn animal! Do you think I'd have come this far if I weren't sure?"

"Yes," said Del, "I think perhaps you would."

They reached the blue moss. Rita shuffled it about with her feet and then sank gracefully down to it. Barbara stood alone in the shadows of the willow grove. Del thumped gently at an aspen with his fist. Rita, smiling, arranged the bridle to cast, and laid it across her lap.

The rabbits stayed hid. There was an uneasiness about the grove. Barbara sank to her knees, and put out her hand. A chipmunk ran to nestle in it.

This time there was a difference. This time it was not the slow silencing of living things that warned of his approach, but a sudden babble from the people on the ridge.

Rita gathered her legs under her like a sprinter, and held the bridle poised. Her eyes were round and bright, and the tip of her tongue showed between her white teeth. Barbara was a statue. Del put his back against his tree, and became as still as Barbara.

Then from the ridge came a single, simultaneous intake of breath, and silence. One knew without looking that some stared speechless, that some buried their faces or threw an arm over their eyes.

He came.

He came slowly this time, his golden hooves choosing his paces like so many embroidery needles. He held his splendid head high. He regarded the three on the bank gravely, and then turned to look at the ridge for a moment. At last he turned, and came round the pond by the willow grove. Just on the blue moss, he stopped to look down into the pond. It seemed that he drew one deep clear breath. He bent his head then, and drank, and lifted his head to shake away the shining drops.

He turned toward the three spellbound humans and looked at them each in turn. And it was not Rita he went to, at last, nor Barbara. He came to Del, and he drank of Del's eyes with his own just as he had partaken of the pool— deeply and at leisure. The beauty and wisdom were there, and the compassion, and what looked like a bright white point of anger. Del knew that the creature had read everything then, and that he knew all three of them in ways unknown to human beings.

There was a majestic sadness in the way he turned then, and dropped his shining head, and stepped daintily to Rita. She sighed, and rose up a little, lifting the bridle. The unicorn lowered his horn to receive it—

—and tossed his head, tore the bridle out of her grasp, sent the golden thing high in the air. It turned there in the sun, and fell into the pond.

And the instant it touched the water, the pond was a bog and the birds rose mourning from the trees. The unicorn looked up at them, and shook himself. Then he trotted to Barbara and knelt, and put his smooth, stainless head in her lap.

Barbara's hands stayed on the ground by her sides. Her

gaze roved over the warm white beauty, up to the tip of the golden horn and back.

The scream was frightening. Rita's hands were up like claws, and she had bitten her tongue; there was blood on her mouth. She screamed again. She threw herself off the now withered moss toward the unicorn and Barbara. "She can't be!" Rita shrieked. She collided with Del's broad right hand. "It's wrong, I tell you, she, you, I . . ."

"I'm satisfied," said Del, low in his throat. "Keep away, squire's daughter."

She recoiled from him, made as if to try to circle him. He stepped forward. She ground her chin into one shoulder, then the other, in a gesture of sheer frustration, turned suddenly and ran toward the ridge. "It's mine, it's mine," she screamed. "I tell you it can't be hers, don't you understand? I never once, I never did, but she, but she—"

She slowed and stopped, then, and fell silent at the sound that rose from the ridge. It began like the first patter of rain on oak leaves, and it gathered voice until it was a rumble and then a roar. She stood looking up, her face working, the sound washing over her. She shrank from it.

It was laughter.

She turned once, a pleading just beginning to form on her face. Del regarded her stonily. She faced the ridge then, and squared her shoulders, and walked up the hill, to go into the laughter, to go through it, to have it follow her all the way home and all the days of her life.

Del turned to Barbara just as she bent over the beautiful head. She said, "Silken-swift . . . go free."

The unicorn raised its head and looked up at Del. Del's mouth opened. He took a clumsy step forward, stopped again. "You!"

Barbara's face was set. "You weren't to know," she

choked. "You weren't ever to know . . . I was so glad you were blind, because I thought you'd never know."

He fell on his knees beside her. And when he did, the unicorn touched her face with his satin nose, and all the girl's pent-up beauty flooded outward. The unicorn rose from his kneeling, and whickered softly. Del looked at her, and only the unicorn was more beautiful. He put out his hand to the shining neck, and for a moment felt the incredible silk of the mane flowing across his fingers. The unicorn reared then, and wheeled, and in a great leap was across the bog, and in two more was on the crest of the farther ridge. He paused there briefly, with the sun on him, and then was gone.

Barbara said, "For us, he lost his pool, his beautiful pool."

And Del said, "He will get another. He must." With difficulty he added, "He couldn't be . . . punished . . . for being so gloriously Fair."

Introduction to
L. Sprague de Camp's
"Eudoric's Unicorn":

Like Sturgeon, L. Sprague de Camp is a seminal figure, one whose career spans almost the entire development of modern fantasy and SF. Much of the luster of the "Golden Age" of *Astounding* during the late thirties and the forties is due to the presence in those pages of de Camp, along with his great contemporaries Robert A. Heinlein, Theodore Sturgeon, and A. E. Van Vogt. Important as de Camp was to *Astounding,* though, he was indispensible to *Unknown, Astounding's* sister fantasy magazine—it was in *Unknown* that de Camp's talent really blossomed, and it was there that much of his best work saw print. In fact, great as de Camp's impact on SF was, his impact on the development of fantasy was incalculably greater, and it is impossible to imagine the shape of modern fantasy without him. De Camp's stories for *Unknown* are among the best short fantasies ever written, and include such classics as "The Wheels of If" (one of the first alternate worlds stories), "Divide and Rule," "The Gnarly Man," "None but Lucifer" (with Horace L. Gold), as well as novels such as *Solomon's Stone* and the brilliant *Lest Darkness Fall,* (another alternate worlds story, and one of the three or four best novels ever written on that subject). It would

be the "Harold Shea" stories, though, written in collaboration with Fletcher Pratt (the first of which was "The
Roaring Trumpet" in 1939) that would have the greatest
effect on subsequent work. Collected into book form in
1940 as *The Incomplete Enchanter,* and followed a year
later by a sequel, *The Castle of Iron,* the two Harold Shea
novels (they were collected in an omnibus volume, *The
Compleat Enchanter* in 1975) are truly landmarks of modern fantasy. (It is also interesting to note that the magazine
stories that would make up *The Incomplete Enchanter*
were published almost simultaneously with T. H. White's
The Sword in the Stone, the first section of *The Once and
Future King,* and that both works were charming, intelligent, and highly literate fantasies that depended heavily
for their effect on whimsy and deliberate—and very
funny—anachronism; obviously some special kind of
muse was in the air that particular year.)

De Camp is also in large part responsible for the current
flourishing popularity of "sword and sorcery" or "heroic
fantasy": in 1963 he edited an anthology called *Swords
and Sorcery* in an attempt to preserve and revive a long-
forgotten and "endangered" sub-genre of heroic fantasy,
and in so doing exposed modern readers for the first time
to some of the older giants of fantasy, some of whom had
been out-of-print entirely since before World War II; de
Camp also helped to start the big *Conan* boom of the
sixties and seventies, and has himself converted a number
of uncompleted Robert E. Howard manuscripts into
Conan stories and novels. He has also published some of
the major critical books *about* fantasy, notably *Literary
Swordsmen and Sorcerers* and the definitive *Lovecraft: A
Biography.* De Camp's other books include *Rogue Queen,
The Tower of Zanid, The Search for Zei/The Hand of Zei,
Land of Unreason* (with Fletcher Pratt), *The Glory That
Was.* His most recent books are *The Great Fetish,* and

the collections *The Purple Pterodactyls* and *The Best of L. Sprague de Camp*.

Wry humor mixed with fast-paced and vividly colored adventure has always been de Camp's forte, and the story that follows is no exception, as he turns his sharp satirist's eye toward the unicorn legend . . .

EUDORIC'S UNICORN

L. Sprague de Camp

WHEN Sir Eudoric Dambertson's stagecoach line was running smoothly, Eudoric thought of expansion. He would extend the line from Kromnitch to Sogambrium, the capital of the New Napolitanian Empire. He would order a second coach. He would hire a scrivener to relieve him of the bookkeeping . . .

The initial step would be to look over the Sogambrian end of the route. So he posted notices in Zurgau and Kromnitch that, on a certain day, he would instead of turning around at Kromnitch to come back to Zurgau, continue on to Sogambrium, carrying those who wished to pay the extra fare.

Eudoric got a letter of introduction from his silent partner, Baron Emmerhard of Zurgau, who once had almost become Eudoric's father-in-law. The letter presented Eudoric to the Emperor's brother, the Archduke Rolgang.

"For a gift," said Emmerhard, fingering his graying beard, "I'll send one of my best hounds with thee. Nought is done at court without presents."

"Very kind of you, sir," said Eudoric.

"Not so kind as all that. Be sure to debit the cost of the bitch to operating expenses."

"At what value?"

"Klea should fetch at least fifty marks—"

"Fifty! Good my lord, that's absurd. I can pick up—"

"Be not impertinent with me, puppy! Thou knowest nought of dogs . . ."

After an argument, Eudoric got Klea's value down to thirty marks, which he still thought much too high. A few days later, he set out with a cage, containing Klea, lashed to the back of the coach. In seven days the coach, with Eudoric's helper Jillo driving, rolled into Sogambrium.

Save once when he was an infant, Eudoric had never seen the imperial capital. By comparison, Kromnitch was but a small town and Zurgau, a village. The slated gables seemed to stretch away forever, like the waves of the sea.

The hordes who seethed through the flumelike streets made Eudoric uneasy. They wore fashions never seen in rural parts. Men flaunted shoes with long, turned-up toes, attached by laces to the wearer's legs below the knee; women, yard-high conical hats. Everyone seemed in a hurry. Eudoric had trouble understanding the metropolitan dialect. The Sogambrians slurred their words, dropped whole syllables, and seldom used the old-fashioned, familiar "thou" and "thee."

Having taken quarters at an inn of middling grade, Eudoric left Jillo to care for the coach and team. Leading Klea, he made his way through a gray drizzle to the archducal palace. He tried on one hand to take in all the sights but, on the other, not conspicuously to stare, gape, and crane his neck.

The palace, sheathed in stonework carved in fantastic curlicues, in the ornate modern style, rose adjacent to the Cathedral of the Divine Pair. Eudoric had had enough to do with the court of his own sovran, King Valdhelm III of Locania, to know what to expect at the palace: endless delays, to be shortened only by generous tipping of flunkies. Thanks to this strategy, Eudoric got his audience with the Archduke on the second day.

"A bonny beast," said Rolgang, stroking Klea's head. Clad in gold-and-purple Serican silks, the Archduke was a fat man with beady, piercing little eyes. "Tell me, Sir Eudoric, about this coach-wagon enterprise."

Eudoric told of encountering regular coach service,

unknown in the Empire, on his journey to Pathenia. He recounted bringing the concept back to his home in Arduen, Barony of Zurgau, County of Treveria, Kingdom of Locania, and of having a coach of Pathenian style constructed by local wainwrights.

"This bears thinking on," said the Archduke. "I can foresee some effects adverse to good government. Miscreants could use your coach to flee from justice. Bankrupts could leave the site of their indebtedness and set up in business elsewhere. Subversive agitators could travel 'bout, spreading discontent and rousing the rabble 'gainst their betters."

"On the other hand, Your Highness," said Eudoric, "if the business prosper, you may be able to tax it some day."

The beady eyes lit up. "Aha, young sir! Ye've a shrewd instinct for the jugular vein! With that consideration in mind, I'm sure his Imperial Majesty will impose no obstacle to your enterprise. I'll tell you. His Imperial Majesty holds a levée at ten tomorrow. Be there with this pass, and I'll present you to my 'perial brother."

Leaving the palace cheered by this unexpected stroke of good fortune, Eudoric thought of buying a fashionable new suit, although his thrifty nature winced at the thought of spending capital on another such garment before his present best had begun to show wear. He cheered up at the thought that he might well make a better impression as an honest rustic, clean and decent if not stylish, than as an inept imitation of a metropolitan dandy.

Next morning Eudoric, stocky, dark, square-jawed, and of serious mien, stood in plain russet and black, in line with half a hundred other gentry of the Empire. Emperor Thorar IX and his brother passed slowly down the line, while an official introduced each man:

"Your Imperial Majesty, let me present Baron Gutholf

of Drin, who fought in the Imperial forces to put down the late rebellion in Aiona. Now he doth busy himself with the reconstruction of his holding, dyking and draining a new polder."

"Good, my lord of Drin!" said the Emperor. "We must needs show our deluded subjects, stirred to rebellion by base-born agitators, that we love 'em in spite of all." Thorar was tall, thin, and stooped, with a gray goatee, an obvious hair piece, and a creaky voice. He was clad all in black, against which blazed a couple of jeweled decorations.

"Your Imperial Majesty," said the usher, "this is Sir Eudoric Dambertson of Arduen. He hath instituted the coach line from Zurgau to Kromnitch."

"'Tis he of whom I told you." said the Archduke.

"Ah, Sir Eudoric!" creaked the Emperor. "We know of your enterprise. We'll see you anon on this matter. But—are ye not that Eudoric who slew a dragon in Pathenia and later fought the monstrous spider in the forest of Dimshaw?"

Eudoric simpered with modesty. "Indeed, 'twas I, Your Imperial Majesty, albeit I came through more by good hap than by good management." He did not add that Jillo had killed the dragon, largely by accident, and that Eudoric, when he had the giant spider Fraka under his crossbow, had let her go on a sentimental whim.

"Stuff, my boy!" said the Emperor. "Good luck comes to those prepared to make the most of it. Since ye've shown such adroitness with strange beasts, we have a task for you." The Emperor turned to the Archduke. "Have ye a half-hour to spare after this, Rolgang?"

"Aye, sire."

"Well, bring the lad to the Chamber of Privy Audience, pray. And tell Heinmar to dig Sir Eudoric's dossier out of the file." The Emperor passed on.

In the Chamber of Privy Audience, Eudoric found the Emperor, the Archduke, the Minister of Public Works, the Emperor's secretary, and two bodyguards in silver cuirasses and crested helms. The Emperor was turning the pages of a slim folder.

"Sit down, Sir Eudoric," said Thorar. "This bids fair to take time, and we'd not needlessly inflict sore knees 'pon loyal subjects. Ye are unwed, we see, albeit nearly thirty. Why is this?"

Eudoric thought, the old boy might give the appearance of doddering, but there was nothing wrong with his wits. He said: "I have been betrothed, Your Imperial Majesty, but chance hath each time snatched away my promised bride. That I am single is not from lack of inclination towards the other sex."

"Hm. We must needs 'mend this condition. Rolgang, is that youngest daughter of yours promised yet?"

"Nay, sire."

The Emperor turned back. "Sir Eudoric, the gist is this. Next month, the Grand Cham of the Pantorozians comes on a visit of state, bringing a young dragon to add to the 'perial menagerie. As ye may've heard, our zoological collection is, after the welfare of the empire, our greatest passion. But, for the honor of the Empire, we can't let this heathen Easterling outdo us in generosity.

"Dragons are extinct in the Empire, unless a few still lurk in the wilder wastes. We're told, howsomever, that west of Hessel, in your region, lies the wilderness of Bricken, where dwell many curious beasts. Amongst these is the unicorn."

Eudoric raised his eyebrows. "Your Imperial Majesty wants a unicorn to give to this Pantorozian?"

"Aye, sir; ye've put the bolt in the gold. How 'bout it?"

"Why—ah—sensible though I be of the great honor,

Your Imperial Majesty, I know not whether I could manage it. As I told you, my previous escapes were more by luck than by skill or might. Besides, my coach line, requiring constant attention to detail, takes all my time—''

"Oh, stuff, my boy! Ye crave a just wage for your labor, as do we all, however we bluebloods affect to be above base thought of material gain. Eh, Rolgang?"

The Emperor winked. Eudoric found this ruler's genial cynicism refreshing after the elaborate pretence of the country gentry, among whom he lived, to care nothing for vulgar money. Thorar continued:

"Well, at the moment we have no vacant baronies or counties to bestow, but my brother hath a nubile daughter. She's not the fairest of the fair—"

"Petrilla's a *good* girl!" the Archduke broke in.

"None denies it, none denies it. Neither doth anyone propose her for the Crown of Beauty at tournaments. Well, Sir Eudoric, how about it? One unicorn for the hand of Petrilla Rolgangsdaughter?"

Eudoric took his time about answering. "The young lady would have to give her free consent. May I have the honor of meeeting her?"

"Certes. Rolgang, arrange it, if you please."

Eudoric had been in love several times, but the outcomes of these passions had given him a cynical, practical view of the battle of the sexes. He had never found fat girls attractive, and Petrilla was fat—not grossly so yet, but give her a few years. She was dark, dumpy, blunt of feature, and given to giggles.

Sighing, Eudoric totted up the advantages and disadvantages of being joined with this unglamorous if supremely well-connected young woman. For a career of courtier and magnate, the virtues of being the Archduke's son-in-law overbore all else. After all, Petrilla seemed healthy and good-natured. If she proved too intolerable a bore, he could doubtless find consolation elsewhere.

Back in Arduen, Eudoric sought out his old tutor, Doctor Baldonius, now living in semi-retirement in a cabin in the woods. A wizardly scholar who eked out his pension by occasional theurgies, Baldonius got out his huge encyclopedia and unlocked its iron clasps.

"Unicorn," he said, turning pages of crackling parchment. "Ah, here we are. 'The unicorn, *Dinohyus helicornus,* the last surviving member of the family Entelodontidae. The spirally twisted horn, rising from the animal's forehead, is actually not one horn. This would be impossible because of the frontal suture, along the mid-line of the forehead. It is, instead, a pair of horns conjoined and twisted into a single spike. The legend that the beast can be rendered mild and tractable by a human virgin appears to have a basis in fact. According to the story . . .' But ye know the tale, Eudoric."

"Aye," said Eudoric. "You get a virgin—if you can find one—and have her sit under a tree in a wood frequented by unicorns. The beast will come up and lay its head in her lap, and the hunters can rush out and spear the quarry with impunity. How could that be?"

Baldonius: "My colleague Doctor Bobras hath published a monograph—let me look—ah, here 'tis." Baldonius pulled a scroll out of a cabinet of pigeonholes. "His theory, whereon he hath worked since we were students at Saalingen together, is that the unicorn is unwontedly sensitive to odors. With that great snout, it could well be. Bobras deduces that a virgin hath a smell different from that of a non-virgin human female, and that this effluvium nullifies the brute's ferocious instincts. *Fieri potest.*"

"Very well," said Eudoric. "Assuming I can find me a virgin willing to take part in this experiment, what next? It's one thing to rush upon the comatose beast and plunge a boar spear into its vitals and quite another to capture it alive and unharmed and get it to Sogambrium."

"Alas! I fear I have no experience in such things. As a vegetarian, I have avoided all matters of chase and venery. I use the latter word in its hunting sense; albeit, *scilicet*, the other meaning were also apt for an adept like myself."

"Then who could advise me in this matter?"

Baldonius pondered, then smiled through his waterfall of beard. "There's an unlikely expert dwelling nigh unto Baron Rainmar's demesne, namely and to wit: my cousin Svanhalla."

"The witch of Hesselbourn?"

"The same, but don't let her hear you call her that. A witch, she insists, is a practitioner, of either sex, of black, illegal goëtics, whereas she's a respectable she-wizard or enchantress, whose magics are all beneficient and lawful. My encyclopedia traces the derivation of these words—"

"Never mind," said Eudoric hastily, as Baldonius began to turn the pages. "I've not met her, but I've heard. She's a crankly old puzzle, they say. What would she know of the techniques of hunting?"

"She knows surprising things. 'Twas always said in the fraternity, if ye wish some utterly useless bit of odd information, which nobody on earth could rightly be expected to have—say, for example, what Count Holmer the pretender had for breakfast the day they cut off's head—go ask Svanhalla. I'll give you a letter to her. I haven't seen her for years, for fear of her raspy tongue."

"So ye be a knight now?" said Svanhalla, sitting with Eudoric in the gloom of her hut. "Not by any feats of chivalry, ta-rah! ta-rah! But by shrewdly taking advantage of what luck hath brought you, heh? I know the tale of how ye slew that Pathenian dragon—how ye missed clean with the Serican thunder-tube and ran for your life, and how Jillo by chance touched off the sack of fire-powder just as the beast waddled o'er it.''

Silently cursing Jillo's loose tongue, Eudoric kept his temper. ''Had I been twice as brave and thrice as adept with the thunder weapon, Madam, 'twould have availed us nought had luck been against us. We should have made but toothsome morsels for the reptile. But let's to business. Baldonius says you can advise me on the capture of unicorns in Bricken.''

''I mought, if ye made it worth me while.''

''How much?''

After a haggle, Eudoric and Svanhalla agreed on a fee of sixty marks, half then and the rest when the unicorn was secured. Eudoric paid.

''First,'' said the witch of Hesselbourn, ''ye must needs find a virgin, of above fifteen years. If the tales I hear be true, that may take some doing in Arduen, what with you and your lecherous bretheren . . .''

''Madam! I have not carnally known any local lasses for nigh a year—''

''Aye, aye, I ken. When the lust becomes too great, ye fare to the whores of Kromnitch. Ye should be respectably wived by now, but the girls all think you a cold-blooded opportunist. Therein, they're not altogether wrong; for whilst ye love women, ye love your gold even more, heh!''

''You needn't rub it in,'' said Eudoric. ''Besides, I seek advice on hunting, not love.''

''Heh! Well then, your brother Olf doth cut a veritable swath amid the maids of Arduen. Not that I blame the lad overmuch. He's good-looking, and too many peasant maids think to catch a lordling with their coyntes for bait. They hope, if not for lawful wedlock, at least for affluent concubinage. So they all but shout: 'Come, take me, fair sir!' 'Tis a rotten, degenerate age we live in.''

"Since you know so much about affairs in Arduen, who, then *is* still a virgin?"

"For that, I must needs consult my familiar." She issued further instructions on the mechanics of capture, ending: "Come back on the morrow. Meanwhile go to Frotz the rope-maker to order your net and Karlvag the wainwright for your wheeled cage. Be sure they be big and strong enough, else ye may have less luck than ye had with the dragon, heh!''

When Eudoric returned to Svanhalla's house, he found her talking to a bat the size of an eagle. This creature hung upside down from her rafters, along with smoked hams, bags of onions, and other edibles. When Eudoric jumped back, the witch cackled.

"Fear not Nigmalkin, brave and mighty hero! She's as sweetly loving a little demon as ye shall find in the kingdom, heh. Moreover, she tells me what ye be fain to know.''

"And that is?"

"That in all of Arduen, there's but one wench that would fill your bill. True, there be other virgins in fact, but none suitable. Cresseta Almundsdaughter is ill and like to die; Greda Paersdaughter's father is a religious fanatic who won't let her out of his sight; and so on.''

"Then who is available?"

"Bertrud, daughter of Ulfred the Unwashed.''

"Oh, gods! She takes after her sire; one can detect her down-wind at half a mile. Is that the best you can do, Svanhalla?''

"So it is. Take it or leave it. After all, a proud, fierce adventurer like yourself shouldn't mind a few little stenches, now should he?"

Eudoric sighed. "Well, I shall imagine myself back in that prison cell in Pathenia. It stank even worse."

Bertrud Ulfredsdaughter would, if cleaned up, have been a handsome girl; some would say, even beautiful. Ulfred the Unwashed had once been told by a fortune-teller that he would die of a tisick caught from washing. He had therefore forsworn all external contact with water, and his daughter had fallen into similar habits.

Eudoric rode roundabout from Arduen back to the wilderness of Bricken. He avoided the demesnes of his old foe, Baron Rainmar of Hessel, and tried to keep on the windward side of Bertrud.

Besides Bertrud, with Eudoric rode Jillo's younger brother, a simple farm worker named Theovic Godmarson, to help with the heavy work. Jillo followed, driving the wheeled cage. Eudoric left Jillo with this vehicle at the edge of the forest, into which no road wide enough for it ran.

After a day of searching, while watching cautiously for the nearly-invisible webs of the giant spiders, Eudoric chose a spot. Here grew a giant beech, with enough boughs near the ground to make for easy climbing. It also stood near an affluent of the Lupa, by which they pitched their camp.

It took the rest of the day to rig the net, attaching it by slip knots to the higher branches of the beech and two nearby trees, so that one good pull on the release lanyard would bring the whole thing down. Leaden weights along the edges of the net assured that, when it fell, it would envelop the prey. They made the net heavy, and the summer day was hot. By the time they completed their task, Eudoric and Theovic were bathed in sweat. They threw themselves down and lay panting and listening to the buzz and chirp of insects.

"I'm for a bath," said Eudoric. "You too, Theovic? Bertrud, if you go round yonder bend in the stream, you'll find a pool where you can wash in privacy. 'Twould do you no scathe."

"Me, wash?" said the girl. "'Tis an unwholesome habit. An ye'd risk your death of cold, 'tis your affair."

During the night, Eudoric heard the snort of a unicorn. The next morning, therefore, he caused Bertrud to sit at the base of the beech, while he and Theovic climbed the tree and waited. Peering through the bronze-green leaves, Eudoric held the lanyard that would release the net. Bertrud languidly waved away the cloud of flies that seemed to follow her as a permanent escort.

When it arrived, in the afternoon, the unicorn did not look much like the dainty creatures, half horse and half gazelle, shown on tapestries in the Emperor's palace. Its body and limbs were like those of a buffalo, six feet at the shoulder hump, while its huge, warty head bore some resemblance to that of a gigantic hog. The twisted horn sprouted from its head above the eyes.

The unicorn approached the great beech, under which Bertrud sat. The beast moved cautiously, one step at a time. When it was almost under the net, it halted, sniffing with big, flaring nostrils.

It sniffed some more. Then it threw up its head and gave a colossal grunt, like a lion's roar but more guttural. It rolled its eyes and pawed the earth with cloven forehooves.

"Bertrud!" Eudoric called. "It's going to charge! Get up the tree, forthwith!"

As the unicorn bounded forward, the girl, who had

watched it with increasing dismay on her soil-caked face, scrambled to her feet and swarmed up the low branches. The beast skidded to a halt, glaring about with bloodshot eyes.

Eudoric pulled the lanyard. As the net began to fall, the unicorn sprang forward again, swerved to miss the tree, and continued on. One of the leaden weights of the net struck the unicorn's rump as the net settled to the ground.

With a frightful bellow, the unicorn whirled, champing its great dog-teeth or tusks. Seeing no foe, it galloped off into the forest. The crashing and drumming of its passage died away.

When the unicorn-hunters were back on the ground, Eudoric said: "That settles it. Baldonius said these creatures are sensitive to odors. You, my dear Bertrud, have odor for six. Theovic, you shall go to Hessel Minor and buy a cake of soap and a sponge. Here's money."

"Wouldn't ye rather go and leave me to guard the lass, me lord?" said Theovic with a cunning gleam.

"Nay. If I were recognized, Rainmar would have his bully boys after us; so keep a close mouth whilst there. Go, and with luck you'll be back for dinner."

With a sigh, Theovic saddled his horse and trotted off. With a trembling lip, Bertrud asked: "What—what will ye do to me, sir? Am I to be beaten or raped?"

"Nonsense, wench! I won't hurt a hair of your head. Don't think that, because I have a 'Sir' before my name, I go about bullying the commonality. I try to treat folk as they merit, be they serf or king."

"What will ye do, then?"

"You shall see."

"Ye mean to wash me, that's what! I'll not endure it! I'll run away into the wildwood—"

"With unicorns and other uncanny beasts lurking about? Methinks not."

"I'll show thee! I go—"

She started off at random. Eudoric imitated the grunt of the unicorn. Bertrud shrieked, ran back, and threw her arms around Eudoric's neck. Eudoric firmly unpeeled her, saying:

"When you're cleaned up and the unicorn's caught, then, if you're fain to play such games, we shall see."

Theovic returned at sunset, saying: "Here's your soap and all, me lord. Jillo asked after you, and I told him all went well."

Since Bertrud was cooking their supper, Eudoric let the bath go until morning. Then, stripped to his breech clout and with gleeful help from Theovic, he pushed and hauled Bertrud, struggling and weeping, down to the branch of the Lupa. They pulled off her skirt and blouse and forced her into the water. She shrieked:

"Gods, that's cold!"

"'Tis the best we have, my lady," said Eudoric, scrubbing vigorously. "By the Divine Pair, wench, you have layers of dirt over layers of dirt! Hold still, damn your arse! . . . Hand me the comb, Theovic. I'd get some of the tangles out of this hair. All right, I can manage the rest. It's time you fed the horses."

Theovic started back towards the camp. Eudoric continued soaping, scrubbing, and ducking his victim.

"Now," he said, "does that feel so dreadful?"

"I—I know not, sir. 'Tis a feeling I never have felt ere now. But I'm cold; let me warm myself against you. My, beant you the strong fellow, though?"

"You're no weakling yourself," said Eudoric, "after the struggle I had to get you in here."

"I work hard. There's none to do the chores, since me mother ran away with that pedlar, but me father and me. What thews!"

She felt his biceps, inching closer until her big, firm

teats rubbed his chest. Eudoric felt a familiar stirring in his loin cloth.

"Now, now, my dear," he said. "I said, *after* the brute's captured, not before." When she continued her attentions and started to explore Eudoric's person, he barked: "I said nay!" and pushed her away.

He pushed harder than he intended, so that she fell backwards and got another ducking. When she scrambled up, her expression had changed.

"So!" she said. "The high and mighty knight won't look at a poor peasant lass! Too grand for aught but them perfumed, painted whores of the courts! Ye may take them all to Hell with you, for all of me!"

She strode out of the pool, picked up her garments, and vanished towards the camp.

Eudoric looked after her with a troubled smile. He devoted himself to his own bath until the smell of breakfast reminded him of the passage of time.

He and Theovic rigged the net again. This time, the unicorn came around noon. As before, it seemed about to approach the seated Bertrud but then went into a frenzy of rage. Again, Bertrud had to scramble up the tree to safety.

This time, the unicorn did not even wait for Eudoric to pull the lanyard. It blundered off into the forest at once.

Eudoric sighed. "At least, we shan't have to haul that damned net up into the trees again. But what could have gone wrong this time? . . ." He caught a faint smirk on Theovic's face. "Oho, so thither lies the wind, eh? Whilst I was bathing this morn, you were futtering our frail, so she's no more a virgin!"

Theovic and Bertrud giggled.

"I'll show you two witlings!" howled Eudoric.

He whipped out his hunting falchion and started for the pair. Although he meant only to spank them with the flat, they fled with shrieks of mortal terror. Eudoric ran after them, brandishing the short, curved sword, until he tripped over a root and then fell sprawling. When he had pulled himself together again, Theovic and Bertrud were out of sight.

On the borders of the wilderness, Eudoric told Jillo: "When that idiot brother of yours comes in, tell him, if he wants his pay, to return to finish his task. Nay, I won't hurt him, for all his loonery. I should have foreseen what would happen. Now I must needs leave these nags with you whilst I ride Daisy back to Svanhalla's hut."

When Eudoric came again to the cabin of the witch of Hesselbourn, Svanhalla cackled. "Ah, well, ye did your best. But, when the devil of carnal desire reaves a youth or a maid, it takes one of monkish humor to withstand it. That's something neither of those twain possesses."

"All very true, Madam," said Eudoric, "but what next? Where shall I find another virgin, sound of wind and limb?"

"I'll send me familiar, Nigmalkin, out to scout the neighboring holdings. Baron Rainmar's daughter Maragda's a filly unridden, but she's to wed in a month. Besides, I misdoubt ye'd find her suitable."

"I should say not! Rainmar would hang me if he could lay hands on me. But . . . Harken, Madam Svanhalla, would not *you* qualify for the part?"

The witch's bony jaw sagged. "Now that, Sir Eudoric, is something I should never have hit upon. Aye, for all these years—an hundred and more—I have forsworn such carnal delights in pursuit of the highest grades of magical wisdom. For a price, mayhap . . . . But how would ye get an ancient bag of bones like me to yonder wildwood? I'm spry enough around this little cabin, but not for long tramps or horseback rides."

"We'll get you a horse litter," said Eudoric. "Bide you here, and I shall soon be back."

Thus it came to pass that, half a month later, the aged witch of Hesselbourn sat at the foot of the same beech tree on which Eudoric had rigged his net. After a day's wait, the unicorn approached, sniffed, then knelt in front of Svanhalla and laid its porcine head in her bony lap.

Eudoric pulled the lanyard. The net fell. As Svanhalla scrambled to safety, the unicorn surged up, shaking its head and snorting. Its efforts to free itself only got it more entangled. Eudoric dropped down from the branches, unslung the hunting horn from his back, and blew a blast to summon Jillo.

Eudoric, Jillo, and the forgiven Theovic rolled the beast, exhausted, but still struggling, on an ox hide. Avoiding thrashing hooves and foaming jaws, they lashed it down. Then the hide was hitched to three horses, which towed the ungainly bundle along the trail to where they had left the wheeled cage.

It took most of a day to get the animal into the cage. Once it almost got away from them, and a soaking thunderstorm made their task no easier. At last the brute was securely locked in.

Eudoric and his helpers shoved armfulls of fresh-cut grain stalks through the bars. The unicorn, which had not eaten in two days, fell to.

The Archduke Rolgang said: "Sir Eudoric, ye've done well. The Emperor is pleased—nay, delighted. In sooth, he so admires your beast that he's decided to keep the monster in his own menagerie, 'stead o' sending it off to the Cham of the Pantorozians."

"I am gratified, Your Highness," said Eudoric. "But

meseems there was nother matter, touching your daughter Petrilla, was there not?''

The fat Archduke coughed behind his hand. ''Well, now, as to that, ye put me in a position of embarrassment. Ye see, the damsel's no longer to be had, alas, no matter how noble and virtuous her suitor.''

''Not dead?'' cried Eudoric.

''Nay; quite otherwise. I'd have saved her for you, but my duty to the Empire overbore my private scruples.''

''Will you have the goodness to explain, my lord?''

''Aye, certes. The Grand Cham paid his visit, as planned. No sooner, howsomever, had he set eyes 'pon Petrilla than he was smitten with a romantical passion. Nor was she 'verse.

''Ye see, laddie, she's long complained that no gallant gentleman of the Empire could ever love a squatty, swarthy, full-bodied lass like her. But here comes the mighty Cham Czik, master of hordes of fur-capped nomads. He, too, is a short, stout, swart, bowlegged wight. So 'twas love at first sight.''

''I thought,'' said Eudoric, ''she and I had exchanged mutual promises—not publicly, but—''

''I reminded her of that, also. But, if ye'll pardon my saying so, that was a hard-faced commercial deal, with no more sentiment than a turnip hath blood.''

''And she's—''

''Gone off with the Grand Cham to his home on the boundless steppes, to be his seventeenth—or mayhap eighteenth, I forget which—wife. Not the husband I'd have chosen for her, being a heathen and already multiply wived; but she'd made up her mind. That's why my 'perial brother did not deem it necessary to send the Cham your unicorn, since Lord Gzik had already received from us an unthridden pearl of great price.

"But, even if Petrilla be no longer at hand, my brother and I mean not to let your service go unrewarded. Stand up, Sir Eudoric! In the name of His Imperial Majesty, I hereby present you with the Grand Cross of the Order of the Unicorn, with oak leaves and diamonds.''

"Ouch!" said Eudoric. "Your Highness, is it necessary to pin the medal to my skin as well as my coat?''

"Oh, your pardon, Sir Eudoric." The Archduke fumbled with fat fingers and finally got the clasp locked. "There ye are, laddie! Take a look in the mirror."

"It looks splendid. Pray convey to His Imperial Majesty my undying thanks and gratitude.''

Privately, Eudoric fumed. The medal was pretty; but he was no metropolitian courtier, swanking at imperial balls in shining raiment. On his plain rustic garb, the bauble looked silly. While he could let Petrilla go without uncontrollable grief, he thought that, if they were going to reward him, a neat life pension would have been more to the point, or at least the repayment of his expenses in unicorn-hunting. Of course, if times got hard and the order were neither lost nor stolen, he could pawn or sell it. . . .

He said nothing of all this, however, endeavoring to look astonished, awed, proud, and grateful all at the same time. Rolgang added:

"And now, laddie, there's the little matter we spake of aforetime. Ye are authorized to extend your coach line to Sogambrium, and beyond, if ye can manage it. By a decree of His Imperial Majesty, howsomever, all fares collected for such scheduled carriage shall henceforth be subject to a tax of fifty per centum; payable monthly. . . .''

Introduction to
Larry Niven's
"The Flight of the Horse":

When is a horse not a horse? This is a metaphysical question obscure enough to baffle a medieval theologian, let alone Svetz, the hapless, harried, and overworked Time Retrieval Expert who must deal with it in the fine and funny story that follows.

Larry Niven made his first sale to *Worlds of If* magazine in 1964, and soon established himself as one of the best new writers of "hard" science fiction since Heinlein. By the end of the seventies, Niven had won several Hugo and Nebula Awards, published *Ringworld,* one of the most acclaimed technological novels of the decade, had written several best-selling novels in collaboration with Jerry Pournelle, including the well-known *The Mote in God's Eye,* and had also established himself as a fantasy writer of some note with his novel *The Magic Goes Away.* His other books include the novels *Protector, World of Ptavvs,* and *A Gift from Earth,* and the collections *Tales of Known Space, Neutron Star, Inconstant Moon, The Long ARM of Gil Hamilton,* and *The Flight of the Horse.* His most recent books are *Ringworld Engineers, Oath of Fealty* (with Jerry Pournelle), and the collection *Convergent Series.*

THE FLIGHT OF THE HORSE

Larry Niven

THE year was 750AA (AnteAtomic) or 1200 AD (Anno
Domini), approximately. Hanville Svetz stepped out of
the extension cage and looked about him.

To Svetz the atomic bomb was eleven hundred years old
and the horse was a thousand years dead. It was his first
trip into the past. His training didn't count; it had not
included actual time travel, which cost several million
commercials a shot. Svetz was groggy from the peculiar
gravitational side effects of time travel. He was high on
pre-industrial-age air, and drunk on his own sense of
destiny; while at the same time he was not really convinced that he had *gone* anywhere. Or anywhen. Trade
joke.

He was not carrying the anaesthetic rifle. He had come
to get a horse; he had not expected to meet one at the door.
How big was a horse? Where were horses found? Consider
what the Institute had had to go on: a few pictures in a
salvaged children's book, and an old legend, not to be
trusted, that the horse had once been used as a kind of
animated vehicle!

In an empty land beneath an overcast sky, Svetz braced
himself with one hand on the curved flank of the extension
cage. His head was spinning. It took him several seconds
to realize that he was looking at a horse.

It stood fifteen yards away, regarding Svetz with large
intelligent brown eyes. It was much larger than he had
expected. Further, the horse in the picture book had had a
glossy brown pelt with a short mane, while the beast now
facing Svetz was pure white, with a mane that flowed like
a woman's long hair. There were other differences . . .

but no matter, the beast matched the book too well to be anything but a horse.

To Svetz it seemed that the horse watched him, waited for him to realize what was happening. Then, while Svetz wasted more time wondering why he wasn't holding a rifle, the horse laughed, turned and departed. It disappeared with astonishing speed.

Svetz began to shiver. Nobody had warned him that the horse might have been sentient! Yet the beast's mocking laugh had sounded far too human.

Now he knew. He was deep, deep in the past.

Not even the horse was as convincing as the emptiness the horse had left behind. No reaching apartment towers clawed the horizon. No contrails scratched the sky. The world was trees and flowers and rolling grassland, innocent of men.

The silence—It was as if Svetz had gone deaf. He had heard no sound since the laughter of the horse. In the year 1100 PostAtomic, such silence could have been found nowhere on Earth. Listening, Svetz knew at last that he had reached the British Isles before the coming of civilization. He had traveled in time.

The extension cage was the part of the time machine that did the traveling. It had its own air supply, and needed it while being pushed through time. But not here. Not before civilization's dawn; not when the air had never been polluted by fission wastes and the combustion of coal, hydrocarbons, tobaccos, wood, et al.

Now, retreating in panic from that world of the past to the world of the extension cage, Svetz nonetheless left the door open behind him.

He felt better inside the cage. Outside was an unexplored planet, made dangerous by ignorance. Inside the cage it was no different from a training mission. Svetz had spent hundreds of hours in a detailed mockup of this cage, with a computer running the dials. There had even been artificial gravity to simulate the peculiar side effects of motion in time.

By now the horse would have escaped. But he now knew its size, and he knew there were horses in the area. To business, then . . .

Svetz took the anaesthetic rifle from where it was clamped to the wall. He loaded it with what he guessed was the right size of soluble crystalline anaesthetic needle. The box held several different sizes, the smallest of which would knock a shrew harmlessly unconscious, the largest of which would do the same for an elephant. He slung the rifle and stood up.

The world turned grey. Svetz caught a wall clamp to stop himself from falling.

The cage had stopped moving twenty minutes ago. He shouldn't still be dizzy!—But it had been a long trip. Never before had the Institute for Temporal Research pushed a cage beyond zero PA. A long trip and a strange one, with gravity pulling Svetz's mass uniformly toward Svetz's navel . . .

When his head cleared, he turned to where other equipment was clamped to a wall.

The flight stick was a lift field generator and power source built into five feet of pole, with a control ring at one end, a brush discharge at the other, and a bucket seat and seat belt in the middle. Compact even for Svetz's age, the flight stick was a spinoff from the spaceflight industries.

But it still weighed thirty pounds with the motor off. Getting it out of the clamps took all his strength. Svetz felt queasy, very queasy.

He bent to pick up the flight stick, and abruptly realized that he was about to faint.

He hit the door button and fainted.

* * *

"We don't know where on Earth you'll wind up," Ra Chen had told him. Ra Chen was the Director of the Institute for Temporal Research, a large round man with gross, exaggerated features and a permanent air of disapproval. "That's because we can't focus on a particular time of day—or on a particular year, for that matter. You won't appear underground or inside anything because of energy considerations. If you come out a thousand feet in the air, the cage won't fall; it'll settle slowly, using up energy with a profligate disregard for our budget . . ."

And Svetz had dreamed that night, vividly. Over and over his extension cage appeared inside solid rock, exploded with a roar and a blinding flash.

"Officially the horse is for the Bureau of History," Ra Chen had said. "In practice it's for the Secretary-General, for his twenty-eighth birthday. Mentally he's about six years old, you know. The royal family's getting a bit inbred these days. We managed to send him a picture book we picked up in 130 PA, and now the lad wants a horse . . ."

Svetz had seen himself being shot for treason, for the crime of listening to such talk.

" . . . Otherwise we'd never have gotten the appropriation for this trip. It's in a good cause. We'll do some cloning from the horse before we send the original to the UN. Then—well, genes are a code, and codes can be broken. Get us a male, and we'll make all the horses anyone could want."

But why would anyone want even one horse? Svetz had studied a computer duplicate of the child's picture book that an agent had pulled from a ruined house a thousand years ago. The horse did not impress him.

Ra Chen, however, terrified him.

"We've never sent anyone this far back," Ra Chen had told him the night before the mission, when it was too late to back out with honor. "Keep that in mind. If something goes wrong, don't count on the rule book. Don't count on your instruments. Use your head. Your head, Svetz. Gods know it's little enough to depend on . . ."

Svetz had not slept in the hours before departure.

"You're scared stiff," Ra Chen had commented just before Svetz entered the extension cage. "And you can hide it, Svetz. I think I'm the only one who's noticed. That's why I picked you, because you can be terrified and go ahead anyway. Don't come back without a horse . . ."

The Director's voice grew louder. "Not without a horse, Svetz. Your *head*, Svetz, your **HEAD** . . ."

Svetz sat up convulsively. The air! Slow death if he didn't close the door! But the door was closed, and Svetz was sitting on the floor holding his head, which hurt.

The air system had been transplanted intact, complete with dials, from a martian sandboat. The dials read normally, of course, since the cage was sealed.

Svetz nerved himself to open the door. As the sweet, rich air of twelfth-century Britain rushed in, Sveta held his breath and watched the dials change. Presently he closed the door and waited, sweating, while the air system replaced the heady poison with its own safe, breathable mixture.

When next he left the extension cage, carrying the flight stick, Svetz was wearing another spinoff from the interstellar exploration industries. It was a balloon, and he wore it over his head. It was also a selectively permeable membrane, intended to pass certain gasses in and others out, to make a breathing-air mixture inside.

It was nearly invisible except at the rim. There, where light was refracted most severely, the balloon showed as a narrow golden circle enclosing Svetz's head. The effect was not unlike a halo as shown in medieval paintings. But Svetz didn't know about medieval paintings.

He wore also a simple white robe, undecorated, constricted at the waist, otherwise falling in loose folds. The Institute thought that such a garment was least likely to violate taboos of sex or custom. The trade kit dangled loose from his sash: a heat-and-pressure gadget, a pouch of corundum, small phials of additives for color.

Lastly he wore a hurt and baffled look. How was it that he could not breathe the clean air of his own past?

The air of the cage was the air of Svet's time, and was nearly four percent carbon dioxide. The air of 750 AnteAtomic held barely a tenth of that. Man was a rare animal here and now. He had breathed little air, he had destroyed few green forests, he had burnt scant fuel since the dawn of time.

But industrial civilization meant combustion. Combustion meant carbon dioxide thickening in the atmosphere many times faster than the green plants could turn it back to oxygen. Svetz was at the far end of two thousand years of adaptation to air rich in CO_2.

It takes a concentration of carbon dioxide to trigger the autonomic nerves in the lymph glands in a man's left armpit. Svetz had fainted because he wasn't breathing.

So now he wore a balloon, and felt rejected.

He straddled the flight stick and twisted the control knob on the fore end. The stick lifted under him, and he wriggled into place on the bucket seat. He twisted the knob further.

He drifted upward like a toy balloon.

He floated over a lovely land, green and untenanted, beneath a pearl-grey sky empty of contrails. Presently he found a crumbling wall. He turned to follow it.

He would follow the wall until he found a settlement. If the old legend was true—and, Svetz reflected, the horse had certainly been *big* enough to drag a vehicle—then he would find horses wherever he found men.

Presently it became obvious that a road ran along the wall. There the dirt was flat and bare and consistently wide enough for a walking man; whereas elsewhere the land rose and dipped and tilted. Hard dirt did not a freeway make; but Svetz got the point.

He followed the road, floating at a height of ten meters.

There was a man in worn brown garments. Hooded and barefoot, he walked the road with patient exhaustion, propping himself with a staff. His back was to Svetz.

Svetz thought to dip toward him to ask concerning horses. He refrained. With no way to know where the cage would alight, he had learned no ancient languages at all.

He thought of the trade kit he carried, intended not for communication, but instead of communication. It had never been field-tested. In any case it was not for casual encounters. The pouch of corundum was too small.

Svetz heard a yell from below. He looked down in time to see the man in brown running like the wind, his staff forgotten, his fatigue likewise.

"Something scared him," Svetz decided. But he could see nothing fearful. Something small but deadly, then.

The Institute estimated that man had exterminated more than a thousand species of mammal and bird and insect— some casually, some with malice—between now and the distant present. In this time and place there was no telling what might be a threat. Svetz shuddered. The brown man with the hairy face might well have run from a stinging thing destined to kill Hanville Svetz.

Impatiently Svetz upped the speed of his flight stick. The mission was taking far too long. Who would have guessed that centers of population would have been so far apart?

*   *   *

Half an hour later, shielded from the wind by a paraboloid force field, Svetz was streaking down the road at sixty miles per hour.

His luck had been incredibly bad. Wherever he had chanced across a human being, that person had been just leaving the vicinity. And he had found no centers of population.

Once he had noticed an unnatural stone outcropping high on a hill. No law of geology known to Svetz could have produced such an angular, flat-sided monstrosity. Curious, he had circled above it—and had abruptly realized that the thing was hollow, riddled with rectangular holes.

A dwelling for men? He didn't want to believe it. Living within the hollows of such a thing would be like living underground. But men tend to build at right angles, and this thing was *all* right angles.

Below the hollowed stone structure were rounded, hairy-looking hummocks of dried grass, each with a man-sized door. Obviously they must be nests for very large insects. Svetz had left that place quickly.

The road rounded a swelling green hill ahead of him. Svetz followed, slowing.

A hilltop spring sent a stream bubbling downhill to break the road. Something large was drinking at the stream.

Svetz jerked to a stop in midair. *Open water: deadly poison.* He would have been hard put to say which had startled him more: the horse, or the fact that it had just committed suicide.

The horse looked up and saw him.

It was the same horse. White as milk, with a flowing abundance of snowy mane and tail, it almost had to be the horse that had laughed at Svetz and run. Svetz recognized

the malignance in its eyes, in the moment before it turned
its back.

But how could it have arrived so fast?

Svetz was reaching for the gun when the situation
turned upside down.

The girl was young, surely no more than sixteen. Her
hair was long and dark and plaited in complex fashion. Her
dress, of strangely stiff blue fabric, reached from her neck
to her ankles. She was seated in the shadow of a tree, on
dark cloth spread over the dark earth. Svetz had not
noticed her, might never have noticed her . . .

But the horse walked up to her, folded its legs in
alternate pairs, and laid its ferocious head in her lap.

The girl had not yet seen Svetz.

"Xenophilia!" Svetz snarled the worst word he could
think of. Svetz hated aliens.

The horse obviously belonged to the girl. He could not
simply shoot it and take it. It would have to be purchased
. . . somehow.

He needed time to think! And there was no time, for the
girl might look up at any moment. Baleful brown eyes
watched him as he dithered . . .

He dared waste no more time searching the countryside
for a wild horse. There was an uncertainty, a Finagle
factor in the math of time travel. It manifested itself as an
uncertainty in the energy of a returning extension cage,
and it increased with time. Let Svetz linger too long, and
he could be roasted alive in the returning cage.

Moreover, the horse had drunk open water. It would
die, and soon, unless Svetz could return it to 1100 Post-
Atomic. Thus the beast's removal from this time could not
change the history of Svetz's own world. It was a good
choice . . . if he could conquer his fear of the beast.

The horse was tame. Young and slight as she was, the
girl had no trouble controlling it. What was there to fear?

But there was its natural weaponry . . . of which Ra Chen's treacherous picture book had shown no sign. Svetz surmised that later generations routinely removed it before the animals were old enough to be dangerous. He should have come a few centuries later . . .

And there was the look in its eye. The horse hated Svetz, and it knew Svetz was afraid.

Could he shoot it from ambush?

No. The girl would worry if her pet collapsed without reason. She would be unable to concentrate on what Svetz was trying to tell her.

He would have to work with the animal watching him. If the girl couldn't control it—or if he lost her trust—Svetz had little doubt that the horse would kill him.

The horse looked up as Svetz approached, but made no other move. The girl watched too, her eyes round with wonder. She called something that must have been a question.

Svetz smiled back and continued his approach. He was a foot above the ground, and gliding at dead slow. Riding the world's only flying machine, he looked impressive as all hell, and knew it.

The girl did not smile back. She watched warily. Svetz was within yards of her when she scrambled to her feet.

He stopped the flight stick at once and let it settle. Smiling placatorily, he removed the heat-and-pressure device from his sash. He moved with care. The girl was on the verge of running.

The trade kit was a pouch of corundum, Al_2O_3, several phials of additives, and the heat-and-pressure gadget. Svetz poured corundum into the chamber, added a dash of chromic oxide, and used the plunger. The cylinder grew warm. Presently Svetz dropped a pigeon's-blood star ruby into his hand, rolled it in his fingers, held it to the sun. It was red as dark blood, with a blazing white six-pointed star.

It was almost too hot to hold.

Stupid! Svetz held his smile rigid. Ra Chen should have warned him! What would she think when she felt the gem's unnatural heat? What trickery would she suspect?

But he had to chance it. The trade kit was all he had.

He bent and rolled the gem to her across the damp ground.

She stooped to pick it up. One hand remained on the horse's neck, calming it. Svetz noticed the rings of yellow metal around her wrist; and he also noticed the dirt.

She held the gem high, looked into its deep red fire.

''Ooooh,'' she breathed. She smiled at Svetz in wonder and delight. Svetz smiled back, moved two steps nearer, and rolled her a yellow sapphire.

How had he twice chanced on the same horse? Svetz never knew. But he soon knew how it had arrived before him . . .

He had given the girl three gems. He held three more in his hand while he beckoned her onto the flight stick. She shook her head; she would not go. Instead she mounted the animal.

She and the horse, they watched Svetz for his next move.

Svetz capitulated. He had expected the horse to follow the girl while the girl rode behind him on the flight stick. But if they both followed Svetz it would be the same.

The horse stayed to one side and a little behind Svetz's flight stick. It did not seem inconvenienced by the girl's weight. Why should it be? It must have been bred for the task. Svetz notched his speed higher, to find how fast he could conveniently move.

Faster, he flew, and faster. The horse must have a limit . . .

He was up to eighty before he quit. The girl lay flat along the animal's back, hugging its neck to protect her face from the wind. But the horse ran on, daring Svetz with its eyes.

How to describe such motion? Svetz had never seen ballet. He knew how machinery moved, and this wasn't it. All he could think of was a man and a woman making love. Slippery-smooth rhythmic motion, absolute single-minded purpose, motion for the pleasure of motion. It was terrible in its beauty, the flight of the horse.

The word for such running must have died with the horse itself.

The horse would never have tired, but the girl did. She tugged on the animal's mane, and it stopped. Svetz gave her the jewels he held, made four more and gave her one.

She was crying from the wind, crying and smiling as she took the jewels. Was she smiling for the jewels, or for the joy of the ride? Exhausted, panting, she lay with her back against the warm, pulsing flank of the resting animal. Only her hand moved, as she ran her fingers repeatedly through its silver mane. The horse watched Svetz with malevolent brown eyes.

The girl was homely. It wasn't just the jarring lack of makeup. There was evidence of vitamin starvation. She was short, less than five feet in height, and thin. There were marks of childhood disease. But happiness glowed behind her homely face, and it made her almost passable, as she clutched the corundum stones.

When she seemed rested, Svetz remounted. They went on.

He was almost out of corundum when they reached the extension cage. There it was that he ran into trouble.

The girl had been awed by Svetz's jewels, and by Svetz himself, possibly because of his height or his ability to fly. But the extension cage scared her. Svetz couldn't blame her. The side with the door in it was no trouble: just a seamless spherical mirror. But the other side blurred away in a direction men could not visualize. It had scared Svetz spitless the first time he saw the time machine in action.

He could buy the horse from her, shoot it here and pull it inside, using the flight stick to float it. But it would be so much easier if . . .

It was worth a try. Svetz used the rest of his corundum. Then he walked into the extension cage, leaving a trail of colored corundum beads behind him.

He had worried because the heat-and-pressure device would not produce facets. The stones all came out shaped like miniature hen's-eggs. But he was able to vary the color, using chromic oxide for red and ferric oxide for yellow and titanium for blue; and he could vary the pressure planes, to produce cat's-eyes or star gems at will. He left a trail of small stones, red and yellow and blue . . .

And the girl followed, frightened, but unable to resist the bait. By now she had nearly filled a handkerchief with the stones. The horse followed her into the extension cage.

Inside, she looked at the four stones in Svetz's hand: one of each color, red and yellow and light blue and black, the largest he could make. He pointed to the horse, then to the stones.

The girl agonized. Svetz perspired. She didn't want to give up the horse . . . and Svetz was out of corundum . . .

She nodded, one swift jerk of her chin. Quickly, before she could change her mind, Svetz poured the stones into her hand. She clutched the hoard to her bosom and ran out of the cage, sobbing.

The horse stood up to follow.

Svetz swung the rifle and shot it. A bead of blood appeared on the animal's neck. It shied back, then sighted on Svetz along its natural bayonet.

Poor kid, Svetz thought as he turned to the door. But she'd have lost the horse anyway. It had sucked polluted water from an open stream. Now he need only load the flight stick aboard . . .

Motion caught the corner of his eye.

A false assumption can be deadly. Svetz had not waited for the horse to fall. It was with something of a shock that he realized the truth. The beast wasn't about to fall. It was about to spear him like a cocktail shrimp.

He hit the door button and dodged.

Exquisitely graceful, exquisitely sharp, the spiral horn slammed into the closing door. The animal turned like white lightning in the confines of the cage, and again Svetz leapt for his life.

The point missed him by half an inch. It plunged past him and into the control board, through the plastic panel and into the wiring beneath.

Something sparkled and something sputtered.

The horse was taking careful aim, sighting along the spear in its forehead. Svetz did the only thing he could think of. He pulled the home-again lever.

The horse screamed as it went into free fall. The horn, intended for Svetz's navel, ripped past his ear and tore his breathing-balloon wide open.

Then gravity returned; but it was the peculiar gravity of an extension cage moving forward through time. Svetz and the horse were pulled against the padded walls. Svetz sighed in relief.

He sniffed again in disbelief. The smell was strong and strange, like nothing Svetz had ever smelled before. The animal's terrible horn must have damaged the air plant.

Very likely he was breathing poison. If the cage didn't return in time . . .

But would it return at all? It might be going anywhere, anywhen, the way that ivory horn had smashed through anonymous wiring. They might come out at the end of time, when even the black infrasuns gave not enough heat to sustain life.

There might not even be a future to return to. He had left the flight stick. How would it be used? What would they make of it, with its control handle at one end and the brush-style static discharge at the other and the saddle in the middle? Perhaps the girl would try to use it. He could visualize her against the night sky, in the light of a full moon . . . and how would that change history?

The horse seemed on the verge of apoplexy. Its sides heaved, its eyes rolled wildly. Probably it was the cabin air, thick with carbon dixoide. Again, it might be the poison the horse had sucked from an open stream.

Gravity died. Svetz and the horse tumbled in free fall, and the horse queasily tried to gore him.

Gravity returned, and Svetz, who was ready for it, landed on top. Someone was already opening the door.

Svetz took the distance in one bound. The horse followed, screaming with rage, intent on murder. Two men went flying as it charged out into the Institute control center.

"It doesn't take anaesthetics!" Svetz shouted over his shoulder. The animal's agility was hampered here among the desks and lighted screens, and it was probably drunk on hyperventilation. It kept stumbling into desks and men. Svetz easily stayed ahead of the slashing horn.

A full panic was developing . . .

"We couldn't have done it without Zeera," Ra Chen told him much later. "Your idiot tanj horse had the whole

Center terrorized. All of a sudden it went completely tame, walked up to that frigid bitch Zeera and let her lead it away."

"Did you get it to the hospital in time?"

Ra Chen nodded gloomily. Gloom was his favorite expression and was no indication of his true feelings. "We found over fifty unknown varieties of bacteria in the beast's bloodstream. Yet it hardly looked sick! It looked healthy as a . . . healthy as a . . . it must have tremendous stamina. We managed to save not only the horse, but most of the bacteria too, for the Zoo."

Svetz was sitting up in a hospital bed, with his arm up to the elbow in a diagnostician. There was always the chance that he too had located some long-extinct bacterium. He shifted uncomfortably, being careful not to move the wrong arm, and asked, "Did you ever find an anaesthetic that worked?"

"Nope. Sorry about that, Svetz. We still don't know why your needles didn't work. The tanj horse is simply immune to tranks of any kind.

"Incidentally, there was nothing wrong with your air plant. You were smelling the horse."

"I wish I'd known that. I thought I was dying."

"It's driving the interns crazy, that smell. And we can't seem to get it out of the Center." Ra Chen sat down on the edge of the bed. "What bothers me is the horn on its forehead. The horse in the picture book had no horns."

"No, sir."

"Then it must be a different species. It's not really a horse, Svetz. We'll have to send you back. It'll break our budget, Svetz."

"I disagree, sir—"

"Don't be so tanj polite."

"Then don't be so tanj stupid, sir." Svetz was *not* going back for another horse. "People who kept tame horses must have developed the habit of cutting off the horn when the animal was a pup. Why not? We all saw how dangerous that horn is. Much too dangerous for a domestic animal.''

''Then why does our horse have a horn?''

''That's why I thought it was wild, the first time I saw it. I suppose they didn't start cutting off horns until later in history.''

Ra Chen nodded in gloomy satisfaction. ''I thought so too. Our problem is that the Secretary-General is barely bright enough to notice that his horse has a horn, and the picture-book horse doesn't. He's bound to blame me.''

''Mmm.'' Svetz wasn't sure what was expected of him.

''I'll have to have the horn amputated.''

''Somebody's bound to notice the scar,'' said Svetz.

''Tanj it, you're right. I've got enemies at court. They'd be only too happy to claim I'd mutilated the Secretary-General's pet.'' Ra Chen glared at Svetz. ''All right, let's hear *your* idea.''

Svetz was busy regretting. Why had he spoken? His vicious, beautiful horse, tamely docked of its killer horn . . . He had found the thought repulsive. His impulse had betrayed him. What could they do but remove the horn?

He had it. ''Change the picture book, not the horse. A computer could duplicate the book in detail, but with a horn on every horse. Use the Institute computer, then wipe the tape afterward.''

Morosely thoughtful, Ra Chen said, ''That might work. I know someone who could switch the books.'' He looked up from under bushy black brows. ''Of course, you'd have to keep your mouth shut.''

''Yes, sir.''

''Don't forget.'' Ra Chen got up. ''When you get out of the diagnostician, you start a four-week vacation.''

*   *   *

"I'm sending you back for one of these," Ra Chen told him four weeks later. He opened the bestiary. "We picked up the book in a public park around ten PostAtomic; left the kid who was holding it playing with a corundum egg."

Svetz examined the picture. "That's *ugly*. That's really ugly. You're trying to balance the horse, right? The horse was so beautiful, you've got to have one of these or the universe goes off balance."

Ra Chen closed his eyes in pain. "Just go get us the Gila monster, Svetz. The Secretary-General wants a Gila monster."

"How big is it?"

They both looked at the illustration. There was no way to tell.

"From the looks of it, we'd better use the *big* extension cage."

Svetz barely made it back that time. He was suffering from total exhaustion and extensive second-degree burns. The thing he brought back was thirty feet long, had vestigial batlike wings, breathed fire, and didn't look very much like the illustration; but it was as close as anything he'd found.

The Secretary-General loved it.

Introduction to
Harlan Ellison's
"On the Downhill Side":

One of the most acclaimed and controversial figures in modern letters, Harlan Ellison has produced thirty-seven books and over nine hundred stories, articles, essays, film and television scripts. He is the editor of *Dangerous Visions; Again, Dangerous Visions;* and *The Last Dangerous Visions*. His short story collections include *Partners in Wonder, Alone Against Tomorrow, The Beast that Shouted Love at the Heart of the World, Approaching Oblivion, Deathbird Stories, Strange Wine,* and *Shatterday*. A multiple award winner, he has won Nebula, Hugo, and Edgar Awards, and three Writers Guild of America Awards for Most Outstanding Television Script.

In the story that follows, he envisions for us a ghostly kind of courtship played out against the feverdream streets and dangerous satin darkness of the French Quarter of modern-day New Orleans . . . .

ON THE DOWNHILL SIDE

Harlan Ellison

"In love, there is always one who kisses and one who offers the cheek."

—French proverb

I KNEW she was a virgin because she was able to ruffle the silken mane of my unicorn. Named Lizette, she was a Grecian temple in which no sacrifice had ever been made. Vestal virgin of New Orleans, found walking without shadow in the thankgod coolness of cockroach-crawling Louisiana night. My unicorn whinnied, inclined his head, and she stroked the ivory spiral of his horn.

Much of this took place in what is called the Irish Channel, a strip of street in old New Orleans where the lace curtain micks had settled decades before; now the Irish were gone and the Cubans had taken over the Channel. Now the Cubans were sleeping, recovering from the muggy today that held within its hours the *déjà vu* of muggy yesterday, the *déjà rêvé* of intolerable tomorrow. Now the crippled bricks of side streets off Magazine had given up their nightly ghosts, and one such phantom had come to me, calling my unicorn to her—thus, clearly, a virgin—and I stood waiting.

Had it been Sutton Place, had it been a Manhattan evening, and had we met, she would have kneeled to pet my dog. And I would have waited. Had it been Puerto Vallarta, had it been 20° 36′ N, 105° 13′W, and had we met, she would have crouched to run her fingertips over the oil-slick hide of my iguana. And I would have waited. Meeting in streets requires ritual. One must wait and not breathe too loud, if one is to enjoy the congress of the nightly ghosts.

She looked across the fine head of my unicorn and smiled at me. Her eyes were a shade of gray between onyx and miscalculation. "Is it a bit chilly for you?" I asked.

"When I was thirteen," she said, linking my arm, taking a tentative two steps that led me with her, up the street, "or perhaps I was twelve, well no matter, when I was that approximate age, I had a marvelous shawl of Belgian lace. I could look through it and see the mysteries of the sun and the other stars unriddled. I'm sure someone important and very nice has purchased that shawl from an antique dealer, and paid handsomely for it."

It seemed not a terribly responsive reply to a simple question.

"A queen of the Mardi Gras Ball doesn't get chilly," she added, unasked. I walked along beside her, the cool evasiveness of her arm binding us, my mind a welter of answer choices, none satisfactory.

Behind us, my unicorn followed silently. Well, not entirely silently. His platinum hoofs clattered on the bricks. I'm afraid I felt a straight pin of jealousy. Perfection docs that to me.

"When were you queen of the Ball?"

The date she gave me was one hundred and thirteen years before.

It must have been brutally cold down there in the stones.

There is a little book they sell, a guide to manners and dining in New Orleans: I've looked: nowhere in the book do they indicate the proper responses to a ghost. But then, it says nothing about the wonderful cemeteries of New Orleans' West Bank, or Metairie. Or the gourmet dining at such locations. One seeks, in vain, through the mutable, mercurial universe, for the compleat guide. To everything. And, failing in the search, one makes do the best one can. And suffers the frustration, suffers the ennui.

Perfection does that to me.

We walked for some time, and grew to know each other, as best we'd allow. These are some of the high points. They lack continuity. I don't apologize, I merely point it out, adding with some truth, I feel, that *most* liaisons lack continuity. We find ourselves in odd places at various times, and for a brief span we link our lives to others—even as Lizette had linked her arm with mine—and then, our time elapsed, we move apart. Through a haze of pain occasionally; usually through a veil of memory that clings, then passes; sometimes as though we have never touched.

"My name is Paul Ordahl," I told her. "And the most awful thing that cver happcncd to mc was my first wife, Bernice. I don't know how else to put it—even if it sounds melodramatic, it's simply what happened—she went insane, and I divorced her, and her mother had her committed to a private mental home."

"When I was eighteen," Lizette said, "my family gave me my coming-out party. We were living in the Garden District, on Prytania Street. The house was a lovely white Plantation—they call them antebellum now—with Grecian pillars. We had a persimmon-green gazebo in the rear gardens, directly beside a weeping willow. It was six-sided. Octagonal. Or is that hexagonal? It was the loveliest party. And while it was going on, I sneaked away with a boy . . . I don't remember his name . . . and we went into the gazebo, and I let him touch my breasts. I don't remember his name."

We were on Decatur Street, walking toward the French Quarter; the Mississippi was on our right, dark but making its presence known.

"Her mother was the one had her committed, you see. I only heard from them twice after the divorce. It had been four stinking years and I really didn't want any more of it. Once, after I'd started making some money, the mother

called and said Bernice had to be put in the state asylum.
There wasn't enough money to pay for the private home
any more. I sent a little; not much. I suppose I could have
sent more, but I was remarried, there was a child from her
previous marriage. I didn't want to send any more. I told
the mother not to call me again. There was only once after
that . . . it was the most terrible thing that ever happened
to me."

We walked around Jackson Square, looking in at the
very black grass, reading the plaques bolted to the spear-
topped fence, plaques telling how New Orleans had once
belonged to the French. We sat on one of the benches in
the street. The street had been closed to traffic, and we sat
on one of the benches.

"Our name was Charbonnet. Can you say that?"

I said it, with a good accent.

"I married a very wealthy man. He was in real estate.
At one time he owned the entire block where the *Vieux
Carré* now stands, on Bourbon Street. He admired me
greatly. He came and sought my hand, and my *maman* had
to strike the bargain because my father was too weak to do
it; he drank. I can admit that now. But it didn't matter, I'd
already found out how my suitor was set financially. He
wasn't common, but he wasn't quality, either. But he was
wealthy and I married him. He gave me presents. I did
what I had to do. But I refused to let him make love to me
after he became friends with that awful Jew who built the
Metairie Cemetery over the race track because they
wouldn't let him race his Jew horses. My husband's name
was Dunbar. Claude Dunbar, you may have heard the
name? Our parties were *de rigueur*."

"Would you like some coffee and *beignets* at Du
Monde?"

She stared at me for a moment, as though she wanted me
to say something more, then she nodded and smiled.

We walked around the Square. My unicorn was waiting at the curb. I scratched his rainbow flank and he struck a spark off the cobblestones with his right front hoof. "I know," I said to him, "we'll soon start the downhill side. But not just yet. Be patient. I won't forget you."

Lizette and I went inside the Café Du Monde and I ordered two coffees with warm milk and two orders of *beignets* from a waiter who was originally from New Jersey but had lived most of his life only a few miles from College Station, Texas.

There was a coolness coming off the levee.

"I was in New York," I said. "I was receiving an award at an architects' convention—did I mention I was an architect—yes, that's what I was at the time, an architect—and I did a television interview. The mother saw me on the program, and checked the newspapers to find out what hotel we were using for the convention, and she got my room number and called me. I had been out quite late after the banquet where I'd gotten my award, quite late. I was sitting on the side of the bed, taking off my shoes, my tuxedo tie hanging from my unbuttoned collar, getting ready to just throw clothes on the floor and sink away, when the phone rang. It was the mother. She was a terrible person, one of the worst I ever knew, a shrike, a terrible, just a terrible person. She started telling me about Bernice in the asylum. How they had her in this little room and how she stared out the window most of the time. She'd reverted to childhood, and most of the time she couldn't even recognize the mother; but when she did, she'd say something like, 'Don't let them hurt me, Mommy, don't let them hurt me.' So I asked her what she wanted me to do, did she want money for Bernice or what . . . Did she want me to go see her since I was in New York . . . and she said God no. And then she did an awful thing to me. She said the last time she'd been to see Bernice, my

ex-wife had turned around and put her finger to her lips
and said, 'Shhh, we have to be very quiet. Paul is working.' And I swear, a snake uncoiled in my stomach. It was
the most terrible thing I'd ever heard. No matter how
secure you are that you honest to God had *not* sent someone to a madhouse, there's always that little core of doubt,
and saying what she'd said just burned out my head. I
couldn't even think about it, couldn't even really *hear* it,
or it would have collapsed me. So down came these iron
walls and I just kept on talking, and after a while she hung
up.

"It wasn't till two years later that I allowed myself to
think about it, and then I cried; it had been a long time
since I'd cried. Oh, not because I believed that nonsense
about a man isn't supposed to cry, but just because I guess
there hadn't been anything that important to cry *about*. But
when I let myself hear what she'd said, I started crying,
and just went on and on till I finally went in and looked into
the bathroom mirror and I asked myself face to face if I'd
done that, if I'd ever made her be quiet so I could work on
blueprints or drawings . . . .

"And after a while I saw myself shaking my head no,
and it was easier. That was perhaps three years before I
died."

She licked the powdered sugar from the *beignets* off her
fingers, and launched into a long story about a lover she
had taken. She didn't remember his name.

It was sometime after midnight. I'd thought midnight
would signal the start of the downhill side, but the hour
had passed, and we were still together, and she didn't
seem ready to vanish. We left the Café Du Monde and
walked into the Quarter.

I despise Bourbon Street. The strip joints, with the
pasties over nipples, the smell of need, the dwarfed souls
of men attuned only to flesh. The noise.

We walked through it like art connoisseurs at a showing of motel room paintings. She continued to talk about her life, about the men she had known, about the way they had loved her, the ways in which she had spurned them, and about the trivia of her past existence. I continued to talk about my loves, about all the women I had held dear in my heart for however long each had been linked with me. We talked across each other, our conversation at right angles, only meeting in the intersections of silence at story's end.

She wanted a julep and I took her to the Royal Orleans Hotel and we sat in silence as she drank. I watched her, studying that phantom face, seeking for even the smallest flicker of light off the ice in her eyes, hoping for an indication that glacial melting could be forthcoming. But there was nothing, and I burned to say correct words that might cause heat. She drank and reminisced about evenings with young men in similar hotels, a hundred years before.

We went to a night club where a Flamenco dancer and his two-woman troupe performed on a stage of unpolished woods, their star-shining black shoes setting up resonances in me that I chose to ignore.

Then I realized there were only three couples in the club, and that the extremely pretty Flamenco dancer was playing to Lizette. He gripped the lapels of his bolero jacket and clattered his heels against the stage like a man driving nails. She watched him, and her tongue made a wholly obvious flirtatious trip around the rim of her liquor glass. There was a two-drink minimum, and as I have never liked the taste of alcohol, she was more than willing to prevent waste by drinking mine as well as her own. Whether she was getting drunk or simply indulging herself, I do not know. It didn't matter. I became blind with jealousy, and dragons took possession of my eyes.

When the dancer was finished, when his half hour show

was concluded, he came to our table. His suit was skin tight and the color of Arctic lakes. His hair was curly and moist from his exertions, and his prettiness infuriated me. There was a scene. He asked her name, I interposed a comment, he tried to be polite, sensing my ugly mood, she overrode my comment, he tried again in Castilian, *th*-ing his *esses*, she answered, I rose and shoved him, there was a scuffle. We were asked to leave.

Once outside, she walked away from me.

My unicorn was at the curb, eating from a porcelain *Sévres* soup plate filled with *flan*. I watched her walk unsteadily up the street toward Jackson Square. I scratched my unicorn's neck and he stopped eating the egg custard. He looked at me for a long moment. Ice crystals were sparkling in his name.

We were on the downhill side.

"Soon, old friend," I said.

He dipped his elegant head toward the plate. "I see you've been to the Las Americas. When you return the plate, give my best to *Señor* Pena."

I followed her up the street. She was walking rapidly toward the Square. I called to her, but she wouldn't stop. She began dragging her left hand along the steel bars of the fence enclosing the Square. Her fingertips thudded softly from bar to bar, and once I heard the chitinous *clak* of a manicured nail.

"Lizette!"

She walked faster, dragging her hand across the dark metal bars.

"Lizette! Damn it!"

I was reluctant to run after her; it was somehow terribly demeaning. But she was getting farther and farther away. There were bums in the Square, sitting slouched on the benches, their arms out along the backs. Itinerants, kids with beards and knapsacks. I was suddenly frightened for her. Impossible. She had been dead for a hundred years. There was no reason for it . . . I was afraid for her!

I started running, the sound of my footsteps echoing up and around the Square. I caught her at the corner and dragged her around. She tried to slap me, and I caught her hand. She kept trying to hit me, to scratch my face with the manicured nails. I held her and swung her away from me, swung her around, and around, dizzyingly, trying to keep her off balance. She swung wildly, crying out and saying things inarticulately. Finally, she stumbled and I pulled her in to me and held her tight against my body.

"Stop it! Stop, Lizette! I . . . *Stop it!*" She went limp against me and I felt her crying against my chest. I took her into the shadows and my unicorn came down Decatur Street and stood under a streetlamp, waiting.

The chimera winds rose. I heard them, and knew we were well on the downhill side, that time was growing short. I held her close and smelled the woodsmoke scent of her hair. "Listen to me," I said, softly, close to her. "Listen to me, Lizette. Our time's almost gone. This is our last chance. You've lived in stone for a hundred years; I've heard you cry. I've come there, to that place, night after night, and I've heard you cry. You've paid enough, God knows. So have I. We can *do* it. We've got one more chance, and we can make it, if you'll try. That's all I ask. Try."

She pushed away from me, tossing her head so the auburn hair swirled away from her face. Her eyes were dry. Ghosts can do that. Cry without making tears. Tears are denied us. Other things; I won't talk of them here.

"I lied to you," she said.

I touched the side of her face. The high cheekbone just at the hairline. "I know. My unicorn would never have let you touch him if you weren't pure. I'm not, but he has no choice with me. He was assigned to me. He's my familiar and he puts up with me. We're friends.''

"No. Other lies. My life was a lie. I've told them all to you. We can't make it. You have to let me go.''

I didn't know exactly where, but I knew how it would happen. I argued with her, trying to convince her there was a way for us. But she couldn't believe it, hadn't the strength or the will or the faith. Finally, I let her go.

She put her arms around my neck, and drew my face down to hers, and she held me that way for a few moments. Then the winds rose, and there were sounds in the night, the sounds of calling, and she left me there, in the shadows.

I sat down on the curb and thought about the years since I'd died. Years without much music. Light leached out. Wandering. Nothing to pace me but memories and the unicorn. How sad I was for *him*; assigned to me till I got my chance. And now it had come and I'd taken my best go, and failed.

Lizette and I were the two sides of the same coin; devalued and impossible to spend. Legal tender of nations long since vanished, no longer even names on the cracked papyrus of cartographers' maps. We had been snatched away from final rest, had been set adrift to roam for our crimes, and only once between death and eternity would we receive a chance. This night . . . this nothing-special night . . . this was our chance.

My unicorn came to me, then, and brushed his muzzle against my shoulder. I reached up and scratched around the base of his spiral horn, his favorite place. He gave a long, silvery sigh, and in that sound I heard the sentence I was serving on him, as well as myself. We had been linked, too. Assigned to one another by the one who had ordained this night's chance. But if I lost out, so did my unicorn; he who wandered with me through all the sound-less, lightless years.

I stood up. I was by no means ready to do battle, but at least I could stay in for the full ride . . . all the way on the downhill side. "Do you know where they are?"

My unicorn started off down the street.

I followed, hopelessness warring with frustration. Dusk to dawn is the full ride, the final chance. After midnight is the downhill side. Time was short, and when time ran out there would be nothing for Lizette or me or my unicorn *but* time. Forever.

When we passed the Royal Orleans Hotel I knew where we were going. The sound of the Quarter had already faded. It was getting on toward dawn. The human lice had finally crawled into their flesh-mounds to sleep off the night of revelry. Though I had never experienced directly the New Orleans in which Lizette had grown up, I longed for the power to blot out the cancerous blight that Bourbon Street and the Quarter had become, with its tourist filth and screaming neon, to restore it to the colorful yet healthy state in which it had thrived a hundred years before. But I was only a ghost, not one of the gods with such powers, and at that moment I was almost at the end of the line held by one of those gods.

My unicorn turned down dark streets, heading always in the same general direction, and when I saw the first black shapes of the tombstones against the night sky, the *lightening* night sky, I knew I'd been correct in my assumption of destination.

The Saint Louis Cemetery.

Oh, how I sorrow for anyone who has never seen the world-famous Saint Louis Cemetery in New Orleans. It is the perfect graveyard, the complete graveyard, the finest graveyard in the universe. (There is a perfection in some designs that informs the function totally. There are Danish chairs that could be nothing *but* chairs, are so totally and completely *chair* that if the world as we know it ended, and a billion years from now the New Orleans horsy cockroaches became the dominant species, and they dug down through the alluvial layers, and found one of those chairs, even if they themselves did not use chairs, were not constructed physically for the use of chairs, had never seen a chair, *still* they would know it for what it had been made to be: a chair. Because it would be the essence of *chairness*. And from it, they could reconstruct the human race in replica. *That* is the kind of graveyard one means when one refers to the world-famous Saint Louis Cemetery.)

The Saint Louis Cemetery is ancient. It sighs with shadows and the comfortable bones and their afterimages of deaths that became great merely because those who died went to be interred in the Saint Louis Cemetery. The water table lies just eighteen inches below New Orleans—there are no graves in the earth for that reason. Bodies are entombed aboveground in crypts, in sepulchers, vaults, mausoleums. The gravestones are all different, no two alike, each one a testament to the stonecutter's art. Only secondarily testaments to those who lie beneath the markers.

We had reached the moment of final nightness. That ultimate moment before day began. Dawn had yet to fill the eastern sky, yet there was a warming of tone to the night; it was the last of the downhill side of my chance. Of Lizette's chance.

We approached the cemetery, my unicorn and I. From deep in the center of the skyline of stones beyond the fence I could see the ice-chill glow of a pulsing blue light. The light one finds in a refrigerator, cold and flat and brittle.

I mounted my unicorn, leaned close along his neck, clinging to his mane with both hands, knees tight to his silken sides, now rippling with light and color, and I gave a little hiss of approval, a little sound of go.

My unicorn sailed over the fence, into the world-famous Saint Louis Cemetery.

I dismounted and thanked him. We began threading our way between the tombstones, the sepulchers, the crypts.

The blue glow grew more distinct. And now I could hear the chimera winds rising, whirling, coming in off alien seas. The pulsing of the light, the wail of the winds, the night dying. My unicorn stayed close. Even we of the spirit world know when to be afraid.

After all, I was only operating off a chance; I was under no god's protection. Naked, even in death.

There is no fog in New Orleans.

Mist began to form around us.

Except sometimes in the winter, there is no fog in New Orleans.

I remembered the daybreak of the night I'd died. There had been mist. I had been a suicide.

My third wife had left me. She had gone away during the night, while I'd been at a business meeting with a client; I had been engaged to design a church in Baton Rouge. All that day I'd steamed the old wallpaper off the apartment we'd rented. It was to have been our first home together, paid for by the commission. I'd done the steaming myself, with a tall ladder and a steam condenser and two flat pans with steam holes. Up near the ceiling the heat had been so awful I'd almost fainted. She'd brought me lemonade, freshly squeezed. Then I'd showered and changed and gone to my meeting. When I'd returned, she was gone. No note.

Lizette and I were two sides of the same coin, cast off after death for the opposite extremes of the same crime. She had never loved. I had loved too much. Overindulgence in something as delicate as love is to be found monstrously offensive in the eyes of the God of Love. And some of us—who have never understood the salvation in the Golden Mean—some of us are cast adrift with but one chance. It can happen.

Mist formed around us, and my unicorn crept close to me, somehow smaller, almost timid. We were moving into realms he did not understand, where his limited magics were useless. These were realms of potency so utterly beyond even the limbo creatures—such as my unicorn— so completely alien to even the intermediary zone wanderers—Lizette and myself—that we were as helpless and without understanding as those who live. We had only one advantage over living, breathing, as yet undead humans: we *knew* for certain that the realms on the other side existed.

Above, beyond, deeper:where the gods live. Where the one who had given me my chance, had given Lizette *her* chance, where He lived. Undoubtedly watching.

The mist swirled up around us, as chill and final as the dust of pharaoh's tombs.

We moved through it, toward the pulsing heart of blue light. And as we came into the penultimate circle, we stopped. We were in the outer ring of potency, and we saw the claiming things that had come for Lizette. She lay out on an altar of crystal, naked and trembling. They stood around her, enormously tall and transparent. Man shapes without faces. Within their transparent forms a strange, silvery fog swirled, like smoke from holy censers. Where eyes should have been on a man or a ghost, there were only dull flickering firefly glowings, inside, hanging in the smoke, moving, changing shape and position. No eyes at all. And tall, very tall, towering over Lizette and the altar.

For me, overcommitted to love, when dawn came without salvation, there was only an eternity of wandering, with my unicorn as sole companion. Ghost forevermore.

Incense chimera viewed as dust-devil on the horizon, chilling as I passed in city streets, forever gone, invisible, lost, empty, helpless, wandering.

But for her, empty vessel, the fate was something else entirely. The God of Love had allowed her the time of wandering, trapped by day in stones, freed at night to wander. He had allowed her the final chance. And having failed to take it, her fate was with these claiming creatures, gods themselves . . . of another order . . . higher or lower I had no idea. But terrible.

"Lagniappe!" I screamed the word. The old Creole word they use in New Orlenas when they want a little extra; a bonus of *croissants,* a few additional carrots dumped into the shopping bag, a larger portion of clams or crabs or shrimp. *"Lagniappe!* Lizette, take a little more! Try for the extra! Try . . . demand it . . . there's time . . . you have it coming to you . . . you've paid . . . I've paid . . . it's ours . . . *try!"*

She sat up, her naked body lit by lambent fires of chill blue cold from the other side. She sat up and looked across the inner circle to me, and I stood there with my arms out, trying desperately to break through the outer circle to her. But it was solid and I could not pass. Only virgins could pass.

And they would not let her go. They had been promised a feed, and they were there to claim. I began to cry, as I had cried when I finally heard what the mother had said, when I finally came home to the empty apartment and knew I had spent my life loving too much, demanding too much, myself a feeder at a board that *could* be depleted and emptied and serve up no more. She wanted to come to me, I could *see* she wanted to come to me. But they would have their meal.

Then I felt the muzzle of my unicorn at my neck, and in

a step he had moved through the barrier that was impenetrable to me, and he moved across the circle and stood waiting. Lizette leaped from the altar and ran to me.

It all happened at the same time. I felt Lizette's body anchor into mine, and *we* saw my unicorn standing over there on the other side, and for a moment *we* could not summon up the necessary reactions, the correct sounds. We knew for the first time in either our lives or our deaths what it was to be paralyzed. Then reactions began washing over me, we, us in wave after wave: cascading joy that Lizette had come to . . . us; utter love for this Paul ghost creature; realization that instinctively part of us was falling into the same pattern again; fear that part would love too much at this mystic juncture; resolve to temper our love; and then anguish at the sight of our unicorn standing there, waiting to be claimed . . . .

We called to him . . . using his secret name, one we had never spoken aloud. We could barely speak. Weight pulled at his throat, our throats. "Old friend . . ." We took a step toward him but could not pass the barrier. Lizette clung to me, Paul held me tight as I trembled with terror and the cold of that inner circle still frosting my flesh.

The great transparent claimers stood silently, watching, waiting, as if content to allow us our moments of final decision. But their impatience could be felt in the air, a soft purring, like the death rattle always in the throat of a cat. "Come back! Not for me . . . don't do it for me . . . it's not fair!"

Paul's unicorn turned his head and looked at us.

My friend of starless nights, when we had gone sailing together through the darkness. My friend who had walked with me on endless tours of empty places. My friend of gentle nature and constant companionship. Until Lizette, my friend, my only friend, my familiar assigned to an onerous task, who had come to love me and to whom I had belonged, even as he had belonged to me.

I could not bear the hurt that grew in my chest, in my stomach; my head was on fire, my eyes burned with tears first for Paul, and now for the sweetest creature a god had ever sent to temper a man's anguish . . . and for myself. I could not bear the thought of never knowing—as Paul had known it—the silent company of that gentle, magical beast.

But he turned back, and moved to them, and they took that as final decision, and the great transparent claimers moved in around him, and their quickglass hands reached down to touch him, and for an instant they seemed to hesitate, and I called out, "Don't be afraid . . ." and my unicorn turned his head to look across the mist of potency for the last time, and I saw he *was* afraid, but not as much as he would have been if I had not been there.

Then the first of them touched his smooth, silvery flank and he gave a trembling sigh of pain. A ripple ran down his hide. Not the quick flesh movement of ridding himself of a fly, but a completely alien, unnatural tremor, containing in its swiftness all the agony and loss of eternities. A sigh went out from Paul's unicorn, though he had not uttered it.

We could feel the pain, the loneliness. My unicorn with no time left to him. Ending. All was now a final ending; he had stayed with me, walked with me, and had grown to care for me, until that time when he would be released from his duty by that special God; but now freedom was to be denied him; an ending.

The great transparent claimers all touched him, their ice fingers caressing his warm hide as we watched, helpless, Lizette's face buried in Paul's chest. Colors surged across my unicorn's body, as if by becoming more intense the chill touch of the claimers could be beaten off. Pulsing waves of rainbow color that lived in his hide for moments, then dimmed, brightened again and were bled off. Then the colors leaked away one by one, chroma weakening: purple-blue, manganese violet, discord, cobalt blue, doubt, affection, chrome green, chrome yellow, raw sienna, contemplation, alizarin crimson, irony, silver, severity, compassion, cadmium red, white.

They emptied him . . . he did not fight them . . . going colder and colder . . . flickers of yellow, a whisper of blue, pale as white . . . the tremors blending into one constant shudder . . . the wonderful golden eyes rolled in torment, went flat, brightness dulled, flat metal . . . the platinum hoofs caked with rust . . . and he stood, did not try to escape, gave himself for us . . . and he was emptied. Of everything. Then, like the claimers, we could see through him. Vapors swirled within the transparent husk, a fogged glass, shimmering . . . then nothing. And then they absorbed even the husk.

The chill blue light faded, and the claimers grew indistinct in our sight. The smoke within them seemed thicker, moved more slowly, horribly, as though they had fed and were sluggish and would go away, back across the line to that dark place where they waited, always waited, till their hunger was aroused again. And my unicorn was gone. I was alone with Lizette. I was alone with Paul. The mist died away, and the claimers were gone, and once more it was merely a cemetery as the first rays of the morning sun came easing through the tumble and disarray of headstones.

We stood together as one, her naked body white and virginal in my weary arms; and as the light of the sun struck us we began to fade, to merge, to mingle our bodies and our wandering spirits one into the other, forming one spirit that would neither love too much, nor too little, having taken our chance on the downhill side.

We faded and were lifted invisibly on the scented breath

of that good God who had owned us, and were taken away from there. To be born again as one spirit, in some other human form, man or woman we did not know which. Nor would we remember. Nor did it matter.

This time, love would not destroy us. This time out, we would have luck.

The luck of silken mane and rainbow colors and platinum hoofs and spiral horn.

Introduction to
Thomas Burnett Swann's
"The Night of the Unicorn":

The late Thomas Burnett Swann was a fantasist who composed a rich body of pastoral novels and stories about the fabulous creatures that inhabited the old worlds of Rome ("Where is the Bird of Fire?"), Egypt (*The Minikins of Yam*), Minoan Crete (*Day of the Minotaur*), Persia ("Vashi"), and Medieval England ("The Manor of Roses," probably his best story, and one of the best of all modern fantasy novellas). Here, in a departure from his other work, he takes us instead to the New World, to the hot, dusty streets of the Yucatán village during festival time, where we learn that perfection, like beauty, is to be found in the eye of the beholder.

Swann's other books include *The Goat Without Horns, Cry Silver Bells, Green Phoenix, The Forest of Forever, Lady of the Bees, Where is the Bird of Fire?, The Werewoods, The Dolphin and the Deep,* and *Queens Walk in the Dust.*

THE NIGHT OF THE UNICORN
Thomas Burnett Swann

IT was the night of the unicorn, and the villagers of
Cozumel, the capital and only town of a small island off
the Yucatán peninsula, had begun to gather in the square.
The maidens wore their brightest prints, lemon and tur-
quoise and hyacinth, so that the animal could see their
dresses even if not their virginal countenances and give
them the approval of his notice. Somewhat more sedate in
dress, their mothers maintained that haughty vigilance
which had thus far safeguarded the daughters for marriage, while the young men of the town, casual in figured
American sport shirts, looked impishly at the girls who
would one day become their wives.

Maria stood in the doorway of her basket shop, debating
if she should join the rest. The night of the unicorn! The
words sang themselves in her brain, like an old Mayan
chant to the god of swallows. It was said that a hundred
years ago, a unicorn had emerged from the Mayan-
haunted jungles of the interior and walked through the
town, acknowledging the purest women with a nod of his
golden horn or the press of his warm muzzle. He had never
returned. But the villagers still celebrated in the hope that
they could once again lure him from the jungle. Besides,
Maria guessed, they loved a holiday and the chance to
wear finery.

"Shall we go?" asked Mico, appearing quietly beside
Maria in the door. At seventeen, his face looked adoles-
cent but his eyes, gray and deep and a little sad, looked
forty. He was small and copper-skinned like most of the
islanders, with short-cut prickly hair. Also like them, he
worked for tourists in the season, gigging lobsters or

guiding photographers into the interior of the island where
Mayan temples still thrust their stone jaguars through
matted lianas. But a seriousness of purpose, almost a
solemnity, distinguished him from the other youths, who
laughed when he drew out his English grammar and announced that one day he would go to school in America.
Maria loved him as a brother. Only Mico had befriended
her since she had come to the island a year ago to open her
shop.

"Shall we go?" he repeated. "The unicorn may truly
come this year. My father saw strange tracks beside the
Temple to the Jaguar."

"It is my dream to see the unicorn," Maria sighed.
"But he will probably ignore me." It was not a secret that
Maria, in Mérida, had sold her body and thus amassed the
money with which, at forty-one, she had come to Cozumel
to open a basket shop. She had come to forget her tawdry
past. But the men of Cozumel remembered her from
Mérida. Since she was still beautiful, with the slenderest
figure on the island and with curious slanted eyes as purple
as a murex shell, they paid her unpleasant attentions. What
was worse, their jealous wives refused to buy her baskets,
and her shop was threatened with failure. With a few
hundred dollars, she could purchase curios for the tourist
trade; but she lacked such a sum and the poor baskets she
imported from Mérida were fit only for the islanders who
refused to buy them. Her money would soon be gone.
What then? The prospect of returning to Mérida alarmed
her.

"He will not pass you by," said Mico firmly. "If he
comes at all, he will come to you."

She touched his cheek and smiled. "Let us go."

He took her arm and they walked toward the square. A
breeze from the sea brought the stench of lobster shells
rotting in the harbor. Was there something else, Maria

asked herself, a fragrance of jungle flowers and the sweet moistness of buried temples? For an instant, figures tumbled to clarity within her mind, a silken unicorn surrounded by jaguars, boars, and coatis. When the unicorn raised his head, the scythe of his golden horn flashed in the green light.

"Mico, is there something in the air tonight?"

Mico sniffed. "Yes," he said matter-of-factly. "There are pigs and chickens and asses—" Indeed, they were passing a wire-fenced yard where children huddled with pigs under sapodilla trees and roosters drowsed in the branches. Ahead of them in the street, an ass and a mongrel sniffed at a tuft of garbage.

"You're right, of course. I thought for a moment—"

"You thought it was the unicorn," said Mico, apologetic because he had not guessed her meaning. "Tonight he will surely come."

"What will he look like, Mico?" Sometimes she tried to draw him into moods of fantasy, though she loved him no less because he was more a realist than a dreamer.

"A lordly beast, my father says. His horn will catch the lamplight and gleam like a crescent moon above the white clouds of his mane. He will move up the street like a Mayan priest in a sacred procession. And he will pause beside the innocent—"

"If I could only glimpse him," she sighed. "Just a glimpse, no more."

"When he comes," Mico continued, "he will pause beside *you*." Maria claimed Mayan blood, and Mico had often compared her to the ancient corn goddesses who came from the jungle to teach the natives agriculture. "He will pause and dip his horn—"

"Maria, go home," screeched a female voice, its owner concealed in a blur of faces. "You will frighten the unicorn!"

Suddenly Maria saw that the people in the street, both men and women, were staring at her. The men spoke loudly, careful that she should catch their gross compliments:

"Maria's kiss is worth a dozen unicorns. . . ."

"In Mérida they called her the Crimson One. . . ."

Maria lowered her head but she did not turn aside or slow her pace. "We will stand apart," she whispered to Mico. "There is no need that the unicorn see us. Only that we see him." They sought the shelter of a bougainvillea bush, its moon-silvered blossoms, purple by daylight, exploding earthward. Beyond the bush a row of streetlights kindled the village to a garish orange. But the sacred circle of the bougainvillea seemed inviolate to the work of man, aloof from his artificial lamps, his overpainted houses, and his strident outcries. Within this circle, companioned only by the moon, Maria and Mico awaited the unicorn.

In the streets, in the doorways of the shops, the crowd continued to chatter, first about the unicorn, then about lobsters and tobacco and silks from Mérida, the tourists who would soon be coming from the United States and the new guest houses built to accommodate them. In a little while they seemed to forget the unicorn. Had anyone really expected to see him after a hundred years, Maria wondered, except herself and Mico? Perhaps even Mico was humoring her out of politeness. A good boy, yes, but practical, his dreams extending no farther than a school in America.

And then she saw the animal in the street. He was walking toward her. He came slowly, deliberately, looking to neither side of him. At first she could not understand why the crowd had failed to take notice, for an unmistakable horn rose above his head.

"The unicorn!" she cried. "It is the unicorn, Mico!"
Why did no one see him? Why did even Mico stare, like a
stupid owl, into the distance? For an instant modesty
restrained her. Then she forgot herself. She began to run,
weaving among the crowd, brushing against the virgins,
who drew back as if she had dirtied their dresses. She
scarcely felt the jagged pebbles under her thin shoes. A
bicycle came toward her and swerved to avoid a collision.
The driver was too astonished to swear.

At last she knelt before the animal and stretched out her
hand to touch his horn. How lordly he looked, even in the
garish lamplight! How imperial was his bearing, how like
a king's! She hesitated, suddenly aware of her daring,
frozen with her fingers inches from his horn. She, the
fallen, importuning a unicorn! But slowly, with infinite
majesty, he pressed his muzzle against her cheek, and she
felt the warm salt wetness of her own tears.

A babble of voices stabbed at her ears. The people are
startled, she thought, because the unicorn has honored me,
the least pure, and overlooked the virgins. The voices rose
into a howling unison, and then she realized that the crowd
was laughing at her. Laughing and calling her unicorn an
ass!

"You profane him," she shouted. "You profane the
holy unicorn!"

Mico hurried to her side. "Are you sure he is a unicorn?" he whispered. "Look at him again."

She looked at the animal closely for the first time, no
longer blinded by tears and wonder. Imperial? On the
contrary, he was small, gray, mottled with age and mud.
There was little to distinguish his body from that of an ass.
But his horn. That was the irrefutable mark of his kingship!
Only a unicorn boasted such a horn. But she looked
again, and she saw that, though he truly held a horn, it was

dirty and crooked, and it might have grown there as a freak of nature or it might have been placed there as a hoax.

Boys, emboldened by their sisters, began to scoop garbage from the street and hurl it at Maria and her unicorn. A banana peel struck her face and another struck the animal where the horn sprouted from his head. He began to look baffled and frightened, not kingly at all. A simple-minded ass in the midst of a hostile crowd, Maria thought. Well, no matter. She would not let the crowd make fun of him. Facing his attackers, she returned the banana peels and shouted, "You leave this animal alone! Whatever he is, you have no right to hurt him!"

She felt Mico's hand on her shoulder. "The animal has gone, Maria. His horn fell off and he ran away." He presented the horn to her, the dirty crescent which somehow had been fastened to the head. She clutched the horn and began to run, tears in her eyes, tears of shame for her own embarrassment and, even more, for the helpless animal harassed by the crowd. She did not stop until she had come to her house and run through the clean, spare kitchen into a garden where a pool, no wider than a well, reflected a mahogany tree, a moon, and a riot of stars. Beside the pool, she fell to her feet and the horn slipped from her fingers. Breathless, Mico overtook her and waited for her to speak. For a long time she was silent. Mico retrieved the horn and began to wash it in the water.

"Why are you doing that?" she asked finally. "You know it is false. Someone has played a trick on me."

"It is very heavy," he said. "I want to see what it is made of."

The hard surface of the horn glittered beneath a coating of mud and filth. In the pool, among a hundred stars and beside the golden scimitar of the moon, a second scimitar materialized, richer than the first.

He handed the horn to Maria. "I believe it is made of gold."

She looked at him, unbelieving. She took the horn in her hand and marveled at its weight and its hard, smooth texture. A small treasure in gold! Her mind leaped: precious curios from the mainland to sell the tourists, an education for Mico.

"But shouldn't we return it to the unicorn?" she asked doubtfully.

"He will grow another. This one he meant for you."

"Then we must thank him! He is probably heading for the interior. If we hurry, we can overtake him."

But they were too late. Beyond the village, they found his tracks vanishing into the jungle and knew that he had eluded them. Swallows and frogs muffled whatever hoof-beats they might have heard.

"We'll never find him now," sighed Maria. "And we never told him how grateful we were."

As if to reassure her, a lordly cry thundered among the orchids and cacti, and briefly, goldenly, a pair of eyes poised in the black and silver night. The swallows and frogs fell silent.

"Good-bye, king unicorn," Maria whispered. "A king has no need of a crown. He carries kingliness in his heart."

"So does a queen," said Mico.

Introduction to
Stephen R. Donaldson's
"Mythological Beast":

Even in the grayest, most institutionalized, and most unsmiling of times, fantasy can still break through in surprising ways, changing all the rules, cancelling all bets, and altering all the odds. Here Stephen R. Donaldson, the author of the best-selling fantasy trilogy *The Chronicles of Thomas Covenant the Unbeliever*, tells a tale of liberation and sudden transcendental change set against the background of a regimented and repressive society where everything is safe and sterile and controlled and there are no surprises left anymore . . . or so it seems.

MYTHOLOGICAL BEAST

Stephen R. Donaldson

NORMAN was a perfectly safe, perfectly sane man. He lived with his wife and son, who were both perfectly safe, perfectly sane, in a world that was perfectly sane, perfectly safe. It had been that way all his life. So when he woke up that morning, he felt as perfect as always. He had no inkling at all of the things that had already started to happen to him.

As usual, he woke up when he heard the signal from the biomitter cybernetically attached to his wrist; and, as usual, the first thing he did was to press the stud which activated the biomitter's LED read-out. The display gleamed greenly for a moment on the small screen. As usual, it said, *You are OK*. There was nothing to be afraid of.

As usual, he had absolutely no idea what he would have done if it had said anything else.

His wife, Sally, was already up. Her signal came before his so that she would have time to use the bathroom and get breakfast started. That way, there would be no unpleasant hurrying. He rolled out of bed promptly and went to take his turn in the bathroom so that he would not be later for work and his son, Enwell, would not be later for school.

Everything in the bathroom was the same as usual. Even though Sally had just used it, the vacuum-sink was spotless. And the toilet was as clean as new. He could not even detect his wife's warmth on the seat. Everything was perfectly safe, perfectly sane. His reflection in the mirror was the only thing that had changed.

The tight lump in the center of his forehead made no sense to him. He had never seen it before. Automatically, he checked his biomitter, but again it said, *You are OK*. That seemed true enough. He did not feel ill—and he was almost the only person he knew who knew what "ill" meant. The lump did not hurt in any way. But still he felt vaguely uneasy. He trusted the biomitter. It should have been able to tell him what was happening.

Carefully, he explored the lump. It was as hard as bone. In fact, it seemed to be part of his skull. It looked familiar; and he scanned back in his memory through some of the books he had read until he found what he wanted. His lump looked like the base of a horn or perhaps the nub of a new antler. He had seen such things in books.

That made even less sense. His face wore an unusual frown as he finished in the bathroom. He returned to the bedroom to get dressed and then went to the kitchen for breakfast.

Sally was just putting his food on the table—the same juice, cereal, and soyham that she always served him—a perfectly safe meal that would give him energy for the morning without letting him gain weight or become ill. He sat down to eat it as he always did. But when Sally sat down opposite him, he looked at her and said, "What's this thing on my forehead?"

His wife had a round bland face, and its lines had slowly become blurred over the years. She looked at his lump vaguely, but there was no recognition in her eyes. "Are you OK?" she said.

He touched the stud of his biomitter and showed her that he was OK.

Automatically, she checked her own biomitter and got the same answer. Then she looked at him again. This time, she, too, frowned. "It shouldn't be there," she said.

Enwell came into the kitchen, and Sally went to get his breakfast. Enwell was a growing boy. He watched the food come as if he were hungry, and then he began to eat

quickly. He was eating too quickly. But Norman did not
need to say anything. Enwell's biomitter gave a low hum
and displayed in kind yellow letters: *Eat more slowly*.
Enwell obeyed with a shrug.

Norman smiled at his son's obedience, then frowned
again. He trusted his biomitter. It should be able to explain
the lump on his forehead. Using the proper code, he
tapped on the face of the display, *I need a doctor*. A doctor
would know what was happening to him.

His biomitter replied, *You are OK*.

This did not surprise him. It was standard procedure—
the biomitter was only doing its job by reassuring him. He
tapped again, *I need a doctor*. This time, the green letters
said promptly, *Excused from work. Go to Medical Building room 218*.

Enwell's biomitter signaled that it was time for him to
go to school. "Got to go," he mumbled as he left the
table. If he saw the lump on his father's forehead, he did
not think enough about it to say anything. Soon he had left
the house. As usual, he was on time.

Norman rubbed his lump. The hard bone nub made him
feel uneasy again. He resisted an urge to recheck his
biomitter. When he had finished his breakfast, he said
good-by to Sally, as he always did when he was going to
work. Then he went out to the garage and got into his
mobile.

After he had strapped himself in, he punched the address of the Medical Building into the console. He knew
where the Medical Building was, not because he had ever
been there before (in fact, no one he knew had ever been
there), but because it was within sight of the National
Library, where he worked. Once the address was locked
in, his mobile left the garage smoothly on its balloon tires
(a perfectly safe design), and slid easily into the perfectly
sane flow of the traffic.

All the houses on this street were identical for a long way in either direction, and as usual Norman paid no attention to them. He did not need to watch the traffic, since his mobile took care of things like that. His seat was perfectly comfortable. He just relaxed in his safety straps and tried not to feel concerned about his lump until his mobile deposited him on the curb outside the Medical Building.

This building was much taller and longer than the National Library; but, apart from that, the two were very much alike. Both were empty except for the people who worked there; and the people worked there because they needed jobs, not because there was any work that needed to be done. And both were similarly laid out inside. Norman had no trouble finding his way to room 218.

Room 218 was in the Iatrogenics Wing. In the outer office was a desk with a computer terminal very much like the one Norman used at the library, and at the desk sat a young woman with yellow hair and confused eyes. When Norman entered her office, she stared at him as if he were sick. Her stare made him touch his lump and frown. But she was not staring at his forehead. After a moment, she said, "It's been so long—I've forgotten what to do."

"Maybe I should tell you my name," he said.

"That sounds right," she said. She sounded relieved. "Yes, I think that's right. Tell me your name."

He told her. She looked around the terminal, then pushed a button to engage some kind of program.

"Now what?" he said.

"I don't know," she said. She did not seem to like being so confused.

Norman did not know, either. But almost at once the door to the inner office opened. The woman shrugged, so Norman just walked through the doorway.

The inner office had been designed to be cozy, but

something had gone wrong with its atmospherics, and now it was deep in dust. When Norman sat down in the only chair, he raised the dust, and the dust made him cough.

"I'm Dr. Brett," a voice said. "You seem to have a cough."

The voice came from a console that faced the chair. Apparently, Dr. Brett was a computer who looked just like the Director of the National Library. Norman relaxed automatically. He naturally trusted a computer like that. "No," he said. "It's the dust."

"Ah, the dust," the computer said. "I'll make a note to have it removed." His voice sounded wise and old and very rusty. After a moment, he went on. "There must be something wrong with my scanners. You look healthy to me."

Norman said, "My biomitter says I'm OK."

"Well, then my scanners must be right. You're in perfect health. Why did you come?"

"I have a lump on my forehead."

"A lump?" Dr. Brett hummed. "It looks healthy to me. Are you sure it isn't natural?"

"Yes." For an instant, Norman felt unnaturally irritated. He touched the lump with his fingers. It was as hard as bone—no, harder, as hard as steel, magnacite. It was as hard as tung-diamonds. He began to wonder why he had bothered to come here.

"Of course, of course," the doctor said. "I've checked your records. You weren't born with it. What do you think it is?"

The question surprised Norman. "How should I know? I thought you would tell me."

"Of course," said the computer. "You can trust me. I'll tell you everything that's good for you. That's what I'm here for. You know that. The Director of the National Library speaks very highly of you. It's in your records."

The machine's voice made Norman's irritation evaporate. He trusted his biomitter. He trusted Dr. Brett. He settled himself in the chair to hear what his lump was. But even that amount of movement raised the dust. He sneezed twice.

Dr. Brett said, "You seem to have a cold."

"No," Norman said. "It's the dust."

"Ah, the dust," Dr. Brett said. "Thank you for coming."

"Thank you for—"?" Norman was surprised. All at once, he felt very uneasy. He felt that he had to be careful. "Aren't you going to tell me what it is?"

"There's nothing to worry about," the doctor said. "You're perfectly healthy. It will go away in a couple of days. Thank you for coming."

The door was open. Norman stared at the computer. The director did not act like this. He was confused. But he did not ask any more questions. Instead, he was careful. He said, "Thank you, Doctor," and walked out of the office. The door closed behind him.

The woman was still sitting at the outer desk. When she saw Norman, she beckoned to him. "Maybe you can help me," she said.

"Yes?" he said.

"I remember what I'm supposed to do now," she said. "After you see the doctor, I'm supposed to get his instructions"—she tapped the console—"and make sure you understand them. But nobody's ever come here before. And when I got this job, I didn't tell them"—she looked away from Norman—"that I don't know how to read."

Norman knew what she meant. Of course, she could read her biomitter—everybody could do that. But except for that, reading was not taught anymore. Enwell certainly was not learning how to read in school. Reading was not needed anymore. Except for the people at the National Library, Norman was the only person he knew who could actually read. That was why no one ever came to use the library.

But now he was being careful. He smiled to reassure the woman and walked around the desk to look at her console. She tapped the display to activate the read-out.

At once, vivid red letters sprang across the screen. They said:

SECRET CONFIDENTIAL PRIVATE PERSONAL SECRETcy UNDER NO CIRCUMSTANCES REPEAT UNDER NO CIRCUMSTANCES SHOW THIS DIAGNOSIS TO PATIENT OR REVEAL ITS CONTENTScyclecycle

Then there was a series of numbers that Norman did not understand. Then the letters said:

ABSOLUTE PRIORITY TRANSMIT AT ONCE TO GENERAL HOSPITAL EMERGENCY DIVISION REPEAT EMERGENCYc DIVISION ABSOLUTE PRIORITY cyclecyclecyclecyclecyclecyclecyclecy

"Transmit," the woman said. "That means I'm supposed to send this to the hospital." Her hand moved toward the buttons that would send the message.

Norman caught her wrist. "No." he said. "That isn't what it means. It means something else."

The woman said, "Oh."

The bright red letters said:

DIAGNOSIS cyclecyclecyclecyclecy PATIENT SUFFERING FROM MASSIVE GENETIC BREAK-

DOWN OF INTERMEDIATE ORIGIN COMPLETE
REPEAT COMPLETE STRUCTURAL TRANSI-
TION IN PROGRESS TRANSMUTATION IR-
REVERSIBLEcyclecyclecyclecyclecyclecyclec PROG-
NOSIScyclecyclecyclecyclecy PATIENT WILL BE-
COME DANGEROUS HIMSELF AND WILL
CAUSE FEAR IN OTHERS REPEAT WILL CAUSE
FEAR TREATMENT cyclecyclecyclecycle STUDY
RECOMMENDED BUT DESTRUCTION IMPERA-
TIVE REPEAT IMPERATIVE REPEAT IMPER-
ATIVE EFFECT SOONEST cyclecyclecyclecyc-
lecyclecyclecy

"What did it say?" the woman said.

For a moment, Norman did not answer. His lump was as
hard as a magnacite nail driven into his skull. Then he
said, "It said I should get some rest. It said I've been
working too hard. It said I should go to the hospital if I
don't feel better tomorrow." Before the woman could stop
him, he pressed the buttons that erased the terminal's
memory. The terminal was just like the one he used in the
National Library, and he knew what to do. After erasing,
he programmed the terminal to cancel everything that had
happened today. Then he fed in a cancel program to wipe
out everything in the terminal. He did not know what good
that would do, but he did it anyway.

He expected the woman to try to stop him, but she did
not. She had no idea of what he was doing.

He was sweating, and his pulse was too fast. He was so
uneasy that his stomach hurt. That had never happened to
him before. He left the office without saying anything to
the woman. His knees were trembling. As he walked
down the corridor of the Iatrogenics Wing, his biomitter
was saying in blue reassuring letters, *You will be OK. You
will be OK.* .

Apparently, his erasures were successful. In the next few days, nothing happened to him as a result of Dr. Brett's report. By the time he had returned home from the Medical Building, his read-out had regained its placid green, *You are OK*.

He did this deliberately. He did not feel OK. He felt uneasy. But he did not want his biomitter to send him to the General Hospital. So while his mobile drove him home, he made an effort to seem OK. The touch of his lump gave him a strange reassurance, and after a while his pulse, blood-pressure, respiration, reflexes had become as steady as usual.

And at home everything seemed perfectly sane, perfectly safe. He woke up every morning at the signal of his biomitter, went to work at the signal of his biomitter, ate lunch at the signal of his biomitter. This was reassuring. It reassured him that his biomitter took such good care of him. Without it, he might have worked all day without lunch, reading, sorting the mountain of discarded books in the storeroom, feeding them into the reference computer. At times like that, his uneasiness went away. He went home again at the end of the day at the signal of his biomitter.

But at home his uneasiness returned. Something was happening inside him. Every morning, he saw in the mirror that his lump was growing. It was clearly a horn now—a pointed shaft as white as bone. It was full of strength. When it was more than four inches long, he tested it on the mirror. The mirror was made of glasteel so that it would never shatter and hurt anybody. But he scratched it easily with the tip of his horn. Scratching it took no effort at all.

And that was not the only change. The soles of his feet were growing harder. His feet seemed to be getting shorter. They were starting to look like hooves.

Tufts of pure white hair as clean as the sky were sprouting from the backs of his calves and the back of his neck. Something that might have been a tail grew out of the small of his back.

But these things were not what made him uneasy. And he was not uneasy because he was thinking that someone from the hospital might come to destroy him. He was not thinking that at all. He was being careful: he did not let himself think anything that might make his biomitter call for help. No, he was uneasy because he could not understand what Sally and Enwell were doing about what was happening to him.

They were not doing anything. They were ignoring the changes in him as if he looked just the same as always.

Everything was perfectly sane, perfectly safe, to them.

First this made him uneasy. Then it made him angry. Something important was happening to him, and they did not even see it. Finally at breakfast one morning he became too irritated to be careful. Enwell's biomitter signaled that it was time for him to go to school. He mumbled, "Got to go," and left the table. Soon he had left the house. Norman watched his son go. Then he said to Sally, "Who taught him to do that?"

She did not look up from her soyham. "Do what?" she said.

"Go to school," he said. "Obey his biomitter. We never taught him to do that."

Sally's mouth was full. She waited until she swallowed. Then she said, "Everybody does it."

The way she said it made his muscles tighten. A line of sweat ran down his back. For an instant, he wanted to hit the table with his hand—hit it with the hard flat place on the palm of his hand. He felt sure he could break the table.

Then his biomitter signaled to him. Automatically, he left the table. He knew what to do. He always knew what to do when his biomitter signaled. He went out to the garage and got into his mobile. He strapped himself into the seat. He did not notice what he was doing until he saw that his hands had punched in the address of the General Hospital.

At once, he canceled the address, unstrapped himself and got out of the mobile. His heart was beating too fast. His biomitter was saying without being asked, *Go to the Hospital. You will be OK*. The letters were yellow.

His hands trembled. But he tapped onto the display, *I am OK*. Then he went back into the house.

Sally was cleaning the kitchen, as she always did after breakfast. She did not look at him.

"Sally," he said. "I want to talk to you. Something's happening to me."

"It's time to clean the kitchen," she said. "I heard the signal."

"Clean the kitchen later," he said. "I want to talk to you. Something's happening to me."

"I heard the signal," she said. "It's time to clean the kitchen now."

"Look at me," he said.

She did not look at him. Her hands were busy wiping scraps of soyham into the vacuum-sink, where they were sucked away.

"Look at me," he said. He took hold of her shoulders with his hands and made her face him. It was easy. He was strong. "Look at my forehead."

She did not look at him. Her face screwed up into tight knots and ridges. It turned red. Then she began to cry. She wailed and wailed, and her legs did not hold her up. When he let her go, she sank to the floor and folded up into a ball and wailed. Her biomitter said to her in blue, *You will be OK. You will be OK*. But she did not see it. She cried as if she were terrified.

Norman felt sick in his stomach. But his carefulness had come back. He left his wife and went back to the garage. He got into his mobile and punched in an address only ten houses away down the road. His mobile left the garage smoothly and eased itself into the perfectly sane flow of the traffic. When it parked at the address he had given it, he did not get out. He sat in his seat and watched his house.

Before long, an ambulance rolled up to his house. Men in white coats went in. They came out carrying Sally in a stretcher. They loaded her carefully into the ambulance and drove away.

Because he did not know what else to do, he punched the address of the National Library into the console of his mobile and went to work. The careful part of him knew that he did not have much time. He knew (everyone knew) that his biomitter was his friend. But now he also knew that it would not be long before his biomitter betrayed him. The rebellion in his genes was becoming too strong. It could not stay secret much longer. And he still did not know what was happening to him. He wanted to use the time to find out, if he could. The library was the best place for him to go.

But when he reached his desk with its computer console like the one in Dr. Brett's outer office, he did not know what to do. He had never done any research before. He did not know anyone who had ever done any research. His job was to sort books, to feed them into the reference computer. He did not even know what he was looking for.

Then he had an idea. He keyed his terminal into the reference computer and programmed it for autoscan. Then he tapped in his question, using the "personal information" code which was supposed to keep his question and answer from tying up the general circuits of the library and bothering the director. He asked:

I have hooves, a tail, white hair, and a horn in the middle of my forehead. What am I?

After a short pause, the display ran numbers which told Norman his answer was coming from the 1976 *Encyclopedia Americana*. That encyclopedia was a century out of date, but it was the most recent one in the library. Apparently, people had not bothered to make encyclopedias for a long time.

Then the display said:

ANSWERcycleUNICORNcyclecycl
DATA FOLLOWScyclecyclecyclecy

His uneasiness became suddenly sharper. There was a sour taste in his mouth as he scanned the read-out.

THE UNICORN IS A MYTHOLOGICAL BEAST USUALLY DEPICTED AS A LARGE HORSE WITH A SINGLE HORN ON ITS FOREHEADcyclecyclecyclecyclecyc

Sweat ran into his eyes. He missed a few lines while he blinked to clear his sight.

IT REPRESENTED CHASTITY AND PURITY THOUGH ITcWOULD FIGHT SAVAGELY WHEN CORNERED IT COULD BE TAMED BY A VIRGIN'S TOUCH IN SOME INTERPRETATIONS THE UNICORN IS ASSOCIATED WITH THE VIRGIN MARY IN OTHERS IT REPRESENTS CHRIST THE REDEEMERcyclecyclecyclecyclecyclecyclecyclecycl

Then, to his surprise, the display showed him a picture of a unicorn. It was prancing high on its strong clean legs, and its coat was pure as the stars, and its eyes shone. Its mane flew like the wind. Its long white horn was as strong as the sun. At the sight, all his uneasiness turned into joy. The unicorn was beautiful. It was beautiful. He was going to be beautiful. For a long time, he made the display hold that picture, and he stared at it and stared at it.

But after his joy receded a little and the display went blank, he began to think. He felt that he was thinking for the first time in his life. His thoughts were clear and necessary and quick.

He understood that he was in danger. He was in danger from his biomitter. It was a hazard to him. It was only a small thing, a metasensor that monitored his body for signs of illness; but it was linked to the huge computers of the General Hospital; and when his metabolism passed beyond the parameters of safety, sanity, his biomitter would summon the men in white coats. For the first time in his life, he felt curious about it. He felt that he needed to know more about it.

Without hesitation, he tapped his question into the reference computer, using his personal information code. He asked:

Origin of biomitter?

The display ran numbers promptly and began a readout.

WORLDWIDE VIOLENCE CRIME WAR INSANITY OF 20TH CENTURY SHOWED HUMANS CAPABLE OF SELFEXTERMINATION OPERATIVE CAUSE WAS FEAR REPEAT FEAR RESEARCH DEMONSTRATED HUMANS WITHOUT FEAR NONVIOLENT SANEcyclec POLICE EDUCATION PEACE TREATIES INADEQUATE TO CONTROL FEAR OF INDIVIDUAL HUMANS BUT SANE INDIVIDUAL HUMANS NOT PRONE TO VIOLENCE WAR TREATIES POLICE WEAPONS

UNNECESSARY IF INDIVIDUALS NOT AFRAID
cyclecyclecyclecyclecyclecy TREATMENTcyclecyc-
lecyclecyclec BIOMITER MEDICOMPUTER NET-
WORK INITIATED FORc ALL INDIVIDUALS
MONITOR PHYSIOLOGICAL SIGNS OF EMO-
TION STRESS ILLNESS CONDITIONED RE-
SPONSES INBRED TO CONTROL BEHAVIOR
FEAR*** CROSSREFERENCE PAVLOV BE-
HAVIOR MODIFICATION SUBCONSCIOUS
HYPNOTISMcyclecyclecyclecyclecyclecy SUCCESS
OF BIOMITTER PROGRAM DEMONSTRATES
FEAR DOES NOT EXIST WHERE CONTROL
ORDER

Abruptly, the green letters flashed off the display, and
the terminal began to read-out a line' of red.

DATA CANCEL REPEAT CANCELcyclecyclecyc-
lecyclecyclecyclecy MATERIAL CLASSIFICATION
RESTRICTED NOT AVAILABLE WITHOUT AP-
PROVAL DIRECTOR NATIONAL LIBRARY FILE
APPROVAL CODE BEFORE REACTIVATING RE-
FERENCE PROGRAMcyclecycle cyclecyclecycl

Norman frowned around his horn. He was not sure what
had happened. Perhaps he had accidentally stumbled upon
information that was always restricted and had automatically triggered the reference computer's cancellation
program. Or perhaps the director had just now succeeded
in breaking his personal information code and had found
out what he was doing. If the interruption had been automatic, he was still safe. But if the director had been
monitoring him personally, he did not have much time. He
needed to know.

He left his desk and went to the director's office. The
director looked very much like Dr. Brett. Norman be-

lieved that he could break the director with one kick of his hard foot. He knew what to do. He said, "Director."

"Yes, Norman?" the director said. His voice was warm and wise, like Dr. Brett's. Norman did not trust him. "Are you OK? Do you want to go home?"

"I am OK," Norman said. "I want to take out some books."

"Take out some books'?" the director said. "What do you mean?"

"I want to withdraw some books. I want to take them home with me."

"Very well," the director said. "Take them with you. Take the rest of the day off. You need some rest."

"Thank you," Norman said. He was being careful. Now he had what he wanted. He knew that the director had been watching him. He knew that the director had deliberately broken his personal information code. He knew that the director had transmitted his information to the General Hospital and had been told that he, Norman, was dangerous. No one was allowed to take books out of the National Library. It was forbidden to withdraw books. Always. Even the director could not override that rule, unless he had been given emergency programming.

Norman was no longer safe. But he did not hurry. He did not want the General Hospital to think that he was afraid. The men in white coats would chase him more quickly if they thought he was afraid of them. He walked calmly, as if he were perfectly safe, perfectly sane, to the stacks where the books were kept after they had been sorted and fed into the reference computer.

He did not try to be thorough or complete. His time was short. He took only the books he could carry, only the books he was sure he wanted: He took *The Mask, the Unicorn, and the Messiah;* the *Index to Fairy Tales,*

Myths, and Legends; Barbarous Knowledge; the *Larousse Encyclopedia of Mythology; The Masks of God;* and *The Book of Imaginary Beings.* He would need these books when his transformation was complete. They would tell him what to do.

He did not try to find any others. He left the National Library, hugging the books to his broad chest like treasure.

The careful part of him expected to have trouble with his mobile, but he did not. It took him home exactly as it always did.

When he entered his house, he found that Sally had not been brought back. Enwell had not come home. He did not think that he would ever see them again. He was alone.

He took off his clothes because he knew that unicorns did not wear clothes. Then he sat down in the living room and started to read his books.

They did not make sense to him. He knew most of the words, but he could not seem to understand what they were saying. At first he was disappointed in himself. He was afraid that he might not make a very good unicorn. But then he realized the truth. The books did not make sense to him because he was not ready for them. His transformation was not complete yet. When it was complete, he would be able to understand the books. He bobbed his horn joyfully. Then, because he was careful, he spent the rest of the day memorizing as much as he could of the first book, *The Book of Imaginary Beings.* He wanted to protect himself in case his books were lost or damaged.

He was still memorizing after dark, and he was not tired. His horn filled him with strength. But then he began to hear a humming noise in the air. It was soft and soothing, and he could not tell how long it had been going on. It was coming from his biomitter. It found a place deep inside him that obeyed it. He laid down on the couch and went to sleep.

But it was not the kind of sleep he was used to. It was not calm and safe. Something in him resisted it, resisted the reassuring hum. His dreams were wild. His emotions were strong, and one of them was uneasiness. His uneasiness was so strong that it must have been fear. It made him open his eyes.

All the lights were on in the living room, and there were four men in white coats around him. Each of them carried a hypogun. All the hypoguns were pointed at him.

"Don't be afraid," one of the men said. "We won't hurt you. You're going to be all right. Everything is going to be OK."

Norman did not believe him. He saw that the men were gripping their hypoguns tightly. He saw that the men were afraid. They were afraid of him.

He flipped off the couch and jumped. His legs were immensely strong. His jump carried him over the heads of the men. As he passed, he kicked one of the men. Blood appeared on his forehead and spattered his coat, and he fell down and did not move.

The nearest man fired his hypogun. But Norman blocked the penetrating spray with the hard flat heel of his palm. His fingers curled into a hoof, and he hit the man in the chest. The man fell down.

The other two men were trying to run away. They were afraid of him. They were running toward the door. Norman jumped after them and poked the nearest one with his horn. The man seemed to fly away from the horn. He crashed into the other man, and they both crashed against the door and fell down and did not move again. One of them had blood all over his back.

Norman's biomitter was blaring red: *You are ill. You are ill.*

The man Norman had punched was still alive. He was gasping for breath. His face was white with death, but he was able to tap a message into his biomitter. Norman could read his fingers. He was saying, *Seal the house. Keep him trapped. Bring nerve gas.*

Norman went to the man. "Why?" he said. "Why are you trying to kill me?"

The man looked at Norman. He was too close to dying to be afraid anymore. "You're dangerous," he said. He was panting, and blood came out of his mouth. "You're deadly."

"Why?" Norman said. "What's happening to me?"

"Transmutation," the man said. "Atavism. Psychic throwback. You're becoming something. Something that never existed."

" 'Never existed'?" Norman said.

"You must've been buried," the man said. "In the subconscious. All this time. You never existed. People made you up. A long time ago. They believed in you. Because they needed to. Because they were afraid."

More blood came out of his mouth. "How could it happen?" he said. His voice was very weak. "We put fear to sleep. There is no more fear. No more violence. How could it happen?" Then he stopped breathing. But his eyes stayed open, staring at the things he did not understand.

Norman felt a deep sorrow. He did not like killing. A unicorn was not a killing beast. But he had had no choice. He had been cornered.

His biomitter was shouting, *You are ill.*

He did not intend to be cornered again. He raised his wrist and touched his biomitter with the tip of his horn. Pieces of metal were torn away, and the bright blood ran down his arm.

After that, he did not delay. He took a slipcover from the couch and used it as a sack to carry his books. Then he went to the door and tried to leave his house.

The door did not open. It was locked with heavy steel bolts that he had never seen before. They must have been built into the house. Apparently, the men in white coats, or the medicomputers, were prepared for everything.

They were not prepared for a unicorn. He attacked the door with his horn. His horn was as hard as steel, as hard as magnacite. It was as hard as tung-diamonds. The door burst open, and he went out into the night.

Then he saw more ambulances coming down the road. Ambulances were converging on his house from both directions. He did not know where to run. So he galloped across the street and burst in the door of the house opposite his. The house belonged to his friend, Barto. He went to his friend for help.

But when Barto and his wife and his two daughters saw Norman, their faces filled with fear. The daughters began to wail like sirens. Barto and his wife fell to the floor and folded up into balls.

Norman broke down the back door and ran out into the service lane between the rows of houses.

He traveled the lane for miles, After the sorrow at his friend's fear came a great joy at his strength and swiftness. He was stronger than the men in white coats, faster than ambulances. And he had nothing else to be wary of. The medicomputers could not chase him themselves. With his biomitter gone, they could not even tell where he was. And they had no weapons with which to fight him except men in white coats and ambulances. He was free and strong and exhilarated for the first time in his life.

When daylight came, he climbed up onto the roofs of the houses. He felt safe there, and when he was ready to rest, he slept there alone, facing the sky.

He spent days like that—traveling the city, reading his books and committing them to memory—waiting for his transformation to be complete. When he needed food, he raided grocery stores to get it, though the terror of the people he met filled him with sorrow. And gradually his food-need changed. Then he did not go to the grocery stores anymore. He pranced in the parks at night and cropped the grass and the flowers and ran nickering among the trees.

And his transformation continued. His mane and tail grew thick and exuberant. His face lengthened, and his teeth became stronger. His feet became hooves, and the horny part of his hands grew. White hair the color of moonlight spread across his body and limbs, formed flaring tufts at the backs of his ankles and wrists. His horn grew long and clean and perfectly pointed.

His joints changed also and began to flex in new ways. For a time, this gave him some pain, but soon it became natural to him. He was turning into a unicorn. He was becoming beautiful. At times, there did not seem to be enough room in his heart for the joy the change gave him.

Yet he did not leave the city. He did not leave the people who were afraid of him, though their fear gave him pangs of a loneliness he had never felt before. He was waiting for something. There was something in him that was not complete.

At first, he believed that he was simply waiting for the end of his transformation. But gradually he came to understand that his waiting was a kind of search. He was alone—and unicorns were not meant to be alone, not like this. He was searching the city to see if he could find other people like him, people who were changing.

And at last one night he came in sight of the huge, high

structure of the General Hospital. He had been brought there by his search. If there were other people like him, they might have been captured by the men in white coats. They might be prisoners in the Emergency Division of the hospital. They might be lying helpless while the medicomputers studied them, plotting their destruction.

His nostrils flared angrily at the thought. He stamped his foreleg. He knew what he had to do. He put his sack of books in a place of safety. Then he lowered his head and charged down the road to attack the General Hospital.

He broke down the front doors with his horn and pounded into the corridors. People fled from him in terror. Men and women grabbed hypoguns and tried to fire at him, but he flicked them with the power of his horn, and they fell down. He rampaged on in search of the Emergency Division.

The General Hospital was designed just like the Medical Building and the National Library. He was able to find his way without trouble. Soon he was among the many rooms of the Emergency Division. He kicked open the doors, checked the rooms, checked room after room. They were full of patients. The Emergency Division was a busy place. He had not expected to find that so many people were ill and dangerous. But none of them were what he was looking for. They were not being transformed. They were dying from physical or mental sickness. If any people like him had been brought here, they had already been destroyed.

Red rage filled his heart. He charged on through the halls.

Then suddenly he came to the great room where the medicomputers lived. Rank on rank, they stood before him. Their displays glared evilly at him, and their voices shouted. He heard several of them shout together, "Absolute emergency! Atmospheric control, activate all nerve gas! Saturation gassing, all floors!''

They were trying to kill him. They were going to kill everybody in the hospital.

The medicomputers were made of magnacite and plasmium. Their circuits were fireproof. But they were not proof against the power of his horn. When he attacked them, they began to burn in white fires, as incandescent as the sun.

He could hear gas hissing into the air. He took a deep breath and ran.

The gas was hissing into all the corridors of the hospital. Patients began to die. Men and women in white coats began to die. Norman began to think that he would not be able to get out of the hospital before he had to breathe.

A moment later, the fire in the medicomputers ignited the gas. The gas burned. Oxygen tanks began to explode. Dispensaries went up in flames. The fire extinguishers could not stop the intense heat of burning magnacite and plasmium. When the cylinders of nerve gas burst, they had enough force to shatter the floors and walls.

Norman flashed through the doors and galloped into the road with the General Hospital raging behind him like a furnace.

He breathed the night air deep into his chest and skittered to a stop on the far side of the road to shake the sparks out of his mane. Then he turned to watch the hospital burn.

At first he was alone in the road. The people who lived nearby did not come to watch the blaze. They were afraid of it. They did not try to help the people who escaped the flames.

But then he saw a young girl come out from between the houses. She went into the road to look at the fire.

Norman pranced over to her. He reared in front of her.

She did not run away.

She had a lump on her forehead like the base of a horn or the nub of a new antler. There was a smile on her lips, as if she were looking at something beautiful.

And there was no fear in her eyes at all.

Introduction to
Eric Norden's
"The Final Quarry":

The hunt is in our blood, as much today as in prehistoric times when our ancestors painted animals on cave walls to propiate the gods, and insure dinner. But while we once hunted to survive, most of us now hunt for sport, or to satisfy our greed; and in our insatiable hunger for more trophies, pelts, and tusks, we've wiped entire species from the face of the earth forever. The list of creatures hunted to extinction by mankind is long—the dodo, the passenger pigeon, the aurochs—and the list of those creatures now tottering on the brink of extinction is longer still—the Indian Rhinoceros, the sea otter, the bald eagle, the elephant, the whooping crane, the blue whale . . . .

Here Eric Norden, a frequent contributor to *The Magazine of Fantasy and Science Fiction* and *Playboy*, and the author of the collection *Starsongs and Unicorns*, suggests that the unicorn might be about to be added to that dreary list, and that (as is also true of all the other creatures on the list) we won't fully realize just what we have lost until after it is gone.

THE FINAL QUARRY
Eric Norden

THE last unicorn on earth lay dozing in the sun on a hilltop in northern Thessaly, memories buzzing softly through his brain like the murmur of distant bees. As unicorns go, he was not a noticeably distinguished specimen, for age had dulled the gloss of his ivory pelt, and here and there along his withered flanks tufts of hair had fallen out, lending him a patched, faintly moth-eaten quality. But his eyes, even now when filmed with dream, were luminous with wisdom, as if they had drunk in the centuries like dew, and his imperious spiral horn rested lightly on the grass, a gleaming golden icicle in the summer sunlight. He stirred once in his sleep, as the thoughts of a child in the valley reached him, crystalline as the chime of a steeple bell, and then, replenished lapsed into deeper slumber. The dark, demanding voices of the earth no longer spoke to him, and it had been a thousand years since silent wings beat the air above his head, or tingling laughter pealed in ageless mockery as he sipped from the waterfall below the gorge, but the old unicorn did not begrudge the new masters of earth, and was content to savor the endless tapestry of his dreams. A zephyr prematurely tinged with autumn brushed his horn gently as a butterfly's wings, perhaps in warning, but he slept on.

The older and immeasurably grosser of the two Englishmen shoved his plate of cold stuffed eggplant across the rough-planked wooden table with a violent, stabbing motion and snarled at the innkeeper.

"If this is the best you have to offer us, we shall ride on to Pharanakos tonight!"

150

His florid face was suffused with a darker flush of fury as he wrenched the coarse linen napkin from his neck and hurled it to the packed dirt floor. His companion, a slim youth in his early twenties, elegantly attired in a fawn-grey cheviot lounge suit of a cut popularized by the late king and a resplendent waistcoat of brocaded maroon silk, languidly surveyed the room and tapped a cone of ash from his think black cheroot onto the remains of his own dinner.

"My dear Marius," he drawled, "for once I do wish you could forget your belly and remember the purpose of our visit. We are not here as scouts for the *Guide Michelin,* and as for myself, I should rather grub like a pig for roots than spend one more hour in that infernal coach."

As the innkeeper hastily snatched the plate from the table and scurried towards the kitchen amidst a flurry of apologies in broken English, Sir Marius Wallaby, Bart., turned his wrath on his traveling companion.

"God's blood, Deverish, don't let me hear from you what the purpose of this journey is. If I hadn't been gulled by your mad tale back in Athens, I wouldn't be sitting in this miserable excuse for an inn, two hundred miles from the last pretense of civilization, feeding on warmed-over table scraps and guzzling mare's piss for wine." He groaned piteously. "And my last bottle of hock gone two days back, with no decent cellars between here and the coast."

Nigel Deverish sipped with overtly sadistic relish from his glass of white *Retzina.*

"As for myself, I rather enjoy its clean, piney bite," he said. "But then I am obviously no connoisseur in such matters."

"The matters in which you are a connoisseur I tremble to contemplate." The older man's anger crumpled abruptly as his huge frame slumped back into a rickety rattan chair precariously accommodating his twenty stone, and

he ran one hand, plump and livid as a baby lobster,
through thinning sandy hair before speaking in a voice
thickly edged with fatigue.

"I must caution you I don't intend going on like this
much longer, Deverish. Don't think I'm not up to it
physically—God knows. I've been on treks in Africa and
Brazil that makes this expedition look like a walking tour
of Surrey." He grimaced wearily. "But then I was always
after something tangible, something that left a spoor I
could follow, something I could fix in the sights of my
rifle. We must have passed through thirty of these half-
arsed villages in the past three weeks and no one even
knows what we're talking about. The whole idea is so
damned vague, it's like trying to grab a handful of smoke,
and it's getting on my nerves, Deverish, I'm not ashamed
to confess."

Nigel Deverish eyed his companion with thinly veiled
contempt. Sir Marius Wallaby was a huge, corpulent man
in his early fifties, with a flaccid basketball of a head,
candid, hyperthyroid eyes of a pale, china-blue prominent
in his ruddy face, now stubbled by a two-day growth of
orangy beard, and a mouth pursed like a querulous
rosebud. He was dressed with customary carelessness in a
rumpled Norfolk hacking jacket, multidarned cardigan of
muddy-brown wool, heather-green tweed knickers, and
battered Peal's brogues. Hardly the picture, Deverish reflected grimly, of a man worth half a million if a guinea,
but Wallaby cared nothing for appearances, or money. His
only passions were, in interchangeable order, the table,
the hunt, and the bottle. Wallaby's tempers were fierce but
transient, for like a toothless dog he had learned long ago
to rely on his bark. He was as petulant as a child, Deverish
had perceived on their first meeting, and as innocent; an
easy man to use, but only if one were willing to cosset him
like a nanny. "My dear Marius," he now soothed, "no

one understands better than I your disappointment. But surely, for the man of idomitable will, such frustrations only serve to redouble the determination to succeed. Had Stanley given up before Victoria Falls . . ." He let the sentence trail off meaningfully, mildly sickened by the ingenuousness of his appeal, but equally convinced of its effectiveness.

"Yes, yes, I suppose you're quite right," Wallaby murmured, sitting imperceptibly straighter. "It doesn't do to get discouraged too quickly on these things." He sipped distastefully from his wine glass. "Years ago in Mombasa I ran into a dicey old Dutchman who swore he'd seen a white rino in the Gambezi. He'd been tracking it off and on for years whenever he could steer a safari into the area, and everyone thought he was crackers, of course, but one day he walked right into Starrs', threw the skin on the bar, and ordered drinks for the house. Showed us all, he did. Never forgot it." Wallaby scowled darkly. "Which is probably why I'm here with you today instead of enjoying a bottle of decent hock in Athens."

The innkeeper moved deferentially to their table and placed a worn copper platter before Sir Marius. "This looks a bit better," the Englishman grunted as he dubiously surveyed an array of *media dolma* and *moussaka,* a local dish of beef cunningly cooked with aubergines, mushrooms and tomatoes, and smothered in a simmering souffle of *feta* cheese. The elderly Greek smiled encouragingly and placed another bottle of *Retzina* on the table.

"You enjoy, *Kyrios,* you enjoy." Panayotis beamed proudly. "I know how to cook for English. I work in Athens three years. That's where I learn your language, also French and a little Turkish." The innkeeper had regaled them earlier with his travels, for as the only local man to venture forth as far as fabled Athens and the sea, he was a minor celebrity, and served as mayor of the cluster of rude stone-and-wattle cottages comprising the hamlet of Theodorina. "You will find the best food in the Pindus mountains right here, here with Panayotis, milord."

"I don't question that," Sir Marius grunted, tentatively slipping a fork into a mussel entwined with grape leaves, "only whether it's a recommendation." But after one bite, he smiled abruptly, like ice melting, and nodded approval to the innkeeper, who half giggled with relief and obsequiously bobbed his grizzled head in an awkward half-bow. Why do the peasants always fawn on the hulking, ill-mannered boor, Deverish reflected bitterly, when it's so obvious I'm the sole gentleman in our party? He gulped his *Retzina* convulsively, and lit another cheroot, gratefully dragging the harsh smoke into his lungs.

After the meal was over and cloyingly sweet honey-and-nut pastries had been washed down with Turkish coffee and ouzo, Wallaby belched contentedly and plucked a cigar from a battered lizard-skin case.

"Doubtless have indigestion later on, but at least I feel halfway human for the time being," he grumbled. Panayotis diffidently presented a bill, and Wallaby, without examining it, tossed a jumble of fifty-drachma notes onto the table.

"Take our rooms from that and keep the change."

The innkeeper's eyes fixed hotly on the bills for a long moment before he scrabbled them up with trembling hands, his mumbled words of gratitude cut short by Wallaby's roar for a bottle of Metaxa. Deverish choked back the bile in his throat. Of course the old fool could afford to throw away his money—he'd never had to sweat for it. He cursed for the thousandth time the perverse law of nature ordaining that cretins like Wallaby be blessed with wealth, while the rare man of genius must grovel in muck for the offal of everyday existence, lyric words and vaulting imagery strangled stillborn. Deverish stared at Wallaby guzzling brandy like a bloated pig greedily snuffling for truffles, and his hand involuntarily strayed to the sheaf of poems in his jacket pocket. It would not be long now. His eyes slivered as he smiled suddenly, exultantly, and when he spoke he no longer had to struggle to keep the hatred from his voice.

"Don't you think you overpaid that chap a bit, old boy?"

Wallaby looked up from his brandy and scowled.

"You're bad enough as a guide, Deverish, don't start doubling as my accountant. In any case, the draft from Athens gives me enough to buy and sell this whole pigsty of a town—not that I'd want it, God knows." He slurped noisily from his glass and wiped his moist forehead with a tattered red bandana. "And another thing, Deverish, once and for all stop calling me 'old boy', and trotting out your whole insufferably tatty Oxbridge act. I don't give a damn about a man's birth, and I've always held Debrett's the least reliable stud-book of the lot, but the pose bores me to tears and will only get you laughed at back in London." His eyes suddenly softened. "I don't mean that harshly, Deverish. Just be yourself, that's all. You'll get along better that way."

Deverish stood up abruptly, his sallow cheeks flaming. Wallaby's insult he could have almost savored, on account so to speak, but the gratuitous fillip of condescension was intolerable. His fists tightened into balls and he spoun on his heels to hide his face from Wallaby's eyes.

"I'll speak to the innkeeper now and see if he knows anything," Deverish said tautly, his words barely above a whisper.

"All right, all right, we've gone this far, go ahead." Wallaby belched, and took a long pull from his glass. "Though I'm beginning to think that photograph of yours was some kind of forgery or perhaps just a shot of an ibex or aurochs. You probably wouldn't know the difference anyway."

With a surge of secret satisfaction, Deverish composed himself. He, after all, was the master of this situation. There had never been any photograph, merely the maudlin mumblings of an old Greek in a Salonika bar drunkenly bemoaning his native Karanakis where unicorns still lived and flited through the forest glades. Deverish had been amused at first, but the old man's words held the germ of an idea. He had met Sir Marius Wallaby for the first time the day before at the Travellers' Club, where he had eloquently requested the wealthy baronet's backing to publish a volume of his verse, only to be summarily rebuffed and packed off like a beggar with a fiver stuffed in his pocket as a token of Wallaby's largess—which, to make it worse, he was forced by dint of circumstances to accept. But Deverish knew of Wallaby's reputation as a hunter; the old man had stalked everything from elephants in Africa to cougars in Peru, and photo stories of his expeditions appeared regularly in the lurid illustrated press. If the opportunity to bag the greatest game of all—the last surviving unicorn—presented itself, could the cold fool resist the temptation? Wallaby's childlike credulity needed little priming from Deverish, and the baronet accepted the tale eagerly, immediately moving to outfit an expedition. Now, three weeks later, the two of them were alone in one of the most desolate areas of Greece, two hundred miles from the nearest police station, in a mountainous countryside where accidents were bound to occur, particularly to someone fat, clumsy and slow of foot—someone, above all, with the equivalent of two thousand English pounds in Greek drachmas stuffed in his pockets.

Breaking off his reverie, Deverish strode to the kitchen and peremptorily ordered the innkeeper to their table.

Panayotis followed, but not, Deverish noted irritably, with the alacrity he displayed in response to even the rudest of Wallaby's summonses. Once seated, the old Greek gratefully accepted a glass of Metaxa and listened closely as Deverish explained their quest in fluent Greek, frowning thoughtfully before finally replying in tortured English—Wallaby didn't know a word of any foreign language not featured on menus—that he had never heard of such an animal.

"But, milord," Panayotis continued haltingly, addressing only Wallaby as was his custom, "there is an old man, a priest, who lives in the woods. He stayed many years in a monastery on Mount Athos and is now what you would call *hermetos,* for he exists only on nuts and berries, and will kill no living thing for food. There are some who say he is mad—" Panayotis crossed himself surreptitiously at the blasphemy—"but I see much truth in his eyes. He lives in a cave at the foot of Karajides mountain, but once in awhile he comes here, and I give him bread and wine." He took another sip of Metaxa. "This priest knows the woods and mountains like none of us, who are all farmers and seldom wander far from our fields. I have seen him in the forest once or twice, and the animals follow him, even the deer, and are not afraid. He feeds them and sometimes he talks to them." Panayotis looked momentarily embarrassed fearful the Englishman would despise his credulity. "Of course, milord, for all I know he is not even a real priest; the priest at Calabaris in the valley comes here once a month to preach since we have no church of our own and he says he knows nothing of this *hermetos.* But I think he is a holy man."

Wallaby gestured impatiently with one pudgy hand.

"I don't care if he's a saint or a highwayman. If he knows the woods and mountains of this territory, I want to speak to him. We've been going around in circles for three weeks because your damned peasants have eyes for nothing beyond their bloody turnip plots. Can you bring him to us?''

The innkeepers' brow furrowed doubtfully.

"That I do not think, milord. He visits here only when he desires, and you could wait weeks before he come again.'' He brightened preceptibly. "But I could lead you to his cave—it is not a long walk.''

Wallaby heaved agonizedly out of his chair and began waddling towards the stairs, the bottle of Metaxa dangling loosely from one hand.

"All right, we'll leave at seven in the morning. Wake me at six, prepare a warm bath, and for breakfast fry me six eggs, coffee, some toasted bread, and a side of bacon.'' He cut off the innkeeper's protest. "Then kill the pig, I'll pay you for it. Seven o'clock.'' He nodded curtly to Deverish and hauled his bulk laboriously up the stairs.

Deverish sat hunched over his brandy for at least another hour, and the innkeeper was puzzled by the Englishman's sporadic bouts of smirking laughter. Yes indeed, he thought, savoring the words, do kill the pig. And you will pay for it, dear Marius, you will surely pay for it.

Deverish awoke after a restless night on a hard pallet-like bed and shaved painfully in cold water brought him in a chipped porcelain basin by the innkeeper's eldest son, a handsome boy in his late teens with tousled coal-black hair, smooth olive skin, and the classic features of a young Homeric prince. He eyed the youth appraisingly for a moment, and then dismissed the thought. Later back in Athens or elsewhere on the Continent, but not here not now. He could afford no taint of suspicion, much less scandal—the stakes were too high.

Downstairs, Wallaby crouched over a three-week-old copy of the *Times* he had purchased in Ioannina, the last stage of their journey maintaining vestigial contact with the outside world. He had already polished off his breakfast, and looked up irritably as Deverish took his place at the table and accepted a steaming mug of harsh black tea from the innkeeper.

"Can't you ever be on time, man? I said we'd depart at seven, and seven it is, whether you've eaten or not. Hurry up with that breakfast!" Panayotis, who had been hovering over Wallaby's shoulder, resignedly padded out to the kitchen, no trace of resentment on his face, and Wallaby immersed himself in the paper for a few more moments before hurling it to the table with a muted imprecation.

"Must know the damned thing by heart now," he growled. "I can recite King George's movements from morning to night, and throw in a verbatim report of the Kaiser's speech at Potsdam." He looked accusingly at Deverish. "If I'd known we'd be running about half of Greece on this mad chase of yours, I'd have taken some serious reading matter along."

Deverish's lip curled imperceptibly. Wallaby's idea of serious literature was the latest issue of the *Strand*, and the peregrinations of Conan Doyle's absurd fictional fabrication—or, on a more refined level, the muddled bleats of eunuchs such as George Manville Fenn, Dick Donovan and W. Clark Russell. For hours on the coach from Athens, Wallaby had rattled on with indefatigable enthusiasm over the latest literary excretions of those favored pygmies—all the while oblivious to the presence at his side of one who could burn his words into the ages if only freed from the material shackles binding lesser men and allowed to breathe, to move, to create. Once, at the very outset of the trip, when his plan had not as yet fully crystallized, Deverish granted Wallaby a second chance to become his patron and read the fool several of his best poems. Wallaby had listened abstractedly, finally nodding judiciously and patting Deverish on the shoulder. "Nice stuff, I'm sure, but I prefer poets who make themselves clear, like Kipling or Housman. All this agonizing over life and death is a bit deep for me. But keep at it, old boy, by all means keep at it.'' Wallaby had returned with evident relief to his copy of *Nature*, and neither of them referred to the subject again.

Under Wallaby's impatient eye, Deverish wolfed an indifferent breakfast of lumpy porridge and cold slabs of greasy bacon and then departed with the innkeeper for the hermit's cave. As the small party left the village and passed through the open fields of the valley, Deverish's spirits failed to lighten, although it was a cool, antiseptic morning, with a clean summer breeze rippling the air and scudding ragged tufts of cloud across a sky of the washed metallic blue found only in the Mediterranean. Deverish wanted Wallaby alone high in the mountains, not on a hiking trip through the forest in quest of some half-crazed recluse, but he had waited this long, and could afford to wait a few hours or a few days longer.

A short journey it might be to the innkeeper, but for Deverish the trek appeared interminable, burdened as he was with both their hunting rifles and a rucksack containing rations and extra cartridges. For all his bulk Wallaby pressed on relentlessly through the fields and into the thick woods of hawthorn and birch lapping at the foot of the more lightly forested mountain slopes, his plump cheeks redder than usual from exertion, intermittently whistling bawdy tunes and pausing only for an occasional swift swig of brandy from his capacious silver flask. Deverish was consistently astounded and repelled by the man's insatiable appetite for liquor, and by the fact that it never exacted a toll the following morning, whereas his own four brandies of the night before had bequeathed him an aching head and churning stomach, tinged with the bleak edge of nervous despair always attendant to his hangovers.

Wallaby, predictably enough, was in the best of spirits and insisted on regaling Deverish with his hunting exploits.

"Only thing I've never killed is a fox," he said as the old Greek led them through a copse of silver birch and into a small sun-swept clearing at the foot of a rugged, barren hillside. "No sport there, the poor terrified beast doesn't have a chance, run to ground by a pack of bloody baying hounds and a hundred horsemen. A coward's pastime, if you ask me—I always give my game a sporting chance." He pulled out his flask again and took a quick, slobbering gulp, wiping his mouth with the back of one scarlet hand. "Whatever else they say about that fellow Wilde, he had the fox hunter's number: 'the unspeakable in pursuit of the uneatable.' Eh?" Wallaby burst into a sudden peal of laughter and slapped one meaty thigh, as if the words had been his own spontaneous observation. Deverish merely grimaced—there was something blasphemous at the words of Wilde dribbling from the flaccid lips of this great oaf—and joined the old Greek, who had halted in the middle of the clearing.

"The holy man lives here," Panayotis whispered reverently, as Wallaby lumbered to his side, "in that cave there, milord." He pointed to a black gash in the pitted face of the hill. "I will go on ahead and see if he will talk with you." Panayotis dropped his pack to the ground and extracted two bottles of wine and a sack stuffed with flat bread, dates, *feta* cheese, and pungent black Calamaris olives—it had been decided that a bit of discreet bribery might lubricate the priest's tongue—and entered the cave.

Wallaby and Deverish stood together without speaking in the clearing for several moments after the innkeeper left them. Deverish was restless and nervy, and the insistent glare of sunlight pained his eyes. He was suddenly conscious of the intensity of bird song in the surrounding trees, and as he looked closely he saw hundreds of different

birds arrayed in the branches, their voices beating out
to serenade the men in the clearing. Under ordinary circumstances it would have been a pleasant scene, but now
the noise was too orchestral, too insistent, and Deverish
found it vaguely disturbing, if not actively tinged with
menace. There were too many birds for such a small
clearing, and he had a tingling sensation of their *aware-
ness,* as if their tiny eyes were all fixed on his, the jarring
cacophony of bird song directed at him alone. He jerked
around to face the cave, sweat springing out on his
brow, just as Panayotis emerged and waved them to
enter.

Deverish followed Wallaby and the innkeeper into a
dank warren littered with scraps of food and fouled linen.
The air was so noxious Deverish almost choked, and
abruptly he experienced a wild impulse to flee back into
the sunlit glade. But then he saw the man huddled in one
corner, and his artist's fascination with the grotesque
dispelled all fear. The hermit was tall, at least six feet four,
and incredibly filthy, his bony frame draped in the tattered
remnants of a *soutane,* a huge, hand-carved wooden
crucifix dangling from his neck. His hands and feet were
polished black with a solid patina of filth, and greasy,
tangled dark locks fell below his shoulders. The hermit's
beard was a living thing, a coiled snake dangling to his
waist, encrusted with grime and particles of food, but his
teeth, when he smiled to greet them, were startingly white,
and his eyes were the clear light blue of the bleached sky
outside. The man should have been repellent, but even to
Deverish he was strangely impressive. He did not rise but
remained crouched in the corner, extending both hands in
a mute gesture of welcome. Deverish wondered if they
were expected to sit on the filthy floor of the cave, but
Wallaby merely squatted on his haunches before the old
man and motioned Deverish to explain their mission,
while Panayotis hovered edgily by the entrance, occasion-

ally casting awe-struck glances at the hermit. Deverish explained that he and Wallaby had heard reports of a unicorn surviving in these remote hills, and wished to verify them. The old man was silent for a long moment, his eyes cast down and pensive, before he looked directly up at Deverish and spoke softly. Deverish couldn't follow him at first, but finally he realized the old man was speaking classical Greek, the words pure and clean as a mountain stream.

"But are not unicorns mythical beasts, stranger?" The old man employed the word *barbaros,* a proper classical usage, but with a faint underlay of emphasis that vaguely disturbed Deverish.

"Who can say for sure what is myth and what reality, father?" he replied carefully, the ancient words creaking with disuse on his tongue. "We seek only truth."

The old man's smile faded, and he sighed. Deverish watched with loathing as a louse crawled from the tangled mat of hair under his armpit and struggled laboriously along the tattered remnants of one sleeve.

"If you seek only truth," the hermit continued. "then I shall answer you with truth. But first I must know more of your purpose in coming here. Is it only the search for knowledge that impels you?"

The startlingly blue eyes fixed on his, and suddenly the facile words caught in Deverish's throat. He could only nod feebly, and the old man sighed again.

"I can call no man a liar, because there are too many truths. So to answer you, yes, there is such a beast in these hills, the very last one in the entire world. He is old and tired, and sleeps much in the sun, but sometimes we meet and share our thoughts. He feeds on goodness, and that is why he is old and infirm, and soon shall die, for it is a meager diet today."

The old priest was obviously mad, but Deverish continued in order to keep Wallaby's flickering interest in their quest alive, for with the sportsman's intuitive flair, the fat Englishman had sensed the spoor of his elusive quarry and now was glancing back and forth at the two of them like a spectator at a match of lawn tennis, hoping by sheer intensity of will to fathom the alien words.

"Where can we find this beast?" Deverish asked, choking back a smile. The momentary sense of discontinuity he'd experienced earlier had dissolved, and now he felt only contempt tinged with pity for the pathetic demented fool before him.

"He lives on the slopes above Thanatakis mountain, five miles to the south of here. His legs are weak, and he seldom ventures far from his waterfall. He will not flee from you, for he is very tired and does not know fear."

Deverish turned to Wallaby and gave him a quick digest of their conversation, registering with satisfaction the glint of excitement in the other man's eyes. Wallaby pulled himself to his feet and started towards the cave door, but before he could follow, the hermit's hand shot out and clutched at his sleeve. Deverish noted with disgust that the fingernails were long, talon-like, and reamed in filth. He tried to shake his arm free, but the old man's grip was inordinately strong, and suddenly the deep, distant eyes fastened on his, and again Deverish felt a vague disorientation, a falling away from reality.

The old man spoke softly, never looking from Deverish's face.

"You are here to kill the unicorn, are you not?"

For one irrational moment Deverish accepted the reality of the hunt as passionately as Wallaby. The priest repeated his question quietly, and Deverish did not have the strength to lie. He felt suddenly nauseous, and the hermit's eyes were like twin stakes impaling him. He nodded weakly, and the old man shook his head and clasped his one free hand to the wooden crucifix about his neck.

"I had known you were coming for some time now. The birds told me."

His grip tightened on Deverish's arm.

"I cannot stop you, for these things are ordained," the old man whispered, "but I must tell you this: you go to slay the most precious creature left on earth."

He paused, and Deverish again felt the eyes tearing into his mind like arrows. Wallaby called something impatiently from the doorway, but he could not move.

"Listen to me, my son," the priest continued, the ancient words falling with liquid precision from his lips, "this beast you seek to slay is the last guardian of man's innocence. Unicorns live on thoughts of beauty, and the radiance of their souls has fallen like sunlight on the world for thousands of years, even before the Old Ones were dreamed into substance on Olympus." The priest's voice fell even lower and the mad eyes filmed with grief. "But the day Christ died on the cross the king of the Unicorns took it upon his race to suffer penance for the act, for otherwise God's wrath delivered on the heads of man would indeed have been terrible. And so on that day, while the heavens shook and the earth trembled on the brink of chaos, he ordered all the females of his race to die, and in great silver flocks they mounted the heights of Thessaly and threw themselves to death on the crags below, singing the ancient songs as they fell. Their voices reached the ear of God, and the tears of Christ rained upon Greece for three days and three nights, and beauty crept into the dreams of everyone."

He is mad, thought Deverish feebly, why does he keep looking at me, why does he not let me out into the sunlight?

"Since then," the priest went on, "the remaining unicorns have died one by one, always by the violence of man's hand, because Christ in his love has spared them pain or illness or suffering or death, save that inflicted by his own tormentors. And with the death of each unicorn over the centuries, something of beauty, something of innocence, has gone out of the world, and a candle has been extinguished in the heart of every man, and the darkness has grown. This poor tired beast you plan to kill is the sole custodian of that ancient, guttering flame. When he is slain the last light of God's mercy is snuffed out, and even children's hearts shall become soiled, and wonder will die slowly, strangled until it becomes only a word, and innocence shall never return. A vast darkness hovers over the earth, peopled with the horrors of the apocalypse, and this beast is man's last solitary light. So God intended it and so shall it be. Go and destroy him.''

The bony fingers released Deverish's sleeve, and he was free. With a wrenching effort he staggered forward and rejoined Panayotis and Wallaby. The priest's eyes followed him, but at a slightly wrong angle, and it was only then that he realized that the old man was blind.

As Deverish stumbled into the sunlight, Wallaby looked at him inquisitively.

"What was the old beggar whispering to you about just now?" he enquired, and then scowled as he saw Deverish's face. "You look white as a ghost, man. Have a swig of cognac, it'll do you good."

Deverish accepted numbly, noticing with clinical detachment as he raised the flask to his lips that his hands were trembling. His legs felt like jelly, but he followed Panayotis and Wallaby across the clearing, and it was only when they reached the edge of the copse of white spruce trees that he realized all the birds in the glen had fallen silent.

Wallaby was anxious to set out at once on foot for Thanatakis mountain and the lair of his quarry, but Panayotis dissuaded him.

"For such a trip you need pack animals, milord," he

protested. ''I have a cousin with a farm less than a kilometer away and I will go fetch mules and more supplies. While I am gone, rest here and eat so you will be strong for your journey.''

Wallaby negligently tossed him a five hundred drachma note to pay his cousin, and the old Greek scampered off gleefully. Deverish had little desire to remain in such close proximity to the madman in the cave—he could still feel those dead, empty eyes fastened on him as if they could read his soul—but the experience had been so unsettling and had so jarred his already taut nerves that he could not have continued in any case, and now he eased himself gratefully to the ground at the foot of a birch, the tension gradually seeping from his body until he lay in a luxuriantly languid stupor in the dappled pool of shade beneath the tree. Wallaby lay stretched out beside him, gorging on a packed lunch of cold lamb, goat's cheese, olives and brandy, but Deverish had no appetite.

Panayotis returned within the hour, just as Deverish had begun to doze, leading on a tether two bony mules that appeared barely capable of supporting Deverish's weight, let alone Wallaby's twenty stone.

''My cousin let you keep these for two days, if you wish to stay overnight, but he say you should come back before sunset because the spirits of the old gods still walk the high hills at night and are sometimes thirsty for Christian blood.'' He crossed himself and then grimaced self-consciously. ''My cousin is superstitious, of course, milord—he is just an uneducated man, he speaks no English.''

Wallaby ignored the Greek's chatter but looked quizzically at the decrepit mules.

''Why have you brought only two animals?''

Panayotis' eyes shifted from Wallaby's and he shuffled his right foot nervously.

''Milord, it is impossible for me to go with you. You

understand, there is the inn, I must be there in case other travelers come. . . ."

"The inn!" Wallaby roared, his face flaming, the cheeks puffing like twin blood sausages. "That flea-bitten hovel! Your only customers are a few pig farmers guzzling your foul pine-cone wine, and there are no travelers in this area except ourselves. You're our guide, man, albeit a paltry excuse for one at best." His voice dropped and he looked almost imploringly at Panayotis. "Without you we'll never find this place the priest spoke of. Surely you will not desert us now, just when we're so close to our goal?"

Panayotis was shamefaced. "Perhaps I can lead you to the foot of the mountain, milord, but no farther." The faintest edge of a whine tinged his voice. "From there you will have no trouble finding this place by the waterfall of which you speak. But I cannot go up the mountain with you."

Panayotis cast a quick fearful look over his shoulder at his holy man's cave, and Deverish realized with a surge of elation that the innkeeper had somehow picked up the old priest's apprehensions about their journey and was reluctant to be further involved. Deverish struggled lest his face register his joy, for this meant that at least he would be alone in the mountains with Wallaby.

He called Panayotis aside, cutting off Wallaby's sputtered protests over the guide's desertion, and spoke swiftly in colloquial Greek, striving to impart an earnest ring to his words.

"My dear Panayotis, I wish you would accompany us all the way up the mountain. My friend does not like to admit that he is no longer a young or agile man, and a climb like this could prove too much for him. With the two of us along the chances of any ill befalling him lessen appreciably."

He watched the Greek's face with wry amusement as servile respect for Wallaby struggled with superstitious awe of his cherished holy man in the cave. As Deverish had known, the latter conquered.

"It is impossible, *Kyrios*," he muttered miserably, looking down at his feet. "I do not know why you have come here, but I cannot accompany you beyond the foot of the mountain." He looked up anxiously. "Perhaps you can convince milord to call off this trip, since you feel he is not strong enough for it." His eyes brightened. "You come back to the tavern and I will prepare a fine meal with much wine and brandy. He forget about the mountain then, no?"

Deverish spoke with quiet sincerity. "No Panayotis, I am afraid he will not forget. We must go on. I only pray he will not injure himself again, as he has in the past on mere piddling slopes. But you have done your best, and I am grateful for your presence on the initial stage of our journey."

As Panayotis dejectedly led the mules from the hermit's glen, Deverish reflected with fierce elation that it would come as no surprise to the old innkeeper when he returned alone.

The journey took the better part of the day, and when they finally reached the foot of Thanatakis mountain, Deverish was soaking with sweat. Wallaby's scarecrow mule had miraculously accommodated its rider's bulk, although the beast's belly sagged and nearly scraped the ground as they proceeded up the lowland slopes, luxuriantly carpeted with wild flowers, and reached the more rugged terrain leading to the Kanakatos mountain range. Unable to adjust comfortably to the jarring gait of his beast, Deverish had walked most of the way, and by the time they approached the mountain his feet were numb and his legs moved with the jerky, automation stride of a mechanical toy. The cool, pine-scented air was honied with bee song, and the countryside was a study in brilliant color, its blues and greens scraped fresh from a painter's palette, but Deverish stumbled on obliviously, anxious only to reach their destination and to be alone at last with Wallaby.

The climb had been uphill all the way, but never steeply, and it was difficult for Deverish to imagine they were really in the mountains unless he assayed a glance down into the valley and saw the cluster of rude cottages, in Panayotis' village, as if through the wrong end of a telescope, the inn itself a dollhouse study in miniature. Then Panayotis finally halted the party before a small gorge slashed into the barren face of the hillside. The sky was paling to rose and a breeze tinged with evening coolness lightly stirred the pines. The old Greek, anxious to depart, doffed his hat obsequiously to Wallaby.

"Whatever you search for, milord, I hope you find. I return now to the village to keep your rooms in readiness for your return." He glanced anxiously at Wallaby, who in fact had weathered the journey far better than Deverish and was now breathing in the cool air with greedy gulps, and added in humble benediction: "May God be with you both."

"Well, Deverish," Wallaby bellowed as the Greek departed, slapping his hands together in eager anticipation, "you're the unicorn expert. What now? Is he a nocturnal beastie, or shall we make camp and wait for morning?"

Deverish looked around him, at the empty gray crags thrusting desolate fingers into the darkening sky, and then let his eyes travel down past the rocky hillside, bare save for a few sparse pines, and on to the thickly forested valley below. Once Panayotis was well on his way there would be no other human being within miles of them, but this business was still best done at night.

"It's best we fortify ourselves with a light meal and proceed forthwith," Deverish told him. "I fear my expertise is less than you imagine, but once in the beast's territory I advise we strike quickly, lest he become alarmed by our presence."

"Good, good," Wallaby cried, "the sooner the better! This shall be a splendid hunt, my dear Deverish, a positively splendid hunt."

His eagerness dissolved abruptly, the beetling eyebrows knitted, and he scowled.

"If, of course, that holy man of Panayotis isn't just a lunatic amusing himself by inventing tales to send us traipsing down the garden path."

"My dear Marius," Deverish swiftly appeased him, "I can assure you the old priest knows this countryside as no one else, and claims with certitude to have seen such a beast. Wrong he may conceivably be, but of his sincerity there can be no doubt."

And thank God, Deverish added fervently to himself, that this tiresome child's charade shall soon be done for good and all.

His words served to rekindle Wallaby's enthusiasm, and they both wolfed a quick meal of goat's cheese and dates. Deverish's appetite had returned; the doubts and fears that inexplicably assailed him in the presence of the old hermit had dissolved like mountain mist the moment Panayotis departed and he was now exultant in anticipation of his final triumph.

As the sun passed below the pines and darkness settled gently over the peaks, Wallaby and Deverish tethered the mules, left behind the better part of their supplies, and proceeded through the gorge and up a hilly slope surmounted by a small clearing sentried by a solitary ring of stunted spruce trees. The carpet of grass in the glade had been beaten flat, obviously by the feet of living creatures, and was curiously free of wild flowers and weeds, as if cleared by the pruning hand of man. Deverish looked about uneasily for a moment, but nothing moved in the foliage, and the light of the full moon illuminated the hillside in photographic clarity.

Wallaby walked ahead gingerly, for all his bulk still nimble on his toes, clutching his Mauser .465 in both hands, while Deverish's own rifle remained slung negligently over one shoulder.

"Go softly now," Wallaby murmured, his eyes bright. "This is our quarry's terrain and one careless move may warn him off for good."

As they passed through the glade a faint murmuring broke the preternatural stillness, which Wallaby swiftly traced to a small stream meandering along the rocky hillside.

"You said the priest spoke of a waterfall," Wallaby whispered, and Deverish nodded contemptuously. It would be over soon now, but to fully savor his victory he must play the game out a bit longer.

They followed the stream for a few hundred more yards, as the whisper of running water rapidly swelled to a muted thunder. Deverish heard Wallaby's grunt of excitement ahead as they passed through a small grove of spruce trees and found themselves in another clearing facing on a steep ravine, where the stream ended in a foaming miniature white waterfall churning gently over a brief expanse of rocky hillside to form a tiny pool of clear crystal water.

Wallaby held Deverish back and scrutinized the area closely before scrabbling down the cliff side.

"Look!" he exclaimed, pointing at some imprints in the moist earth by the edge of the pool. "Hoofprints!"

Wallaby bent down to look closer, and his voice sang with excitement.

"Cloven hoofs! And no deer this far up! We've found him!"

Deverish held the rock he'd picked up as they passed through the gorge lovingly in his right hand, its roughly pitted surface sensuously caressing his palm.

"Deverish, my dear fellow," Wallaby cried exultantly, still on his knees, "you were right after all! I never should have doubted you." He turned his beaming face towards Deverish, as the younger man had hoped, and the eager, innocent child's eyes blinked only once as the rock struck down into his forehead, the jagged point splitting open the great ruddy face from hairline to the bridge of the nose, and exploding a slimy pudding of brain matter onto Deverish's hands. Wallaby died instantly, but Deverish was impelled to strike and strike again, until nothing remained of the face but a ripe pulp the color and consistency of the scooped innards of an autumn pumpkin. Finally, exhausted and alternately laughing and sobbing, Deverish rose to his feet and with considerable difficulty dragged the great body back across the clearing and to a steeper cliff face plunging into a black ravine at least three hundred feet deep, and at the bottom studded with needle-like crags.

He extracted Wallaby's billfold from the inside jacket pocket and rifled tenderly through the sheaf of bills, almost five thousand drachma, and another thousand back at the inn where he, as Wallaby's grief-stricken comrade, would soon have access to it.

Deverish tumbled the bloated body over the edge and listened with satisfaction to the seconds that elapsed before it landed with a soft plop on the rocks below. It was done.

Deverish turned, picked up his rucksack and rifle, and

as an afterthought tossed Wallaby's gun over the edge of
the ravine, sighing deeply as his lungs drew in the cool
night air tinged with the clean, heady scent of pine. He
looked out over the ravine for a long, final moment and
was about to light a cheroot before returning to the rough
camp at the foot of the gorge, when he experienced a
disconcerting sensation of eyes fixed hotly on the back of
his neck. It was absurd, of course, an obvious trick of
nerves, but he turned and sighed with relief when he saw
there was nothing.

Deverish was halfway back towards the gorge when he
felt the same prickling sensation again. He swung around,
annoyed at his ready indulgence of such fancies, and a
scream gurgled silently in his throat. Less than five feet
away a silver shadow gleamed in the moonlight, its con-
tours indistinguishable save for two huge, luminous eyes
looking imploringly into and through his, just as the old
priest's had, and registering incomprehension tinged with
a pity more terrifying than any accusation. Deverish
jerked the rifle to his shoulder and convulsively snapped
off three shots.

The creature made no sound but sank to its knees,
dipping a slender spiral horn to the earth as if in salutation,
or relief. Deverish covered his eyes with his hands, but
when he finally stopped trembling and looked again, there
was nothing on the ground before him; and when he
staggered forward and closely scrutinized the spot where
the thing had been, nothing remained but a tiny mound of
silvery dust, which the breeze quickly snatched away in
coruscating swirls that sparkled oddly in the moonlight.

Deverish returned, shaken, to the camp, the money in
his pocket momentarily forgotten, as the wind grew in
intensity and howled through the trees with manic frenzy
before waning at midnight to a gentle breeze whispering
through the forest like a sigh. Across Europe, in that

summer of 1914, birds cried in the darkness, and new dreams crept into men's minds as old dreams died; while four hundred and twenty miles from the mountains of Thessaly, in the city of Sarajevo, the Serbian nationalist Gavrilo Princip passed a restless night loading and unloading his automatic pistol.

Introduction to
Vonda N. McIntyre's
"Elfleda":

Vonda N. McIntyre was trained as a geneticist, taking a BS degree from the University of Washington, but embarked on a writing career instead shortly after attending the famous Clarion Writer's Workshop. She first came to prominence in 1974, when her novelette "Of Mist, and Grass, and Sand," won the Nebula Award. By 1979, her novel *Dreamsnake* had won the Nebula and the Hugo Award, as well as selling to paperback for a high five-figure advance, and she had become one of the most popular, as well as one of the most critically-acclaimed, of all the "new" SF writers of the seventies. Her newest book is *Fireflood and Other Stories,* a collection. Her other books include a novel, *The Exile Waiting,* as well as an anthology she co-edited with Susan Janice Anderson, *Aurora: Beyond Equality.*

Here she uses her knowledge of genetics to tell a haunting and melancholy tale of those who are forever doomed to a strange and painful kind of exile . . . .

ELFLEDA
Vonda N. McIntyre

I LOVE her. And I envy her, because she is clever enough, defiant enough, to outwit our creators. Or most of them. She is not a true unicorn: many of us have human parts, and she is no exception. The reconnections are too complicated otherwise. Our brilliant possessors are not quite brilliant enough to integrate nerves directly from the brain.

So Elfleda is, as I am, almost entirely human from the hips up. Below that I am equine: a centaur. She is a unicorn, for her hooves are cloven, her tail is a lion's, and from her brow sprouts a thin straight spiral horn. Her silver forelock hides the pale scar at its base; the silver hair drifts down, growing from her shoulders and spine. Her coat is sleek and pale grey, and great dapples flow across her flanks. The hair on the tip of her tail is quite black. For a long time I thought some surgeon had made a mistake or played her a joke, but eventually I understood why this was done, as from afar I watched her twitching her long black-tipped tail like a cat. My body has no such artistic originality. I hate everything about me as much as I love everything about Elfleda.

She will talk to me from a distance; I think she pities me. When the masters come to our park she watches them, lashes her tail, and gallops away. Sometimes she favors them with a brief glimpse of her silver hide. Her inaccessibility makes her the most sought-after of us all. They follow after her, they call her, but only a few can touch or move her. She is the only one of us who can ever resist their will. Even this freedom was their creation; they are so powerful they can afford to play with the illusion of defiance.

177

But the rest of us, the other centaurs, the satyrs, nymphs, merfolk, we strut and prance across the meadows or wait in the forest or gently splash the passersby, hoping to be noticed.

We dare not complain. Indeed, we should not, we should be grateful. Our lives have been saved. Every one of us would have died if the masters had not accepted us and taken us in. We owe them our lives, and that is the payment they exact. Sometimes I think the price too high, but though nothing prevents me from leaping off the mountainside or eating poison flowers, I am still alive.

The noon sun is warm in the meadow, so I walk toward the forest through the high grass. A small creature leaps from his sleeping-place and flees, as startled by me as I by him. Galloping, he surges into the air: one of the small pegasoi. His feathered wings seem much too large in proportion to his body. That is the reason only the smallest pegasoi can fly at all. This one is a miniature appaloosa pony, not as tall as my knee. Half the meadow away he touches down and trots off, folding his blue-grey wings against his spotted sides. The larger pegasoi, the ones my size, are spectacular but earthbound; they seek flight but never find it. I have watched one standing in the wind, neck arched, nostrils flaring, tail high. She spread her wings and raised them, cantered against the wind, galloped, ran, but the wings were not large enough to lift her. Our masters use their beasts as they use those of us part human: for amusement, for beauty. It would not occur to them that a flying horse's heart might break because she could not fly.

The shade of the forest envelops me with a cool scent of pine and humus. The loam beneath my hooves is soft. I can feel its resilience, but not its texture. When first I rose, after the operations, the healing, the pain, I could not walk properly. I stumbled and fell and was threatened with punishment if I scarred my bright bay hide. After that I walked slowly but learned quickly. Human beings did not evolve to articulate six limbs, but we are adaptable. I learned to walk, to trot, to run, and I even learned to move my arms simultaneously, with not too much gracelessness. I did not scar myself, and now my skin—my human skin—is tanned almost as dark as my red-gold coat. My mane and tail and lower legs are black.

The stream ripples by, loud with snow-water. It splashes down a rock slide into a mountain lake that reflects in its depths another, freer world. There the purple-blue mountains are valleys which could be reached if one could find them. The mountains themselves cannot be crossed. One of the large pegasoi, seeking the sky, climbed only halfway to a summit before his hooves slipped on the sheer rock and he fell. He broke his leg. Equine legs are a great trouble to heal, so he was put to death, humanely. As humanely as he had been given this life.

The pond's surface moves and breaks, and one of the mer-people glides onto stones dampened by mist. It is the water-folks' favorite place to sun themselves when the icy water chills their memories of being warm-blooded. I think the being is a mermaid, but I cannot be sure from this distance. They are all slender and lithe, with narrow shoulders and long bright hair. The women have hardly any breasts at all, and the men have no proper genitals. They all have only slits, like fishes, half-concealed among the multicolored scales on their abdomens. I have never seen them copulate with each other, so perhaps the opening is only for excretion and for our owners to use when pleasuring themselves. The mer-people are as deformed one way as I am the other. They have no genitals at all, while I have two sets. I am sure some biological engineer received a prize for clever design. My human penis hangs in its accustomed human place, but above the front legs of a bay horse. My stallion parts are much more discreet, tucked away between my hind legs.

The mermaid flicks her tail, the filmy fin sending out rainbow drops of spray. Another of the merfolk casts himself up beside her. But they do not touch; no intimacy exists between them. Perhaps the feeling has been taken from them, or the cold water slows their passion as much as their bodies.

But, oh, they are lovely. When I wade out to drink, I can sometimes see them beneath the water, swimming together in their own inexplicable patterns, hair streaming gold, silver, scarlet, scales rippling blue, orange, black, all with a metallic sheen. Their tailfins are like gauze, like lace, transparent silk, translucently veined. Their gill slits make vermilion lines across their chests and backs and throats.

They never speak.

If I moved from my hiding place of shadows, the mermaid and merman would disappear beneath the silver surface of the ice-blue water, marring it with ripples. Two sets of concentric circles would touch, and interact, and fade away, and I would be alone again. I do not move. I watch the beautiful creatures sunning themselves, occasionally flicking water over their scales with their fins or their long narrow hands.

I envy their contentment with solitude, their independence, as I envy Elfleda. She and they are never touched by the games our masters play with us. Elfleda watches from a high pinnacle where only she can climb. The merfolk participate when they are called and commanded, but their eyes are blank. I think by the next day they have already forgotten.

I never forget. I remember every incident that has occurred since I was brought here. Soon it will all happen again.

One of the merfolk swims away, then the other. The forest has chilled me, and I am hungry. The sun bursts warm on my back as I leave deep shade and cross the meadow to the orchard.

Light through the mottled ceiling of leaves dapples my flanks. The lazy buzz of a black fly does not disturb me. Having a long tail, I must confess, can be convenient.

A nymph and a satyr copulate beneath a plum tree, oblivious to my presence. They are as brazen as the merfolk are shy. The satyr's short furry tail jerks up and down as she mounts the nymph and clasps him with her hairy legs. His green hands grasp her hips and move up to caress her pink human flesh. On either side of her spine's erect crest of brown bristles her back is slightly sunburned. The nymph arches himself into her and she grunts, twining her fingers in his curly green-black hair. His heels press the ground, his toes curl; her cloven goat-hooves dig up bits of sod. The nymph moans and clasps the satyr to him. Our creators have no respect for the traditional gender of their creatures. They please only themselves, never myth or legend.

I wheel and gallop away to escape the frantic plunging and gasps and groans in the orchards. I have coupled with the satyr myself, gods help me.

The meadow grass parts before me and the air flows through my mane like water. The birds are silent in the heat but the cicadas' shrill afternoon song urges me onward. My hooves pound the earth, crushing flowers, cutting the turf. Sweat sparkles in my eyes. I pull my elbows close to my sides against the pain of breathing. The air enters in burning gouts. Sweat pours down my chest, breaks out on my flanks, drips down my legs, and flies from the points of my fetlocks as I run. I feel my buttocks rub the sweat into white foam.

The meadow ends and I run among rocks. I leap a huge bounder and come down in scree. The valley narrows, rises, and ends in a sheer wall of stone. I stumble, stop, stand spraddle-legged, knee-locked, and try only to breathe.

Later I realize I still have a plum in one hand and a peach in the other. The juice, where I clasped the fruit, runs between my fingers. I tear the pulp with my teeth and swallow it slowly until all that is left are the seeds. Fruit trees are hybrids; they reproduce only freaks, sports, throwbacks. I fling the seeds among the jumbled rocks, where they will have no chance to grow.

The sweat dries on me as I plod down the mountain. A dull ache creeps up my near hind leg from the center of my hoof: I think I have a stone bruise.

Back in the meadow I lie down in deep cool grass. I am never comfortable sleeping now. When I stand, like a horse, my head droops and I wake with a backache. Lying on my side with my head pillowed on my arm is awkward, and my hand always goes to sleep.

The shadow of the mountain is creeping over me when I wake. It will be dark soon, and the moon will be full. I fling out my forelegs and push myself to my feet.

A flash of white among the trees draws my attention. "Elfleda!"

She stops and turns toward me, tilting her head gracefully to draw the spiral horn from beneath the branches. She has small breasts and long, strong hands. Human skin blends into animal hide at her navel, but like the rest of the equiforms she has human sex organs between the beast forelegs. Our owners must have bred and chosen Elfleda's animal part carefully, for it is both horse and deer, with a musky taint of goat. She lashes her tail.

"Hello, Achilleus. What do you want?"

"I . . ." But I want nothing from her that she will give. She is not cruel, only detached. She does not feel for me and I have no reason or excuse to expect her to.

"They'll come again soon," she says.

"I hope not."

"They will."

"And you'll watch for them."

"Yes," she says. I do not understand, since she can ignore almost all of them, why she does not disappear into the forest when they come. Instead she watches, and our masters see her and grow jealous of her freedom. What they give, they can take back.

Elfleda flicks her tail again. The black tip touches the point of her horse-shoulder, her withers, her flanks. The wind lifts her short fine hair away from her head, away from her back, haloing her in silver light. I step toward her, and she does not back away. But I am covered with sweat and dust and I smell like hot horse, hot human. I am embarrassed to approach her like this. She watches me, waiting, unafraid. She knows she could outrun me if she had to. They made me large, taller than I was in life—in real life—but she is quick and her hooves are sharp; and they did not take away so much of my humanity that I would force myself on her. That would be bitter love indeed.

"I wasn't thought ugly before—" My voice is querulous. I should not speak to her like this, as if I would be content if she took me out of pity.

She frowns, then her brow clears and she steps toward me. "If you were, Achilleus, you know it wouldn't make any difference to me." She reaches out: I can feel the heat of her hand near my face. She has never touched me before.

I draw back and turn away. "You still don't find me attractive."

"That isn't fair."

And even now I do not look at her, though I know she is right. "You've accepted their rules. Nothing holds us to them."

"Do you think not?"

"What keeps you from loving me?"

"We love, or we do not love."

"We let them control us."

"We cannot stop them," she says, and again I know she is right. Between the times of their coming I want to believe we could all resist them, if we tried, and I blame our obedience on our weaknesses and our guilt, our willingness to be controlled and thereby absolved of all responsibility. But when the compulsions come to me—

Elfleda touches my arm and I start violently. She jumps back, as surprised as I, her other hand still raised, pointing toward the sky where she sought to draw my attention.

"Look."

Darkness has fallen. I look at the stars and see a brilliant multicolored light approaching. Above us, our masters ride in a great dirigible that floats majestically over the crest of the mountains. Its engines are nearly silent. Lights festoon its cabin and illuminate the treetops below. It passes directly over us and we hear music and faint laughter. I look down at Elfleda. The lights paint her, red, violet, blue, green. Her expression is wistful, hopeful. She does not look at me.

A sharp cry of delight or distress draws my attention back to the dirigible. When I look down again, Elfleda is gone.

But what does it matter? What does she matter? Others desire me, if she does not. If I felt tired and spent a moment ago, I am excited and powerful now. Half the forest lies between me and the meadow, and if I do not hurry I will be late. But the distance is nothing. Evergreen branches brush me with their fragrance as I run. The ache in my hoof is no more than an insect bite.

All of us gather in the meadow, beast and beast-human alike. The little pegasoi cavort and scamper among us and over us, while the flightless ones display their plumage. A gryphon sitting on its haunches on a boulder roars and screeches, and the unearthly light of the aircraft shimmers around us all. The dirigible descends slowly, so immense it blots out the stars. I catch one tether-rope and the centaur Hekate takes another. Hekate pulls harder than I, the muscles in her haunches bulging like fists. The dirigible tilts down on her side and she laughs. We drag the craft to earth against its lifting force, glorying in our strength, and bind the ropes to trees. Our masters step down upon the ground.

They are ordinary humans, as ordinary as we were before they changed us. They look so strange, walking normally on two legs, hoofless, clawless, hairless. They are small, weak, omnipotent. They smile on us and we wait, hoping to be chosen. They are all as beautiful as flowers. The gryphon bounds down and rubs felinely against their legs.

A silhouetted figure stands in the hatchway of the aircraft, hanging back. He steps down and hesitates with the light flowing across him. His face is coarse, his expression uncertain. He is both curious and frightened.

"Hekate!"

The ugly boy vanishes from my mind. One of our masters is calling dark Hekate, and she obeys, her black hair streaming in the wind of her speed. Her great hooves plough the ground as she stops before the slender young woman. Her horse-part is heavy through the shoulders and haunches, powerful and immense, ebony highlighted through the spectrum by the dirigible's illumination. In her other life she must have been a formidable and stunning woman, for she is a compelling myth. The young human leaps upon her back and drums her bare heels against her sides, laughing. Hekate wheels and bolts across the meadow, her tail held high like a plume. The vibration of her hoofbeats echoes around us.

Two satyrs bound along beside her, as fleet and randy as goats. Their musk mingles in the air with the pungent sweat of Hekate.

A light pressure on my back: "Run, Achilleus, follow them." A nymph clasps me with his long pale arms, his fingers across my belly. I can feel his slender legs around my ribs, but he is weightless. "Run, or they'll leave us behind."

I obey as if he were a master. I follow Hekate's path easily through the trampled grass and silver darkness. I leap an obstruction and realize later it was nothing but the human's flimsy robe. I gallop through a shallow extrusion of the lake, flinging spray in all directions, passing naked humans who wade toward the rocks of the languorous merfolk.

Hekate and the human stand gilded by moonlight. They embrace, the human standing on Hekate's broad back, leaning over her shoulder, bending around to hold and kiss her. They glance toward me. The human woman laughs.

"What shall we do with them?"

"Exhaust them." Hekate's laugh is low and full. "Exhaust them, and go back to what we were doing."

Copulating in the grass, the two satyrs ignore us all. The nymph slips from my back as I prance toward Hekate. The human turns and sits astride her, facing backwards. She holds out her arms to me; I rear, I mount Hekate as a stallion and embrace the human as a man. She slides her heels over my forelegs and pulls herself onto me. As she draws me down to kiss her I see Hekate bend likewise, as she shifts her haunches beneath me, to caress the gold-green nymph. He is light and thin, but tall enough for her. His fingers clench, nails digging into Hekate's shoulder blades. The human moans and slips her hand down my stomach. I thrust in a single rhythm, and Hekate groans as pleasure washes her in double waves.

Many combinations occur between us. My memory is like diamond-bearing stone, opaque, with sparks of crystal clarity. The human finishes with me, kisses me one last gentle time, and slips from Hekate's withers. When the human draws the nymph away, Hekate leans back against me. Beings move and laugh and touch all around us, forming some immense incomprehensible dance. One of the other centaurs gallops by and throws us a leather flask. I hold it for Hekate, and drink from it myself. The warm wine cools me, and I let it dribble down my chin, drip on my chest and into Hekate's long mane. The taste is strong and sour and the intoxication hits us quickly. Revitalized, I rear back and return to the ground, and Hekate and I canter through the meadow, playing like foals, rearing and striking at a night-pony who sails between us, black bat-wings sharp as knives. Under a tree we face each other and couple again, while nearby a fully human pair watches and laughs.

The energy of intoxication lasts a few minutes, and quite suddenly drains away as Hekate chases me through the trees. I stumble and slow; she passes me, calls to me, but when I do not follow she snorts and gallops away. I sink down in the soft cushion of pine needles, enveloped by a pleasant lethargy. While I doze, the gold-green nymph returns to me and curls up against my side, trustful among my hooves.

I dream of Elfleda, but the dream dissolves as I am about to touch her, as she reaches for me. I half-wake and see her, real, before me, half-hidden by a growth of ferns. She does not know I am here.

The ugly human boy is standing before her, head down, hair falling across his face as if to hide it. Elfleda says something to him that I cannot hear, and he looks up and smiles. All his movements and expressions are hesitant. Elfleda takes his hand. He reaches up, touches her breast, her throat, her forehead, her spiral horn. She touches its point to his shoulder and lifts her head again. Together they walk away into the forest. I shiver, close my eyes, and try to sleep again, making myself believe I never really woke.

While it is still dark Hekate returns and lies beside me, back to back to we can lean on each other and have a little more comfort. I expected her to stay with the human.

"Couldn't you find her?"

"I found her," Hekate says. I wait; finally she continues. "She sent me away. I suppose she had something better to do." Her low voice is well-suited for anger, but not for disappointment. She mutters a few more words as we fit ourselves against each other for sleep. In the meadow, only the humans and perhaps a few satyrs will still be stirring. I cannot understand what drew the human from Hekate; I would be offended, too, if one of the humans left me for one of the hairy creatures. Nevertheless we obey our masters as long as we are able, whether the orders are to serve or leave them.

Obedience and the night are over for me; I am spent.

The nymph snores and Hekate shifts and sighs in her sleep. I hear laughter, giggling, the command to hush, but the sounds pass over me like a breeze. It must be the humans, searching in a pack for something to entertain them, and I am beyond entertaining.

We have few storms here, but when they come they are violent and long. We know now when to seek shelter, for the gentle wind that precedes them through the mountain peaks has a certain coolness, a certain flavor. My hair rises, all down my spine, for the storm-wind and the breeze of words are all too similar.

I move my legs carefully so I will not hurt the snoring nymph, then lurch to my feet. Hekate stirs but does not wake. I am already stiff and sore, and my hoof aches fiercely. But I remember the direction Elfleda and the ugly boy walked, and I remember the way the humans crept, after her.

I followed the bruised leaves of their passing, too frightened to call out. Elfleda could be beyond the sound of my warning, and the humans could come back and silence me. I climb as fast as I am able. The ache spreads into my haunches and along the vertebrae strained by my unnatural construction.

The trees end suddenly. Moonlight throws my long shadow against pale granite. The mountain peak is still far above, separated from me by ridges, flat sheets of rock, sheer walls.

I climb the first ridge, my hooves scraping the bare stone. When I reach the top I can see Elfleda and the boy, gilt in the midst of shadows. His hands are twined in her mane and her arms around his naked body. He moves against her.

They are safe, and alone. I am spying on them, up here silhouetted against the sky, and I am ashamed. I will go back to Hekate's solid warm side—

The moon reflects from ornament or weapon.

"Elfleda!"

As she throws up her head at my warning the humans rush her. The boy jumps away, surprised and embarrassed. The other humans are all around, yelling in triumph, holding nets and ropes to take back the defiance they gave her. The ugly boy looks from one face to another, confused, humiliated: at least he did not know what use they planned for his initiation. He sees the ropes, and strikes one angrily away. Elfleda rears and another misses her. She charges the humans' head down, and they scatter away from her sharp horn. She is trapped by the mountain and the waiting nets.

I gallop down the side of the ridge. A noose settles over Elfleda's head, around her throat, and slides tight. She turns, flinching, grasps the rope and sets herself back on her haunches, pulling the human off balance. She tears the rope away and flings it to the ground, but another settles around her shoulders. One strikes her hind legs like a snake. Startled, she springs away, and the tension of the rope halts her in mid-arc and pulls her down. She lies stunned, a scarlet burn on her throat, blood trickling from one leg where the rope has cut it.

Laughing, the humans close a circle around her as I near, my hoofbeats echoing on the stone. To our masters, this is adventure. Between them I see Elfleda raise her head. She tosses it, as a human approaches her, and her horn opens a deep wound. I reach the crowd and scatter our frail creators with my shoulders. I charge the human who holds the trip-rope; I pick her up and throw her down on the stones.

Our masters have stopped laughing.

Elfleda kicks off the loosened rope and pulls away the other, struggling to her feet. She menaces the humans with her horn and I with my fists, my hooves. They stand back, milling around us. We are all at bay.

"Achilleus!"

She bounds forward and I follow. The humans are raising nets, crying to each other to hurry. One snare drapes low, rippling and tangled. As it rises Elfleda leaps it. I gather speed, collect myself, and jump. The strands graze my forelegs—they must entrap my hind legs—but I kick back and up, the rough cords scrape me, and I am free!

I plunge after Elfleda's pale form. Our retreat to the

park, where we could hide and hope the masters might forget their anger, is cut off. Elfleda flees toward the mountain and the impassable ridges.

She starts to climb, hesitating when she no longer hears me behind her. "Achilleus, come on!"

"But where will we go?"

"Anywhere but back—if we want to live. Hurry!"

She reaches toward me in encouragement: she is too high above actually to reach me.

"There's nothing out there for us."

She looks beyond me. I turn. The masters are very near, now, confident of their prey.

"Hurry!" Elfleda says again, and I put one hoof on the steep rock. This is desperation. I begin to climb. I scrabble on the stone, straining upward. My hooves are made for meadows and prairies. I can hear the masters just behind me. Trying to go faster, I slip and fall to my knees, crying out at the wave of pain, reaching with my hands to keep from falling. Granite soaks up my blood.

Elfleda is almost close enough to touch me. Did she descend to help me climb?

"I can't—"

"Try," she says. "Just try . . ."

Shining in the failing moonlight, a rope slips over her head as she grasps my hand.

Another noose falls around my throat and jerks me backwards. I fumble at it, struggling to free myself and climb. The rope jerks me again, much harder, pulling me down, cutting off my breath. My bruised hoof slams against a rock spur. The pain completes my disorientation. I stumble again, falling and sliding on the stone. I am lost.

When next I am aware of anything I feel warm droplets falling on my shoulder. I open my eyes, and see the masters leading Elfleda back down the mountain. She is at the center of a web of ropes, around her throat, her arms,

her waist, binding her hands, but she holds her head erect.
One of the humans reaches out and pulls her black-tipped
tail. She lashes out with a sharp hind hoof and half-turns
toward him, but the other humans drag her around.

I lunge up. The ugly human boy reaches out to stop me,
too late. I scream and fall back, shuddering, panting,
suddenly cold and wet with sweat. When I lie still the pain
is only a great throbbing.

"I'm sorry," the boy whispers. "I didn't know . . ."

I push myself slowly up on one elbow, straining to see
yet not move my hindquarters. Blood is black in the
moonlight, but dawn will soon turn the patch beneath me
scarlet. I can see the bones protruding from my shattered
leg.

Elfleda and the humans disappear among the trees as I
sink back to the ground. I can only see the paling sky and
the single human. "Help me . . . please help me . . ."
But he is wiping the tears from his cheeks, pushing the hair
from his forehead. It must be the kind moonlight and dawn
that make him appear less coarse, less uncertain. There is
no magic here.

"Elfleda," I whisper, and the boy gazes blankly down,
as if he never knew her name.

Behind me I can hear the footsteps of two more humans,
as they approach me one last time.

Introduction to
Ursula K. Le Guin's
"The White Donkey":

Here is a subtle and evocative story about the loss of innocence by multiple award-winner Ursula K. Le Guin, one of the major writers of our times, author of such landmark books as *The Left Hand of Darkness*, *The Dispossessed*, *The Lathe of Heaven*, *The Wizard of Earthsea*, and the recent *The Beginning Place*.

THE WHITE DONKEY
Ursula K. Le Guin

THERE were snakes in the old stone place, but the grass grew so green and rank there that she brought the goats back every day. "The goats are looking fat," Nana said. "Where are you grazing them, Sita?" And when Sita said, "At the old stone place, in the forest," Nana said, "It's a long way to take them," and Uncle Hira said, "Look out for snakes in that place," but they were thinking of the goats, not of her; so she did not ask them, after all, about the white donkey.

She had seen the donkey first when she was putting flowers on the red stone under the pipal tree at the edge of the forest. She liked that stone. It was the Goddess, very old, round, sitting comfortably among the roots of the tree. Everybody who passed by there left the Goddess some flowers or poured a bit of water on her, and every spring her red paint was renewed. Sita was giving the Goddess a rhododendron flower when she looked round, thinking one of the goats was straying off into the forest; but it wasn't a goat. It was a white animal that had caught her eye, whiter than a Brahminee bull. Sita followed, to see what it was. When she saw the neat round rump and the tail like a rope with a tassel, she knew it was a donkey; but such a beautiful donkey! And whose? There were three donkeys in the village, and Chandra Bose owned two, all of them grey, bony, mournful, laborious beasts. This was a tall, sleek, delicate donkey, a wonderful donkey. It could not belong to Chandra Bose, or to anybody in the village, or to anybody in the other village. It wore no halter or harness. It must be wild; it must live in the forest alone.

194

Sure enough, when she brought the goats along by whistling to clever Kala, and followed where the white donkey had gone into the forest, first there was a path, and then they came to the place where the old stones were, blocks of stone as big as houses all half-buried and over-grown with grass and kerala vines; and there the white donkey was standing looking back at her from the darkness under the trees.

She thought then that the donkey was a god, because it had a third eye in the middle of its forehead like Shiva. But when it turned she saw that that was not an eye, but a horn—not curved like a cow's or a goat's horns, a straight spike like a deer's—just the one horn, between the eyes, like Shiva's eye. So it might be a kind of god donkey; and in case it was, she picked a yellow flower off the kerala vine and offered it, stretching out her open palm.

The white donkey stood a while considering her and the goats and the flower; then it came slowly back among the big stones towards her. It had split hooves like the goats, and walked even more neatly than they did. It accepted the flower. Its nose was pinkish-white, and very soft where it snuffled on Sita's palm. She quickly picked another flower, and the donkey accepted it too. But when she wanted to stroke its face around the short, white, twisted horn and the white, nervous ears, it moved away, looking sidelong at her from its long dark eyes.

Sita was a little afraid of it, and thought it might be a little afraid of her; so she sat down on one of the half-buried rocks and pretended to be watching the goats, who were all busy grazing on the best grass they had had for months. Presently the donkey came close again, and standing beside Sita, rested its curly-bearded chin on her lap. The breath from its nostrils moved the thin glass bangles on her wrist. Slowly and very gently she stroked the base of the white, nervous ears, the fine, harsh hair at the base of the horn, the silken muzzle; and the white donkey stood beside her, breathing long, warm breaths.

Every day since then she brought the goats there, walking carefully because of snakes; and the goats were getting fat; and her friend the donkey came out of the forest every day, and accepted her offering, and kept her company.

"One bullock and one hundred rupees cash," said Uncle Hira, "you're crazy if you think we can marry her for less!"

"Moti Lal is a lazy man," Nana said. "Dirty and lazy."

"So he wants a wife to work and clean for him! And he'll take her for only one bullock and one hundred rupees cash!"

"Maybe he'll settle down when he's married," Nana said.

So Sita was betrothed to Moti Lal from the other village, who had watched her driving the goats home at evening. She had seen him watching her across the road, but had never looked at him. She did not want to look at him.

"This is the last day," she said to the white donkey, while the goats cropped the grass among the big, carved, fallen stones, and the forest stood all about them in the singing stillness. "Tomorrow I'll come with Uma's little brother to show him the way here. He'll be the village goatherd now. The day after tomorrow is my wedding day."

The white donkey stood still, its curly, silky beard resting against her hand.

"Nana is giving me her gold bangle," Sita said to the donkey. "I get to wear a red sari, and have henna on my feet and hands."

The donkey stood still, listening.

"There'll be sweet rice to eat at the wedding," Sita said; then she began to cry.

"Goodbye, white donkey," she said. The white donkey looked at her sidelong, and slowly, not looking back, moved away from her and walked into the darkness under the trees.

Introduction to
Roger Zelazny's
"Unicorn Variations":

Like a number of other writers, Roger Zelazny began publishing in 1962 in the pages of Cele Goldsmith's *Amazing*. This was the so-called "Class of '62," whose membership also included Thomas M. Disch, Keith Laumer, and Ursula K. Le Guin. Everyone in that "class" would eventually achieve prominence, but some of them would achieve it faster than others, and Roger Zelazny's subsequent career would be one of the most meteoric and dazzling in the history of SF. The first Zelazny story to attract wide notice was "A Rose for Ecclesiastes," published in 1963 (and since reprinted in the *SFWA Hall of Fame* anthology, where it had been selected by vote of the SFWA membership as one of the best SF stories of all time). By the end of the decade, he had won two Nebula Awards and two Hugo Awards, and was widely regarded as one of the two most important and influential American SF writers of the sixties (the other was Samuel R. Delany). Since then, he has won several more awards, and his series of novels about the enchanted land of Amber—beginning with *Nine Princes in Amber*—has made him one of the best-selling SF and fantasy writers of our times, and inspired fanclubs and fanzines across the country. His books include *This Immortal, The Dream Master, Lord of Light, Isle of the Dead,* and the collection of *The Doors of His Face, the Lamps of His Mouth, and Other Stories*. His most recent books are *Madwand* and *The Last Defender of Camelot*, a collection.

Here, with his customary wit and elan, he examines the consequences of the unicorn's well-known fondness for playing chess . . . . What, you didn't *know* about the unicorn's fondness for playing chess? Well, read on . . . .

UNICORN VARIATIONS
Roger Zelazny

A BIZARRERIE of fires, cunabulum of light, it moved with a deft, almost dainty deliberation, phasing into and out of existence like a storm-shot piece of evening; or perhaps the darkness between the flares was more akin to its truest nature—swirl of black ashes assembled in prancing cadence to the lowing note of desert wind down the arroyo behind buildings as empty yet filled as the pages of unread books or stillnesses between the notes of a song.

Gone again. Back again. Again.

Power, you said? Yes. It takes considerable force of identity to manifest before or after one's time. Or both.

As it faded and gained it also advanced, moving through the warm afternoon, its tracks erased by the wind. That is, on those occasions when there were tracks.

A reason. There should always be a reason. Or reasons.

It knew why it was there—but not why it was *there,* in that particular locale.

It anticipated learning this shortly, as it approached the desolation-bound line of the old street. However, it knew that the reason may also come before, or after. Yet again, the pull was there and the force of its being was such that it had to be close to something.

The buildings were worn and decayed and some of them fallen and all of them drafty and dusty and empty. Weeds grew among floorboards. Birds nested upon rafters. The droppings of wild things were everywhere, and it knew them all as they would have known it, were they to meet face to face.

It froze, for there had come the tiniest unanticipated sound from somewhere ahead and to the left. At that moment, it was again phasing into existence and it released its outline which faded as quickly as a rainbow in hell, that but the naked presence remained beyond subtraction.

Invisible, yet existing, strong, it moved again. The clue. The cue. Ahead. *A gauche*. Beyond the faded word SALOON on weathered board above. Through the swinging doors. (One of them pinned alop.)

Pause and assess.

Bar to the right, dusty. Cracked mirror behind it. Empty bottles. Broken bottles. Brass rail, black, encrusted. Tables to the left and rear. In various states of repair.

Man seated at the best of the lot. His back to the door. Levi's. Hiking boots. Faded blue shirt. Green backpack leaning against the wall to his left.

Before him, on the tabletop, is the faint, painted outline of a chessboard, stained, scratched, almost obliterated.

The drawer in which he had found the chessmen is still partly open.

He could no more have passed up a chess set without working out a problem or replaying one of his better games than he could have gone without breathing, circulating his blood or maintaining a relatively stable body temperature.

It moved nearer, and perhaps there were fresh prints in the dust behind it, but none noted them.

It, too, played chess.

It watched as the man replayed what had perhaps been his finest game, from the world preliminaries of seven years past. He had blown up after that—surprised to have gotten even as far as he had—for he never could perform well under pressure. But he had always been proud of that one game, and he relived it as all sensitive beings do certain turning points in their lives. For perhaps twenty minutes, no one could have touched him. He had been shining and pure and hard and clear. He had felt like the best.

It took up a position across the board from him and stared. The man completed the game, smiling. Then he set up the board again, rose and fetched a can of beer from his pack. He popped the top.

When he returned, he discovered that White's King's Pawn had been advanced to K4. His brow furrowed. He turned his head, searching the bar, meeting his own puzzled gaze in the grimy mirror. He looked under the table. He took a drink of beer and seated himself.

He reached out and moved his Pawn to K4. A moment later, he saw White's King's Knight rise slowly into the air and drift forward to settle upon KB3. He stared for a long while into the emptiness across the table before he advanced his own Knight to his KB3.

White's Knight moved to take his Pawn. He dismissed the novelty of the situation and moved his Pawn to Q3. He all but forgot the absence of a tangible opponent as the White Knight dropped back to its KB3. He paused to take a sip of beer, but no sooner had he placed the can upon the tabletop than it rose again, passed across the board and was upended. A gurgling noise followed. Then the can fell to the floor, bouncing, ringing with an empty sound.

"I'm sorry," he said, rising and returning to his pack. "I'd have offered you one if I'd thought you were something that might like it."

He opened two more cans, returned with them, placed one near the far edge of the table, one at his own right hand.

"Thank you," came a soft, precise voice from a point beyond it.

The can was raised, tilted slightly, returned to the tabletop.

"My name is Martin," the man said.

"Call me Tlingel," said the other. "I had thought that perhaps your kind was extinct. I am pleased that you at least have survived to afford me this game."

"Huh?" Martin said. "We were all still around the last time that I looked—a couple of days ago."

"No matter. I can take care of that later," Tlingel replied. "I was misled by the appearance of this place."

"Oh. It's a ghost town. I backpack a lot."

"Not important. I am near the proper point in your career as a species. I can feel that much."

"I am afraid that I do not follow you."

"I am not at all certain that you would wish to. I assume that you intend to capture that pawn?"

"Perhaps. Yes, I do wish to. What are you talking about?"

The beer can rose. The invisible entity took another drink.

"Well," said Tlingel, "to put it simply, your— successors—grow anxious. Your place in the scheme of things being such an important one, I had sufficient power to come and check things out."

" 'Successors'? I do not understand."

"Have you seen any griffins recently?"

Martin chuckled.

"I've heard the stories," he said, "seen the photos of the one supposedly shot in the Rockies. A hoax, of course."

"Of course it must seem so. That is the way with mythical beasts."

"You're trying to say that it was real?"

"Certainly. Your world is in bad shape. When the last grizzly bear died recently, the way was opened for the griffins—just as the death of the last aepyornis brought in the yeti, the dodo the Loch Ness creature, the passenger pigeon the sasquatch, the blue whale the kraken, the American eagle the cockatrice—''

''You can't prove it by me.''

''Have another drink.''

Martin began to reach for the can, halted his hand and stared.

A creature approximately two inches in length, with a human face, a lion-like body and feathered wings was crouched next to the beer can.

''A mini-sphinx,'' the voice continued. ''They came when you killed off the last smallpox bacillus.''

''Are you trying to say that whenever a natural species dies out a mythical one takes its place?'' he asked.

''In a word—yes. Now. It was not always so, but you have destroyed the mechanisms of evolution. The balance is now redressed by those others of us, from the morning land—we, who have never truly been endangered. We return, in our time.''

''And you—whatever you are, Tlingel—you say that humanity is now endangered?''

''Very much so. But there is nothing that you can do about it, is there? Let us get on with the game.''

The sphinx flew off. Martin took a sip of beer and captured the Pawn.

''Who,'' he asked then, ''are to be our successors?''

''Modesty almost forbids,'' Tlingel replied. ''In the case of a species as prominent as your own, it naturally has to be the loveliest, most intelligent, most important of us all.''

''And what are you? Is there any way that I can have a look?''

''Well—yes. If I exert myself a trifle.''

The beer can rose, was drained, fell to the floor. There followed a series of rapid rattling sounds retreating from the table. The air began to flicker over a large area opposite Martin, darkening within the growing flamework. The outline continued to brighten, its interior growing jet black. The form moved, prancing about the saloon, multitudes of tiny, cloven hoofprints scoring and cracking the floorboards. With a final, near-blinding flash it came into full view and Martin gasped to behold it.

A black unicorn with mocking, yellow eyes sported before him, rising for a moment onto its hind legs to strike a heraldic pose. The fires flared about it a second longer, then vanished.

Martin had drawn back, raising one hand defensively.

"Regard me!" Tlingel announced. "Ancient symbol of wisdom, valor and beauty, I stand before you!"

"I thought your typical unicorn was white," Martin finally said.

"I am archetypical," Tlingel responded, dropping to all fours, "and possessed of virtues beyond the ordinary."

"Such as?"

"Let us continue our game."

"What about the fate of the human race? You said—"

" . . . And save the small talk for later."

"I hardly consider the destruction of humanity to be small talk."

"And if you've any more beer . . ."

"All right," Martin said, retreating to his pack as the creature advanced, its eyes like a pair of pale suns. "There's some lager."

Something had gone out of the game. As Martin sat before the ebon horn on Tlingel's bowed head, like an insect about to be pinned, he realized that his playing was off. He had felt the pressure the moment he had seen the beast—and there was all that talk about an imminent doomsday. Any run-of-the-mill pessimist could say it without troubling him, but coming from a source as peculiar as this . . .

His earlier elation had fled. He was no longer in top form. And Tlingel was good. Very good. Martin found himself wondering whether he could manage a stalemate.

After a time, he saw that he could not and resigned.

The unicorn looked at him and smiled.

"You don't really play badly—for a human," it said.

"I've done a lot better."

"It is no shame to lose to me, mortal. Even among mythical creatures there are very few who can give a unicorn a good game."

"I am pleased that you were not wholly bored," Martin said. "Now will you tell me what you were talking about concerning the destruction of my species?"

"Oh, that," Tlingel replied. "In the morning land where those such as I dwell, I felt the possibility of your passing come like a gentle wind to my nostrils, with the promise of clearing the way for us—"

"How is it supposed to happen?"

Tlingel shrugged, horn writing on the air with a toss of the head.

"I really couldn't say. Premonitions are seldom specific. In fact, that is what I came to discover. I should have been about it already, but you diverted me with beer and good sport."

"Could you be wrong about this?"

"I doubt it. That is the other reason I am here."

"Please explain."

"Are there any beers left?"

"Two, I think."

"Please."

Martin rose and fetched them.

"Damn! The tab broke off this one," he said.

"Place it upon the table and hold it firmly."

"All right."

Tlingel's horn dipped forward quickly, piercing the can's top.

" . . . Useful for all sorts of things," Tlingel observed, withdrawing it.

"The other reason you're here . . ." Martin prompted.

"It is just that I am special. I can do things that the others cannot."

"Such as?"

"Find your weak spot and influence events to exploit it, to—hasten matters. To turn the possibility into a probability, and then—"

"*You* are going to destroy us? Personally?"

"That is the wrong way to look at it. It is more like a game of chess. It is as much a matter of exploiting your opponent's weaknesses as of exercising your own strengths. If you had not already laid the groundwork I would be powerless. I can only influence that which already exists."

"So what will it be? World War III? An ecological disaster? A mutated disease?"

"I do not really know yet, so I wish you wouldn't ask me in that fashion. I repeat that at the moment I am only observing. I am only an agent—"

"It doesn't sound that way to me."

Tlingel was silent. Martin began gathering up the chessmen.

"Aren't you going to set up the board again?"

"To amuse my destroyer a little more? No thanks."

"That's hardly the way to look at it—"

"Besides, those are the last beers."

"Oh." Tlingel stared wistfully at the vanishing pieces, then remarked, "I would be willing to play you again without additional refreshment . . ."

"No thanks."

"You are angry."

"Wouldn't you be, if our situations were reversed?"

"You are anthropomorphizing."

"Well?"

"Oh, I suppose I would."

"You could give us a break, you know—at least, let us make our own mistakes."

"You've hardly done that yourself, though, with all the creatures my fellows have succeeded."

Martin reddened.

"Okay. You just scored one. But I don't have to like it."

"You are a good player. I know that . . ."

"Tlingel, if I were capable of playing at my best again, I think I could beat you."

The unicorn snorted two tiny wisps of smoke.

"Not *that* good," Tlingel said.

"I guess you'll never know."

"Do I detect a proposal?"

"Possibly. What's another game worth to you?"

Tlingel made a chuckling noise.

"Let me guess: You are going to say that if you beat me you want my promise not to lay my will upon the weakest link in mankind's existence and shatter it."

"Of course."

"And what do I get for winning?"

"The pleasure of the game. That's what you want, isn't it?"

"The terms sound a little lopsided."

"Not if you are going to win anyway. You keep insisting that you will."

"All right. Set up the board."

"There is something else that you have to know about me first."

"Yes?"

"I don't play well under pressure, and this game is going to be a terrific strain. You want my best game, don't you?"

"Yes, but I'm afraid I've no way of adjusting your own reactions to the play."

"I believe I could do that myself if I had more than the usual amount of time between moves."

"Agreed."

"I mean a lot of time."

"Just what do you have in mind?"

"I'll need time to get my mind off it, to relax, to come back to the positions as if they were only problems . . ."

"You mean to go away from here between moves?"

"Yes."

"All right. How long?"

"I don't know. A few weeks, maybe."

"Take a month. Consult your experts, put your computers onto it. It may make for a slightly more interesting game."

"I really didn't have that in mind."

"Then it's time that you're trying to buy."

"I can't deny that. On the other hand, I will need it."

"In that case, I have some terms. I'd like this place cleaned up, fixed up, more lively. It's a mess. I also want beer on tap."

"Okay. I'll see to that."

"Then I agree. Let's see who goes first."

Martin switched a black and a white pawn from hand to hand beneath the table. He raised his fists then and extended them. Tlingel leaned forward and tapped. The black horn's tip touched Martin's left hand.

"Well, it matches my sleek and glossy hide," the unicorn announced.

Martin smiled, setting up the white for himself, the black pieces for his opponent. As soon as he had finished, he pushed his Pawn to K4.

Klingel's delicate, ebon hoof moved to advance the Black King's Pawn to K4.

"I take it that you want a month now, to consider your next move?"

Martin did not reply but moved his Knight to KB3. Tlingel immediately moved a Knight to QB3.

Martin took a swallow of beer and then moved his Bishop to N5. The unicorn moved the other Knight to B3. Martin immediately castled and Tlingel moved the Knight to take his Pawn.

"I think we'll make it," Martin said suddenly, "if you'll just let us alone. We do learn from our mistakes, in time."

"Mythical beings do not exactly exist in time. Your world is a special case."

"Don't you people ever make mistakes?"

"Whenever we do they're sort of poetic."

Martin snarled and advanced his Pawn to Q4. Tlingel immediately countered by moving the Knight to Q3.

"I've got to stop," Martin said, standing. "I'm getting mad, and it will affect my game."

"You will be going, then?"

"Yes."

He moved to fetch his pack.

"I will see you here in one month's time?"

"Yes."

"Very well."

The unicorn rose and stamped upon the floor and lights began to play across its dark coat. Suddenly, they blazed and shot outward in all directions like a silent explosion. A wave of blackness followed.

Martin found himself leaning against the wall, shaking. When he lowered his hand from his eyes, he saw that he was alone, save for the knights, the bishops, the kings, the queens, their castles and both the kings' men.

He went away.

Three days later Martin returned in a small truck, with a generator, lumber, windows, power tools, paint, stain, cleaning compounds, wax. He dusted and vacuumed and replaced rotted wood. He installed the windows. He polished the old brass until it shone. He stained and rubbed. He waxed the floors and buffed them. He plugged holes and washed glass. He hauled all the trash away.

It took him the better part of a week to turn the old place from a wreck back into a saloon in appearance. Then he drove off, returned all of the equipment he had rented and bought a ticket for the Northwest.

The big, damp forest was another of his favorite places for hiking, for thinking. And he was seeking a complete change of scene, a total revision of outlook. Not that his next move did not seem obvious, standard even. Yet, something nagged . . .

He knew that it was more than just the game. Before that he had been ready to get away again, to walk drowsing among shadows, breathing clean air.

Resting, his back against the bulging root of a giant tree, he withdrew a small chess set from his pack, set it up on a rock he'd moved into position nearby. A fine, mist-like rain was settling, but the tree sheltered him, so far. He reconstructed the opening through Tlingel's withdrawal of the Knight to Q3. The simplest thing would be to take the Knight with the Bishop. But he did not move to do it.

He watched the board for a time, felt his eyelids drooping, closed them and drowsed. It may only have been for a few minutes. He was never certain afterwards.

Something aroused him. He did not know what. He blinked several times and closed his eyes again. Then he reopened them hurriedly.

In his nodded position, eyes directed downward, his gaze was fixed upon an enormous pair of hairy, unshod feet—the largest pair of feet that he had ever beheld. They stood unmoving before him, pointed toward his right.

Slowly—very slowly—he raised his eyes. Not very far, as it turned out. The creature was only about four and a half feet in height. As it was looking at the chessboard rather than at him, he took the opportunity to study it.

It was unclothed but very hairy, with a dark brown pelt, obviously masculine, possessed of low brow ridges, deep-set eyes that matched its hair, heavy shoulders, five-fingered hands that sported opposing thumbs.

It turned suddenly and regarded him, flashing a large number of shining teeth.

"White's pawn should take the pawn," it said in a soft, nasal voice.

"Huh? Come on," Martin said. "Bishop takes knight."

"You want to give me black and play it that way? I'll walk all over you."

Martin glanced again at its feet.

". . . Or give me white and let me take that pawn. I'll still do it."

"Take white," Martin said, straightening. "Let's see if you know what you're talking about." He reached for his pack. "Have a beer?"

"What's a beer?"

"A recreational aid. Wait a minute."

Before they had finished the six-pack, the sasquatch—whose name, he had learned, was Grend—

had finished Martin. Grend had quickly entered a ferocious midgame, backed him into a position of swindling security and pushed him to the point where he had seen the end and resigned.

"That was one hell of a game," Martin declared, leaning back and considering the ape-like countenance before him.

"Yes, we Bigfeet are pretty good, if I do say it. It's our one big recreation, and we're so damned primitive we don't have much in the way of boards and chessmen. Most of the time, we just play it in our heads. There're not many can come close to us."

"How about unicorns?" Martin asked.

Grend nodded slowly.

"They're about the only ones can really give us a good game. A little dainty, but they're subtle. Awfully sure of themselves, though, I must say. Even when they're wrong. Haven't seen any since we left the morning land, of course. Too bad. Got any more of that beer left?"

"I'm afraid not. But listen, I'll be back this way in a month. I'll bring some more if you'll meet me here and play again."

"Martin, you've got a deal. Sorry. Didn't mean to step on your toes."

He cleaned the saloon again and brought in a keg of beer which he installed under the bar and packed with ice. He moved in some bar stools, chairs and tables which he had obtained at a Goodwill store. He hung red curtains. By then it was evening. He set up the board, ate a light meal, unrolled his sleeping bag behind the bar and camped there that night.

The following day passed quickly. Since Tlingel might show up at any time, he did not leave the vicinity, but took his meals there and sat about working chess problems. When it began to grow dark, he lit a number of oil lamps and candles.

He looked at his watch with increasing frequency. He began to pace. He couldn't have made a mistake. This was the proper day. He—

He heard a chuckle.

Turning about, he saw a black unicorn head floating in the air above the chessboard. As he watched, the rest of Tlingel's body materialized.

"Good evening, Martin." Tlingel turned away from the board. "The place looks a little better. Could use some music . . ."

Martin stepped behind the bar and switched on the transistor radio he had brought along. The sounds of a string quartet filled the air. Tlingel winced.

"Hardly in keeping with the atmosphere of the place."

He changed stations, located a Country & Western show.

"I think not," Tlingel said. "It loses something in transmission."

He turned it off.

"Have we a good supply of beverage?"

Martin drew a gallon stein of beer—the largest mug that he could locate, from a novelty store—and set it upon the bar. He filled a much smaller one for himself. He was determined to get the beast drunk if it were at all possible.

"Ah! Much better than those little cans," said Tlingel, whose muzzle dipped for but a moment. "Very good."

The mug was empty. Martin refilled it.

"Will you move it to the table for me?"

"Certainly."

"Have an interesting month?"

"I suppose I did."

"You've decided upon your next move?"

"Yes."

"Then let's get on with it."

Martin seated himself and captured the Pawn.

"Hm. Interesting."

Tlingel stared at the board for a long while, then raised a cloven hoof which parted in reaching for the piece.

"I'll just take that bishop with this little knight. Now I suppose you'll be wanting another month to make up your mind what to do next."

Tlingel leaned to the side and drained the mug.

"Let me consider it," Martin said, "while I get you a refill."

Martin sat and stared at the board through three more refills. Actually, he was not planning. He was waiting. His response to Grend had been Knight takes Bishop, and he had Grend's next move ready.

"Well?" Tlingel finally said. "What do you think?"

Martin took a small sip of beer.

"Almost ready," he said. "You hold your beer awfully well."

Tlingel laughed.

"A unicorn's horn is a detoxicant. It's possession is a universal remedy. I wait until I reach the warm glow stage, then I use my horn to burn off any excess and keep me right there."

"Oh," said Martin. "Neat trick, that."

". . . If you've had too much, just touch my horn for a moment and I'll put you back in business."

"No, thanks. That's all right. I'll just push this little pawn in front of the queen's rook two steps ahead."

"Really . . ." said Tlingel. "That's interesting. You know, what this place really needs is a piano—rinkytink, funky . . . Think you could manage it?"

"I don't play."

"Too bad."

"I suppose I could hire a piano player."

"No. I do not care to be seen by other humans."

"If he's really good, I suppose he could play blind-folded."

"Never mind."

"I'm sorry."

"You are also ingenious. I am certain that you will figure something out by next time."

Martin nodded.

"Also, didn't these old places used to have sawdust all over the floors?"

"I believe so."

"That would be nice."

"Check."

Tlingel searched the board frantically for a moment.

"Yes. I meant 'yes'. I said 'check'. It means 'yes' sometimes, too."

"Oh. Rather. Well, while we're here . . ."

Tlingel advanced the Pawn to Q3.

Martin stared. That was not what Grend had done. For a moment, he considered continuing on his own from here. He had tried to think of Grend as a coach up until this point. He had forced away the notion of crudely and crassly pitting one of them against the other. Until P-Q3. Then he recalled the game he had lost to the sasquatch.

"I'll draw the line here," he said, "and take my month."

"All right. Let's have another drink before we say good night. Okay?"

"Sure. Why not?"

They sat for a time and Tlingel told him of the morning land, of primeval forests and rolling plains, of high craggy mountains and purple seas, of magic and mythic beasts.

Martin shook his head.

"I can't quite see why you're so anxious to come here,"
he said, "with a place like that to call home."

Tlingel sighed.

"I suppose you'd call it keeping up with the griffins. It's the thing to do these days. Well. Till next
month . . ."

Tlingel rose and turned away.

"I've got complete control now. Watch!"

The unicorn form faded, jerked out of shape, grew
white, faded again, was gone, like an afterimage.

Martin moved to the bar and drew himself another mug.
It was a shame to waste what was left. In the morning, he
wished the unicorn were there again. Or at least the horn.

It was a gray day in the forest and he held an umbrella
over the chessboard upon the rock. The droplets fell from
the leaves and made dull, plopping noises as they struck
the fabric. The board was set up again through Tlingel's
P-Q3. Martin wondered whether Grend had remembered,
had kept proper track of the days . . .

"Hello," came the nasal voice from somewhere behind
him and to the left.

He turned to see Grend moving about the tree, stepping
over the massive roots with massive feet.

"You remembered," Grend said. "How good! I trust
you also remembered the beer?"

"I've lugged up a whole case. We can set up the bar
right here."

"What's a bar?"

"Well, it's a place where people go to drink—in out of
the rain—a bit dark, for atmosphere—and they sit up on
stools before a big counter, or else at little tables—and

they talk to each other—and sometimes there's music—
and they drink.''

"We're going to have all that here?"

"No. Just the dark and the drinks. Unless you count the
rain as music. I was speaking figuratively.''

"Oh. It does sound like a very good place to visit,
though.''

"Yes. If you will hold this umbrella over the board, I'll
set up the best equivalent we can have here.''

"All right. Say, this looks like a version of that game
we played last time.''

"It is. I got to wondering what would happen if it had
gone this way rather than the way that it went.''

"Hmm. Let me see . . .''

Martin removed four six-packs from his pack and
opened the first.

"Here you go.''

"Thanks.''

Grend accepted the beer, squatted, passed the umbrella
back to Martin.

"I'm still white?"

"Yeah.''

"Pawn to King six.''

"Really?"

"Yep.''

"About the best thing for me to do would be to take this
pawn with this one.''

"I'd say. Then I'll just knock off your knight with this
one.''

"I guess I'll just pull this knight back to K2.''

" . . . And I'll take this one over to B3. May I have
another beer?''

An hour and a quarter later, Martin resigned. The rain
had let up and he had folded the umbrella.

"Another game?" Grend asked.

"Yes."

The afternoon wore on. The pressure was off. This one was just for fun. Martin tried wild combinations, seeing ahead with great clarity, as he had that one day . . .

"Stalemate," Grend announced much later. "That was a good one, though. You picked up considerably."

"I was more relaxed. Want another?"

"Maybe in a little while. Tell me more about bars now."

So he did. Finally, "How is all that beer affecting you?" he asked.

"I'm a bit dizzy. But that's all right. I'll still cream you the third game."

And he did.

"Not bad for a human, though. Not bad at all. You coming back next month?"

"Yes."

"Good. You'll bring more beer?"

"So long as my money holds out."

"Oh. Bring some plaster of paris then. I'll make you some nice footprints and you can take casts of them. I understand they're going for quite a bit."

"I'll remember that."

Martin lurched to his feet and collected the chess set.

"Till then."

"Ciao."

Martin dusted and polished again, moved in the player piano and scattered sawdust upon the floor. He installed a fresh keg. He hung some reproductions of period posters and some atrocious old paintings he had located in a junk shop. He placed cuspidors in strategic locations. When he was finished, he seated himself at the bar and opened a bottle of mineral water. He listened to the New Mexico wind moaning as it passed, to grains of sand striking against the windowpanes. He wondered whether the whole world would have that dry, mournful sound to it if Tlingel found a means for doing away with humanity, or—disturbing thought—whether the successors to his own kind might turn things into something resembling the mythical morning land.

This troubled him for a time. Then he went and set up the board through Black's P-Q3. When he turned back to clear the bar he saw a line of cloven hoofprints advancing across the sawdust.

"Good evening, Tlingel," he said. "What is your pleasure?"

Suddenly, the unicorn was there, without preliminary pyrotechnics. It moved to the bar and placed one hoof upon the brass rail.

"The usual."

As Martin drew the beer, Tlingel looked about.

"The place has improved, a bit."

"Glad you think so. Would you care for some music?"

"Yes."

Martin fumbled at the back of the piano, locating the switch for the small, battery-operated computer which controlled the pumping mechanism and substituted its own memory for rolls. The keyboard immediately came to life.

"Very good," Tlingel stated. "Have you found your move?"

"I have."

"Then let us be about it."

He refilled the unicorn's mug and moved it to the table, along with his own.

"Pawn to King six," he said, executing it.

"What?"

"Just that."

"Give me a minute. I want to study this."

"Take your time."

"I'll take the pawn," Tlingel said, after a long pause and another mug.

"Then I'll take this knight."

Later, "Knight to K2," Tlingel said.

"Knight to B3."

An extremely long pause ensued before Tlingel moved the Knight to N3.

The hell with asking Grend, Martin suddenly decided. He'd been through this part any number of times already. He moved his Knight to N5.

"Change the tune on that thing!" Tlingel snapped.

Martin rose and obliged.

"I don't like that one either. Find a better one or shut it off!"

After three more tries, Martin shut it off.

"And get me another beer!"

He refilled their mugs.

"All right."

Tlingel moved the Bishop to K2.

Keeping the unicorn from castling had to be the most important thing at the moment. So Martin moved his Queen to R5. Tlingel made a tiny, strangling noise, and when Martin looked up smoke was curling from the unicorn's nostrils.

"More beer?"

"If you please."

As he returned with it, he saw Tlingel move the Bishop to capture the Knight. There seemed no choice for him at that moment, but he studied the position for a long while anyhow.

Finally, "Bishop takes bishop," he said.

"Of course."

"How's the warm glow?"

Tlingel chuckled.

"You'll see."

The wind rose again, began to howl. The building creaked.

"Okay," Tlingel finally said, and moved the Queen to Q2.

Martin stared. What was he doing? So far, it had gone all right, but—He listened again to the wind and thought of the risk he was taking.

"That's all, folks," he said, leaning back in his chair. "Continued next month."

Tlingel sighed.

"Don't run off. Fetch me another. Let me tell you of my wanderings in your world this past month."

"Looking for weak links?"

"You're lousy with them. How do you stand it?"

"They're harder to strengthen than you might think. Any advice?"

"Get the beer."

They talked until the sky paled in the east, and Martin found himself taking surreptitious notes. His admiration for the unicorn's analytical abilities increased as the evening advanced.

When they finally rose, Tlingel staggered.

"You all right?"

"Forgot to detox, that's all. Just a second. Then I'll be fading."

"Wait!"

"Whazzat?"

"I could use one, too."

"Oh. Grab hold, then."

Tlingel's head descended and Martin took the tip of the

horn between his fingertips. Immediately, a delicious, warm sensation flowed through him. He closed his eyes to enjoy it. His head cleared. An ache which had been growing within his frontal sinus vanished. The tiredness went out of his muscles. He opened his eyes again.

"Thank—"

Tlingel had vanished. He held but a handful of air.

"—you."

"Rael here is my friend," Grend stated. "He's a griffin."

"I'd noticed."

Martin nodded at the beaked, golden-winged creature.

"Pleased to meet you, Rael."

"The same," cried the other in a high-pitched voice. "Have you got the beer?"

"Why—uh—yes."

"I've been telling him about beer," Grend explained, half-apologetically. "He can have some of mine. He won't kibitz or anything like that."

"Sure. All right. Any friend of yours . . ."

"The beer!" Rael cried. "Bars!"

"He's not real bright," Grend whispered. "But he's good company. I'd appreciate your humoring him."

Martin opened the first six-pack and passed the griffin and the sasquatch a beer apiece. Rael immediately punctured the can with his beak, chugged it, belched and held out his claw.

"Beer!" he shrieked. "More beer!"

Martin handed him another.

"Say, you're still into that first game, aren't you?" Grend observed, studying the board. "Now, *that* is an interesting position."

Grend drank and studied the board.

"Good thing it's not raining," Martin commented.

"Oh, it will. Just wait a while."

"More beer!" Rael screamed.

Martin passed him another without looking.

"I'll move my pawn to N6," Grend said.

"You're kidding."

"Nope. Then you'll take that pawn with your bishop's pawn. Right?"

"Yes . . ."

Martin reached out and did it.

"Okay. Now I'll just swing this knight to Q5."

Martin took it with the Pawn.

Grend moved his Rook to K1.

"Check," he announced.

"Yes. That *is* the way to go," Martin observed.

Grend chuckled.

"I'm going to win this game another time," he said.

"I wouldn't put it past you."

"More beer?" Rael said softly.

"Sure."

As Martin poured him another, he noticed that the griffin was now leaning against the treetrunk.

After several minutes, Martin pushed his King to B1.

"Yeah, that's what I thought you'd do," Grend said. "You know something?"

"What?"

"You play a lot like a unicorn."

"Hm."

Grend moved his Rook to R3.

Later, as the rain descended gently about them and Grend beat him again, Martin realized that a prolonged period of silence had prevailed. He glanced over at the griffin. Rael had tucked his head beneath his left wing, balanced upon one leg, leaned heavily against the tree and gone to sleep.

"I told you he wouldn't be much trouble," Grend remarked.

Two games later, the beer was gone, the shadows were lengthening and Rael was stirring.

"See you next month?"

"Yeah."

"You bring my plaster of paris?"

"Yes, I did."

"Come on, then. I know a good place pretty far from here. We don't want people beating about *these* bushes. Let's go make you some money."

"To buy beer?" Rael said, looking out from under his wing.

"Next month," Grend said.

"You ride?"

"I don't think you could carry both of us," said Grend, "and I'm not sure I'd want to right now if you could."

"Bye-bye then," Rael shrieked, and he leaped into the air, crashing into branches and treetrunks, finally breaking through the overhead cover and vanishing.

"There goes a really decent guy," said Grend. "He sees everything and he never forgets. Knows how everything works—in the woods, in the air—even in the water. Generous, too, whenever he has anything."

"Hm," Martin observed.

"Let's make tracks," Grend said.

"Pawn to N6? Really?" Tlingel said. "All right. The bishop's pawn will just knock off the pawn."

Tlingel's eyes narrowed as Martin moved the Knight to Q5.

"At least this is an interesting game," the unicorn remarked. "Pawn takes knight."

Martin moved the Rook.

"Check."

"Yes, it is. This next one is going to be a three flagon move. Kindly bring me the first."

Martin thought back as he watched Tlingel drink and ponder. He almost felt guilty for hitting it with a powerhouse like the sasquatch behind its back. He was convinced now that the unicorn was going to lose. In every variation of this game that he'd played with Black against Grend, he'd been beaten. Tlingel was very good, but the sasquatch was a wizard with not much else to do but mental chess. It was unfair. But it was not a matter of personal honor, he kept telling himself. He was playing to protect his species against a supernatural force which might well be able to precipitate World War III by some arcane mind-manipulation or magically induced computer foulup. He didn't dare give the creature a break.

"Flagon number two, please."

He brought it another. He studied it as it studied the board. It was beautiful, he realized for the first time. It was the loveliest living thing he had ever seen. Now that the pressure was on the verge of evaporating and he could regard it without the overlay of fear which had always been there in the past, he could pause to admire it. If something *had* to succeed the human race, he could think of worse choices . . .

"Number three now."

"Coming up."

Tlingel drained it and moved the King to B1.

Martin leaned forward immediately and pushed the Rook to R3.

Tlingel looked up, stared at him.

"Not bad."

Martin wanted to squirm. He was struck by the nobility of the creature. He wanted so badly to play and beat the unicorn on his own, fairly. Not this way.

Tlingel looked back at the board, then almost carelessly moved the Knight to K4.

"Go ahead. Or will it take you another month?"

Martin growled softly, advanced the Rook and captured the Knight.

"Of course."

Tlingel captured the Rook with the Pawn. This was not the way that the last variation with Grend had run. Still . . .

He moved his Rook to KB3. As he did, the wind seemed to commence a peculiar shrieking, above, amid, the ruined buildings.

"Check," he announced.

The hell with it! he decided. I'm good enough to manage my own endgame. Let's play this out.

He watched and waited and finally saw Tlingel move the King to N1.

He moved his Bishop to R6. Tlingel moved the Queen to K2. The shrieking came again, sounding nearer now. Martin took the Pawn with the Bishop.

The unicorn's head came up and it seemed to listen for a moment. Then Tlingel lowered it and captured the Bishop with the King.

Martin moved his Rook to KN3.

"Check."

Tlingel returned the King to B1.

Martin moved the Rook to KB3.

"Check."

Tlingel pushed the King to N2.

Martin moved the Rook back to KN3.

"Check."

Tlingel returned the King to B1, looked up and stared at him, showing teeth.

"Looks as if we've got a drawn game," the unicorn

stated. "Care for another one?"

"Yes, but not for the fate of humanity."

"Forget it. I'd given up on that a long time ago. I decided that I wouldn't care to live here after all. I'm a little more discriminating than that.

"Except for this bar." Tlingel turned away as another shriek sounded just beyond the door, followed by strange voices. "What is that?"

"I don't know," Martin answered, rising.

The doors opened and a golden griffin entered.

"Martin!" it cried. "Beer! Beer!"

"Uh—Tlingel, this is Rael, and, and—"

Three more griffins followed him in. Then came Grend, and three others of his own kind.

"—and that one's Grend," Martin said lamely. "I don't know the others."

They all halted when they beheld the unicorn.

"Tlingel," one of the sasquatches said. "I thought you were still in the morning land."

"I still am, in a way. Martin, how is it that you are acquainted with my former countrymen?"

"Well—uh—Grend here is my chess coach."

"Aha! I begin to understand."

"I am not sure that you really do. But let me get everyone a drink first."

Martin turned on the piano and set everyone up.

"How did you find this place?" he asked Grend as he was doing it. "And how did you get here?"

"Well . . ." Grend looked embarrassed. "Rael followed you back."

"Followed a jet?"

"Griffins are supernaturally fast."

"Oh."

"Anyway, he told his relatives and some of my folks about it. When we saw that the griffins were determined to visit you, we decided that we had better come along to keep them out of trouble. They brought us.''

"I—see. Interesting . . .''

"No wonder you played like a unicorn, that one game with all the variations.''

"Uh—yes.''

Martin turned away, moved to the end of the bar.

"Welcome, all of you,'' he said. "I have a small announcement. Tlingel, awhile back you had a number of observations concerning possible ecological and urban disasters and lesser dangers. Also, some ideas as to possible safeguards against some of them.''

"I recall,'' said the unicorn.

"I passed them along to a friend of mine in Washington who used to be a member of my old chess club. I told him that the work was not entirely my own.''

"I should hope so.''

"He has since suggested that I turn whatever group was involved into a think tank. He will then see about paying something for its efforts.''

"I didn't come here to save the world,'' Tlingel said.

"No, but you've been very helpful. And Grend tells me that the griffins, even if their vocabulary is a bit limited, know almost all that there is to know about ecology.''

"That is probably true.''

"Since they have inherited a part of the Earth, it would be to their benefit as well to help preserve the place. Inasmuch as this many of us are already here, I can save myself some travel and suggest right now that we find a meeting place—say here, once a month—and that you let me have your unique viewpoints. You must know more about how species become extinct than anyone else in the business.''

"Of course,'' said Grend, waving his mug, "but we really should ask the yeti, also. I'll do it, if you'd like. Is that stuff coming out of the big box music?''

''Yes.''

''I like it. If we do this think tank thing, you'll make enough to keep this place going?''

''I'll buy the whole town.''

Grend conversed in quick gutturals with the griffins, who shrieked back at him.

''You've got a think tank,'' he said, ''and they want more beer.''

Martin turned toward Tlingel.

''They were your observations. What do you think?''

''It may be amusing,'' said the unicorn, ''to stop by occasionally.'' Then, ''So much for saving the world. Did you say you wanted another game?''

''I've nothing to lose.''

Grend took over the tending of the bar while Tlingel and Martin returned to the table.

He beat the unicorn in thirty-one moves and touched the extended horn.

The piano keys went up and down. Tiny sphinxes buzzed about the bar, drinking the spillage.

Introduction to
Gardner Dozois'
"The Sacrifice":

Gardner Dozois is the author or editor of fourteen books, including the novel *Strangers,* the collection *The Visible Man,* and the annual anthology series *Best Science Fiction Stories of the Year*. His short fiction has appeared in *Playboy, Penthouse, Omni,* and nearly all the major SF magazines and anthologies.

THE SACRIFICE

Gardner Dozois

THERE were four of them who entered the haunted darkness of the Old Forest that night, but only three who would return, because three was a magic number.

Featherflower walked silently beside her father Nightwind, her head high, trying not to stumble over the twisted, snakelike roots that seemed to snatch at her legs, trying not to flinch or start at the sinister noises of the forest, the wailing and hooting of things that might be birds, the rustling and crackling of the undergrowth as unseen bodies circled around them in the secret blackness of the night. Her heart was pounding like a fist inside her, but she would not let herself show fear—she was a chief's daughter, after all, and though he led her now to an almost certain death, she would not betray his dignity or her own. Firehair walked slightly ahead of them, as befitted a young war leader in the prime of his strength, but his steps were slow and sometimes faltering, the whites of his eyes showing as he looked around him, and Featherflower took a bitter and strength-giving pleasure from the unspoken but undeniable fact that he was more afraid than she was. Grim old Lamefoot brought up the rear, his scarred and graying body moving silently as a ghost, imperturbable, his steps coming no faster or slower than they ever did.

They had been silent since the trees had closed out the sky overhead—the Old Forest at night had never been a place that encouraged inconsequential chatter, but this silence was heavy and sour and unyielding, pressing down upon them more smotheringly even than the fay and enchanted darkness that surrounded them. Featherflower could sense her father's agony, the grief and guilt that

232

breathed from him like a bitter wind, but she would not make it easier for him by deed or gesture or word. She was the one who was to be sacrificied—why should she comfort *him*? She knew her duty as well as he knew his, had been born to it, and she would not fight or seek to escape, but it hurt her in her heart that Nightwind—her *father*— would do this thing to her, however grave the need, and she would not make it easier for him. Let it be hard, as it soon would be hard for her, let him hurt and sweat and cry aloud with the hardness of it.

So they walked through the forest in silence and guilty enmity and fear, the great and living darkness walking with them, a-bristle with watching eyes, until ahead there was a glitter of light.

The forest opened up around them into a small meadow, drenched with brilliant silver moonlight. At the far end of the meadow rose an enormous oak tree, a giant of the forest, its huge branches spread high above them like waiting, encircling arms.

"Here," said old Lamefoot the wizard. "He will come *here*."

When they had crossed the meadow and stood beneath the arms of the oak tree, Featherflower said quietly, "Father, must this be?"

Nightwind sighed. "The trees do not bloom, the streams dry up, the grass is sere . . . It has been long and long since such a thing was done, and I had hoped my time would pass before it was again needful, but clearly the gods have turned their faces away . . ." He fell silent again, looking very old. "*He* will come here," Lamefoot said in his grim gray voice, "and if he accepts you, then the powers will smile on us again . . ." Firehair looked guiltily away from her, glanced nervously around him with wide frightened eyes and said only "It is for the good of the Folk . . ."

She blew out her lips at him in scorn, snorting derisively. "Then for the good of the Folk, I will stay," she said, and sat herself down beneath the giant old oak.

Lamefoot studied her closely. "You will not run away, child?"

"No," she said calmly. "I will not run away . . ."

They watched her for awhile longer then, but there was nothing more for anyone to say, and so at last they went away and left her there, Nightwind giving one last agonized look back before the darkness swallowed them.

She was alone in the Old Forest.

Trembling, she waited beneath the ancient oak. Never had she been so afraid. The dark shapes of the trees seemed to press menacingly close around the meadow, kept at bay only by the silver moonlight. A bat flittered by through that moonlight, squeaking, and she flinched away from it. Something howled away across the cold and silent reaches of the forest, howled again in a voice like rusty old iron. Featherflower's head turned constantly as she sought to look in all directions at once, straining wide-eyed to pierce the gloom beneath the trees. She would not give way to fear, she would not give way to fear . . . but her defenses were crumbling, being sluiced away by a rising flood of terror.

A crashing in the forest, growing louder, coming nearer, the sound of branches bending and snapping, leaves rustling, the sound of some large body forcing its brute way through the entangling undergrowth . . .

She looked away, fear choking her like a hand, stopping her breath.

Something *coming* . . .

There was movement among the trees, the bare branches stirring gently as though moved by the ghost of the wind, and when she looked again *he* was there, seeming to materialize from the dappled leaf-shadows, his head held high, paler than the moonlight, clothed in the awful glory of his flesh, so noble and swift-moving and puissant, so proud and lordly of bearing that all fear vanished from her and she felt her heart melt within her with poignant and unbearable love.

Their eyes met, hers shy and guileless, his bright and clear and wild, liquid as molten gold. She tossed her own head back, moonlight gleaming from the long white horn that protruded from her forehead, and pawed nervously at the ground with a tiny silver hoof.

He came to her then across the broken ground, the human, moving as lightly and soundlessly as mist, and laid his terrible head in her lap.

Introduction to
Frank Owen's
"The Unicorn":

We tend to think of the unicorn in a medieval European setting, but in actuality the unicorn is a symbol that can be found all over the world, in Jewish and Hindu mythologies as well as Christian folklore, and even in the tales and legends of China and Japan. In China, the unicorn is sometimes called the k'i-lin. According to Chinese legend, the unicorn is such a gentle creature that it will not even eat live grass for fear of harming something that lives. It is considered to be the finest of creatures that lives on the land, an animal of good omen which brings good fortune to anyone lucky enough to be under its benign protection.

Yet, as we shall see, even this gentle creature has its dark side . . . .

The late Frank Owen specialized in writing oriental fantasy, and in effect created his own sub-genre. Most of his stories, which were usually set in China, appeared in *Weird Tales*, and can be found in now-rare collections such as *A Husband for Kutani*, *The Porcelain Magician*, and *The Wind that Tramps the World: Splashes of Chinese Color*. His novels include *Rare Earth*, *Madonna of the Damned*, and *The Scarlet Hill*. He was also the co-author of *The Blue Highway*, a juvenile, in collaboration with Anna Owen.

THE UNICORN
Frank Owen

THERE was a woman of Hangchow who had a singular adventure. Her name was Lin Mie. Some would have considered her poor but she believed she was rich, glorying in the love of her husband Lin Wong. She had been married ten years but she was still childless. In China this is considered tragedy indeed. Her husband had longed for a son but he had not taken a secondary wife. Not always does a woman of China live little better than a slave existence, under the thumb of her mother-in-law. On the contrary, history records many instances of women completely dominating men, for example the love of the King of Wu for Hsi Shih, and Ming Huang's adoration of Yang Kwei-fei who permitted herself to be hanged to save her Emperor. This happened twelve hundred years ago but it is still lamented by poets as "the everlasting wrong." Usually the love which a Chinese has for his wife is something precious which he keeps within the walls of his garden. Truly written are the words, "A woman's hair draws more than a team of oxen."

One day when Lin Mie had been working long hours in the fields, she stopped for a moment to rest beneath a willow tree. A misty rain was falling, the soft, gentle rain of China that is unlike any other rain the world over. The air was fragrantly cool, and very silent, as though all nature were poised on tip-toe. Lin Mie was so very tired. Her arms ached and she folded them in her lap. Whether she slept or not she did not know but suddenly she realized that she was holding a sleeping child in her arms, a very little boy, about three years old. His hair was jet black, his nose was well-formed, his complexion was so pale he

might not have been a Chinese at all. He was so handsome,
like the child about whom she had always dreamed. Then
he opened his eyes, they were blue, as blue as the early
evening sky. This frightened her, for a person with blue
eyes in China is usually blind. The child smiled and the
radiance of his smile put the sun to shame.

"Mama," he said, and snuggled up to her.

"Who are you, little one?" she asked gently.

"I'm your boy," said he, "and you haven't given me a
name. Besides I'm hungry. I haven't had morning rice."

So she took him into the house and cooked rice for him.
As he ate she clasped her hands on the table before her.
Was it only her imagination? Her hands were pale and
delicately beautiful, not a trace of toil did they show. Even
the nails were pointed and unbroken.

The boy said, "The rice is good."

"Rice is life," she said, "and life is good."

They named the boy Lin Mu, or rather the mother did,
for Lin Wong showed a strange reluctance to call the boy
his son, though he was happy that the little one had chosen
to live with them. The name was very appropriate for Mu
meant tree and by coincidence the family name, Lin,
meant forest. And the mother thought, "My boy is indeed
like a young tree, slim and strong enough to stand against a
typhoon." Her happiness was complete, her eyes were
large with wonder that such good fortune had befallen her.

One night as she made ready for sleep, there was a
gorgeous bed where the old mattress had formerly been
on the bare floor. And the sheets were of silk, petal soft.
On the teakwood chair beside the bed was a sleeping-robe
of caressive softness. She undressed and put on the silk
robe and slipped between the fragrant sheets. She was so
happy she wondered if this were all a dream and she would
soon awaken to stern reality. Then her little boy crept into

her arms, "Let me stay with you until papa comes," he whispered.

Lin Wong sat smoking before the door until his pipe was exhausted. He retired in the dark. When his body came in contact with the silken sheets, he disliked them immensely, for they were as slippery, he thought, as snake's skin. He was irked by the softness of the bed. After a sleepless hour, he tried the floor and slept at once.

During the following days, the mother seemed to grow younger and slenderer. But little change was to be noticed in the father, Lin Wong.

"How I wish that I could have a water-buffalo to do my plowing," he said. He thought seldom of his bodily comfort but constantly of his fields of millet, rice and turnips. They were a source of pleasure to him, as important as his heart or his lungs.

Toward noon little Mu said to his father, "Here is a unicorn. He can help you plow better than a water-buffalo. See, he is very gentle."

Lin Wong gazed astounded at the unicorn. He remembered all the mythical tales he had heard about that marvelous beast, that it springs from the Central Regions; that it has superior integrity and appears to virtuous people; that the mid-part of its cry is like a monastery bell; that it is the horned beast *par excellence*.

The unicorn had a white horselike body, covered with scales and a crested back; its hoofs were cloven. It had a long, bushy tail. Its head was akin to that of a dragon. From the center of its forehead grew a single horn. Despite its ferocious appearance, it was as docile as a small dog, following little Lin Mu wherever he walked.

In the days that followed the unicorn proved to be as good at drawing a plow as any water-buffalo. The gentleness of the huge animal was beyond belief. Sometimes Lin Wong wondered how it existed, for he never saw it eating or drinking, yet his son assured him the animal wanted nothing.

"He eats the wind," he said. "He chews the sunrise."

News of the presence of the unicorn on the farm of Lin Wong spread throughout the province, and though he did not know it Lin Wong had become famous. For does not the unicorn appear only to virtuous monarchs? Perhaps Lin Wong was a prince in disguise. Fabulous were the stories circulated about him. And at last they came to the ears of a notorious bandit, Loo Tak, who called himself a war lord. He was angered. Why should a simple farmer become so renowned? What had he done to merit it? Far better for him, Loo Tak, to own the unicorn. What man in the province was stronger than he? Although he was only of medium height, he had a giant's strength because he had four huge bodyguards. Now Loo Tak was no more than a festering blight on the face of China. Never had he owned anything that he did not first steal. Force, power, corruption were his gods. He lived ruthlessly, caring not how many people he ruined or despoiled. He had never known the devotion of a good woman. He had great wealth when applied to money and jewels and material things, but mentally he was a beggar. By everyone he was hated but feared. Not even his own bodyguard trusted him. However, he believed he was invincible. What he wanted he took, nor did he hesitate to slay. What idiot would stand up against him? So he decided that he would capture the unicorn. So sure was he of success that he took with him only one bodyguard.

So he went to the farm of Lin Wong. Nobody stood in his way but a very little boy. He stooped to cuff the boy and fell flat on his face. That was ignominy indeed. He couldn't understand it. What had happened? He was angered beyond words and his anger was against the child who was smiling. Again he lunged with his fist. This time he hit the earth with such force he was breathless. He was losing face before his bodyguard. Suddenly he decided to swallow his anger for now the unicorn was coming gently toward him. The little boy slowly approached the animal and stood so close that his body touched the animal.

The bandit smiled. His mission would be as easy as seizing a playful kitten. Despite its size the unicorn was absolutely docile. Loo Tak was without fear as he attempted to grasp the fantastic white animal. It was the last thing he ever did, for the unicorn impaled him on its horn and then tossed him so high that most of his bones were broken as he crashed to the earth. The unicorn stamped him into the soil until not a trace of the mighty war lord remained. Then the boy and the unicorn went back into the field again. The bodyguard fled. He had learned a bitter lesson. It is unwise to attempt to steal a unicorn.

Neither Lin Wong nor his wife were aware of the calamity that had overtaken the bandit who had believed himself to be invincible. Too bad that he did not know that even the tiger and the leopard are perpetually anxious lest they encounter a unicorn.

Now in Hangchow, also, lived the Mandarin Lim, an army general and therefore a Mandarin of the First Rank. On his conical-shaped official hat was an opaque ruby and coral button, an inch in diameter, set on the center of his hat like a knob. His girdle clasp was of jade set in rubies, on his breast and back was a square of silk, a foot in diameter, embroidered with the unicorn, the emblem of his high rank.

Lim did not look like a general for he was short and fat

but he was tall in dignity and very vain. He had the delusion that he presented an impressive figure as his bearers carried his gaudy chair through the streets and lanes of the town. Before his equipage ran a number of criers, screeching discordantly and clapping cymbals so that all might move aside at the approach of such an illustrious person. How were they to know that Lim was a meek, pudgy little fat man who had never distinguished himself in battle. All his high honors were hereditary. About the only thing outstanding about him was his appetite. He disposed of such huge quantities of food even his servants marveled.

He spent most of each day munching kumquats and lichee nuts which were more delicious to him than even his concubines. He knew little of warfare and had no relish for it. He had never led an army in the field, but that did not prevent him from wearing a large variety of medals. He was pompous and vain even though his accomplishments were infinitesimal. His wealth had come to him from many generations of generals but he could not have been prouder of himself if he had earned it all through his military leadership.

Since the unicorn was his rightful emblem, he reasoned that it would be fitting that he own a unicorn. He did not stop to reason that nobody ever owns a unicorn, for a unicorn is one of the four supernatural creatures of which the dragon, the phoenix and the tortoise are the others. The unicorn is the king of all animals, associated with good government or the awakening of spring.

Little Lin Mu's mother used to think of him as a young prince, so perhaps the presence of the unicorn was not so extraordinary.

Meanwhile the Mandarin Lim mulled over his problem as he munched luscious tangerines. Unlike the bandit, he

had no idea of snatching the unicorn. Money enough had
he to buy what he desired. Unwisely he believed that gold
can purchase anything. And yet it cannot cause one extra
bud to appear on a rose bush, nor can it change the
brightness of a single star, nor can it block the course of a
typhoon. When a man is starving, he cannot eat gold, nor
is the touch of gold half as satisfying as the touch of jade.
Too much gold spoils a man's sleep, worrying about being
robbed. To drink gold, is to woo death. There are many
things gold cannot buy, among which is a gentle white
unicorn. But of this the Mandarin Lim was unaware, for
despite the fact he had studied at the Hanlin Academy, he
had little education. His sluggish mind was incapable of
retaining knowledge. How mortified he would have been
had he been capable of realizing that in the things that
count, he was a beggar. Even his dreams were threadbare,
despite the fact that he slept between embroidered sheets
on a teakwood bed.

Meanwhile the Lin family prospered. The crops of rice,
millet and turnips were abundant. The house gradually
changed in appearance. Its austerity vanished.

But there was no change in Lin Wong. True, his farm-
ing was less arduous and he could smoke a pipe of tobacco
without worrying over the cost.

One early evening when Lin Wong sat smoking before
his door, there occurred such a commotion as he had never
heard before. It was the clash of cymbals, the discordant
beating of drums, and the ringing of bells, betokening the
approach of the equipage of the Mandarin Lim as, elabo-
rately gowned in full splendor, gaudy yellow and purple
silk, embroidered with golden thread, and wearing the
squares emblazoned with the unicorn, the emblem of his
rank, he sat squeezed into the narrow confines of his sedan

chair, carried by four bearers, perspiring profusely. Before the house of Lin Wong, the discord stopped, and the Mandarin climbed down from his chair with a sigh of relief.

Lin Wong was amazed at the visit of so high an official and his mouth gaped open.

"Do I address Lin Wong?" asked the Mandarin pompously.

"Yes," was the reply, "but I have done no wrong."

"Be not disturbed, I came as a friend. I have heard that there is a unicorn upon this farm."

"That is true. He draws the plow."

"A menial task indeed."

"But a worthy one."

"Permit me to make known to you that I am the Mandarin Lim, a general whose emblem is the unicorn. Hence my interest."

At that moment a small boy came from in back of the house. He held a gleaming object in his hand. To the Mandarin it seemed to be a gold-piece. He was dismayed. How could he offer Lin Wong gold in exchange for the unicorn if he had so much of it that his little son could play with a gold-piece?

He smiled at the boy and patted his tiny head. Then he attempted to take the gold-piece from the child's hand, but without success. Might as well try to snatch a star from the sky. How could a small one have such strength? Yet he had touched the thing the child was playing with and it was definitely a gold-piece. But now Lin Mu opened his hand and a yellow leaf fell from it to the ground. The Mandarin was amazed. However could he have made such an error? But even as he questioned himself he somehow knew that the leaf only a moment before had been a gold-piece.

It was akin to magic. Nevertheless his determination to

purchase the unicorn was in no way lessened. So he said to Lin Wong, "I would like a buy the unicorn."

"The unicorn is not mine to sell, it belongs to my son."

"How is it that the head of the house of Lin is ruled by so young a boy? It would be well for you to consider my offer, a catty of gold for the noble animal, gold enough to enrich you for the rest of your days. No longer need you toil in the fields."

The temptation was great and Lin Wong could not help mulling over the offer, chewing upon it as though it were a very choice morsel. He had never possessed a gold-piece. Of course, though he thought not of her, he had a beautiful wife who grew younger in appearance every day as the years slipped from her like peach blossoms falling. He had a small son of rare beauty, who when he was with his mother was a veritable chatterbox. A unicorn made his plowing so easy it was almost effortless. And his house had become spacious, luxurious and friendly. Truly he had no need for a catty of gold but it lured him nonetheless. He would be enormously rich, he reasoned, so, at last he accepted the offer of the Mandarin.

But now his wife emerged from the house. She held the little boy by the hand and he was chattering as usual as he skipped along beside her. They passed Lin Wong without noticing him and paid no heed whatever to the mighty Mandarin Lim. His pomp was somewhat deflated and he was angry but he did not show it. He watched, even as did Lin Wong, the quiet way they walked down the long old road over which for centuries countless feet had trod, and on into the distance. Now they seemed to be climbing a hill though Lin Wong knew no hill was there. Was it only his imagination or were they fading from view as though their bodies had the texture of gossamer? A gentle breeze swept the countryside like a broom and then they seemed to be one with the sky and the wind and the evening glow. It was a strange sight to behold, but breathtaking too, like a dream's end or a white moth flying. Lin Wong sighed, and his hands shook. Too late, he realized that a man is not wise who attempts to sell a unicorn.

Introduction to
Gene Wolfe's
"The Woman the Unicorn Loved":

Here's another story in which sophisticated genetic science is employed to create in living flesh the fabulous monsters of fantasy and mythology: centaurs, satyrs, pegasoi . . . and, of course, unicorns. But once you have created such chimeras, what do you *do* with them? Can you chain the basilisk or tame the manticore, or pen a Pegasus up in your back yard? How well do they fit into our hectic modern world of superhighways and shopping centers and condominums, where urban sprawl spreads over the countryside like an oil slick over quiet water, and where even the few remaining "wilderness" areas are crisscrossed by grinning tourists on roaring snowmobiles? What moral responsibility do the creators have for the created? What happens when you tire of your dazzling new toys, and yet they refuse to go quietly back into the box. . . ?

Although he has been seriously underestimated and underappreciated, Gene Wolfe is one of the best—perhaps *the* best—SF and fantasy writers working today. He has written some of the best short fiction of the seventies—stories such as "The Hero as Werewolf," "Seven American Nights," "The Island of Doctor Death and Other Stories," "Tracking Song," and the Nebula-winning

"The Death of Doctor Island." His novel *The Fifth Head of Cerberus* is a recognized classic, and in its original form is probably the single best novella of the seventies. His novel *Peace,* ostensibly a book about the mundane life of a frozen-orange-juice manufacturer, contains enough magic and genuine wonder for a dozen ordinary fantasy novels, and his *The Devil in a Forest* is a vivid and compelling evocation of the medieval world. His tetralogy *The Book of the New Sun* (the first two volumes of which, *The Shadow of the Torturer* and *The Claw of the Conciliator* were released in 1980 and 1981, respectively) is shaping up to be one of the seminal works of science fantasy, perhaps as good—and maybe ultimately as influential—as Tolkein's *Lord of the Rings* or T. H. White's *The Once and Future King.* Wolfe's most recent books are *The Sword of the Lictor* (the third volume of *The Book of the New Sun*), and the collections *The Island of Doctor Death and Other Stories and Other Stories* and *Gene Wolfe's Book of Days.*

THE WOMAN THE UNICORN LOVED
Gene Wolfe

AT the western edge of the campus the parkway sent a river of steel and rubber roaring out of the heart of the city. Fragrant pines fringed the farther side. The unicorn trotted among them, sometimes concealed, sometimes treading the strip of coarse grass that touched the strip of soiled gravel that touched the concrete. That was where Anderson, looking from his office window, first saw him.

Drivers and passengers saw him too. Some waved; no doubt some shouted though their shouts could not be heard. Faces pale and faces brown pressed against glass, but no one stopped. Possibly some trucker with a CB informed the police.

The unicorn was so white he gleamed. His head looked Arabian, but his hooves were darkly red, like pigeon's-blood rubies, and his tail was not like a horse's tail at all, but the kind of tail—like the tail of a bull, but with an additional guidon of hair halfway to the tip—that is seen only in heraldic beasts. His horn shone like polished ivory, straight as the blade of a rapier and as long as a man's arm. Anderson guessed his height at twenty-four hands.

He turned away to lift his camera bag down from the top of the filing cabinet, and when he got back to the window the unicorn was in the traffic. Across two hundred yards of campus lawn he could hear the squealing of brakes.

> *"Pluto, the grisly god, who never spares,*
> *Who feels no mercy, who hears no prayers."*

Anderson recited the couplet to himself, and only as he pronounced the word *prayers* was he aware that he had spoken aloud.

Then the unicorn was safe on the other side, cantering across the shaven grass. (Pluto, it appeared, might hear prayers after all.) As the armed head lifted to test the wind, Anderson's telephone rang. He picked it up.

"Hello, Andy? Dumont. Look out your window."

"I am looking," Anderson said.

"Dropped right into our laps. Can you imagine anybody letting something like that go?"

"Yes, pretty easily. I can also imagine it jumping just about any fence on earth. But if we're going to protect it, we'd better get on the job before the kids run it off." Anderson had found his telephoto zoom and coupled it to the camera body. With the phone clamped between his shoulder and his ear, he took a quick picture.

"I'm going after it. I want a tissue specimen and a blood sample."

"You can get them when Army shoots it."

"Listen, Andy, I don't want to see it shot any more than you do. A piece of work like that? I'm going out there now, and I'll appreciate any help I can get. I've already told my secretary to phone some members. If the military comes in—well, at least you'll be able to get some stills to send the TV people. You coming?"

Anderson came, a big, tawny man of almost forty, with a camera hanging from his neck. By the time he was out of the Liberal Arts Building, there were a hundred or so students around the unicorn. He must have menaced them; their line bent backward, then closed again. His gleaming horn was lifted above their heads for a moment, half playful, half triumphant. Anderson used his size and faculty status to elbow his way to the front of the crowd.

The unicorn stood—no, trotted, almost danced—in the center of a circle fifty feet wide, while the students shouted jokes and cheered. A little group who must have known something of his lore grabbed a blonde in a cheerleader's sweater and pushed her foreward. He put his head down, a lancer at the charge, and she scampered back into the jeering crowd, breasts bobbing.

Anderson lowered his camera.

"Get it?" a student beside him asked.

"I think so."

A Frisbee sailed by the unicorn's ears, and he shied like a skittish horse. Someone threw it back.

Anderson yelled, "If that animal gets frightened, he's going to hurt somebody."

Dumont heard him, whether the students did or not. He waved from the farther side of the circle, his bald head gleaming. As the unicorn trotted past him, he thrust out a loaf of bread and was ignored.

Anderson sprinted across the circle. The students cheered, and several began running back and forth.

"Hi," Dumont said. "That took guts."

"Not really." Anderson found he was puffing. "I didn't come close. If he was angry, none of us would be here."

"I wish none of them were—nobody but you and me. It would make everything a hell of a lot simpler."

"Don't you have that tranquilizer gun?"

"At home. Our friend there would be long gone by the time I got back with it. Maybe I should keep one in the lab, but you know how it is—before this, we've always had to go after them."

Anderson nodded, only half listening as he watched the unicorn.

"We had this bread to feed to mice in a nutrition project. I put some stuff in it to quiet him down. On the spur of the moment, it was the best I could do."

Anderson was wondering who would arrive first—their

Mythic Conservationists with protest signs or the soldiers and their guns. "I doubt that it's going to be good enough," he told Dumont.

A young woman slipped between them. "Here," she asked, "can I try?" Before Dumont could object, she took the bread and jogged to the center of the circle, the wind stirring her short, brown hair and the sunlight flashing from her glasses.

The unicorn came toward her slowly, head down.

Dumont said, "He'll kill her."

The students were almost quiet now, whispering. Anderson had to fight the impulse to dash out, to try to hold back the white beast, to knock him off his feet and wrestle him to the ground if he could. Except that he could not; that a dozen like him could not, no more than they could have overthrown an elephant. If he, or anyone here, were to attempt such a thing now, people would surely die.

The young woman thrust out Dumont's loaf—common white bread from some grocery store. After a moment she crouched to bring her eyes on a level with the unicorn's.

Anderson heard himself murmur,

"Behold a pale horse:
And his name that sat on him was Death."

Then, when tension had been drawn so fine that it seemed to him that he must break, it broke instead. The ivory lance came up, and the shining, impossible lancer trotted forward, nibbled at the bread, nuzzled the young woman's neck. Still quiet, indeed almost hushed, the students surged forward. A boy with a feathery red beard patted the unicorn's withers, and a girl Anderson recognized from one of his classes buried her face in the flowing mane. The young woman herself, the girl with the bread, stroked fierce horn. Anderson found that he was there too, his hand on a gleaming flank.

Then the magic blew away beneath the threshing of a helicopter, dissolved like a dream at cockcrow. It came in low across the park, a dark blue gunship. (Police, Anderson thought crazily, police and not the Army this time.) A dozen people yelled, and the students began to scatter.

It banked in a tight turn and came back trailing a white plume of tear gas. Anderson ran with the rest then, hearing the thunder of the unicorn's hooves over—no, under—the whicker of the four-bladed prop. There was a sputter of fire from some automatic weapon.

Back in the Liberal Arts Building several hours later, he went to the restroom to wash the traces of the gas from his face and hands and put drops in his faintly burning eyes. The smell of the gas was in his trousers and jacket; they would have to be cleaned. He wished vaguely that he had been prescient enough to keep a change of clothes on campus.

When he opened the door to his office, the young woman was there. Absurdly, she rose when he entered, as though sex roles had not just been eliminated but reversed.

He nodded to her, and she extended her hand. "I'm Julie Coronell, Dr. Anderson."

"It's a pleasure," he said. She might have been quite pretty, he decided, if she were not so thin. And so nervous.

"I—I noticed you out there. With the unicorn. I was the one who fed him bread."

"I know you were," Anderson said. "I noticed you, too. Everyone did."

She actually blushed, something he had not seen in years. "I've some more." She lifted a brown paper sack. "The other wasn't mine, really—I got it from some man there. He's in the Biology Department, I think.''

Anderson nodded. "Yes, he is.''

"That was white. That bread. This is pumpernickel. I thought he—the unicorn. I thought he might like it better.''

Anderson could not keep from grinning at that, and she smiled too.

"Well, anyway, *I* like it better. Do you know the story about the general's horse? Or am I being a pest?''

"Not at all. I'd love to hear the story of the general's horse, especially if it has anything to do with unicorns.''

"It doesn't, really. Only with horses, you know, and pumpernickel. The general was one of Napoleon's. I think Bernadotte, and he had a favorite charger named Nicole—we would say Nicholas or Nick. When the Grand Army occupied Germany, and the officers ate at the German country inns, they were served the coarse, brown German bread with their meals. All Frenchmen hate it, and none of them would eat it. But the others saw that Bernadotte slipped it into his pockets, and when they asked him about it, he said it was for his horse—*Pain pour Nicole,* bread for Nick. After that the others joked about the German 'horse bread,' *pain pour Nicole,* and the Germans thought that was the French name for it, and since anything French has always been very posh on menus, they used it.''

Anderson chuckled and shook his head. "Is that what you're going to call him when you find him? Nicholas? Or will it be Nicole?''

"Nick, actually. The story is just folk-etymology, really. But I thought of it, and it seemed to fit. Nick, because we're both Americans now. I was born in New Zealand, and that brings me to one of the things I came to ask you—what nationality are unicorns? I mean originally. Greek?''

"Indian," Anderson told her.

"You're making fun of me."

He shook his head. "Not American Indian, of course. Indian like the tiger. A Roman naturalist called Pliny seems to have begun the story. He said that people in India hunted an animal he called the monoceros. Our word *unicorn* is a translation of that. Both words mean 'one-horned.' "

Julie nodded.

"Pliny said this unicorn had a head like a stag, feet like an elephant, a boar's tail, and the body of a horse. It bellowed, it had one black horn growing from its forehead, and it could not be captured alive."

She stared at him. He stared expressionlessly back, and at last she said, "That's not a unicorn! That's not a unicorn at all. That's a rhinoceros."

"Uh huh. Specifically, it's an Indian rhinoceros. The African ones actually have two horns, one above the other. Pliny's description fell into the hands of the scholars of the dark ages, who knew nothing about rhinoceroses or even elephants, and the unicorn became a one-horned creature that was otherwise much like a horse. Unicorn horn was supposed to neutralize poisons, but the Indians didn't ship their rhinoceros horns west—China was much closer and much richer, and the Chinese thought rhinoceros horn was an aphrodisiac. Narwhale horns were brought in to satisfy the demand, and narwhale horns succeeded wonderfully, because narwhale horns are so utterly fantastic that no one who hasn't seen one can believe in them. They're ivory, and spiraled, and perfectly straight. You know, of course. You had your hand on one today, only it was growing out of a unicorn's head. Dumont would say out of the head of a genetically reengineered horse, but I think we both know better."

Julie smiled. "It's wonderful, isn't it? Unicorns are real now."

"In a way, they were real before. As Chesterton says

somewhere, to think of a cow with wings is essentially to
have met one. The unicorn symbolized masculine
purity—which isn't such a bad thing to symbolize, after
all. Unicorns were painted on shields and sewn into flags.
A unicorn rampant is the badge of Scotland, just as the
bald eagle is the badge of this country, and eventually that
unicorn became one of the supporters of the British arms.
The image, the idea, has been real for a long time. Now
it's tangible.''

"And I'm glad. I like it like that. Dr. Anderson, the real
reason I came to see you was that a friend told me you were
the president of an organization that tries to save these
animals.''

"Most of them are people. All right if I smoke?'' She
nodded, and Anderson took a pipe from his desk and
began to pack it with tobacco. "Many of the creatures of
myth were partly human and had human intelligence—
lamias, centaurs, fauns, satyrs, and so forth. Often that
seems to appeal to the individuals who do this sort of
thing. Then too, human cellular material is the easiest of
all for them to get—they can use their own.''

"Do you mean that I could make one of these mythical
animals if I wanted to? Just go off and do it?''

The telephone rang and Anderson picked it up.

"Hello, Andy?'' It was Dumont again.

"Yep,'' Anderson said.

"It seems to have gotten away.''

"Uh huh. Our bunch certainly couldn't find it, and our
operator said there was nothing on the police radio.''

"Well, it gave them the slip. A student—an under-
graduate, but I know him, and he's pretty reliable—just
came and told me. He saw it over on the far side of the
practice field. He tried to get up close, but it ran behind the
field house and he lost it.''

Anderson covered the mouthpiece with his hand and

said, "Nick's all right. Someone just saw him." He asked Dumont, "You send a bunch to look for him?"

"Not yet. I wanted to talk to you first. I gave the boy the key to my place and asked him to fetch my tranquilizer gun. He's got my van."

"Fine. Come up here and we'll talk. Leave this student a note so he'll know where you are."

"You don't think we ought to send some people out after the unicorn?"

"We've had searchers out after him for a couple of hours, and so have the police. I don't know about you, but while I was beating the bushes, I was wondering just what in the name of Capitoline Jove I was going to do with him if I found him. Try to ride him? Put salt on his tail? We can't do a damn thing until we've got your tranquilizer gun or some other way to control him, and by the time the boy gets back from your house in Brookwood it will be nearly dark."

When he had cradled the telephone, Anderson said, "That should give you an idea of how well organized we are."

Julie shrugged sympathetically.

"In the past, you see, it was always a question of letting the creature get away. The soldiers or the police wanted to kill it, we wanted to see it spared. Usually they head for the most lightly populated area they can find. We should have anticipated that sooner or later we'd be faced with one right here in the city, but I suppose we assumed that in a case like that we'd have no chance at all. Now it turns out that we've got a chance—your friend Nick is surprisingly elusive for such a big beast—and we haven't the least idea of what to do."

"Maybe he was born—do you say born?"

"We usually say created, but it doesn't matter."

"Well, maybe he was created here in the city, and he's

trying to find his way out of it.''

"A creature that size?'' Anderson shook his head. "He's come in from outside, from some sparsely settled rural area, or he'd have been turned in by a nosy neighbor long ago. People can—people do—perform DNA engineering in the city. Sometimes in basements or garages or kitchens, more often on the sly in college labs or some big corporation's research and development facility. They keep the creatures they've made, too; sometimes for years. I've got a sea-horse at home in an aquarium, not one of those fish you buy cast in plastic paperweights in the Florida souvenir shops, but a little fellow about ten inches long, with the head and forelegs of a pony and the hindquarters of a trout. I've had him for a year now, and I'll probably have him for another ten. But suppose he were Nick's size—where would I keep him?''

"In a swimming pool, I imagine,'' Julie said. "In fact, it seems rather a nice idea. Maybe at night you could take him to Lake Michigan and ride him there, in the lake. You could wear scuba gear. I'm not a terribly good swimmer, but I think I'd do it.'' She smiled at him.

He smiled back. "It does sound like fun, when you describe it.''

"Just the same, you think he's escaped from some farm—or perhaps an estate. I should think that would be more likely. The rich must have these poor, wonderful animals made for them sometimes.''

"Sometimes, yes.''

"Unicorns. A sea-horse—that's from mythology too, isn't it?''

Anderson was lighting his pipe; the mingled fumes of sulfur and tobacco filled the office. "Balios and Xantos drew the chariot of Poseidon,'' he said. "In fact, Poseidon was the god of horses as well as of the sea. His herds were the waves, in a mystic sense few people understand today. The whitecaps were the white manes of his innumerable steeds.''

''And you mentioned lamias—those were snake women, weren't they?''

''Yes.''

''And centaurs. And fauns and satyrs. Are all the animals like that, that the biologists make, from mythology?''

Anderson shook his head. ''Not all of them, no. But let me ask you a question, Ms. Coronell—''

''Call me Julie, please.''

''All right, Julie. Now suppose that you were a biologist. In genetic engineering they've reached the stage at which any competent worker with a Master's or a PhD—and a lot of bright undergraduates—can do this sort of thing. What would you make for yourself?''

''I have room for it, and privacy, and lots of money?''

''If you like, yes.''

''Then I'd make a unicorn, I think.''

''You're impressed with them because you saw a beautiful one today. After that. Suppose you were going to create something else?''

Julie paused, looking pensive. ''We talked about riding a sea-horse in the lake. Something with wings, I suppose, that I could ride.''

''A bird? A mammal?''

''I don't know. I'd have to think about it.''

''If you chose a bird, it would have to be much larger, of course, than a natural bird. You'd also find that it could not maintain the proportions of any of the species whose genetic matter you were using. Its wings would have to be much larger in proportion to its body. Its head would not have to be much bigger than an eagle's—and so on. When

you were through and you were spotted sailing among the
clouds, the newspapers would probably call your bird a
roc, after the one that carried Sinbad.''

"I see.''

"If you decided on a winged horse instead, it would be
Pegasus. I've never yet seen one of those that could
actually fly, by the way. A winged human being would be
an angel, or if it were more bird-like, with claws and tail
feathers and so on, perhaps a harpy. You see, it's quite
hard to escape from mythological nomenclature, because
it covers so much. People have already imagined all these
things. It's just that now we—some of us—can make them
come true.''

Julie smiled nervously. "An alligator! I think I'll
choose an alligator with wings. I could make him smarter
at the same time.''

Anderson puffed out a cloud of smoke. "That's a dragon.''

"Wait, I'll—''

The door flew open and Dumont came in. Anderson
said, "Here's the man who can tell you about recombinant
DNA and that sort of thing. I'd only make a hash of it.'' He
stood. "Julie, may I present Henry A. Dumont of Biology, my good friend and occasionally my rival.''

"Friendly rival,'' Dumont put in.

"Also the treasurer and technical director of our little
society. Dumont, this is Julia Coronell, the lady who's
hiding the unicorn.''

For a moment no one spoke. Julie's face was guarded,
expressionless save for tension. Then she said, "How did
you know?''

Anderson sat down again, and Dumont took the office's
last chair. Anderson said, "You came here because you
were concerned about Nick.'' He paused, and Julie nodded. "But you didn't seem to want to *do* anything. If Nick

was running around while the police looked for him, the situation was urgent; but you told me that story about pumpernickel and let me blather on about fauns and centaurs. You were worried, you were under a considerable strain, but you weren't urging me to get busy and reactivate the group we had looking for Nick this afternoon. When Dumont here called, I was very casual about the whole thing and just asked him to come over and talk. You didn't protest, and I decided that you knew where Nick was already. And that he was safe, at least for the time being.''

"I see," Julie whispered.

"I don't," Dumont said. "That boy told me he saw the unicorn."

Anderson nodded. "A friend of yours, Julie?"

"Yes . . ."

Dumont said, "Honey, it's nothing to be ashamed of. We're on your side."

"You hid Nick," Anderson continued, "after the police dropped their tear gas. He was tame with you, as we saw earlier. He may even have eaten enough of Dumont's bread to calm him down a bit—there was a sedative in it. For a while after that, you were probably too frightened to do anything more; you just lay low. Then the police went away and our search parties gave up, and you went off campus to buy that bread you're holding. On the way back to give it to Nick, you met someone who told you about me.''

Dumont asked, "Was it Ed? The boy who told me he saw the unicorn?''

Julie's voice was nearly inaudible. "Yes, it was."

"And between the two of you, you decided it would be smart to start some rumors indicating that Nick was still free and moving in a direction away from the place where you had him hidden.'' Anderson paused to relight his pipe. "So the first report had him disappearing behind the field house. The next one would have put him even farther away, I suppose. But more or less on impulse, you decided that we might help you, so you came up here to wait for me. Anyway, it would be safer for you to take that bread to Nick after dark. All right, we will help you. At least, we'll try. Where is Nick?"

Ed was no more a boy, actually, than Julie Coronell was a girl—a studious looking young man of nineteen or twenty. He had brought Dumont's tranquilizer gun, and Dumont had it now, though all of them hoped it would not be needed. Julie led the way, with Anderson beside her and Dumont and Ed behind them. A softness as of rose petals was in the evening air.

Anderson said, "I've seen you around the campus, haven't I? Graduate school?"

Julie nodded. "I'm working on my doctorate, and I teach some freshman and sophomore classes. Ed's one of my students. Most of the people I meet seem to think I'm a sophomore or a junior myself. How did you know I wasn't?"

"The way you're dressed. I guessed, actually. You look young, but you also look like the sort of woman who looks younger than she is."

"You ought to have been a detective," she told him.

"Yes, anything but this."

The sun had set behind the trees of the park, trees whose long shadows had all run together now, flooding the lawns and walks with formless night. Most of the windows in the buildings the four passed were dark.

"What department?" Anderson asked when Julie said nothing more.

"English. My dissertation will be on twentieth century American novelists."

I should have recognized you, but I'm more than two thousand years behind you.''

"I'm easy to overlook.''

"Let's hope Nick is too." For a moment, Anderson studied the building looming before them. "Why the library?''

"I've been doing research; they let me have a key. I knew it had just closed, and I couldn't think of anything else.'' She held up the key.

A minute or two later, it slid into the lock. The interior was dim but not dark—a scattering of lights, lonely and almost spectral, burned in the recesses of the building, as though the spirits of a few geniuses lingered, still awake.

Dumont said, "You'd better let me go in front," and hurried past them with the tranquilizer gun. The doors closed with a hollow boom; suddenly the air seemed stale.

"Isn't there a watchman?'' Anderson asked.

Julie nodded. She was near enough for Anderson to smell her faint perfume. "You said Ed was a friend of mine. I don't have a lot, but I suppose Bailey—he's the watchman—is a friend too. I'm the only one who never calls him Beetle. I told you Nick was in the Sloan Fantasy Collection. Have you heard of it?''

"Vaguely. My field is classical literature.''

Behind them, Ed said, "That's what fantasy is— classical lit that's still alive. When the people who wrote those stories did it, their books were called fantasy.''

"Ed!'' Julie protested.

"No,'' Anderson said. "He's right.''

"Anyway,'' Julie continued, "the Sloan Collection isn't the best in the country, or even a famous collection. But it's a jolly good one. It's got James Branch Cabell in first editions, for example, and a lot of his letters. And there's some wonderful John Gardner material. So that's where I put Nick.''

Stamping among the books, Anderson thought to himself. Couchant at the frontiers of Overworld and Oz.

> *Pity the Unicorn,*
> *Pity the Hippogriff,*
> *Souls that were never born*
> *Out of the land of If!*

Somewhere ahead, Dumont called, *"He's dead!"* and suddenly all three of them were running, staggering, stumbling down a dark and narrow corridor, guided by the flame of Dumont's lighter.

Anderson heard Julie whisper, "Nick! Oh, God, Nick!" Then she was quiet. The thing on the floor was no white unicorn.

Dumont rasped. "Hasn't anybody got a light?"

"Just matches," Anderson said. He lit one.

Ed told them, "I've got one," and from the pocket of his denim shirt produced a little, disposable pen light.

Julie was bending over the dead man, trying not to step in his blood. There was a great deal of it, and Dumont had stepped in it already, leaving a footprint. Ed played his light upon the dead man's face—cleanshaven; about sixty, Anderson guessed. He had worn a leather windbreaker. There was a hole in it now, a big hole that welled blood.

"It's Bailey," Julie said. And Dumont, thinking that she spoke to him (as perhaps she did), answered, "Is that his name? Everybody called him Beetle."

Bailey had been gored in the middle of the chest, very near the heart, Anderson decided. No doubt he had died instantly, or almost instantly. His face was not peaceful or frightened or anything else; only twisted in the terrible rictus of death. The match burned Anderson's fingers; he shook it and dropped it.

"Nick . . ." Julie whispered. "Nick did this?"

"I'm afraid so," Dumont told her.

She looked around, first at Dumont, then at Anderson. "He's dangerous . . . I suppose I always knew it, but I didn't like to think about it. We'll have to let the police . . ."

Dumont nodded solemnly.

"Like hell," Anderson said, and Julie stared at him. "You put him here, in this room—" Anderson glanced at the half open door, "—and went away and left him. Is that right?"

"Mr. Bailey was with us. He heard us as soon as I brought Nick inside. Nick's hooves made a lot of noise on the terrazzo floor. We took him to this room, and Mr. Bailey locked it for me."

Ed asked, "Hold this, will you, Dr. Dumont?" and handed Dumont the pen light, then took three steps, stooped, and straightened up with a much larger flashlight. After the near darkness, its illumination seemed almost a glare. Dumont let his lighter go out and dropped it into his pocket.

Ed was grinning weakly. "This must be the old man's flash," he said. "I thought I saw something shine over here."

"Yes." Anderson nodded. "He would have had it in his hand. After Julie left he came here to take another look at the unicorn. He opened the door and turned on his flashlight."

Julie shivered. "It could have been me."

"I doubt it. Even if Nick doesn't have human or almost human intelligence—and I suspect he does—he would have winded the watchman and known it wasn't your smell. No matter what kind of brain his creator gave him, his sensory setup must be basically the one that came with his equine DNA. Am I right, Dumont?"

"Right." The biologist glanced at his wrist. "I wish we had more information about the time Beetle died."

Ed asked, "Can't you tell from the clotting of the blood?"

"Not close enough," Dumont said. "Maybe a forensic technician could, but that's not my field. If this were one of those mysteries on TV, we could tell from the time his watch broke. It didn't, and it's still running. Anybody want to guess how far that unicorn's gone since he did this?"

"I will," Anderson told him. "Not more than about two hundred and fifty feet."

They stared at him.

"The front doors were locked when we came in—Julie had to open them for us. I'd bet the side door is locked too, and this building has practically no windows."

"You mean he's still in here?"

"If he's not, how did he get out?"

Julie said, "We'd hear him, wouldn't we? I told you—his hooves made a racket when I led him in."

"He heard them too," Anderson told her. "He wouldn't have to be a tenth as intelligent as he probably is to keep quiet. Almost any animal will do that by instinct. If it can't run—or doesn't think running's a good idea—it freezes."

Ed cleared his throat. "Dr. Anderson, you said he could tell by the smell that Beetle wasn't Julie. He'll know we aren't Julie too."

"Conversely, he'll know that she is. But if we separate to look for him and the wrong party finds him, there could be trouble."

Dumont nodded. "What do you think we ought to do?"

"To start with, give Ed here the keys to your van so he can bring it around front. If we find Nick, we're going to have to have some way to get him out of town. We'll leave the front doors open—"

"And let him get away?"

"No. But we need unicorn bait, and freedom's about as good a bait as anybody's ever found. Nick's probably hungry by now, and he's almost certainly thirsty. My mind runs to quotations anyway, so how about:

> '*One by one in the moonlight there,*
> *Neighing far off on the haunted air,*
> *The unicorns come down to the sea.*'

Do you know that one?"

All three looked blank.

"It's Conrad Aiken, and of course he never saw a unicorn. But there may be some truth in it—in the feeling of it—just the same. We'll prop the doors wide. Dumont, you hide in the darkest shadow you can find there; the open doors should let in enough light for you to shoot by, particularly since you'll be shooting at a white animal. Julie and I will go through the building, turning on lights and looking for Nick. If we find him and he's docile with her, we can just lead him out and put him in the truck. If he runs, you should get him on the way out."

Dumont nodded.

When the two of them were alone, Julie asked, "That gun of Dr. Dumont's won't really hurt Nick, will it?"

"No more than a shot in the arm would hurt you. Less."

The beam of the dead watchman's flashlight probed the corridor, seeming to leave a deeper twilight where it had passed. A few moments before, Anderson had talked of turning on more lights, but thus far they had failed to find the switches. He asked Julie if it were always this dim when she came to do research after the library had closed.

"Bailey used to take care of the lights for me," she said. "But I don't know where. I'd begin setting up my things on one of the tables, my notebooks and so forth, and the lights would come on.'' Her voice caught on *lights*.

She sniffled, and Anderson realized she was crying. He put his arm about her shoulders.

''Oh, rot! Why is it that one can—can try to do something fine, and have—have it end . . .''

He chanted softly:

> *''Twist ye, twine ye! Even so,*
> *Mingled shades of joy and woe,*
> *Hope and fear, and peace, and strife,*
> *In the thread of human life.''*

''That's b—beautiful, but what does it mean? That the good and bad are mixed together so we can't pull them apart?''

''And that this isn't the end. Not for men or women or unicorns. Probably not even for poor old Bailey. Threads are long.''

She put her arms about his neck and kissed him, and he was so busy pressing those soft, fragrant lips in return that he hardly heard the sudden thunder of the unshod hooves.

He pushed her away just in time. The spiraled horn raked his belly like a talon; the beast's shoulder hit him like a football player's, sending him crashing into a high bookcase.

Julie screamed, ''No, Nick! Don't!'' and he tried to stand.

The unicorn was rearing to turn in the narrow aisle, tall as a giant on his hind legs. Anderson clawed at the shelves, bringing down an avalanche of books. He found himself somehow grasping the horn, holding on desperately. A hoof struck his thigh like a hammer and he was careening down some dark passage, half carried, half dragged.

Abruptly, there was light ahead. He tried to shout for Dumont to shoot, but he had no breath, grasping the horn, grappling the tossing white head like a bulldogger. If the soft pluff of the gun ever came, it was lost in the clattering hoofbeats, in the roar of the blood in his ears. And if it came, the dart surely missed.

They nearly fell on the steps. Reeling they reached the bottom like kittens tossed from a sack. Anderson managed then to get his right leg under him, and with the unicorn nearly sprawling, he tried to get his left across the broad, white back and found that leg was broken.

He must have shrieked when the ends of splintered bone grated together, and he must have lost his hold. He lay upon his back, on grass, and heard the gallop of approaching death. Saw Death, white as bone.

Stallions fight, he thought. Fight for mares, kicking and biting. Only men kill other men for a woman.

He lay without moving, his left leg twisted like a broken doll's. Stallions don't kill—not if the other lies down, surrenders.

The white head was silhouetted against the twinkling constellations now, the colors seemingly reversed as in a negative, the longsword horn both new and ancient to the sky of earth.

Later, when he told Julie and Dumont about it, Dumont said, "So he was only a horse after all. He spared you."

"A super horse. A horse armed, with size, strength, grace and intelligence all augmented." They had wanted to carry him somewhere (he doubted if they themselves knew where) but he had stopped them. Now, after Dumont had phoned for an ambulance, they sat beside him on the grass. His leg hurt terribly.

"Which way did he go? The park again?"

"No, the lake shore. 'The unicorns come down to the sea,' remember? You'll have to drum up a group and go after him in the morning."

Julie said, "I'll come, and I'm sure Ed will too."

Anderson managed to nod. "We've got a couple of dozen others. Some here, some in town. Dumont has the phone numbers."

She forced a smile. "Andy—can I call you Andy? You like poems. Do you recall this one?

> *The lion and the unicorn*
> *Were fighting for the crown;*
> *The lion beat the unicorn*
> *And sent him out of town.*
> *Some gave them white bread,*
> *And some gave them brown.*
> *Some gave them plum-cake,*
> *And drummed them out of town.*

We've just had it come true, all except for that bit about the plum-cake."

"And the lion," Anderson said.

Introduction to
Bev Evans'
"The Forsaken":

In the story "On the Last Afternoon," James Tiptree, Jr. says "Man is an animal whose dreams come true and kill him."

Here Beverly G. Evans, a fine new writer whose stories have appeared in *Horrors, Nightmares, Shadows,* and *Terrors,* takes us back to a time when the voices of the gods are becoming silent and the creatures of legend seem to have disappeared, a time when belief itself is a two-edged thing, and dreams are becoming lethal. . . .

EDITOR'S NOTE: This is an original story written expressly for this volume.

THE FORSAKEN
Bev Evans

FINMOLE lay still on his pallet and waited for dawn, making his heartbeat as shallow and soft as a whisper so that not even that would keep him from hearing the morning-song of god-voices in the forest behind his hut. The druid listened in rigid silence until the pain in his chest became more than he could bear; then rolled stiffly onto his side, and stirred the embers on the hearth pit with the end of his walking stick. Again, he thought; again I did not hear them.

Moving slowly, Finmole got to his feet and hobbled about the hut, leaning heavily on the cedar walking-stick that had been worn smooth by time and the constant caressing of his fingers. His back was stooped, so that his sparse grey beard trailed below his girtle, and the weary lid-folds of age nearly covered his pale blue eyes. He opened the door of his hut and looked out over the mountain's flank to where dawn had feathered the sky with crimson and gold. A cool damp breeze came up the slope and stirred his whispy hair.

Below him, the small hamlet of Cannock still smouldered from the midnight raid, and the sunrise was veiled by the soot and ash that rose with the light breeze. The berserkers had come out of the night, their hair stiff with lime, clad only in torque and bracelets, swinging their yard-long swords and screaming death in voices as shrill and pitiless as the crying of sea birds. Now, one by one, the survivors of the raid were coming down from the woods and hills; some weeping, some wounded, most of them silent as they collected their dead and set about salvaging what they could of their hamlet. The berserkers had come before; they would come again. Now was the time to damp out the still-smouldering buildings, to bank the cooking pits with coals so that they would not go out—only later would there be time to mourn.

Finmole sat in the doorway of his hut, casting the onyx stones. The old rituals could not be ignored, even though the inner god-voice that once guided each man now mumbled their wisdom, maundered, laughed madly, or did not sing at all. Throughout his life, the god-voices had been fading; the voices that spoke within each person's mind, guiding, warning, or chiding, as each new situation warranted. Some in Cannock believed that the voices ceased because people had turned from the old ways, leaving them defenseless against berserker raids; all were lost amid the confusion, and turned to the druid. Soon the men from the hamlet would climb the rocky path to his door once again, asking for signs and seeking advice. Finmole coughed, and blood-tinged spittle edged his lips.

Finmole saw the men approaching, their heads bobbing above the low-lying mists as if in time to some dark elfin dance. He blinked and shook his head, taken by the image of the disembodied skulls. The heads seemed to swirl around each other and rise into the air, forming and reforming into first one shape and then another, none lasting longer than the moment it took to recognize each one. There were sprites and laughing faces and grotesque wraiths of death and misfortune. Then they became a full-chested steed surging through the mists . . . the horse with only one leg, impaled on a chariot pole of twisted, burnished oak. On its back was the Earth Mother, and together they raced up the hill as swiftly as the first rush of flame around a bundle of dry straw. The hot breath of the steed warmed the druid's cheeks, and the chariot pole turned so that it seemed to protrude from the beast's forehead. In the last instant, Finmole saw two things: the

steed's chilling blue eyes, and the face of the rider. It had
not been the Earth Mother's, but that of Leandra, a child of
Cannock.

Finmole flushed with heat, and for several moments
could see nothing at all. His head felt light, and there was a
curious high-pitched ringing in his ears. He had never felt
like this after a vision before. What manner of fever-dream
is this, he wondered, that walks during the daylight and
plays tricks with me?

Finmole rubbed his eyes, and saw four men standing a
respectful distance down the path. He stared at them,
almost waiting for their heads to dance once again, but
realized he was making them uncomfortable. He motioned
them to come the rest of the way up the hill, and watched
their faces brighten with interest, for more often than not,
since Samhain, he had waved them away.

The men, blood-flecked and exhausted, sat in a half
circle near the druid. Emer waited with obvious impatience, his thick fingers tugging at a loose end of the goat
skin thong that wrapped his boot leggings tightly against
his calf. His eyes darted from Finmole to the woods behind
the hut and back to Finmole again, as if he expected to see
a vision himself. Next to him sat Jone, cradling his bow in
his lap, waiting with the calm quiet that made him the
hamlet's finest hunter. His hair was dark blond, his beard a
rusty brown; his cheeks were always red with windburn
and sun, and his thin, well-muscled body spoke of energy
even in repose. Kern puffed and wheezed as he labored to
lower his huge frame to the ground. For a man as broad
and strong as an ox, Kern did not have the endurance of the
animal that he had almost come to resemble. Keegan, the
youngest, shook his mane of red hair and eyed the others
with distrust.

"The morning song was sweet," Finmole lied.

"And your vision?" Emer asked, leaning forward with childlike anticipation, his fingers temporarily still.

"I saw no vision."

"There are traces of it in your eyes," Jone said.

Finmole sighed, and silently cursed the man for his powers of observation.

"I have seen the goddess Dana, riding the magic steed."

Three men drew in a breath as one; only Keegan remained unmoved, his eyes fixed squarely on the druid.

"She came riding through the morning mists as you were coming up the path."

All four men involuntarily looked up and around themselves, as if expecting to find the beast's hoofs pawing the air above their heads. It chilled them to think that they had been walking through a dream-vision.

"Is this the vision we've waited for, Finmole?" Jone asked softly.

"I don't know," Finmole said with irritation. "It does not have the feel of a vision. I must think on it."

"No!" Kern cried. "We must have it now. You cannot refuse to tell us what the gods have shown you." Kern's face was red, and he began to wheeze.

Jone laid a hand on Kern's shoulder. "Kern is right," he said. "If the gods' voices have spoken to you with a vision, then we must share it."

Finmole's eyes flickered over the men several times. Was it fever-dream, or vision? he wondered; god-voices or hallucination? Could any of them tell the difference anymore? Could he? Never had he felt his understanding so unsure, his intuition so dimmed. I am old, and ill, he thought, yet still they expect everything from me.

He sighed and closed his eyes. "The face of the goddess was hidden by the mists, but when they cleared, the steed had turned into a unicorn, and the rider's face was that of Leandra.''

"Leandra?" Keegan cried. "What does she have to do with your vision?"

The faces of the other men bespoke surprise and guarded caution. More than the appearance of one of their own in Finmole's dream, the mention of the unicorn stunned them. The most powerful talisman in Cannock was seldom invoked. The unicorn spire in the rock cliff above the chase was the first thing in the hamlet to touch the light of dawn. It was believed to be the horn of a giant unicorn, resting within the rock. The spire was as tall as five men, ridged and weathered smooth so that it gleamed in the morning sun, and glistened when the mists surrounded it. The fairies that lived near the cliff would fling anyone over its edge if they dared to touch the spire.

"We must reach the unicorn and draw from his great powers," Finmole continued, "and the only way to do so is to tempt him with a young virgin. Leandra is the chosen one."

"But Leandra was promised to me last Errl-tide. She is mine!" Keegan, always irascible, paced furiously across the small area in front of Finmole's hut. "You can't have her. She is mine by right!"

"She doesn't want you anyway, Keegan," Emer began, and then bit his lower lip. Jone jabbed him sharply, but Keegan had heard, and whirled to face Emer with fire in his ice-blue eyes.

"That's a lie, Emer, and I'll meet you at the claybank for it, staff for staff," Keegan roared.

Finmole began to speak, but a sudden painful spasm of coughing took his breath away.

"Today," Keegan ordered. "Right now!" He stepped towards Emer, who sat, fearfully gnawing on his lips and looking about for help.

Jone stood up in one smooth motion, placing himself between the two.

"We can go to another hamlet for a bride, if need be, but Leandra has been chosed by the gods," he said.

Keegan regarded Jone for a long, silent moment; then Finmole. Then he spat on the ground in front of the druid, and strode angrily away.

"Is this the vision?" Kern asked.

Suddenly exhausted, Finmole replied; "Sworn by the oak," almost believing it himself.

Leandra sat, wide-eyed and silent, on the floor of Finmole's hut. Usna, Cannock's herbalist, arranged the folds of her robe around her own ample figure, and poured a mug of hot mead for the girl. While Leandra sipped, Usna began to comb the girl's long blond hair, still wet from the ceremonial bath, and redolent of sweet grass.

Finmole threw a handful of dried herbs onto the hearth pit. The hut filled with the heady fragrance of wedgewort and thyme, and the air took on a dusky yellow hue. As he prepared the poultice sack, pausing to search his memory for the proper words, rivulets of sweat traced a ragged path across his brow like morning dew on an autumn leaf.

Usna crooned softly as she began to plait Leandra's hair with colorful strips of linen and sprigs of fresh mistletoe that Finmole had gathered. "Do I look pretty?" Leandra asked, and smiled with sleepy satisfaction when Finmole assured her that she was indeed lovely.

At moonrise, Finmole led the small procession into the deep woods, farther than even Jone had ventured alone before. Emer and Kern followed next, with Jone a step or two behind them. To Finmole's left walked Leandra; the foul-smelling poultice sack slapped her thigh as she moved. No one spoke.

It was dark and eerie in this part of the forest. The men

stubbed their toes on rocks and tree roots, and nervously imagined that it was grinning wood-elves that tripped them and caused them to stumble. Night creatures scurried in the underbrush, and the trees were aglow with watchful, unblinking eyes.

At last they reached the most sacred oak—a massive tree nestled where only druids with their knowledge of elves and fairies could go in safety. Silently the men tethered Leandra to the oak, and removed her coarse woolen sark. Her pale skin rippled with gooseflesh in the damp night air; she looked much younger than her twelve summers beneath the canopy of leaves and shadows.

The men retraced their path through the woods, leaving Leandra for the unicorn that Finmole promised would appear. They would return, but not before the moon had traced a quarter-arc across the glittering night sky.

Leandra waited for the unicorn alone. She had been brave as the men walked away, but soon began to cry. She trembled at every night-sound, fully expecting to see all the demons of her dreams. Spriggans, wild boars, and one-eyed, one-footed fachans flitted through the shadows of her imagination. She could remember the whispered warnings of the women of Cannock. They said that the unicorn had the tail of a lion, the beard of a goat, and hoofs sharp enough to rip an elephant's belly. His horn was long and sharp and twisted; white at the base, black at the middle, and red at the tip. His eyes, they said, were a cold, deadly blue, and could tell truth from lie at a glance. The women winked knowingly at Leandra when they said that, and she realized they were telling her she had best be the virgin they all thought her to be. Usna's assurances that the unicorn was a gentle and noble beast were soon buried under the deepening layers of silence and midnight mist. Finally, despite her fear, she drifted into a fitful sleep, broken by her nightmare cries that floated eerily among the trees like the song of a phantom nightingale.

Leandra opened her eyes and shivered. She knelt on the ground, hugging her arms to her sides for warmth. She felt chilled beyond the coolness of the night air, and briefly wished for her sark, until the feeling that prickled her skin like winter's sleet, crystalized into pure fear, and she knew she was no longer alone in the clearing.

Ten paces away, a pair of clear blue eyes stared evenly at her from beneath a long, pointed horn; and around those, an ethereal white mist glowed with a light all its own. Leandra could not make out any other part clearly, could not piece together the descriptions she had heard to match what stood before her. But the eyes were unmistakable: as cold an azure blue as the color locked within an icicle.

Leandra sat as still as she could, barely breathing, afraid to move lest the unicorn disappear as quickly as it had come; afraid lest it discover some secret flaw in her, some hidden, lustful dream, and kill her on the spot.

Several minutes passed, and neither girl nor beast moved. Leandra's leg began to tingle and feel numb. As she stared into the unicorn's eyes, she sensed a calmness . . . almost a sadness. Through the shifting white glow, she could see first one part of the unicorn, and then another, but never, it seemed, the whole beast at once. When the light revealed its flank pierced and bleeding, Leandra gasped, but the unicorn did not shy away. It continued to stare at her with wide, solemn eyes, and her fear lessened bit by bit.

She waited for the unicorn to come forward and rest its head in her lap as Finmole had said it would. It seemed magnificent and more beautiful than she had imagined; not at all ferocious, but more to be pitied for its wound. But when she heard the rustlings of the men returning, she became afraid again. Afraid, because the unicorn had not lain in her lap as expected . . . and then afraid that if it did, the men would harm it. She leapt to her feet, and whispered to the beast, "You must either come to me now, or run away . . . quickly, make up your mind."

Familiar faces appeared one by one in the bushes around the clearing. Kern strode into the clearing first, staff in hand.

"Where is the unicorn?" he demanded.

The other men stepped forward quietly, scanning the underbrush, and looking to Finmole for guidance.

"Why, it stands right before you, there!" Leandra pointed at the unicorn. "It has stood there for hours, and would not lie in my lap. Finmole, have I done something wrong?"

"I see no unicorn," Emer said.

"Nor I," said Kern, swishing the air before him with his staff. "Jone?"

The hunter paced the clearing, bending low to the ground looking for any kind of spoor.

"I see no unicorn," he said with a sigh, and turned to Finmole.

"But it's here, can't you see it? Emer, you're standing right by its side," Leandra cried, amazed that the men did not see.

Emer jumped and looked about him, but said to the others, "There is no unicorn here. The child lies."

"Finmole?" Jone said.

"Finmole sees, don't you, Finmole?" Leandra said, reaching to touch the druid's cloak, but held back by the tether at her ankle.

The druid rubbed his eyes and blinked several times. A slow wave of fear began at the base of his spine, sending blades of fiery pain across his back and shoulders. He cursed silently. *Where is it?* he thought.

He stared through narrowed lids at the place where Leandra pointed. Nothing. He searched the clearing and the trees beyond. The men began to stir impatiently. Soon their confusion would turn to disappointment, and then to anger. Finmole could already feel the air broiling with their frustration, and for the first time, he feared the men of Cannock.

"The unicorn is here," Finmole said at last. The men froze, still alarmed, but the mood in the clearing eased.

"You cannot see it, for it has powers of invisibility. You must leave, and wait for us to follow. Go quickly," he ordered.

The men moved slowly, not quite convinced, but, still, unwilling to disobey. Finmole waited until he no longer heard their passage through the woods, and let several minutes pass beyond that. Then he turned to Leandra.

"You're lying," he said.

Her expression of relief turned to one of shock.

"But, I'm not. You said . . ."

"I sent them away to save us both. There is nothing here." Finmole began to pace, his walking stick leaving small indentations in the forest floor. "Lying bitch," he cried in anger.

Leandra dropped to the ground, covered her head with her arms, and began to weep.

A spasm of coughing overtook the druid, and he leaned against a tree for support. His lungs felt like woolen sacks filled with stones. In his panic, he had said too much—and now Leandra knew that he had not seen the unicorn. *Fool*, he thought, and muttered frantic pleas for guidance from the still silent god-voices. "Damn," he cried out, lashing at the bushes with his cedar stick. Then he turned to leave.

Leandra looked up, her face swollen and red, her body still trembling with little sobs.

"Finmole, where are you going?" she asked.

The druid did not answer.

"Wait . . . don't leave me here . . . come back!" She tugged at the tether, and tore at the knot with her fingers. "Don't leave me. Please. . . *Finmole*!"

Her screams followed him through the woods until the sounds were lost amid his muffled footfalls and the mossy, ancient trees.

Finmole stepped quietly out of his hut, and started down the hill. It was less than a mile to the unicorn spire. The night was as black as a spriggan's heart, and a thin mist covered the ground. He turned east, just short of the tiny, conical-roofed huts, and skirted the hamlet on a path that wound among the choke-berries and young rowans at the edge of the woods.

Finmole's knees ached as he began the walk to the peak. He gripped his cedar stick tightly, and had to stop twice for the wheezing in his chest to subside before he had gone even fifty paces. He felt feverish, just as he had when he had seen the dream. Vision . . . or fever-dream? he asked himself yet again. He felt as if Leandra's eyes were following him, boring into his soul, perched on his left shoulder like glowing coals. But her eyes lied, he reassured himself.

He reached the base of the outcropping, and looked up at the spire. Dawn would be coming soon, and he left his walking-stick on the ground so that he could use both hands to search for holds across the jagged rock face. The muscles in his legs began to tremble, and his fingers scratched the rock for a solid ridge. His chest burned, and he coughed. Scrabbling for purchase, Finmole began his climb.

Behind him, the hamlet of Cannock was beginning to stir. Soft sounds of the new day, muffled by the mist, drifted up in fragments, as if they were torn by strong winds along the way. Soon Maude, Leandra's mother, would begin grinding at her quern, crushing grain that she used for barter. Finmole imagined her sitting in front of her hut, her head tilted perpetually to the right, deferring to the veined, purple goiter that hung from her neck, and had become half as large as her head despite the poultices from Usna. No-one in Cannock need know that the vision had not been true. Not even Maude. He would go to the spire and bargain with the power of the unicorn himself. And Leandra? No-one dared travel to the sacred oak; she would die there, and he would say she had become the bride of the unicorn, that it had ridden away with her, far into the woods.

Finmole sighed and thought of Usna: Usna, his friend, his bitterest enemy, and, sometimes, his lover, but that had been long ago. Jagged ridges scraped skin from his fingers, and he breathed in dirt and chalky rock dust. His mouth felt parched and his lips dry. Usna would have thought to bring a skin of mead to quench my thirst . . . but I would not have accepted it, he admitted to himself. Together we lead the people of Cannock: a tattooed old whore with waning second sight, and an aging priest, as lost amid the confusion as the ones we try to lead.

Finmole pulled himself up onto a small ledge, bare legs dangling over the edge, bleeding and bruised. He had lost one sandal, and the other was attached to his foot only by the ankle thong. His hair was matted with dirt and perspiration, and his breath came in painful, wrenching gasps. The spire was still fifteen feet beyond him, and whirling winds drifted down to chill the sweat from his body.

From the ledge, he could see all of Cannock and the hills beyond. The river north of the hamlet ran muddy from mountain storms, and raced furiously between its banks. As he sat, he thought of Leandra. Could she have really seen the unicorn? he wondered. Could my powers be so

diminished that it was actually there, but only she could
see it . . .? No. If it had been there, *I* would have been
the one to know, Finmole thought. Leandra was no priest-
ess, no link to the gods. It was nonsense to think that a
mere child could have powers that he no longer commanded. But still, the thought made him uneasy, and he
fought to mask his feelings. He was nearer the unicorn
spire, and dared not approach it with the stink of fear about
him, for the sprites that guarded the spire were capricious,
and could twist a mind already clouded with doubt. Just a
few seconds more, he bargained with himself, and then I'll
continue.

He groaned aloud and resumed his climb. Dawn was
only minutes away, and he had no time to lose. The wind
that swept around the spire buffetted his hair and made him
dizzy. Dizzy, that's what Leandra had felt after Usna had
given her the mead.

Finmole stood at the base of the unicorn spire. His blood
pounded in his ears, and he needed to steady himself, but
would not touch the spire. Suddenly, he twisted around
and looked intently in the direction of the sacred oak, as if
he could see through to the heart of the forest. Then,
slowly, he turned to the spire, stunned, staggered by the
first certainty he had felt in a long time.

"I didn't believe," he said to the spire. "I truly didn't
believe the girl saw you, but now I know. She saw you,
and I could not; not because I lacked the power, but
because I lacked the faith. You denied your manifestation
to me. To *me*!" he cried out in anguish.

"And I came here to wrest your powers from you
. . ." he continued wryly, "to produce a sign for the
people of Cannock to believe in, some evidence to prove
my vision was true—when it is *I* who hesitated to believe." He laughed bitterly. "I pretend to lead them with
the guidance of god-voices I no longer hear. My dreams

and visions and fantasies have all merged together so that I no longer know what is real and what is false . . ."

Finmole removed a vial of poison from his tunic and removed its stopper.

"This vial was to be Cannock's miracle," he cried to the spire. "Now it shall be mine. It is said the touch of your horn can render poison harmless."

Finmole touched the vial to the spire and held it aloft with trembling hands in an awkward salute. The spire sprites whipped the wind around him, creating dust devils that brought tears to his eyes and choked his throat.

"I believe," he whispered, "I believe, I believe . . ."

The winds swirled along the spire, following the spiral ridges all the way to its tip. Finmole's tunic flapped around him, and he was blinded with his own wispy hair. He raised the vial and drank the bitter liquid in one swallow, as the unicorn spire glowed in the first golden rays of dawn.

Introduction to
T. H. White's
"The Unicorn":

Born in 1906, the late T. H. White was perhaps the most talented and widely-acclaimed creator of whimsical fantasy since Lewis Carroll. and probably did more to mold the popular image of King Arthur than any other writer since Twain. Although he published other well-received fantasy novels such as *Mistress Masham's Repose* and *The Elephant and the Kangaroo,* White's major work—and the work on which almost all of his present-day reputation rests—was the massive Arthurian tetrology, *The Once and Future King.* Begun in 1939 with the publication of the first volume *(The Sword in the Stone,* itself well-known as an individual novel, and later made into a Disney animated film), the tetrology was published in an omnibus volume in 1958, became a nationwide best-seller, inspired the musical *Camelot,* one of the most popular shows in the history of Broadway, and was later made into a big-budget (and not terribly successful) movie. Gloriously eccentric and full of whimsy and delightful anachronism, hilarious and melancholy by turns, poetically written and peopled with compassionately-drawn characters, *The Once and Future King* is probably one of the two or three best fantasies of the last half of the twentieth century, seriously rivaled for widespread impact only by J.R.R. Tolkien's *Lord of the Rings*; it also takes its place with works by Mallory, Tennyson, and Twain as one of the major reworkings and interpretations of the Arthurian legends.

"The Unicorn" is an excerpt from *The Once and Future King,* but it also stands alone as an individual short story, and was once published as such by White. As either excerpt or story, though, it remains one of the most sensitive and beautiful renditions of the unicorn theme ever written.

T.H. White died in 1964. *The Book of Merlyn,* a never-before-published "alternate" ending to *The Once and Future King,* was published posthumously in 1980.

THE UNICORN

T. H. White

THE situation at Dunlothian was complicated. Nearly every situation tended to be when it was connected with King Pellinore, even in the wildest North. In the first place, he was in love—that was why he had been weeping in the boat. He explained it to Queen Morgause on the first opportunity—because he was lovesick, not seasick.

What had happened was this. The King had been hunting the Questing Beast a few months earlier, on the south coast of Gramarye, when the animal had taken to the sea. She had swam away, her serpentine head undulating on the surface like a swimming grass-snake, and the King had hailed a passing ship which looked as if it were off to the Crusades. Sir Grummore and Sir Palomides had been in the ship, and they had kindly turned it round to pursue the Beast. The three of them had arrived on the coast of Flanders, where the Beast had disappeared in a forest, and there, while they were staying at a hospitable castle, Pellinore had fallen in love with the Queen of Flanders' daughter. This was fine so far as it went—for the lady of his choice was a managing, middle-aged, stout-hearted creature, who could cook, ride a straight line, and make beds—but the hopes of all parties had been dashed at the start by the arrival of the magic barge. The three knights had got into it, and sat down to see what would happen, because knights were never supposed to refuse an adventure. But the barge had promptly sailed away of its own accord, leaving the Queen of Flanders' daughter anxiously waving her pocket handkerchief. The Questing Beast had thrust her head out of the forest before they lost sight of land, looking, so far as they could see at the distance, even more surprised than the lady. After that, they had gone on sailing till they arrived in the Out Isles, and the further they went the more lovesick the King had become, which made his company intolerable. He spent the time writing poems and letters, which could never be posted, or telling his companions about the princess, whose nickname in her family circle was Piggy.

A state of affairs like this might have been bearable in England, where people like the Pellinores did sometimes turn up, and even won a sort of tolerance from their fellow men. But in Lothian and Orkney, where Englishmen were tyrants, it achieved an almost supernatural impossibility. None of the islanders could understand what King Pellinore was trying to cheat them out of—by pretending to be himself—and it was thought wiser and safer not to acquaint any of the visiting knights with the facts about the war against Arthur. It was better to wait until their plots had been penetrated.

On top of this, there was a trouble which distressed the children in particular. Queen Morgause had set her cap at the visitors.

"What was our mother at doing," asked Gawaine, as they made their way toward St. Toirdealbhach's cell one morning, "with the knights on the mountain?"

Gaheris answered with some difficulty, after a long pause: "They were at hunting a unicorn."

"How do you do that?"

".There must be a virgin to attract it."

"Our mother," said Agravaine, who also knew the details, "went on a unicorn hunt, and she was the virgin for them."

His voice sounded strange as he made this announcement.

Gareth protested: "I did not know she was wanting a unicorn. She has never said so."

Agravaine looked at him sideways, cleared his throat and quoted: "Half a word is sufficient to the wise man."

"How do you know this?" asked Gawaine.

"We listened."

They had a way of listening on the spiral stairs, during the times when they were excluded from their mother's interest.

Gaheris explained, with unusual freedom since he was a taciturn boy:

"She told Sir Grummore that this King's lovesick melancholy could be dispelled by interesting him in his old pursuits. They were as saying that this King is in the habit of hunting a Beast which has become lost. So she said that they were to hunt a unicorn instead, and she would be the virgin for them. They were surprised, I think."

They walked in silence, until Gawaine suggested, almost as if it were a question: "I was hearing it told that the King is in love with a woman out of Flanders, and that Sir Grummore is married already? Also the Saracen is black in his skin?"

No answer.

"It was a long hunt," said Gareth. "I heard they did not catch one."

"Do these knights enjoy to be playing this game with our mother?"

Gaheris explained for the second time. Even if he were silent, he was not unobservant.

"I do not think they would be understanding at all."

They plodded on, reluctant to disclose their thoughts.

St. Toirdealbhach's cell was like an old-fashioned straw beehive, except that it was bigger and made of stone. It had no windows and only one door, through which you had to crawl.

"Your Holiness," they shouted when they got there,

kicking the heavy unmortared stones. "Your Holiness, we have come to hear a story."

He was a source of mental nourishment to them—a sort of guru, as Merlyn had been to Arthur, who gave them what little culture they were ever to get. They resorted to him like hungry puppies anxious for any kind of eatable, when their mother had cast them out. He had taught them to read and write.

"Ah, now," said the saint, sticking his head out of the door. "The prosperity of God on you this morning."

"The selfsame prosperity on you."

"Is there any news at you?"

"There is not," said Gawaine, suppressing the unicorn. St. Toirdealbhach heaved a deep sigh.

"There is none at me either," he said.

"Could you tell us a story?"

"Thim stories, now. There doesn't be any good in them. What would I be wanting to tell you a story for, and me in my heresies? 'Tis forty years since I fought a natural battle, and not a one of me looking upon a white colleen all that time—so how would I be telling stories?"

"You could tell us a story without any colleens or battles in it."

"And what would be the good of that, now?" he exclaimed indignantly, coming out into the sunlight.

"If you were to fight a battle," said Gawaine, but he left out about the colleens, "you might feel better."

"My sorrow!" cried Toirdealbhach. "What do I want to be a saint for at all, is my puzzle! If I could fetch one crack at somebody with me ould shillelagh"—here he produced a frightful-looking weapon from under his gown—"wouldn't it be better than all the saints in Ireland?"

"Tell us about the shillelagh."

They examined the club carefully, while his holiness

told them how a good one should be made. He told them
that only a root growth was any good, as common
branches were apt to break, especially if they were of
crab-tree, and how to smear the club with lard, and wrap it
up, and bury it in a dunghill while it was being
straightened, and polish it with black-lead and grease. He
showed the hole where the lead was poured in, and the
nails through the end, and the notches near the handle
which stood for ancient scalps. Then he kissed it reverently and replaced it under his gown with a heartfelt
sigh. He was play-acting, and putting on the accent.

"Tell us the story about the black arm which came
down the chimney."

"Ah, the heart isn't in me," said the saint. "I haven't
the heart of a hare. It's bewitched I am entirely."

"I think we are bewitched too," said Gareth. "Everything seems to go wrong."

"There was this one in it," began Toirdealbhach, "and
she was a woman. There was a husband living in Malainn
Vig with this woman. There was only one little girl that
they had between them. One day the man went out to cut in
the bog, and when it was the time for his dinner, this
woman sent the little girl out with his bit of dinner. When
the father was sitting to his dinner, the little girl suddenly
made a cry, 'Look now, father, do you see the large ship
out yonder under the horizon? I could make it come in to
the shore beneath the coast.' 'You could do that,' said
the father. 'I am bigger than you are, and I could not do it
myself.' 'Well, look at me now,' said the little girl. And
she went to the well that was near there, and made a
stirring in the water. The ship came in at the coast."

"She was a witch," explained Gaheris.

"It was the mother was the witch," said the saint, and
continued with his story.

" 'Now,' says she, 'I could make the ship be struck against the coast.' 'You could not do that,' says the father. 'Well, look at me now,' says the little girl, and she jumped into the well. The ship was dashed against the coast and broken into a thousand pieces. 'Who has taught you to do these things?' asked the father. 'My mother. And when you do be at working she teaches me to do things with the Tub at home.' "

"Why did she jump into the well?" asked Agravaine. "Was she wet?"

"Hush."

"When this man got home to his wife, he set down his turf-cutter and put himself in his sitting. Then he said, 'What have you been teaching to the little girl? I do not like to have this piseog in my house, and I will not stay with you any longer.' So he went away, and they never saw a one of him again. I do not know how they went on after that."

"It must be dreadful to have a witch for a mother," said Gareth when he had finished.

"Or for a wife," said Gawaine.

"It's worse not to be having a wife at all," said the saint, and he vanished into his beehive with startling suddenness, like the man in the Swiss weather clock who retires into a hole when it is going to be fine.

The boys sat round the door without surprise, waiting for something else to happen. They considered in their minds the questions of wells, witches, unicorns and the practices of mothers.

"I make this proposition," said Gareth unexpectedly, "my heroes, that we have a unicorn hunt of our own!"

They looked at him.

"It would be better than not having anything. We have not seen our Mammy for one week."

"She has forgotten us," said Agravaine bitterly.

"She has not so. You are not to speak in that way of our mother."

"It is true. We have not been to serve at dinner even."

"It is because she has a necessity to be hospitable to these knights."

"No, it is not."

"What is it, then?"

"I will not say."

"If we could do a unicorn hunt," said Gareth, "and bring this unicorn which she requires, perhaps we would be allowed to serve?"

They considered the idea with a beginning of hope.

"St. Toirdealbhach," they shouted, "come out again! We want to catch a unicorn."

The saint put his head out of the hole and examined them suspiciously.

"What is a unicorn? What are they like? How do you catch them?"

He nodded the head solemnly and vanished for the second time, to return on all fours in a few moments with a learned volume, the only secular work in his possession. Like most saints, he made his living by copying manuscripts and drawing pictures for them.

"You need a maid for bait," they told him.

"We have goleor of maids," said Gareth. "We could take any of the maids, or cook."

"They would not come."

"We could take the kitchenmaid. We could make her to come."

"And then, when we have caught the unicorn which is wanted, we will bring it home in triumph and give it to our mother! We will serve at supper every night!"

"She will be pleased."

"Perhaps after supper, whatever the event."

"And Sir Grummore will knight us. He will say, 'Never has such a doughty deed been done, by my halidome!' "

St. Toirdealbhach laid the precious book on the grass outside his hole. The grass was sandy and had empty snail shells scattered over it, small yellowish shells with a purple spiral. He opened the book, which was a Bestiary called *Liber de Natura Quorundam Animalium*, and showed that it had pictures on every page.

They made him turn the vellum quickly, with its lovely Gothic manuscript, skipping the enchanting Griffins, Bonnacons, Cocodrills, Manticores, Chaladrii, Cinomulgi, Sirens, Peridexions, Dragons, and Aspidochelones. In vain for their eager glances did the Antalop rub its complicated horns against the tamarisk tree—thus, entangled, becoming a prey to its hunters—in vain did the Bonnacon emit its flatulence in order to baffle the pursuers. The Peridexions, sitting on trees which made them immune to dragons, sat unnoticed. The Panther blew out his fragrant breath, which attracted his prey, without interest for them. The Tigris, who could be deceived by throwing down a glass ball at its feet, in which, seeing itself reflected, it thought to see its own cubs—the Lion, who spared prostrate men or captives, was afraid of white cocks, and brushed out his own tracks with a foliated tail—the Ibex, who could bound down from mountains unharmed because he bounced upon his curly horns—the Yale, who could move his horns like ears—the She-Bear who was accustomed to bear her young as lumps of matter and lick them into whatever shape she fancied afterwards—the Chaladrius bird who, if facing you when it sat on your bedrail, showed that you were going to die—the Hedgehogs who collected grapes for their progeny by rolling on them, and brought them back on the end of their prickles—even the Aspidochelone, who was a large whale-like creature with seven fins and a sheepish expression, to whom you were liable to moor your boat in mistake for an island if you were not careful: even the Aspidochelone scarcely detained them. At last he found them the place at the Unicorn, called by the Greeks, Rhinoceros.

It seemed that the Unicorn was as swift and timid as the Antalop, and could only be captured in one way. You had to have a maid for bait, and, when the Unicorn perceived her alone, he would immediately come to lay his horn in her lap. There was a picture of an unreliable-looking virgin, holding the poor creature's horn in one hand, while she beckoned to some spearmen with the other. Her expression of duplicity was balanced by the fatuous confidence with which the Unicorn regarded her.

Gawaine hurried off, as soon as the instructions had been read and the picture digested, to fetch the kitchen-maid without delay.

"Now then," he said, "you have to come with us on the mountain, to catch a unicorn."

"Oh Master Gawaine," cried the maid he had caught hold of, whose name was Meg.

"Yes, you have. You are to be the bait whatever. It will come and put its head in your lap."

Meg began to weep.

"Now then, do not be silly."

"Oh, Master Gawaine, I do not want a unicorn. I have been a decent girl, I have, and there is all the washing up to do, and if Mistress Truelove do catch me playing at truant I shall get stick, Master Gawaine, that I will."

He took her firmly by the plaits and led her out.

In the clean bog-wind of the high tops, they discussed the hunt. Meg, who cried incessantly, was held by the hair to prevent her from running away, and occasionally passed from one boy to the other, if the one who was holding her happened to want both hands for gestures.

"Now then," said Gawaine. "I am the captain. I am the oldest, so I am the captain."

"I thought of it," said Gareth.

"The question is, it says in the book that the bait must be left alone."

"She will run away."

"Will you run away, Meg?"

"Yes, please, Master Gawaine."

"There."

"Then she must be tied."

"Oh, Master Gaheris, if it is your will, need I be tied?"

"Close your mouth. You are only a girl."

"There is nothing to tie her with."

"I am the captain, my heroes, and I command that Gareth runs back home to fetch some rope."

"That I will not."

"But you will destroy everything, if you do not do so."

"I do not see why I should have to go. I thought of it."

"Then I command our Agravaine to go."

"Not I."

"Let Gaheris go."

"I will not."

"Meg, you wicked girl, you are not to run away, do you hear?"

"Yes, Master Gawaine. But, oh, Master Gawaine . . ."

"If we could find a strong heather root," said Agravaine, "we could tie her pigtails together, round the other side of it."

"We will do that."

"Oh, oh!"

After they had secured the virgin, the four boys stood round her, discussing the next stage. They had abstracted real boar-spears from the armoury, so they were properly armed.

"This girl," said Agravaine, "is my mother. This is what our Mammy was at doing yesterday. And I am going to be Sir Grummore."

"I will be Pellinore."

"Agravaine can be Grummore if he wants to be, but the bait has got to be left alone. It says so in the book."

"Oh, Master Gawaine, oh, Master Agravaine!"

"Stop howling. You will frighten the unicorn."

"And then we must go away and hide. That is why our mother did not catch it, because the knights stayed with her."

"I am going to be Finn MacCoul."

"I shall be Sir Palomides."

"Oh, Master Gawaine, pray do not leave me alone."

"Hold in your noise," said Gawaine. "You are silly. You ought to be proud to be the bait. Our mother was, yesterday."

Gareth said, "Never mind, Meg, do not cry. We will not let it hurt you."

"After all, it can only kill you," said Agravaine brutally.

At this the unfortunate girl began to weep more than ever.

"Why did you say that?" asked Gawaine angrily. "You always try to frighten people. Now she is at howling more than before."

"Look," said Gareth. "Look, Meg. Poor Meg, do not cry. It will be with me to let you have some shots with my catapult, when we go home."

"Oh, Master Gareth!"

"Ach, come your ways. We cannot bother with her."

"There, there!"

"Oh, oh!"

"Meg," said Gawaine, making a frightful face, "if you do not stop squealing, I will look at you like this."

She dried her tears at once.

"Now," he said, "when the unicorn comes, we must all rush out and stick it. Do you understand?"

"Must it be killed?"

"Yes, it must be killed dead."

"I see."

"I hope it will not hurt it," said Gareth.

"That is the sort of foolish hope you would have," said Agravaine.

"But I do not see why it should be killed."

"So that we may take it home to our mother, you amadan."

"Could we catch it," asked Gareth, "and lead it to our mother, do you think? I mean, we could get Meg to lead it, if it was tame."

Gawaine and Gaheris agreed to this.

"If it is tame," they said, "it would be better to bring it back alive. That is the best kind of Big Game Hunting."

"We could drive it," said Agravaine. "We could hit it along with sticks.

"We could hit Meg, too," he added, as an afterthought.

Then they hid themselves in their ambush, and decided to keep silence. There was nothing to be heard except the gentle wind, the heather bees, the skylarks very high, and a few distant snuffles from Meg.

When the unicorn came, things were different from what had been expected. He was such a noble animal, to begin with, that he carried a beauty with him. It held all spellbound who were within sight.

The unicorn was white, with hoofs of silver and a graceful horn of pearl. He stepped daintily over the heather, scarcely seeming to press it with his airy trot, and the wind made waves in his long mane, which had been freshly combed. The glorious thing about him was his eye.

There was a faint bluish furrow down each side of his nose, and this led up to the eye-sockets, and surrounded them in a pensive shade. The eyes, circled by this sad and beautiful darkness, were so sorrowful, lonely, gentle and nobly tragic, that they killed all other emotion except love.

The unicorn went up to Meg the kitchenmaid, and bowed his head in front of her. He arched his neck beautifully to do this, and the pearl horn pointed to the ground at her feet, and he scratched in the heather with his silver hoof to make a salute. Meg had forgotten her tears. She made a royal gesture of acknowledgment, and held her hand out to the animal.

"Come, unicorn," she said. "Lay your head in my lap, if you like."

The unicorn made a whinny, and pawed again with his hoof. Then, very carefully, he went down first on one knee and then on the other, till he was bowing in front of her. He looked up at her from this position, with his melting eyes, and at last laid his head upon her knee. He stroked his flat, white cheek against the smoothness of her dress, looking at her beseechingly. The whites of his eyes rolled with an upward flash. He settled his hind quarters coyly, and lay still, looking up. His eyes brimmed with trustfulness, and he lifted his near fore in a gesture of pawing. It was a movement in the air only, which said, "Now attend to me. Give me some love. Stroke my mane, will you, please?"

There was a choking noise from Agravaine in the ambush, and at once he was rushing toward the unicorn, with the sharp boar-spear in his hands. The other boys squatted upright on their heels, watching him.

Agravaine came to the unicorn, and began jabbing his spear into its quarters, into its slim belly, into its ribs. He squealed as he jabbed, and the unicorn looked to Meg in anguish. It leaped and moved suddenly, still looking at her reproachfully, and Meg took its horn in one hand. She seemed entranced, unable to help it. The unicorn did not seem able to move from the soft grip of her hand on its horn. The blood, caused by Agravaine's spear, spurted out upon the blue-white coat of hair.

Gareth began running, with Gawaine close after him. Gaheris came last, stupid and not knowing what to do.

"Don't!" cried Gareth. "Leave him alone. Don't!" Don't!"

Gawaine came up, just as Agravaine's spear went in under the fifth rib. The unicorn shuddered. He trembled in all his body, and stretched his hind legs out behind. They went out almost straight, as if he were doing his greatest leap—and then quivered, trembling in the agony of death. All the time his eyes were fixed on Meg's eyes, and she still looked down at his.

"What are you doing?" shouted Gawaine. "Leave him alone. No harm at him."

"Oh, Unicorn," whispered Meg.

The unicorn's legs stretched out horizontally behind him, and stopped trembling. His head dropped in Meg's lap. After a last kick they became rigid, and the blue lids rose half over the eye. The creature lay still.

"What have you done?" cried Gareth. "You have killed him. He was beautiful."

Agravaine bawled, "This girl is my mother. He put his head in her lap. He had to die."

"We said we would keep him," yelled Gawaine. "We said we would take him home, and be allowed to supper."

"Poor unicorn," said Meg.

"Look," said Gaheris, "I am afraid he is dead."

Gareth stood square in front of Agravaine, who was three years older than he was and could have knocked him down quite easily. "Why did you do it?" he demanded. "You are a murderer. It was a lovely unicorn. Why did you kill it?"

"His head was in our mother's lap."

"It did not mean any harm. Its hoofs were silver."

"It was a unicorn, and it had to be killed. I ought to have killed Meg too."

"You are a traitor," said Gawaine. "We could have taken it home, and been allowed to serve at supper."

"Anyway," said Gaheris, "now it is dead."

Meg bowed her head over the unicorn's forelock of white, and once again began to sob.

Gareth began stroking the head. He had to turn away to hide his tears. By stroking it, he had found out how smooth and soft its coat was. He had seen a near view of its eye, now quickly fading, and this had brought the tragedy home to him.

"Well, it is dead now, whatever," said Gaheris for the third time. "We had better take it home."

"We managed to catch one," said Gawaine, the wonder of their achievement beginning to dawn on him.

"It was a brute," said Agravaine.

"We caught it! We of ourselves!"

"Sir Grummore did not catch one."

"But we did."

Gawaine had forgotten about his sorrow for the unicorn. He began to dance round the body, waving his boar-spear and uttering horrible shrieks.

"We must have a gralloch," said Gaheris. "We must do the matter properly, and cut its insides out, and sling it over a pony, and take it home to the castle, like proper hunters."

"And then she will be pleased!"

"She will say, God's Feet, but my sons are of mickle might!"

"We shall be allowed to be like Sir Grummore and King Pellinore. Everything will go well with us from now."

"How must we set about the gralloch?"

"We cut out its guts," said Agravaine.

Gareth got up and began to go away into the heather. He said, "I do not want to help cut him. Do you, Meg?"

Meg, who was feeling ill inside herself, made no answer. Gareth untied her hair—and suddenly she was off, running for all she was worth away from the tragedy, toward the castle. Gareth ran after her.

"Meg, Meg!" he called. "Wait for me. Do not run."

But Meg continued to run, as swiftly as an antalop, with her bare feet twinkling behind her, and Gareth gave it up. He flung himself down in the heather and began to cry in earnest—he did not know why.

At the gralloch, the three remaining huntsmen were in trouble. They had begun to slit at the skin of the belly, but they did not know how to do it properly and so they had perforated the intestines. Everything had begun to be horrible, and the once beautiful animal was spoiled and repulsive. All three of them loved the unicorn in their various ways, Agravaine in the most twisted one, and, in proportion as they became responsible for spoiling its beauty, so they began to hate it for their guilt. Gawaine particularly began to hate the body. He hated it for being dead, for having been beautiful, for making him feel a beast. He had loved it and helped to trap it, so now there was nothing to be done except to vent his shame and hatred of himself upon the corpse. He hacked and cut and felt like crying too.

"We shall not ever get it done," they panted. "How can we ever carry it down, even if we manage the gralloch?"

"But we must," said Gaheris. "We must. If we do not, what will be the good? We must take it home."

"We cannot carry it."

"We have not a pony."

"At a gralloch, they sling the beast over a pony."

"We must cut his head off," said Agravaine. "We must cut its head off somehow, and carry that. It would be enough if we took the head. We could carry it between us."

So they set to work, hating their work, at the horrid business of hacking through its neck.

Gareth stopped crying in the heather. He rolled over on his back, and immediately he was looking straight into the sky. The clouds which were sailing majestically across its endless depth made him feel giddy. He thought: How far is it to that cloud? A mile? And the one above it? Two miles? And beyond that a mile and a mile, and a million million miles, all in the empty blue. Perhaps I will fall off the earth now, supposing the earth is upside down, and then I shall go sailing and sailing away. I shall try to catch hold of the clouds as I pass them, but they will not stop me. Where shall I go?

This thought made Gareth feel sick, and, as he was also feeling ashamed of himself for running away from the gralloch, he became uncomfortable all over. In these circumstances, the only thing to do was to abandon the place in which he was feeling uncomfortable, in the hope of leaving his discomfort behind him. He got up and went back to the others.

"Hallo," said Gawaine, "did you catch her?"

"No, she escaped away to the castle."

"I hope she will not tell anybody," said Gaheris. "It has to be a surprise, or it is no good for us."

The three butchers were daubed with sweat and blood, and they were absolutely miserable. Agravaine had been sick twice. Yet they continued in their labour and Gareth helped them.

"It is no good stopping now," said Gawaine. "Think how good it will be, if we can take it to our mother."

"She will probably come upstairs to say good night to us, if we can take her what she needs."

"She will laugh, and say we are mighty hunters."

When the grisly spine was severed, the head was too heavy to carry. They got themselves in a mess, trying to lift it. Then Gawaine suggested that it had better be dragged with rope. There was none.

"We could drag it by the horn," said Gareth. "At any rate we could drag and push it like that, so long as it was downhill."

Only one of them at a time could get a good hold on the horn, so they took it in turns to do the hauling, while the others pushed behind when the head got snagged in a heather root or a drain. It was heavy for them, even in this way, so that they had to stop every twenty yards or so, to change over.

"When we get to the castle," panted Gawaine, "we will prop it up in the seat in the garden. Our mother is bound to walk past there, when she goes for a walk before supper. Then we will stand in front of it until she is ready, and all will suddenly step back at once, and there it will be."

"She will be surprised," said Gaheris.

When they had at last got it down from the sloping ground, there was another hitch. They found that it was no longer possible to drag it on the flat land, because the horn did not give enough purchase.

In this emergency, for it was getting near to suppertime, Gareth voluntarily ran ahead to fetch a rope. The rope was tied round what remained of the head, and thus at last, with eyes ruined, flesh bruised and separating from the bones, the muddy, bloody, heather-mangled exhibit was con-

veyed on its last stage to the herb garden. They heaved it to
the seat, and arranged its mane as well as they could.
Gareth particularly tried to prop it up so that it would give a
little idea of the beauty which he remembered.

The magic queen came punctually on her walk, con-
versing with Sir Grummore and followed by her lap dogs:
Tray, Blanche and Sweetheart. She did not notice her four
sons, lined up in front of the seat. They stood respectfully
in a row, dirty, excited, their breasts beating with hope.

"Now!" cried Gawaine, and they stood aside.

Queen Morgause did not see the unicorn. Her mind was
busy with other things. With Sir Grummore she passed by.

"Mother!" cried Gareth in a strange voice, and he ran
after her, plucking at her skirt.

"Yes, my white one? What do you want?"

"Oh, Mother. We have got you a unicorn."

"How amusing they are, Sir Grummore," she said.
"Well, my doves, you must run along and ask for your
milk."

"But, Mammy . . . ."

"Yes, yes," she said in a low voice. "Another time."

And the Queen passed on with the puzzled knight of the
Forest Sauvage, electrical and quiet. She had not noticed
that her children's clothes were ruined: had not even
scolded them about that. When she found out about the
unicorn later in the evening she had them whipped for it,
for she had spent an unsuccessful day with the English
knights.

SELECTED BIBLIOGRAPHY

NOVELS

The Last Unicorn, Peter S. Beagle
A Swiftly Tilting Planet, Madeleine L'Engle
The Young Unicorns, Madeleine L'Engle
The Last Battle, C. S. Lewis
The Siege of Wonder, Mark Geston
Sign of the Unicorn, Roger Zelazny

SHORT STORIES

"The Unicorn in the Garden," James Thurber. *Thurber's Carnival*
"Unicorn Tapestry," Samuel R. Delany. *New American Review 9*
"The Last Unicorns," Edward D. Hoch. *Science Fiction Stories*, February, 1959
"Stand-In," Gregory Benford. *The Magazine of Fantasy and Science Fiction*, June, 1965
"The Hunt of the Unicorn," Joan D. Vinge. *Basilisk*
"What Jorkens Has to Put Up With," Lord Dunsany. *Jorkens Remembers Africa*
"The Unicorn," Edmund Cooper. *Voices in the Dark*

REFERENCE BOOKS

The Lore of the Unicorn, Odell Shepard
The Unicorn, Nancy Hathaway
The Lungfish, the Dodo, and the Unicorn, Willy Ley
The Bestiary: A Book of Beasts, T. H. White
Psychology and Alchemy, C. J. Jung

ART BOOKS

In Pursuit of the Unicorn, Josephine Bradley
A Book of Unicorns, Welleran Poltarnees
The Unicorn Tapestries, Margaret B. Freeman

ABOUT THE EDITORS

GARDNER DOZOIS was born and raised in Salem, Massachusetts, and now lives in Philadelphia. He is the author or editor of fifteen books, including the novel *Strangers* and the collection *The Visible Man;* he also edits the annual series *The Year's Best Science Fiction.* His short fiction has appeared in *Playboy, Penthouse, Omni,* and most of the leading SF magazines and anthologies, and he has many times been a finalist for the Hugo and Nebula awards. His critical work has appeared in *Writer's Digest, Starship, Thrust, Writing and Selling Science Fiction, The Writer's Handbook,* and *Science Fiction Writers,* and he is the author of the critical chapbook *The Fiction of James Tiptree, Jr.* His most recent book is *Magicats!,* an anthology edited in collaboration with Jack Dann. He is currently at work on another novel, *Flash Point.*

JACK DANN is the author or editor of thirteen books, including the novels *Junction* and *Starhiker,* and the collection *Timetipping.* He is the editor of the anthology *Wandering Stars,* one of the most acclaimed anthologies of the 1970's, and several other well-known anthologies, including the recently published *More Wandering Stars.* His short fiction has appeared in *Playboy, Penthouse, Omni, Gallery,* and most of the leading SF magazines and anthologies. He has been a Nebula Award finalist five times, as well as a finalist for the World Fantasy Award and the British Science Fiction Association Award. His critical work has appeared in *Starship, Nickelodeon, The Bulletin of the Science Fiction Writers of America, Empire, Future Life,* and *The Fiction Writer's Handbook,* and he is the author of the chapbook, *Christs and Other Poems.* His most recent books are *Magicats!,* an anthology edited in collaboration with Gardner Dozois, and *The Man Who Melted,* a novel; he is at work on another new novel, *Counting Coup.* Dann lives with his family in Johnson City, New York.

COLLECTIONS OF FANTASY AND SCIENCE FICTION

Fantasy from Ace
fanciful and fantastic!